Starting Over

Starting Over

Ronald Bagliere

For Debbie -

Sometimes life is about starting over and sometimes letting go ...

Acknowledgments

Like any work of art, writing is not done in a void. While the author may be the master of his work, there are many other people who become involved in its creation. These men and women provide of their own free will and time, literary and professional critiques, research, artwork, copy and creative editing, and formatting for final publication. I would like to acknowledge a few of them who have given their precious time in providing insightful critiques and encouragement. They have been an invaluable source to me in the development of this novel. First and foremost – a huge thank you to Paul Baxter for his expertise regarding First Responder protocols and operations. Your insights, comments and suggestions were invaluable. To the Central New York Chapter of the Romance Writers of America, the Downtown Writer's Center, and my monthly critique group; many thanks for all your insightful critiques. And as always, many thanks to my beta readers, editors and to my publisher, Fountain Blue Publishing; as always you are right there to take care of all the little things and bumps in the road. Thank you all. I am forever grateful!

Chapter 1

J ANET DROVE her Highlander alongside the shops and eateries of Lincoln City's Harbor Boulevard. The road running through town was quiet this time of year. The tourists had left, leaving the hardy coastal residents behind to hunker down for the approaching winter. Heading toward Fogarty, she glanced at the blue marble urn on the passenger seat. This year's pilgrimage to the beach where so much of her past had been defined marked yet another turning point in her life.

Her beloved husband, Neil, would be joining her father, their ashes comingling on the beach she loved. But as far as she was concerned, it was too soon. It was hard to believe he'd been gone almost a whole year. She thought about his last days at Hazelnut before his body gave up and finally quit. It had been a long haul for them the last two months before he passed, and she'd been there for all of it, standing beside his bed, holding his hand, whispering how beautiful he was. But that was the price she'd paid for marrying a man twenty-five years older than her.

"Someday we'll be back together again," she muttered, because, yes, she'd come to believe there was something beyond this mortal life even though she didn't know what it was. All she knew was that he believed it, and that was all that mattered.

She came to a stoplight. Closed her eyes.

And then there was Megan.

It hadn't been easy to convince her fifty-four-year-old stepdaughter to agree with her plans for today. In the end, she prevailed. The hardest part was persuading Megan to hang back. She knew it wasn't fair, but she couldn't share her final moments with him with anyone, not even his daughter. To make up for it, she gave Megan his journals revealing his hopes and dreams. Perhaps through his words he might reach out from beyond and bring about peace between his children. Maybe someday, she could convince Megan to forgive her brother Trevor from walking out on his father after their mother died. As matriarch of the family, she owed Neil that.

An hour later, she was walking barefoot on the cool, compacted sand as the ocean pounded the shoreline. This was home, the place where her heart had led her to the only man she'd ever loved. And it was also here where she'd made peace with a father she'd desperately sought acceptance from growing up. Carrying the canvas bag holding the remains of her husband, she followed the shoreline of the sprawling beach, contemplating the final letter she'd write to him. There was so much she wanted to say but didn't know how to put it into words.

The fine, watery mist of Fogarty spritzed her face and the wafting brine wrinkled her nose. She inhaled deeply. "I'm back, Dad," she said to no one, "and I brought someone with me. I'm sure you both have catching up to do. Nate's doing a second tour in Iraq and I'm scared. The world over there is crazy, people hating and killing each other. I wish you were here. If anything were to happen to him, I…" She broke off and fought to contain herself, then turned toward her Altar rock sitting on the bluff. "Anyway, I suppose I should let you two get reacquainted."

With her hair spraying out behind her, she strode to the grotto nestled in the face of the eroded rock wall buttressing the picturesque town from the sprawling beach. The jutting slab of weathered granite she called her Altar rock stood firm amidst the strewn rocks and boulders banked against the towering bluff. She stopped and looked up at it, felt the sacred rock's powerful draw on her heart then climbed up over the pile of jumbled stones and found her place on its outstretched palm.

Here, she stood with eyes closed and listened to the thrum of the waves and the distant echoes of her past. Right below her, she'd married Neil on a bright, sunny day, and down the beach they'd spent weekend afternoons with Nate building sandcastles and playing Frisbee. She drank the memories in, marinating in them until at last she reached down and drew the urn from the bag. Holding the marble vessel in front of her, she opened it and poured the ashes over the rocks to the sand below.

As she watched them tumble down, her throat tightened. There were no words to express how she felt so she placed the urn back in the bag and sat with her journal, trying to write words that wouldn't come. Finally, she closed the book and held it tight to her chest as the unreachable distance between her and Neil widened further than she thought possible. For the last two years, she'd immersed herself in her work and the running of the local Alzheimer's Association, trying to escape the suffocating loneliness stalking her day and night. Her body quaked, and she buried her face in her hands. "It's so hard without you, baby. I know you want me to be happy, but I don't know how to do it. Please help me," she rasped, wiping her eyes.

She rocked back and forth under the brooding sky as the wind died and a faint scent of sandalwood danced in the air. She looked up startled and searching the waves, felt something warm on her shoulder. Setting her journal aside, she jumped up knowing it was crazy to believe he was somehow there with her, but she couldn't help wishing it were so. The scent grew stronger and the cover of her journal flipped back. The pages riffed and when she looked down, the book was open. On the page were the paraphrased words of Gibran she'd written shortly after he died.

If I am to hold the spirit of you my love, I must open my heart wide to the body of life.

A smile blossomed in the depths of her grief. The words she'd written to Neil reminded her what was important. To honor him was to embrace life and that was what she was going to do, but she had no idea where to start. She closed her eyes and imagined him beside her.

"I miss you so much."

With determination and renewed strength, she climbed down and started back to her car. Walking beside the soughing, sweptback dunes, she watched a couple walking hand in hand near the surf. Her throat tightened and again, the tears came. This time they wouldn't stop. Her legs gave way and she collapsed to her knees, breaking into a heaving sob, until a little dog came running out from behind one of the dunes. He grabbed a stick and darted back out of sight. A moment later, the stick came whirling back and landed at her feet with the dog giving chase. She blinked. The little guy could've been her Barney's double. Barney was gone now and was buried behind her house. She rose to a knee and wiped her eyes. "Hey, puppy, what's your name?"

The dog barked as a man sporting a blue vested jacket and jeans called to him. "Jack, come here boy. Leave the lady alone."

"You better get back," she said to the dog, but the little guy stayed put. The man whistled, and the dog jerked his head around then back at her. "Go on, now. Get back to your master."

The dog remained, looking up at her with dark brown eyes.

The man walked toward her. When he came near, he said, "I'm sorry. I don't know what's gotten into him."

Great, I must look like hell, she thought. She stood trying to collect herself. "It's okay, I used to have a dog that looked just like him." She averted her gaze toward the ocean and watched the tide roll in for a moment.

Finally, the man said, "Good day for a walk."

"Yes, it is," she said, and glanced toward the underpass.

"Well, it's the last one I'll be taking here for some time." He grabbed the stick and hurled it down the beach. "You from around here?"

She shook her head as the dog chased after it. "No...the Valley."

He arched his brow "The Valley? You mean the one west of Salem?"

She took a step back. "Yes."

"There's some digs up that way." He paused as the dog came racing back with the stick. As Jack dropped it at their feet, he added, "Name's Andy."

She ignored his extended hand and an awkward moment of silence passed between them. Finally, she said, "Janet."

Pulling his hand back, he pointed toward the dog looking up at her. "Nice to meet ya. Seems he's decided you need a turn at fetch."

She eyed Jack. The dog was wagging his tail and darting a glance back and forth between her and the stick. Setting her bag down, she picked the stick up and tossed it towards the surf.

Andy ran a thick hand through his mop of cinnamon hair. As he did so, she caught a fleeting glance of a tattoo below his elbow... an anchor or a harpoon piercing a globe or something like that. One of her son's tattoos was similar. Obviously, it was some rite of passage in the armed forces. She suppressed an urge to ask about it.

How do I get out of here without looking rude? "How old is the little guy?"

"About two," he replied. "Keeps me on my feet."

Raking a lock of hair from her face, she glanced up and found him staring out over the water and scuffing his feet in the sand.

Suddenly, he turned to her. "So, umm... the 'Valley'... how long ya been there?"

She glanced back at the overpass. "About fifteen years. My husband built us a house there."

"Nice. He a contractor?"

She looked off down the beach where she'd sown his ashes on the sand. "No, an architect."

"Cool... Nice bag."

Janet started then looked down at her canvas tote. "Oh thanks. My son got it for me. He's in the Army."

"I noticed that," he said, nudging the side of the bag with his foot. "The Army Seal sort of gives it away." He crossed his arms over his chest. "Deployed?"

"Yeah."

He glanced at her knowingly. "Where?"

"Iraq," she said as Jack bounded back with his stick. The dog dropped it at her feet and she bent over and picked it up. Handing it to Andy, she drew breath and pasted a smile on her face. "Well, I need to be getting along. You have a good day."

"Yeah, you, too."

Walking away, she felt his gaze on her back.

For the first time, the word 'widow' hit home for Janet. Until now, she'd avoided thinking of herself as one - but no more. She pulled off the highway cutting through the Corvallis countryside and headed for home. When she got there, Megan's car was gone. Her stepdaughter had gone north to Woodburn to see her boyfriend, Ben, for the weekend. For that, she was grateful because talking to Megan right now was the furthest thing from her mind.

She unloaded the car and strode to the front door. The house Neil built loomed before her desolate and empty save for the swaying hawthorns around the front stoop. She opened the front door, tossed her keys on the pedestal table and took a long look around the cavernous Great Room.

Removing her jacket, she tossed it on the recliner and went to the kitchen to let Cleo out of his crate and to get a drink of water. What she ended up with was a bottle of wine. It was a bad idea, but at the moment, she didn't care. She poured herself a tall glass of Pinot and padded to the bookcase flanking the hearth. After turning the stereo on, she grabbed one of her family photo albums. A moment later, Jackson Browne's voice swept over her, saturating her with memory. She skipped to the CD's fourth track, 'Stay' and retreated to the couch.

She was on her second glass with the photo album splayed across her lap when the tears came again. She turned the page and gazed down through the years at the two cornerstones of her life: Neil sitting at his desk with Nate beside him in his little league uniform. Tipping the glass back, she drained it and poured another as night gathered outside the cathedral window. Cleo popped up on the couch beside her as she traced the outline of her husband's face in the photo with her finger.

Laying her head back on the couch, she closed her eyes and felt her body drift to the edge of a dream. From out of the fog, she heard a murmur of a ring tone. The sound grew louder, building into a wave until finally, it crashed in on her. Her eyes shot open and she bolted up. Groping around the couch she searched for her cell phone and found it on the end table.

"Hello?"

"Mom?"

She switched the phone to her other ear. Her son rarely called and when he did, it always alarmed her. "Nate? What's wrong? You all right?" She eyed her watch. 11:30 PM. That made it 'what' in Iraq?

There was a long pause. Finally, he said, "Yeah, I'm fine. Umm...I was just thinking about you and wanted to say, Hi."

Her gut tightened. This wasn't Nate's style, calling in the middle of the night to say hi. "Oh, how sweet of you, honey. I miss you."

"Yeah, I miss you, too."

As Cleo nuzzled her hand, she said, "Are you sure you're all right?" She didn't want to press her son, but she couldn't ignore the red flags waving in her face.

"Yeah, Mom, I'm fine. Really." He paused and she heard people talking in the background...people talking in medical terms. "So, how are you doing?"

"I'm fine," she said, homing in on what was being said in the offing. When she heard the word, radiology, she knew he was hiding something. Suddenly, her heart went into overdrive. "Nate, where are you," she said, a little more forcefully than she intended.

There was another long pause. Finally, he said, "Germany."

"Germany? I thought you-"

He cut her short. "Yeah...look, umm..." She heard him clear his throat. *Here it comes.* "Things are, well...in transition right now?"

She drew breath and snatching the pillow from beside her, clutched it to her chest. "Meaning?"

"Meaning, I'm being shipped home."

"Home!" She was dumbfounded, but despite the joy of hearing it, she knew better. *He's in Germany and he's being discharged. Oh my God, he's injured.* It took all her strength to keep her fears in check. "When?"

"In a couple weeks. Got to deal with paperwork."

She closed her eyes. "Are you in the hospital?"

She waited in the stifling silence for an answer. Finally, he said, "Umm...yeah, but nothing to worry about...just got nicked is all."

"Nicked! What do you mean nicked?" Her stomach flipped as visions of him lying in a hospital bed flashed before her. "Where?"

"My leg...and don't wig out on me. It's nothing," he said. "I'll be needing digs when I get home though. Hope you haven't rented my room out."

Right, like I'd do that. She shook her head, found herself cursing him under her breath. "No, I haven't rented your room out."

"Good...Say, look, chow's here so I gotta skate. Like I said, don't worry about me, okay? I'm fine."

As if that's possible. "I'm your mother! Worrying goes with the territory."

She heard him sigh. "I guess...Anyway, I'll hit you up later."

"When?"

"Soon. Gotta go. Love you."

Chapter 2

ANDY SET his toolbox on the back seat of his Suburban and looked wearily at the old white colonial clapboard house. He'd worked all morning installing a new railing, and replacing an old basement window for the new owners. Once, it had been his and Brenda's home. No more. Now it was just an empty box they'd bumped around in. Why was it every relationship he'd ever had turned to sand, sliding through his fingers? Brenda had hung with him the longest; almost seven years, and he'd really believed he met someone who'd go the distance. What he didn't know was their marriage had fallen apart two years after it began. Looking back, he realized he'd been too wrapped up in the day-to-day emergencies of others to notice her drifting away from him. They'd been going through the motions, like an exercise at the fire station, never getting anywhere until one day, she'd had enough.

It was over an ice cream cone at Sammy's. She said she wanted out. She'd had enough of the *Job*, as she called it. Was tired of the *Job* tearing him away from her at all hours of the night. Tired of him taking care of everyone else but her. It stunned him and he didn't know how to answer for a long time. Finally, he'd said, 'So, you wanna go to a movie?' She'd looked at him as if he'd lost his mind. It wasn't far from the truth at that moment. Going out for ice cream had been their way of reconnecting after a long week of passing each other back and forth doing their jobs – not ending a marriage. How did one throw in the towel on loving each other while eating an ice cream cone? It didn't make sense. Ending a marriage while eating ice cream was just wrong.

Jack popped his head over the front seat and nuzzled his hand. He'd gotten the little beagle pup to fill the empty moments when he was home alone. To a point the little dog did. It was the utter silence of the nights that were the hardest, when dark memories of the accident and his past came roaring back. Yes, it was time to move on like Brenda had said when they met for lunch last week. He looked down at Jack and saw the excitement in the dog's eyes about the impending road trip. Jack loved riding shotgun with his head out the window.

"Yeah, I know, hurry it up and let's get on with it." He shut the back door, got in the car and pulled out of the driveway. A few minutes later, he was in town, driving past the shops, cafés and stores that had been woven into the fabric of his life. As the car rolled along under the bright sunshine, he suddenly felt abandoned; ejected into a new life he had no control over. It'd happened before, a long time ago when he was a toddler. One day, Mom and Dad were there and the next, gone. He passed the First Baptist church where he and Brenda had been married in the summer of '99, tightened his grip on the steering wheel and pushed down on the accelerator.

Fifteen minutes later, he turned onto the Salmon River Parkway, heading for Salem. As he drove along the rural road passing open fields and woods, he settled in for the hour-long ride. Dialing to his favorite radio station, KOAC out of Corvallis, he turned the volume up. Click and Clack, the Tappet Brothers were on. It didn't take long until they had him smiling and laughing along with them as they diagnosed a problem that had nothing to do with cars. A young lady was trying to figure out how to get her handsome mechanic to ask her out for a date.

He turned to Jack. "Maybe I should open a service station. What'd'ya think, boy?" The dog barked and he reached over and patted him on the head. "Yeah, I know, get on with it." Truth was, dating was the furthest thing from his mind. Besides, he had lots of things to keep him busy; a fledgling bookstore he'd started a year ago for one.

He'd always been an avid reader and a bit of a history buff since his discharge from the Marines in '72, and had, from time to time over the years, toyed with the idea of retiring from the Fire Department and giving his dream a shot. But there never seemed to be the right time to roll the dice. The real reason, of course, was there were men who'd depended on him down at the station, along with a steady paycheck to pay the bills. But that was all in the past now. A life he could never go back to.

And then there was the VA where he volunteered on Mondays and Thursdays in the Physical Therapy department. With a strong medical background along with a history of service in Viet Nam, the therapists were glad to have him. Returning soldiers who were injured needed someone who understood; someone they could trust and bond with. Nothing sped the healing process up like having someone helping you who'd been in the trenches.

When he pulled into his driveway on Aspen Street, it was nearing dusk. His small one-story Tudor sat in shadow on the pie shaped lot at the end of the cul-de-sac. A large semi-arched picture window looked out over a front lawn in need of mowing. Flanking the house was a stout Gary Oak that had shed most of its orange and yellow leaves. A swath of mountain laurel and rhododendron backed up against a raised slate porch. He opened the car door and got out with Jack bounding behind him. The street was quiet tonight. *Must be the neighbors are at the jazz festival downtown.*

He grabbed his toolbox from the rear seat and headed to the detached one-car garage, still loaded with boxes waiting to be unpacked. They'd been sitting there since he moved in a year ago. Maybe he'd get to them next weekend. Right now, he had a more pressing matter at hand. He looked down at Jack. "Yes, I know, dinner-time."

Setting the toolbox on the workbench, he set off through the garage for the back door as Jack followed close behind. The Long galley-style kitchen was cluttered. Dirty dishes were scattered on the counter, empty pizza boxes and beer cans on the table. He set a bowl of chow down then went to the fridge and pulled out a bottle of beer and a left-over sandwich. As he stood munching on it, his cell phone vibrated.

"Hey, Matt. This is a surprise." He hadn't heard from Matt Fuller in over two months. For him to call out of the blue was out of character.

"Sorry I've been so out of touch. How's things?"

"They're good. Finished the last of the repairs at the house. Closing this Tuesday. What's up?" Andy said.

The Lincoln City Fire Marshall cleared his throat. "Umm … a problem's come up that we need to deal with. You know me. Never been one to candy-coat things." He paused and for a minute Andy thought the call had been dropped. Finally, Matt came back on and said, "Anyway… Leonard's parents have brought a civil suit against the department and you're named in it. Some ambulance-chasing lawyer must've gotten in their ear. Sorry about this, big guy, but I think you're gonna need to get a lawyer involved."

Andy looked up at the ceiling and sighed. A lawyer was one thing, but going over all the details of the accident again wasn't what he needed right now. "It's all right, Matt. Not your fault." But it wasn't all right and never would be. The events that happened on a sweeping bend of highway leading out of Lincoln City had haunted him relentlessly over the last year and a half. And now, he was going to be put through that wringer all over again.

Andy woke up in a cold sweat as the sounds of shrieking metal and shattering glass faded from his mind. Another dream about the accident! Would the nightly terror ever leave him alone? He flipped the sheet off and sat up rubbing his temples. Bending forward, he pinned his hands on the mattress, drew breath and looked at the alarm clock. 6:30 AM. In four hours, he and his partner Bob Lightfoot would be sitting across a table from a lawyer representing the Stewart family, giving yet another deposition regarding the accident.

Right now, he had to pull himself together, shower and shave. After that, he'd start going over his transcript of the previous deposition testimony he'd given during the initial investigation. Unpleasant business, but necessary. He trudged to the bathroom at the end of the hall with Jack following.

Twenty minutes later, he was slurping coffee at the kitchen table with the file in front of him. Fingering the manila folder, he peered through the rain-spattered sliding-glass doors next to him and thought of Brenda. Even though she'd been on her way to a new life, she'd put her interests aside to take care of him during the hellish six months that followed the accident. Now, there was no one left except Jack to quiet the inner demons, and there were many.

At length, he opened the file and stared at the field report. Flipping the page, he read Bob Lightfoot's account of what happened. A diagram of the accident followed showing how he'd valiantly tried to miss the eight-year-old boy, who had chased a ball out onto the highway. The report indicated the weather had been clear and cool. A slight southeast wind had been blowing across the two-lane highway. The siren and emergency running lights were in full operation. His speed: just a hair over fifty-five. Ten miles per hour over the posted state speed limit. Well within the parameters of rushing to an emergency situation. The only problem was he hadn't seen the 'Deaf Child' sign that had recently been posted a hundred yards from the bend in the road. That was the omission that haunted him.

The next seven pages documented the accident in pictures. Those, he flipped through. The memory of Bob pulling him through the jumbled disarray of fallen medical equipment and oxygen bottles in the overturned truck was plenty. He shook his head and was about to turn the page when his sister called. He flipped his phone open and yawned. "Hey, Panda."

"Hi Bruddy. I just wanted to let you know I'll be there in spirit with you today," his sister, Amanda, said. "Sure you don't want me to come with you?"

"I'll be okay. Bob'll be there. 'Sides, who'd open up the store?"

"Well, Jonah could," she said.

He cocked his brow as he thought of the grizzled Viet Nam war veteran he'd hired six months ago. While Jonah was competent and could easily manage it, he didn't want to push flying solo on the man so soon. Finally, he said, "I know he could, but I don't think he'd be comfortable with that just yet."

"Okay, I was just throwing it out there," she said. "Anyway, I'm here for you and so are Tom and Tuck."

"Thanks, I'll be okay," he said, trying to convince himself of it.

"I worry about you sometimes. By the way, have you told Brenda what's going on?"

"No. Didn't see the need," he replied, knowing his sister hadn't approved of Brenda's coming back to take care of him after the accident.

"Good idea." She paused. "You're not gonna lose the store. You did everything right. It's just a horrible thing that dear child ran out in front of you."

"Yeah, maybe … but doing everything right didn't change a damned thing did it? The boy died and I was behind the wheel, so that makes me a part of it."

He heard her sigh on the other end. "Bruddy, you need to stop beating yourself up." She paused and added, "Maybe you should get back in touch with your therapist."

He shook his head. "Mark's retired. I'll be all right."

"You need to talk to someone," she said. "I know of someone who –"

"Panda, please," he said a little harsher than he intended. He sat back and rubbed his eyes. "I'm fine."

"Okay, okay," she replied with a huff. She was quiet a moment then spoke up. "Look, why don't you and Jack join us for dinner tonight? We'll throw some steaks on the grille and I'll put a tater salad together with something sweet for dessert."

"Now, you're talking! By the way, I scheduled Tyler to come in at four today."

"Good, and he better be on time," she said. "I have to get to the bank to make deposits before it closes. So, when should I expect you?"

Andy paused. "Six-thirty?"

"Don't be late. Love you."

"Ditto." He flipped the phone shut. But getting back at it was the last thing he wanted to do and his expanded vision wasn't helping. He sat back, closed his eyes a moment then turned the page to read the statement he'd written a year ago for the inquiry. The passage of time did little to change how he felt about his role in the accident. He should've seen the 'Deaf Child' sign and been a little easy on the pedal. If he'd only been more careful.

The attorney who'd been coaching him on how to handle certain questions, told him to speak to 'just the facts' and avoid emotional responses. The term, 'I don't recall,' was to be a stock answer for dealing with difficult questions. It was 'cover-your-ass' mentality. He didn't like it. Except this was about money. Where the dollar was concerned, the lines between fact and fiction were blurred. A decision against the department would affect their ability to provide needed services to the community, to say nothing of what the suit was asking from him. Three hundred-fifty thousand! Where was he going to get that kind of cash? It would wipe him out financially. And the award to the family; that would do... what?

How do people put a price on a human life? It was blood money. The only winners as far as he could tell were the lawyers. He shook his head and closed the file. It was like trying to wash his hands and leave the water clean. No matter what he said, it wouldn't set things right.

Chapter 3

J ANET STEPPED out of the shower and wrapped herself in a towel. In four hours, she'd be in Portland to pick Nate up and bring him home. Since she'd found out her son was up for a Distinguished Service Cross Medal for extraordinary heroism, there'd hardly been a moment's rest. The local press was calling non-stop. There was even talk of a parade and a meeting with the governor. Everyone was getting into the act. She hastily dried herself off, pulled on a sweater and a pair of jeans, then headed to the kitchen where she heard Megan taking out plates and silverware. The smell of fresh brewed coffee and a broccoli-cheddar quiche wafted in the air. James Taylor's 'Fire and Rain' murmured from the CD player.

As she walked into the sunlit breakfast nook, Megan dragged a slice of quiche onto her plate. "Morning!"

"That for me?" Janet said, nodding at the entree while heading for the coffee pot.

"Not really," Megan said with a crooked smile, "but sure, you can have it."

Janet poured herself a cup. "Thanks, you ready to go?"

"Other than throwing on my face and a pair of boots, yeah."

When it came to putting on make-up, nothing was quick with Megan, especially since they were going to be the center of attention with the media. "You're sure you have a ride back from Kyle's? After we drop you off, Nate and I are coming straight back."

"Positive," Megan said. "You know, I wish my son would move the wedding down here. It'd be so much easier."

And keep it on your turf, Janet mused. She knew how uncomfortable it was going to be for Megan with her ex around. But Kyle's fiancé's family lived in South Burlingame, and so did a lot of Kyle's friends. And then there were nieces and nephews who were close to Kyle. "Have they booked a place for their reception yet?"

"Not yet. I keep telling him August is on the way. But you know kids... Speaking of which, I wonder how Nate's gonna like being 'man of the hour'. You know how he is. 'Mr. Avoidance'."

"I'm sure he'll do fine," Janet said, not believing it for a moment.

Megan rolled her eyes. "Yeaaah, right. We'll see how that goes." She paused. "And Trevor? I take it he's driving up separately?"

Janet ignored Megan's sarcasm. "Yes, he and Nadia are meeting us at the airport. After we have lunch, they're going to the mountains for the weekend."

Megan's face tightened then relaxed. "You really think we're gonna be able to have a private lunch with all the hoopla?"

"I'm hoping," Janet said. She sipped her coffee and sat down. "Surely, they'll be sympathetic to us wanting our privacy."

"Good luck with that," Megan said. "Anyways, it'll be great seeing Nate. Your heart must be doing cartwheels right now."

"You have no idea," Janet said, digging into her breakfast. The truth was, her heart was doing anything but cartwheels. Instead, she was battling an ominous feeling things weren't as good as Nate would have her believe. She knew her son well. Like his father, he downplayed everything. But downplaying a medal? Even that was a stretch for him. "I'm glad he's out of that damned war. It's taken too much from him."

"I know what you mean," Megan agreed. "But he's coming back with his head held high!" She nibbled a piece of toast and sat back. "You know, he acted weird when I asked him about Tracy."

"Yeah, I know," Janet said. She liked Nate's fiancé. She was good for her son.

"What'd'ya think's going on?" Megan said.

Janet set her fork down. Sipped her coffee. "Don't know, and I wouldn't pester him about it, okay?"

Megan cocked her brow. "Excuse me."

"Sorry. I guess I'm a bit uptight." She sighed, forced a smile and eyed Megan's pale green denim blouse. "So, new shirt?"

"Yep. Forty bucks at Abercrombie and Fitch. On sale."

"I like it. Brings out the red in your hair. Looks great with my jeans, too."

Megan laughed. "All mine are in the wash right now. Hope you don't mind."

"Not at all," Janet said. She sliced into her quiche. After taking a bite, she added, "You ever call Logan's? My camera's in there for repair and I need it back if I decide to take the Merced River gig."

"It's done. You can pick it up tomorrow. So, you're still thinking on going?"

"Depends," Janet said. "Nate comes first."

Megan took a sip of coffee. "The invitations for the Alzheimer's Gala are in. I set the box on your desk."

"Great. You check quantities and dates?" Janet said.

"Three hundred…January 10th, right?"

"Yep, good…We need to set up a meeting with the board for decorations and food. Can you make some phone calls?"

"Sure," Megan said. She bit into her piece of toast and put her finger up. "Oh, I meant to tell you, Don called yesterday."

Janet set her fork down. *Pain in my ass publisher!* "He can wait. I've got a wounded son coming home." She took a couple more bites of her breakfast. "And my galley, did you go over it?"

Megan downed the last bite of her quiche, picked up her plate and took it to the sink. "It's all good." Over her shoulder, she added, "By the way, there's an invitation on the counter from the guild. Apparently, they want you at some trade show as a guest speaker regarding your books."

"I'll look it over later," Janet said, knowing Megan had probably been chatting with Don. Her stepdaughter probably thought she was helping by mentioning the guild to Don, but it was the last thing she needed.

The ride north to Portland dragged despite Megan's prattling on about Ben. And if it wasn't Ben she was talking about, it was Kyle's wedding. But Janet's mind was on Nate. She pulled into the terminal parking garage and parked. Turning the engine off, she pulled the key out of the ignition with trembling hands.

She took a deep breath, and turned to her stepdaughter. "I'm scared, Meg. What if–"

Megan clasped her fingers around Janet's hand and squeezed. "He's gonna be okay, Jan, don't worry."

Janet sat back, wiped her eyes and tried to steady her nerves. "I've waited so long for him to come home, but I never wanted it this way."

"I know. But the important thing is, he's back."

"Yes," Janet said, wanting to believe it. "I just wish I knew what to expect. He was so cryptic about his injury. What if he…"

Megan held Janet with a defiant gaze. "Stop! I refuse to believe the worst. And you need to as well. Now come on, let's go get him."

Janet looked at her stepdaughter, loving her more than she thought possible. For over thirty years they'd been tied together. They were best friends before Megan's father came and changed everything. Falling in love with Megan's father had happened so gradually she hadn't seen it coming. By the time it finally hit her, it was too late to turn back. Suddenly, the tight bond between her and Megan unraveled and for the next twenty-seven years they circled each other like a pair of Tom Cats. In the end though, they built a bridge back to each other and laid a new foundation of trust, putting the past hurts behind them.

If for no other reason, Janet trusted Megan to keep her pointed in the right direction. Nobody knew her better than Megan.

Finally, she said, "Yes, you're right. Let's go get him!"

Janet swept through the front doors of the terminal and panned the expansive Travelport Hall for the incoming arrival's screen. It was shortly after twelve noon and the lines at the ticketing counters were short. She tapped Megan on the arm and pointed to an electronic bulletin board to their left and headed toward it.

"Nate's flight's due to land in ten minutes," she said then turned and hoofed it to the escalators leading to the security checkpoint. With every step, her heart raced and her hands dampened. Normally, she would've looked up at the barrel-vaulted skylight and space frame steel rods – a habit she'd picked up from twenty-five years with her architect husband – but not today. She stepped off the escalator into a sea of reporters. Signs of "WELCOME HOME NATE" and "SALEM'S HERO'S BACK" bobbed up and down in the throng gathered near the TSA exit point. Off to the side, stood Trevor and Nadia. Megan, who was trailing behind her, steered clear of them and immersed herself in the crowd.

Janet pushed through the crowd and joined Trevor, her gaze darting to the exit aisle beside the checkpoint.

Trevor said, "Hey Janet. Hell of a crowd, huh? There must be a hundred people here."

"He's not gonna like this," Janet said.

"No, I don't expect he will. Anyway, I'm going for a cup of coffee." He turned to Nadia. "What about you, hon? Want anything?"

"I'm quite all right for the moment," Nadia said in her exacting German accent. "Janet, why don't you come sit with me?"

"I couldn't if I tried," Janet said. She checked her watch and tried to contain herself. *He should be here by now. Where are you, Nate?*

The overhead intercom squawked, announcing a flight arrival from Chicago. A few minutes later, a stream of incoming travelers poured through the exit aisle. Breathlessly, Janet watched them walk past her on their way to unknown destinations until at last there he was in his army fatigues, hobbling along with another soldier. When he saw her, he waved.

As she ran to him, the crowd surged behind her. Cameras flashed as Nate put his hand up, sheltering his eyes from the lights. The soldier beside him bolted forward and held the crowd at bay as Janet threw her arms around her son. He let her hold him a moment then stepped out of her grasp. The separation stung. She wanted more. Wanted to keep touching his face, inhale the citrus scent of his cologne and inspect him like a newborn baby.

"You must be exhausted," she said, glancing at the brace that went the full length of his leg. She fought the urge to drag him back into her arms and forced herself to smile. That's what she had to do when it came to public affection with Nate. He said it made him feel like a child. Well, he was her child and always would be. Again, not for the first time, she wondered how they'd come to this fencing of emotions. Where did she lose her baby and when? Was it the war or was it the Montgomery family curse, which demanded utmost decorum in all things?

"I'm whipped, but I'll manage," he admitted. He nodded toward his companion. "That's PFC Jennings. We met up in Germany. He lives in Salem so we caught a ride together."

The tall, dark-haired man glanced back from holding the crowd away and put his hand out to Janet. "Nice to meet you ma'am."

She looked back into his transparent blue eyes. Ma'am wasn't a name she was accustomed to hearing herself called. She shook his hand. "Nice to meet you, too. So, were you in Nate's unit?"

The private glanced at Nate. "Umm…"

"No, he was in Alpha company," Nate said, cutting in emphatically. He winked at Jennings. "Careful, she'll put you under a light and interrogate the hell outta you."

"Nathan James Porter, I would do no such thing," she said, aghast.

Just then, Megan popped out of the crowd and ran to them. She hugged Nate and when she pulled away, the questions came from the crowd in a torrent about his heroic deeds and what he had planned for the future. Nate panned the crowd and looked away. Finally, he said, "Thanks for coming everyone. But, hey, it's been a long ride so I'm pretty tired right now. Maybe we can do this another time." To Megan, he said, "Can we get the hell out of here?"

They managed to escape and found a small Italian restaurant on the east side of town. After they ate, Janet dropped Megan off at Kyle's and settled in for the two-hour drive home. As she drove along Interstate 5 under a slate sky, she watched her son from the corner of her eye. His gaze was fixed straight ahead at the passing fields of winter wheat and rye. Whatever was on his mind, it had his complete attention. *Should I say anything? Would it push him further away? The last time I pressed him, he shut down. How long should I wait? Is there ever a right time?*

"So, I assume Tracy knows you're home," she said at last.

He shivered and glanced back at her. "What?"

"Tracy. She knows you've been discharged, right?" She held her breath hoping he wouldn't erect one of his famous barricades around his heart.

He shifted in his seat. "Yeah, she knows," he said, brushing the question away like crumbs off a cheap suit.

"She must be worried."

He averted his attention to his passenger-side window. "I guess."

There it was. Her heart had guessed right. Tracy was no longer part of Nate's future. She ached for him. All she ever wanted was for him to be happy and safe, insulated from the deep bitterness the world was dishing out like breath-mints at a funeral. She blamed herself. Somehow she'd failed him.

For the next twenty minutes, they said nothing until finally, he turned to her. "I've been thinking about getting an apartment. I'd like to do it as soon as possible. You wouldn't mind would you?"

His words slammed into her like a sucker punch, taking her breath away. For a moment she didn't know what to say. The thought of him living on his own so soon after getting home hadn't occurred to her.

Sure, he'd want his own place at some point...but so quickly? She swallowed her surprise and buried her disappointment in a smile. "No, of course not, honey. But I think you're gonna be busy with this medal stuff for a bit. And, you'll need a job at some point and what about your leg? Won't you need–"

"Mom!" His tone was firm, leaving no room for argument. "I don't want talk about it, okay?" He shifted in his seat. "Don't look at me like that. I'm fine."

No, you're not, Nate. She saw his jaw tighten and his shoulder flex. Her grip on the wheel increased. It was taking all her strength to keep from stopping the car and pulling him into her. "I know you are. I just want you to remember you have a home for as long as you want."

"I know."

He turned his face toward her, and for a moment she saw his father's determined frown when he wanted something and nothing was going to get in the way. And now he'd become a sterner version of his father. Rigid and unbendable; his beautiful endearing spirit crammed way deep down, like tattered photos in attic boxes that fade under the dust of years.

Chapter 4

HOLIDAYS FOR Andy were a mixed bag of conflicting emotions due to the absence of family. The question of where his grandparents, aunts, uncles and cousins were when he and his sister were orphaned no longer mattered. At least that's what he told himself on the rare occasions he thought about his origins.

Today, as with every Thanksgiving, he was at his sister's. Unlike every year before, they'd invited a guest. Amanda had suggested asking Jonah to dinner. At the moment, the lanky, gray-haired black veteran was isolating himself on the far end of the couch as if he were preparing to bolt at any minute.

A veteran of the Viet Nam war, Jonah had served in the same company as Andy, albeit three years before he'd touched down on its accursed shores. It didn't matter they hadn't ever met. Their experiences connected them in the silent language of memory. Just a look was enough to know what the other was thinking. But for all the strength of that bond, there were parts Andy knew Jonah kept hidden. There were things soldiers wouldn't admit to anyone.

Now Jonah was staring off through the large bay window. The man was eyeing the swaying chestnut tree in the front yard with ever-watchful brown eyes. What he was thinking, Andy couldn't guess. He was certain it had a lot to do with being around a lot of folks. Jonah didn't like crowds.

"You okay, Bruddy?"

"Uh…yeah." He turned to his sister and eyed the table. It was set for twelve with a highchair at one end. An old wooden box sat in the center of it. The stained mahogany box had been with Amanda for as long as he could remember. As his gaze strayed back to Jonah, he wondered what he'd write on the card going into it this year.

"He'll be all right," Amanda whispered, as if guessing his thoughts. "Why don't you come help me in the kitchen. Get your mind off things."

"Sure, why not?"

He followed her out to the countrified kitchen. Her husband, Tom, had remodeled it a few years back under her supervision. Based on the old farm-style kitchens of the past, it had a Tom Sawyer charm. In the center of the room stood a butcher block table with white lacquered skirting. On it sat a twenty-two-pound bird in a roasting pan.

Amanda handed him a knife. "Get to work, Marine."

He chuckled, and a few minutes later, had several slices piled onto a nearby platter. As he set the knife down, his nephew Tim stepped beside him.

"Th-th-that looks good," Tim said, snatching a piece.

He eyed his sandy-haired nephew, whose six-two, one hundred sixty-five-pound frame swam in a cotton blue and white plaid shirt. The young man was Amanda's youngest of three. Her miracle child had arrived twelve weeks premature on the day before Thanksgiving. What Tim lacked in motor skills, he more than made up for with a keen intellect that had pushed him through OSU by seventeen and grad school a year and a half later. Now, at twenty-one, he'd achieved more degrees than the whole Atkins family combined.

He shot Amanda a passing glance. Since she had her back to them, he nabbed a piece for himself. Leaning close to Tim, he whispered, "Pretty damned good, huh? But we better not let your Mom see us doing this."

Tim put his finger to his mouth and broke into a crooked grin.

Amanda set the casserole she'd taken out of the oven on the counter. Over her shoulder, she said, "Timothy, Bruddy, keep your mitts off that turkey!"

Tim grinned as his head wobbled back and forth. "Snagged!"

She went to the fridge and took out two bottles of beer. Bringing them to Tim, she said, "Here, make yourself useful and take these to your father and Uncle Tuck." She turned to Andy after Tim left the room. "You're not helping. He doesn't need the encouragement."

Andy snatched another piece of turkey and winked.

She swatted his arm. "Stop that already!"

"Ouch!" He feigned injury then laughed. "By the way: good idea inviting Jonah."

"Tell you the truth, I didn't know if he'd come."

He stepped back from the turkey, wiped his hands on a towel. "I don't say this as often as I should, but you're aces."

She eyed him sidelong. "Okay, what are you up to?"

"Nothing." He studied the fine lines around her eyes. When had they happened and why hadn't he noticed them before now?

She pressed her lips together and shook her head. "You're a sappy man, Andy McNamara. But I love you anyway."

Andy spent the next day at the VA where he volunteered in the rehab clinic. He'd enlisted for the job after seeing an ad in the local paper. Today, he'd spent the morning helping a double amputee take his first steps with new legs. Although it was triumph for the young man who was on his way to reclaiming his independence, it was also a grim reminder of what man could do to man.

He stepped into the elevator and punched the button for the first floor. As the car descended, he saw the four Viet Cong soldier boys in his mind's eye. Had killing them really been necessary? It was a question he'd been trying to answer most of his life. Sure, they were the enemy, but could there have been another way? He brushed the memory away.

The elevator dinged and the doors opened. Stepping out, he headed across the busy front lobby. There he saw a woman walking behind a young soldier who'd made quite a splash since coming home. The boy was a hero. Nate, he thought his name was, He waved and got a nod in return. But it was the woman behind the young man that caught his attention. She looked familiar. As he passed them, he gave her a second look. When she glanced back, he realized she was the woman he'd met at Fogarty five weeks before. He hesitated, wondering if he should call out and say hi. But he didn't really know her. Other than the chat they'd had on the beach, what could he talk about afterward – the weather? *Let it go,* he thought, but his legs wouldn't move. There was something about her that resonated and made his heart beat a little faster. Whether she felt him staring after her he didn't know but she looked back again.

Well, this is awkward. Now what do I do?

As recognition spread across her face, he debated if he should wave back. But she looked away just as he was about to call out.

Chapter 5

JANET VEERED off Northside Drive Road onto El Portal Road and headed out of Yosemite National Park toward San Francisco. She'd spent the last ten days here with Nate under the towering rock and stone of the glacier carved valley. The trip was as much to determine shots she wanted to get when she came back in mid-February as it was to give Nate a breather from the local press.

She drove along the tree-lined road in the shadow of the towering granite walls, thinking about what to do regarding Christmas. Her brother, Craig, and his wife and kids were flying in from Florida. Her friend and mentor, Mick Danzer and his wife Sandra were coming in from San Francisco. With Kyle and his fiancé Debbie, along with Trevor and Nadia, she had a full house.

"I love your sister and I try to be sympathetic to her feelings, but this feud with your brother has got to end," she said, slowing down around a sharp bend in the road.

Nate was quiet a minute. "You're obsessing, Mom." He grabbed her CD wallet and slid a disc into the CD player. A moment later, Bono's voice filled the empty spaces.

She frowned. *Obsessing? Really?* "Your father would have wanted it, Nate. And the last thing I need right now is another tension-filled holiday. I'm tired of it. Tired of feeling like a diplomat in my own house. Lord knows your brother's trying."

He dug into the bag of trail mix and popped a hand-full into his mouth. "I suppose…I need to stretch my legs. Mind pulling over at the next turn-off."

She glanced over and saw him rubbing his thigh. "You think you might've over-done it yesterday? Your leg needs time to heal."

"Its fine. Just doesn't like being cooped up in the car is all. Besides, Barry and Andy say I'm making progress."

"Well, that's good to hear," she said and thought about the man she passed in the hospital lobby a couple weeks ago. Might he be the same Andy, Nate was referring to? "So, you have two Physical Therapists?"

"No. Barry's the PT. Andy's a volunteer. Helps out around the clinic and stuff." He cleared his throat and his stoic expression brightened. "He's pretty interesting."

Finally a smile! "Who, Andy?"

"Yeah. He was a gunny in Nam."

"You mean a sniper?"

"No…and yes," he conceded. "They don't like the term. They do what they have to, to protect the men, but it's not who they are, not really."

"I see," she said. A backhoe pulled onto the road ahead. She slowed down, went around it. "Hmm…so what else besides guns do you two talk about?"

He shrugged. "Well, he used to be a paramedic."

"Used to be?"

He shut the trail mix bag and set it on the floor between his legs. "He's retired. Owns a bookstore or something like it in town." He pointed to a rest stop ahead. "There's one."

She eased the car onto the broken macadam ramp and parked. He got out and hobbled over to a picnic table. She switched over to a radio. The station was playing oldies. Sixties and seventies rock and roll. The music of her brother's generation. As she sat listening to Jefferson Airplane protest a war that divided the country, she thought of the war her country was involved in right now. A war where people hijacked planes. Flew them into buildings.

A war that took Nate away from her for five years.

A war that stole precious time from his father.

A war that sent him home *damaged.*

She wanted to think of Nate as *a hero,* but all she could think of were the should'a'beens. But how could he have known what the future held for his father? And how could she blame him for his choices?

In the end it had cost Nate dearly. The physical injuries would heal over time. The emotional ones: not so much. As hard as she'd struggled with her decision to place Neil in Hazelnut, it had been exponentially harder for Nate to deal with being away in an uncertain world. And now, it had spit him out like a wad of gum that no longer served its useful purpose.

She drummed her fingers on the wheel as the late afternoon sun pressed down on the windshield. A destination sign ahead noted they were fifteen miles out of Merced. It would be another four hours and change from there to San Francisco. There, they would stay with her old friend Mick, and his wife Sandra. It had been a while since she'd seen them. Maybe Sandra could reach Nate. She was a therapist; maybe she could get him talking.

As she struggled for answers, the sound of a guitar snuck under her thoughts. She blinked, and for the next a two and a half minutes, Paul McCartney's voice floated out of the radio. Suddenly, she was transported back in time to her wedding on the beach. Her lips formed the words: *And I love her.* The memory of Neil's smiling face gripped her.

That evening, she and Nate joined Mick and his wife out by the pool. There, the conversation bounced from the weather to family to Nate's impending Distinguished Service medal, (which was quickly cut off by Nate) and finally to Mick's latest home improvement projects. She listened as Mick laid out his plans for the back yard.

Sandy broke into Mick's long-winded presentation. "Hey, Jan, it's getting chilly. You want a jacket?"

Janet yawned. "I'm good. What about you, Nate?" When he shook his head, she turned to Mick. "Sounds like you're gonna be busy this summer. Between work and all you have going on, you'll be meeting yourself coming and going."

Mick stood, grabbed his wine glass off the patio table. Taking a healthy gulp, he cleared his throat. "Well, yes and no." He eyed Sandy with a tentative expression. "Sandy and I've been talking over things. I'm not getting any younger. We think it's time to retire."

"Really?" Janet said. She sat back in her chair and crossed her legs. Retirement was not a word that'd ever crossed Mick's lips.

"Yep. Just need to fill my position and I'm outta there."

"Any idea how long it'll take," Janet said.

Mick gulped another swallow of wine and eyed her speculatively. "Could be pretty soon, depending…"

"On what?" Janet said, crossing her arms. She'd seen that look before. It was one Mick gave when he was about to spring something on someone.

He rubbed his chin, looked off over the pool then turned back to her. "Umm… well, I've been talking with Harry and umm … well, your name sort'a came up. Actually, quite a bit."

The wind went out of her and set her glass down. "Mick, what did you do?"

"Nothing … Just talking." He shot her one of his classic, sad-little-boy expressions. "You know, brainstorming."

Janet eyed Sandra, who was sitting in the chair beside her. "Did you know anything about this?"

When Sandy shrugged, Mick continued, "Harry thinks you'd be a good fit, and so do I." Janet glanced at Nate, who was sitting across from her nursing a beer. *There's no way I'm going anywhere.* But Mick went on, "You don't have to make a decision right now. Just think about it. It's a hell of an opportunity."

Janet smiled. "I appreciate the thought, really I do, but I afraid I'm going to have to pass."

Mick drained his glass. "You passed a number of years ago if I remember correctly."

"Well, yeah I did, and I have to admit, I probably made a mistake," Janet confessed. "But things are different now."

"Well, that's true, but–"

"Mick, honey, let it go," Sandra interjected.

But Mick pressed on. "You sure, Jan? Lot of prestige, here."

"And a lot of time away from home," Sandra put in. She gave Janet a knowing glance.

Mick shot Sandra a 'what-are-you-doing-to-me' look. To Janet, he said, "What about moving here? San Fran's a great town. We'd love having you close by."

You don't give up, do you? "I'm sure it is. But I could never sell the house."

"I wasn't insinuating you would," Mick said. "Megan's living with you and Nate's home now, give it to them."

That earned a raised brow from Nate.

Sandra let out a protracted sigh. "Mick, really?" To Janet, she said, "Please excuse my idiot husband. Sometimes he's clueless." She turned to Mick. "Sweetheart, her husband built that house for her. She could no more part with it than I could part with your wedding ring."

Mick frowned. It was obvious he was working out what Sandra meant. To him, a wedding ring could be replaced. He had no clue of the underlying objection Janet had and that his wife understood.

Finally, he shrugged. "I guess I see your point." He turned to Janet. Gave her a look of resignation. Not one she was used to seeing on him. When he wanted something, he didn't give up easily. Finally, he said, "Well, I guess the answer's, no, then, isn't it?"

"I'm afraid so," she said, but she couldn't help seeing her father shaking his head in her mind's eye. *Yes, I know Dad. Never burn your bridges, but helping Nate overrules this hands down.*

When nine o'clock came around, Janet announced she was turning in for the night. She went over to her son, who was chatting Mick up about the Niner's prospects. Giving him a peck on the cheek, she headed for the guest room down the hallway. Sandra followed close behind.

"You want an extra blanket?"

"No, I'm fine, but thanks," Janet said. "Dinner was great. Thanks for having us."

"Not a problem. You two are always welcome here." Sandra lowered her voice. "Would you ever consider leaving Salem?"

Janet shook her head. "Right now, no, but who knows."

Sandra looked back over her shoulder then eyed Janet confidingly. "Keep that under your hat or you'll have you know who breathing down your neck…By the way, how are you? With Nate's coming home a hero and injured along with the anniversary of Neil's passing, you must be in tatters."

"I am. I miss Neil terribly some days, but I'm doing okay. And now that Nate's home, I have my hands full. He's thinking of moving out."

Sandra drew back. "Moving out?"

"Yeah. I don't know what to do about it."

"He's seeing someone about what happened, right?" Sandra said.

Janet shrugged. "He says he is, but I don't know for sure."

Sandra reached out. Clasped hands with Janet. "It takes time. He'll come around."

"On the drive here I was thinking maybe…maybe you could talk to him."

"Oh, I'd love to help, you know I would, but I can't," Sandra said. "If he's seeing someone, he'll be okay. Give it time. Whatever's going on will work itself out. You'll see."

Janet nodded, squeezed Sandra's hand and forced a smile. "I guess."

They started back down the hall. As Sandra opened the linen closet door, she said, "By the way, how goes your work with the local Alzheimer's Association?"

"Challenging, but rewarding."

"And your book?"

"My publisher's a pain in the ass."

Sandra handed her a towel and nodded toward the door. "Let's get you settled."

The two of them went in and pulled the covers back on the bed. As Janet tossed the accent pillows on the chair beside her, the pant leg of her capris pulled back. A long, faint scar showed itself on the side of her leg.

It caught Sandra's attention. "From the accident?"

Janet nodded. "It's my beauty mark." She paused. "Actually, it's more than that. It's my touchstone 'cause it brought my father back into my life."

Mick knocked at the door. "You two gonna cackle all night?"

They looked back at him as he leaned against the doorway wearing a green terrycloth robe. For a moment, Janet saw her father in his expression. It hardly seemed possible he had passed six years ago. Until now, she hadn't realized how little she thought of him over the last year. How did that happen? And why couldn't she remember the sound of his voice? Would the memory of his face soon follow?

Chapter 6

ANDY PULLED into the Townsend Medical Arts Plaza and found a place to park. He turned the engine off and thought about Nate Porter. The young man was recovering physically, but mentally, not so much. He knew he should keep his distance and stay out of the kid's head. Why was Nate different?

The answer to that troubled him. It was because of Nate's *mother*.

She was attractive, but it was something more. Something behind her ever-present 'at ease' expression set his heart soaring. He came to himself and looked at his watch. He was early for his appointment.

Pulling his collar up, he got out of his car. Locking up, he headed for the forest-green entry canopy. Once inside, he took the elevator to the third floor and found the doctor's office down the hall.

He liked Dr. Steffens. She was going the distance for him. The prescription glasses were doing the job. The extraneous visual information had diminished. He opened the door to her suite and checked in with the receptionist. Finding a seat in the small but cheerful waiting room, he sat with eyes closed, trying to ward off the ever-present dull ache in the back of his skull.

"Mr. McNamara? We're ready for you."

He got up and followed the thirty-something blond-haired woman holding his chart. As he went into the exam room, he glanced at a photo of Boiler Bay on the wall. He'd seen it before, and liked it.

"Dr. Steffens will be with your shortly," the woman said. As he entered the room, the intern prattled on. "In the meantime, just a couple of routine questions." She set the chart in her hands on the countertop and opened the file. "So, Mr. McNamara, any changes in your vision since last time?"

He took a seat on the exam chair. "Not really."

She scribbled a note in the open file. "Any prolonged dizziness, headaches?"

He'd answered these questions so many times he felt like a parrot. "Yes, to both. Usually happens when it's bright out or after a long day at the store."

The woman gave him a darting glance. "Okay, it shouldn't be too long." She closed the file and left the room. As he waited for the doctor, he went over and studied the picture. In the lower right hand corner was Janet Porter's signature. He rubbed his chin. Janet seemed to be crossing his path at every turn.

Dr. Steffens pushed through the door. Tall, athletic, and in her late forties (at least that's what he guessed her to be), the blue-eyed brunette had a high-octane can-do personality. She shut the door behind her. "I dropped by your bookstore the other day. It's very nice. How are things going there?"

He sat back in the chair as she opened his file and glanced down at her notes. "We're doing pretty good. I think folks come in for my sister's pastries more than they do my books, but I'm not complaining. Whatever gets them through the door. When were you there? Wish I'd known, I'd have given you a treat on the house."

She looked up. "I'll keep that in mind next time. So, how're the glasses working? And why aren't you wearing them?"

"I do when I'm outside."

"You need to wear them all the time," she said, rolling her stool up next to him.

He shrugged. "They make me look like a bug."

"They don't look that bad. If you want different frames, I can change them out." She fiddled around with the lenses on the optometry machine. Turned the lights off and maneuvered it in front of him. "Okay, why don't we try the fourth through the sixth lines?"

He looked through the lens opening and read the letters.

She pulled the machine away and turned her probe light on, aiming its needle-like beam into his eye. "How are the headaches? Getting worse; better?"

"They come and go," he said. "Usually happen in the morning or after a long day on the computer."

She backed away, turned the probe light off and raised the room lights. "You need to give your eyes frequent breaks. Don't look at me like that. I know you have a business to run, but it's not dependent on the computer. Thirty minutes at a time is enough. Now come over here and let's check your pressure."

He got up and followed her to the large tabletop machine. Taking a seat on the stool in front of it, he nested his face on the padded frame.

"So, I meant to ask you the last time you were here what led you to open your book store after your accident? Seems quite a departure from being a EMT," she said as a burst of air punched his eye.

He jerked back. "I've always been reader. When I was a kid, it was an escape from my pain in the ass brothers."

"Brothers can be merciless. Were you the youngest?"

He shifted in the seat, trying to get comfortable, nodded and cleared his throat. "Yeah. You have brothers?"

"I do...two. Okay, left eye now, please."

After she hit him with another burst of air, he got up and went over for the 'follow-the-little-white-dot' test, as he liked to call it. He climbed into the exam chair as a knock came to the door.

When she pulled it open, he heard the aide's voice on the other side. "Your husband called. He can't make it for lunch. The tractor broke down at Ms. Porter's and he has to run for parts."

"Okay. Tell him I'll call him later."

He glanced at the picture on the wall again and waited for the doctor to return. "I was looking at the photo over there again. I noticed it was taken by Janet Porter."

She brought the optic lens machine over and fitted it to his face. "Yes. She's a client of my husband."

In his mind's eye, Janet's face flashed him. Should he say more? He didn't want to appear nosy, but he couldn't help wanting to know more. He leaned forward, followed the flashing white dot around the wall. "I met her a while ago on a beach of all places."

She pulled the machine away. Turned the lights back on. "Really?"

"Yeah. And her son's an outpatient at the VA. I've been working with him."

She rolled her stool over to the counter where his chart lay opened. "He's been through a lot."

"Yeah, he told me he lost his father while he was over in Iraq. That's tough."

She jotted something down. "Yes, it is…Okay, so, are you using those wipes I gave you?"

I guess that ends that, Andy thought. "Ahh…yeah."

She looked up from writing something. "Really?"

"Most of the time," he said, trailing off.

She set her pen down. "All the time, mister. It's important." She scribbled something on a pad, tore the page off and handed it to him. "This is a referral to a neurologist. I want you to call him for an appointment…soon," she said, emphasizing the last word. "We need to get to the bottom of things here."

He was taken aback. "Something wrong?"

"I don't know, but I don't like your persistent headaches. They've been going on way too long," she said. "I'll see you back here in three weeks. And remember, wear your glasses and take breaks from the computer, you hear?"

"Roger that," he said. He got up, not liking the serious tone of her parting words and headed for the V.A..

Nate grunted. "One more rep. I can do it."

Andy considered the request. He didn't want Nate pushing himself too hard and having a setback. Since Nate had been coming to physical therapy, he'd been a man on a mission. But Andy knew the mission was more than just rehabbing the shattered leg. He put his hand on Nate's dampened back and steadied him as he went downward from his standing position to a squat. The grimace on Nate's face told Andy he was pushing things a little too far.

"Okay, okay, that's enough for today soldier," Andy said. He put his other hand on Nate's bent over chest and helped him back up to a standing position. The kid had determination; he'd give him that. He helped him over to a long wooden bench and had him stretch his leg out in front of him. Kneeling on a mat in front of Nate, he cradled the kid's foot in his lap. Looking up, he said, "You did good today. But this isn't going to get better overnight. Injuries like this take time to heal. You don't want to go backwards by overdoing things."

Nate bit his lip as Andy gently massaged the side of the knee under the long snaking scar that ran from mid-calf to mid-thigh. Three more angry crescent scars dug deep into the top of Nate's upper thigh. Gnarled reminders of what flying shrapnel could do to human flesh. At last Nate said, "I'm good."

"I'm sure you are," Andy replied. "So how was the trip to Yosemite? Been a while since I've been there."

"It was all right, I guess. My mom's doing a shoot down there in February. I wanted to stay home, but she badgered me into tagging along."

Andy squeezed another dab of ointment onto his hand and carefully worked it into the shriveled skin around Nate's kneecap. Without looking up, he said, "Yeah...moms are like that."

Nate shifted his body on the bench so it bore down on the hip of his good leg. "All I know is, she's pestering the shit out of me about it and it's getting old." He looked away and stared out over the scattered treadmills, parallel bar set-ups and other equipment. The look on his face was dull. A gaze Andy had seen more often than he cared to admit. It was the mindset of a soldier. Andy knew to let the silence fill the space, so he kept quiet and continued the rub down. When, and if, Nate was ready to talk, it would come a little bit at a time. Until then, it was *listen*. No questions, no trite or cliché comments, just be there.

He finished up, grabbed Nate's brace and fitted it to the leg, wrapping the straps snug, but not too tight. Nate stood and waited while he retrieved his cane. As he handed it to him, Nate said, "When you came home from 'Nam, did you feel like a stranger to everyone, like you didn't know 'em anymore?"

Andy understood where the kid was coming from, and it pained him to tell him the truth. He rolled a wheelchair over. "For a while, yes. The feeling fades, but it never really goes completely away. One day at a time, soldier, okay?"

"Yeah. Well, we better get out there. I'm sure she's waiting for a report."

Andy smiled as Nate settled into the chair and lifted his feet onto the leg rests. "Be kind to your mom. She's had to endure a long time of worrying about you. She'll ease off, trust me." *That is, once I have a chat with her.*

"We'll see. You don't know her like I do," Nate said.

For the first time in five sessions, Andy saw a smile on Nate's face.

Chapter 7

J ANET SAT at the kitchen island with her laptop open, going over image files of her trip to Yosemite as the morning radio show played in the background. She'd just had another restless night with hardly any sleep. For the last few months the media and the military brass were a constant presence in their lives. She was tired of it. Yes, she was proud of Nate; proud he was being recognized and honored. But lately it was feeling more like a photo opportunity for the Washington D.C. elites and local bigwigs. It was an election year after all.

She closed out of Photoshop, and tapped her pencil on the countertop. She was fairly satisfied with the results of her shoot. Out of two hundred and thirty-four shots she'd taken, thirty of them showed promise for the photo-shoot she'd take in mid-February. That was, providing Nate went with her. Otherwise, it could wait. One of the perks of being an Ansel Adams award winning photographer was having latitude with clients. Of course it had its limitations. She jotted down a few notes and sat back, sipping her coffee. As she considered her plan of attack for the shoot, Megan shuffled into the room. With her shoulder length hair askew and wearing sweats, the woman looked like she'd been dragged through a knothole.

"Morning," Janet said with a lilt in her voice.

For the last five weeks, Megan and her boyfriend, Ben, had been driving the forty-five mile jaunt back and forth between Woodburn and her home in the Heights. They were like teenagers, constantly needing to be together. With each date, the witching hour for Megan getting home got increasingly later.

Megan waved as she went to the cupboard.

Janet eyed her while the woman grabbed a mug down from the cupboard. "Late night, huh?" When Megan nodded, she added, "Why don't you just stay the night with him? Save yourself the drive home."

Megan turned and looked at her sideways. "I've thought about it, but I'm not ready for that yet."

Janet smirked because she firmly believed they were spending time between the sheets. "So, you're not sleeping with him?"

A smile danced across Megan's face. "Let's just say, not in the traditional sense." She nibbled her lip. "I never thought I'd say this again, but I think I'm falling in love. He's so great. Lets me be me, you know."

Janet went over and hugged her. It was good to see her best friend happy. For the first time in two years, Meg was coming out of her shell. It probably meant she'd soon be moving on, but Janet couldn't complain.

"You think I'm going too fast?" Megan said, drawing back. "I mean, I've only been seeing him for a couple months."

"What I think doesn't matter," Janet said. "The only thing that matters is what you think. If you think you're going too fast, slow down."

"I know, but every time I leave him, all I can think about is the next time we're together. It's driving me crazy."

"Not to mention running you into the ground." She patted Megan on the shoulder. "Keep your eyes open and listen to your heart. If you love him, it won't lead you wrong."

"It led me wrong once," Megan said, knitting her brow.

"You were a kid then, Meg. You're a grown woman now. You know the flags to look for."

"Well, so far there haven't been any," Megan conceded. "Were there any with you and Dad?

"Nothing major, other than him being so much older," Janet said. "Seriously though, it was mostly *me* learning to trust."

"For me, it's learning to trust again," Megan said with an edge in her voice. She paused then brightened. "By the way, Don called the other day while you were out. You gonna return his calls or not? You know, if I were a betting gal, I'd say he's sweet on you."

Janet went back to her chair. "Is that what you think?"

Megan took her mug back up, sipped her coffee and cracked a smile. "You could do worse."

Janet groaned. "You know, there's nothing worse than a woman in love, believing she has to fix up the whole world."

"Just saying. He's not hard to look at."

"Right now, Quasimodo wouldn't look half bad to you. But he's way too young."

"Right," Megan said. She grinned. "Says the woman who married my father."

"Don't you have some place to be?"

Once Megan was out of the house, Janet sequestered herself in her office and dialed Don. As the phone rang on the other end, she felt her stomach knot. She really didn't want to have this conversation, but it was necessary. It was time to set things in order between them. On the fifth ring, he picked up.

"Janet. I was beginning to wonder if you were avoiding me," he said with a chipper voice.

"Just been busy is all. What's up," she replied then realized her tone was clipped.

"Well," he said, "you never got back to me about dinner. I have some ideas I want to get in front of you about your books."

She took a deep breath. "My son's back from Iraq and needs me. I don't have time right now to meet."

Silence rang on the other end. Finally Don said, "Janet, I know you're going through things, but I have a lot invested in you. I think you could at least give back a little here."

"I can appreciate that, but my son comes first," she said, hardening her tone.

There was a long pause. "Okay, and how long will that take? I have a lot riding on things. I can't wait forever."

"Meaning?"

"Meaning, if you're not interested in giving me a reasonable date and meeting me half way, then I'll call it a day and you can go somewhere else. Of course, I'll be needing the advance back I gave you …with interest. As for your books, the contracts still hold. And I do believe, if I remember correctly, I have a legal interest in the book you're working on right now."

She bristled. "I don't think so."

"Oh, I would look at the contract if I were you. The way it's written it clearly states you can't go to print with anyone but me until the provisionary contract expires. Simply put, I own the intellectual rights for the book you're working on."

There it was, right out in the open: the one thing that really mattered: intellectual rights. He had her by the throat. She couldn't care less about the money, but his controlling her creative works was more than she could bear. How could she have been so stupid to sign a provisional contract for her work in progress? She gritted her teeth as her gut tightened. "So you're holding my work hostage?"

"I prefer to think of it as protecting my interests."

"I want my rights back, all of them."

"And you'll get them, once the contract is up. Look, this is a lose-lose situation for both of us. All I ask is that you devote some time and effort to this. I don't think it's too much to ask."

She tapped her nails on the old Pilgrim desk that had once been her husband's.

"Janet, you still there?"

"Yeah, I'm here," she said.

"Well, am I asking too much?"

"I suppose not, but like I said, my son's needs come first."

"There you go, then," he said. "So, can you come to Portland, say next week?"

She dragged her day-planner off the shelf. Flipping it open, she said, "I have the afternoon of December 29th and the morning of the 30th open right now...providing..."

"Yes, I know, your son's needs." He paused. Okay, the 29th works for me. How's eleven o'clock?"

"Penciling you in as we speak."

"Great ... In the meantime, give some thought to bringing some creative ideas to the table. I hear the guild wants you to do a presentation. You know, you still have a voice out there. People want to see you, hear you talk about your work. Set up a few book signings and maybe a couple radio interviews."

But she hardly heard a word as the door beside her swung open. Nate came in and sat. She put her finger up and whispered she was almost done then went back to Don. "What? Oh, yeah...fine. We'll talk about it when I come up."

"That's better. Believe me, you won't regret it."

What did I just agree to? she thought as she ended the call. She smiled. "What's up, sweetie?"

He bent forward and put his hands on his knees. Eyeing her with a measured look, he set her on edge. "I was just surfing the web and I found a place I wanna check out. I called and they can show it to me at two. Mind driving me over so I can get a look at it?"

She felt her breath catch. This was too soon. He just got home. She forced a smile as her mind spun like a whirling top. "Sure."

For a moment, he stared at her as if he was unsure he'd heard her right. Finally, he said, "Umm...thanks."

"You're welcome." She got up and patted his shoulder, struggling to keep her fears and wants to herself. There were a million reasons she could think of for him to stay put but in the end she knew it'd be a losing battle. The last thing she wanted was to drive him further away. "I'll be ready whenever you are."

The sound of Nate stirring in his room woke Janet from a restless sleep. She pushed back the snarl of covers, wanting to forget yesterday. Pretend her son hadn't found an apartment. That she hadn't told him she'd buy him a car. The thought of him on his own so soon after she'd just gotten him back left her feeling tight and heavy. But there was nothing she could do about it. He was determined and once he got something in his head there was no persuading him otherwise. She stared off into the ever-brightening dawn sky, wanting to get off this emotional rollercoaster she'd been on since he came home.

Glancing at the LED alarm clock, she saw 6:15 AM blinking back. Sleeping in, as Nate would call it! His physical therapy appointment at the VA wasn't for three hours. More than enough time to get around. She rolled out of bed, stepped into her slippers and threw her bathrobe on. Cinching the belt around the black and white flannel robe, she went and let Cleo out of his crate. Out in the hallway, she heard a door shut. A moment later, the murmuring of a shower being turned on drifted through the crack of her bedroom door. She straightened the covers on her bed and headed for the kitchen.

As usual Nate had made coffee. She took a mug down from the cupboard and poured herself a cup. On the breakfast bar, the morning paper was open to the sports page. She leafed through the pages, took the local news section out and brought it the kitchen table. As she perused the opinion page, her phone rang.

Trevor's name was on the screen.

"Hope I didn't wake you."

She sat back. "No, Nate has PT this morning."

"You all right?"

"Umm…yeah, yeah, I'm fine," she said, realizing her tone was far from cheerful.

"You don't sound it. You sure?"

She looked out the sliding glass doors wondering if she should say anything about Nate's finding an apartment. She really didn't want to dwell on it, but she needed a sympathetic ear. When it came to having someone listen without trying to fix things, Trevor was her go-to person. Finally, she said, "Nate's moving out next month. I'm not ready for this Trev. He just got home. You don't think I'm mothering him too much, do you?"

"Well, you haven't seen him but a handful of times in the last five years. And let's not forget, a mother always worries about her babies."

She smiled. "Thanks. You always know the right things to say."

"I've been trained by the best."

"Nadia's been good for you," she said, knowing very well who he was referring to. "How is she, anyway?"

"She's good." He paused. "Speaking of which, she found something buried in the backyard you need to see."

She sat forward. "Oh?"

"Yeah," he said with an air of caution in his tone. "She's been re-landscaping the backyard. Planting bulbs for next spring. Anyway, can you and Nate shoot by later this week? Her sauerbraten's on the menu."

"Oh, really? Well, I suppose I could manage it. So... what's this thing I need to see," she said as the shower shut off in the bathroom down the hall.

"Better see for yourself," he said.

"Hmm... Okay, Mr. Secretive. How's Friday work, say around five?"

"Friday works fine, and bring your appetites."

Janet followed Nate into the VA clinic and took the elevator up to the second floor. They were early, but being on time was who she was, unlike Megan who got there when she got there. As Nate signed in, Andy came in behind them.

"Morning," he said, taking his jacket off.

"Morning yourself," she replied, slipping off her coat and draping it over the back of a Waiting Room chair. "Chilly one out there this morning."

"Yes, it is," he said. He turned to Nate. "You ready for some hard work?"

"Let's get at it," Nate said

She watched her son follow Andy into the therapy room. After the door shut behind them, she dug through a pile of tattered TIME magazines. Settling on the November issue with Barack Obama on the cover, she leafed through it to an article on whether the black president could heal the racial divide in the country. Half way through it, the double doors to the Therapy Room opened. Looking up, she saw Andy heading her way with a water bottle in hand.

"You have a minute?"

She set the magazine down as he came up beside her. "Sure."

"I thought I'd take a moment to say more than just, 'Hi'. Your son is quite a determined young man." He took a swig of water, capped the bottle and sat.

"Yes, he is." She caught a faint scent of cedar wood cologne. She quite liked it. "Takes after his father."

"He told me a little bit about him. Sorry for your loss," he said, turning toward her.

She managed a meager smile. "Well, it's been a while."

He nodded and an awkward silence passed between them. Finally he said, "So, how are you doing with Nate's transition home?"

How thoughtful. "It's a little trying at times, but we're getting along okay," she said, crossing her leg over her knee. "He tells me you served in Viet Nam."

"I did. It was near the end of the war," he said. "Why?"

"Well, I was just wondering, you being a Vet, maybe you have insights, things I should know to help my son."

He shrugged. "I don't know how insightful I am, other than to tell you not to rush things." He uncapped his water bottle, took a sip and looked at her hard. Finally, he said, "Coming home is never easy. Each of us has our own demons and we deal with them in different ways. For some, it's about control: orders and repetition. Organization in the chaos where you never know from one day to the next if it's going to be your last. For others, it's hiding, wanting to forget. And sometimes it's about hating what you've become, because you realize you're capable of doing the most heinous things when you're scared to death." He paused, seemingly waiting to see if she had something to say. When she didn't, he went on. "It took me a long time to open up and talk to someone after I came home. It's not easy."

She considered his response. Knew what he was hinting at. But Nate wasn't his son so he couldn't know the anguish of a parent being held at arm's length. She'd asked the question though, so she gave him a pass. "I remember my brother when he came home. I was a senior in high school at the time. He was distant. Later on, he told me how the last few weeks were the hardest. The wondering if he was gonna end up in a body bag when he was so close to coming home. I can't imagine what it must've felt like."

He nodded. "Pretty damned scary."

"I couldn't understand what my parents were going through until now. It had to have been nerve racking for yours as well."

He looked off. For a moment she wondered if she'd said something wrong. Finally, he turned back. "Well, I made it back, and that's all that mattered." He was quiet a moment then leaned forward. "So, umm...your son told me he found an apartment."

"Yes...yes, he did."

"You okay? You don't look happy about it."

"Oh, I'm fine," she replied, trying to switch gears. "It's that he just got home, say nothing of being injured." She folded her hands in her lap. "You think that's a good idea, him moving to an apartment?"

"Hard to say," he said. "He's looking to regain his independence. On the other hand, he needs to understand his limitations."

She nodded. "That's what worries me. He's very focused as you're probably finding out."

"That he is. Then again, the Army has a way of focusing you." He smiled and looked at her like Neil used to, really seeing her. It had been a long time since anyone had looked at her like this and she found herself basking in it. She leaned his way and eyed him companionably, wanting to know more about him.

"So, what branch were you in?" She started with things Nate had already told her which would lead to other things.

"Marines, Semper Fi...ooh-rah." He pushed his shoulders back into the upholstered chair, popped his foot up and rested his ankle over his knee.

"And, after you got out?"

He uncapped the bottle and took another swig. "I became a fire-fighter and eventually a paramedic."

"Wow. So, you retired and opened a book store?"

"Something like that." He shifted in his seat, averting his gaze as he flipped the bottle cap over and over in his hand. All at once he got up. "Well, I've got to be getting back in there."

She was taken aback. Had she said something wrong? She looked up. Saw sadness looming behind the smile. What it meant, she didn't know; only that she needed to know where it came from. "Oh. Okay," she said, wishing for something more to say. Something to keep them connected. The only thing that came though was what Nate had told her in the car coming home from Yosemite. "Umm...before you go, where's your bookstore? If I'm in the area, I'd like to stop in."

"It's on Trade Street. McNamara's. Can't miss it. Big green canopy out front. If you stop in, be sure to ask for me. I'll treat you to one of my sister's chocolate chip scones. They're out of this world."

As he walked away, her breath quickened. What was going on? Why was her body stirring? She reminded herself she was here for her son so she forced it out of her mind...sort of.

Chapter 8

THE EARLY morning sun rose over the distant hills, staining the billowing clouds a deep plum hue. Trade Street was quiet as Andy drove past shuttered markets, shops, galleries and office buildings. Here and there, trash cans and boxes stuffed with cardboard gathered on the curbs. Ahead, ornamental cast-iron street lamps were dressed in festive evergreen garlands. Tiny white lights twinkled around them. The city was readying itself for the Christmas holiday.

But he wasn't feeling in the holiday mood this morning. The trial for the civil suit loomed in the near future. He tried to ignore the ominous threat that could unravel the fragile life he'd stitched together since the accident. The crushing headache he had wasn't helping. He kneaded the back of his neck as he cruised down the street with Jack riding shotgun. The dog had his nose poking out the partially open passenger-side window, sniffing the crisp winter air. He reached over and ran his hand over the beagle's smooth tri-color coat and turned the heater down. Even the sound of the fan clanged in his ears.

When he came to 17th Street, he turned left, pointed his Suburban down the wide, empty lane and headed toward his store. Hopefully, Tyler remembered to pick up the repair part from Benjamin's for the latte machine. When he neared the storefront, he saw Amanda's car parked out front. He pulled in behind her Caravan, killed the engine and popped a couple more Tylenol.

"Come on, boy." He opened the car door, letting the dog scramble out. The dog shook himself off, and with tail wagging scooted for Amanda, who was propping the front door open. The savory scent of French Roast coffee swirled out, dragging in the morning crowd. It was one of her proven marketing devices. But it was the homemade cinnamon rolls that really dragged them in. His stomach rumbled as he anticipated biting into one of her fresh baked, warm pastries. They were the best part of his mornings. He grabbed his satchel and shut the car door as Amanda stood wiping her hands on the tail of the towel hanging over her shoulder. She pulled a wisp of hair over her ear and headed toward him. Her printed green and yellow checkerboard apron swished back and forth at the hips. She didn't look happy.

"You need to go to Lonnegan's. We're out of coffee. I would've gone, but Jonah called in; something about having to deal with his benefits package at the VA."

He slumped his shoulders. "That's right. He mentioned something about maybe having to go deal with it." He glanced at his watch. It was ten after six. With a thirty-minute round trip drive to the restaurant supply store and a ten-minute wait, he'd just make it back before the morning rush. He handed her the satchel with the opening cash drawer and marched back to his car. As he got in, he said, "I'll be back in forty. Try to save me a roll, will ya?"

"I'll do my best," she replied over her shoulder as she ushered Jack in ahead of her.

"So much for getting ahead with my inventory," he muttered, starting the car. He pulled away from the curb and cruised down the street that was just waking up with the early morning rush hour traffic. Five minutes later, he was on the arterial heading west. If the lights cooperated, he might slice five minutes off the trip. He moved into the left lane and followed the road as it veered around the office buildings heading toward the Center Street Bridge. On his left, he passed Riverfront City Park. Beyond its sleeping brown lawn was the Willamette River. He glanced nonchalantly over its flowing gray waters and thought about how to handle his undependable young employee, Tyler Evans.

Suddenly, a loud screech and a booming thud ripped his attention back to the road. He hit the brakes. Took in the rising smoke lifting off the crumpled hood of a Caddy that had rammed the driver's side door of an SUV. Then, as always before, his hard-wired reflexes kicked in. He pressed down on the accelerator, and as he headed for the accident, ticked down the list of priorities. First thing was to get emergency response on the way. He pulled his cell phone from his pocket and flipped it open.

"Yes, I'm on the scene of a two vehicle accident. Intersection of Front and..." He paused looking for the street sign. When he saw it, said, "and Chemeketa Street. Late model, white SUV in the median. Older model Caddy across the lane. One driver in the Caddy and ... looks like a driver and a passenger in the SUV ... Unknown injuries." *Oh, shit!* "We have a fire ... Caddy ... hold on." He pulled up twenty yards behind the accident. Went to flip the warning light toggle, which wasn't there of course. *Fuck.* He fumbled for his flashers and after turning them on, parked in the lane to prevent other cars from running into the accident. Putting the cell on speaker mode, he tucked it in his shirt pocket in the open position. Running to the back of his Suburban, he opened the tailgate and fished out three flares and an extinguisher. As he did so, a dump truck pulled up along beside him. The door of the truck opened and a tall, blond man jumped out. When the man started running toward the burning Caddy, Andy whistled.

"Hey, I need you back here, buddy."

The man stopped. Turned and looked at him.

"I'm a paramedic," Andy hollered, waving him over. When the man wavered, he made his voice more emphatic. "Look, you wanna help, you need to listen to me. First we need to make this scene safe."

"What about the guy in that car," the man said coming toward him.

"I'm going after him right now," Andy replied, holding out the flares. "In the meantime, I need you to light these up and space 'em out on the road behind us. And keep people back until emergency response shows up. Can you do that for me?"

"Yeah, sure."

"Good." Andy saw a car heading down the road toward them. Nodding at it, he said, "Better get to it then – looks like we have company coming. Oh, and take my phone here and keep the operator informed."

The man grabbed the flares, took the phone and headed off as Andy ran for the burning Caddy. As he neared the wreckage, he slowed, panning his gaze back and forth over the pavement. A puddle of gas was forming around the front driver's side tire. *Shit!* With the SUV only feet away, his priority was putting out the fire. The problem was he only had a standard two and half pound extinguisher, but this was the hand he was dealt. It was just unfortunate he didn't have four other pairs of hands helping right now. He aimed the nozzle at the flames shooting out from under the crumpled hood of the Caddy and squeezed the trigger. A blast of thick, white powder shot out. As the flames sputtered under the spray, he glanced over at the driver side window. There he saw a man slumped over the wheel with a thin streak of blood running down the side of his face.

He'd witnessed this scene more times than he cared to over his twenty-seven years on the force and knew it wasn't going to end well unless help got there quickly. He glanced over at the SUV and eyed the crushed driver's side door. From what he could see, the passenger was sitting upright. The driver, however, he couldn't see. The flames under the Caddy's hood suddenly flared, drawing his attention from the SUV. He swept the extinguisher's spray over the erupting flames until they died away again. But he knew they could easily come back and with the contents of his extinguisher nearly spent, his decision was made. He reached over and tapped the faded red metal of the Caddy's door with the pad of his finger. It was cool enough, so he grabbed hold and tried to yank it open.

It wouldn't budge. With the smoke starting to ooze out from under the battered hood again, he thought about the passenger side door. But when he saw the pool of gas growing around the front tire, he knew time was running out. He needed more hands on board and he needed them like five minutes ago.

Whether someone upstairs was listening, he didn't know, but suddenly someone ran up beside him and when he looked to his right, saw fierce dark eyes staring back. He nodded at the man and the two of them grabbed the door and pulled. As the door grudgingly started to open, another pair of hands joined in. With a ferocious jerk, the door flung back, almost knocking him down.

"Let's get him over there," Andy said, pointing to the sidewalk across the street. The man beside him put the arms of the injured driver over his shoulder and started dragging him away. As Andy followed along, he got his first good look at the victim. Whoever he was, he'd lived a good life. His old body, though frail, showed signs of being kept up and his face was clean-shaven. But it was the old man's face that struck Andy. It was ashen, bloodied and bruised. The man was heading for a cardiac arrest.

The man set the old guy on the concrete curb in the shade of an office building and laid him down. Andy knelt on the curb and put his fingers to the old man's neck. Feeling a faint pulse, he gritted his teeth and glanced toward the SUV. Three men and a woman were prying open its passenger side door. *Better than nothing*, Andy thought. He turned back to the old man. The man who'd laid the old man down was kneeling by his side, looking up at him. *Damn it; hurry up*, Andy thought, listening for the sound of wailing sirens. But all he heard was the early morning rush hour traffic on the southbound lane across the median.

Andy eyed the old man's ashen face and noticed the light blue cast to the skin. *Damn it.* "He's crashing."

He ripped the man's shirt open and placing his palm on the man's chest with his other hand on top, thumped down. He was on the second stroke when a loud 'foo-ump' erupted behind him. A loud cry went up diverting his glance to the wreckage. The hood of the Caddy was thrown back and flames were licking a thick, black plume of smoke spiraling up into the air. Another loud cry came from inside the SUV as the men and woman worked frantically to get the people out of the car. Andy looked upward as he continued to try and resuscitate his patient. *Jesus, help me here.*

"Whoa, damn," said a man in the gathered crowd.

"I know CPR," said a heavy-set, dark-haired woman. She knelt beside Andy. Gently she lifted the old man's chin and waited for Andy to give her a signal for the right moment. When he nodded, she covered the man's nose and blew into his mouth.

Then finally, the sounds of sirens!

The woman blew three more times again then pulled back.

"Come on guy, don't give up on me!" Andy shouted as a squad of EMS and fire trucks came to a screeching halt behind them. Seconds later, two paramedics came running up. One of them pulled on latex gloves while the other spoke into his shoulder anchored radio.

"We have a white male, approximately 60 years old in cardiac arrest," the paramedic radioed back. He plopped the large, green med-kit bag he was carrying on the curb beside Andy.

"He just crashed," Andy said, thrusting down again on the old man's chest. Without asking, the paramedic with the radio turned and ran back to the truck. The other EMT told him and the woman to continue CPR while he set up. A moment later the paramedic with the radio sprinted back. In his hand was a defibrillator. His partner reached into the airway bag and yanked a stethoscope out. Setting the unit down, the paramedic with the radio flipped a tube of gel to his partner. Andy backed away as the EMT dabbed the gel on the paddles, rubbed them together as the unit charged and placed them on the old man's chest.

"V-fib. 200 joules. Clear!" the paramedic with the radio said, triggering the charge. The old man's chest raised.

The paramedic put his fingers to the old man's carotid artery and checked for a pulse. Shaking his head, he gelled the paddles up again. Another jolt raised the old man. The EMT checked for a pulse. This time there was a thumbs-up. Andy released a breath he didn't know he'd been holding. A minute later, a mask was fixed to the man's face while the EMT's made preparations for his transfer to the hospital.

For the next hour and a half, Andy made himself available to answer questions and helped out wherever he could. As the wrecked vehicles were being towed away, the fire captain came over and stood beside Andy in the grassy median. He extended a thick hand. "I heard you're retired from the force."

As he shook it, Andy looked up into the slate gray eyes of the towering redheaded man. "Yeah, but I guess we never really retire, do we?"

The captain nodded. "Nope." They were quiet a moment, then the man continued. "You did good out there today…oh, by the way, I believe this cell phone is yours?"

"Thanks," Andy said as he slipped it into his pocket. "It turned out a lot better than I thought it was going to. The passengers in the SUV are lucky."

"Lucky indeed," the captain echoed back. "So, where do you work out of?"

There it was. The question he didn't want to answer, especially to the discerning captain beside him. News of past accidents involving paramedics had traveled up and down the state before and became etched into the ironclad memories of those who put their lives on the line for others. He sucked a breath. "Lincoln City."

"Good boys down there from what I understand," the captain said, surveying the accident scene. "So what do you think? The old man was having a heart attack at the time of the crash?"

"Probably," Andy agreed, as the knot in his stomach relaxed. "He was ashen and sweating heavily when we dragged him out of the car. It's a good thing your boys got here when they did." He paused. "Say, I never got the old man's name. I'd like to go see how he's doing later on."

The captain pulled his two-way radio out. "Hey Eddie, real quick. You get the name of the old man?"

The radio hissed. A second later, a voice came back. "Name's Garrett Andersen, Cap."

"Thanks bud." The captain turned to Andy. "Well, there you go. Good luck to you, and drop by some time around lunch. Eddie makes a mean Shepherd's Pie."

"I'll do that," Andy replied. As the captain strode away, he ran his hand through his hair. "Well, this has been one hell of a morning." *Oh, shit, Amanda must be going nuts!*

He pulled his cell phone out and saw four voice messages. Sighing, he punched her number in and waited for her to pick up. When she did, he said, "It's me, and before you drill me, I've been dealing with an accident on Front Street...Yes, I'm all right. I'll tell you about it when I get back. Should be there in thirty. Yes, I'll be careful. You worry too much, Panda ... Okay, I'm out."

Chapter 9

J ANET LAY in bed listening to the tiny creaks and groans of the house. At length, she got up and wrapped a robe around her. As she opened the door to her bedroom, she heard Nate bumping around in the kitchen. Megan was overnighting with Ben again. The fourth time this week! At the rate things were going, Megan would be looking to move out shortly, with Nate following close behind, if not sooner. Then she'd be alone. The thought unsettled her.

Up to recently, she hadn't considered what it'd be like to be alone again. The inevitability made her chest tighten. *This is ridiculous.* She closed her eyes, collected herself and joined Nate in the kitchen. There she poured herself a cup of coffee, toasted a bagel and sat with the Sunday morning paper splayed in front of her.

"I think you're sister's gonna be out the door in the near future, too," she said, peeking at her son from over the top of the paper. "Then I'll have this place back to myself."

Nate looked up from shoveling a spoonful of cereal in his mouth. "Not exactly. You'll have Cleo here. But I get it. You'll be okay."

"Of course I will," she said. "You're coming with me later to your brother's, right?"

"I guess," he said. "Why are we going again?"

She took a sip of coffee and a bite of her bagel. "I guess Nadia found something I need to see."

He set his spoon in his bowl and sat back. "Hmm…"

"What?"

"I guess I don't understand why Trev couldn't have just told you over the phone. But whatever."

"Well, yes, but there's sauerbraten, too," she said.

"There is that." He smiled knowingly, picked up his bowl and shuffled over to the counter. Over his shoulder, he added, "Oh, I meant to tell you, Andy down at the VA scored a couple Trailblazer tickets and invited me go. Game's, next week. The 23rd I think."

"Did he?" She set her paper down. *Inviting my son to a Trailblazers game, are we?* "This is a surprise."

He turned back to her and squared his shoulders. "There a problem?"

"No. Just make sure it's not on Christmas Eve."

Janet and Nate headed for Lincoln City under sunny skies. Balmy days were rare in the Pacific Northwest during the winter and she gladly soaked it up. She glanced over at Nate. He was staring intently out the passenger side window. "So, any guesses on what Trevor found," she said trying to make conversation.

The only reply she got was Cleo yawning in the back seat. She eyed the dog in the rearview mirror and saw him gazing back with droopy brown eyes. He licked his muzzle and flipped his long, floppy ears over his shoulders.

"Nate…hello?"

"I heard you," he said, keeping his gaze pinned to the passing landscape. "I haven't a clue."

She sighed then focusing on the road again, turned the radio up. They listened to the banter of the disc jockey for the next five minutes until he handed his show over to the evening newscaster.

"…The retired paramedic who arrived on the scene of the fiery crash is being hailed as a hero. First responders reported his quick thinking saved the life of folklorist, Garrett Anderson, who'd suffered a heart attack leading to the collision. Mr. McNamara has refused to comment, other than to say, 'It was something you just do.' And now, onto other news, the common council…"

"Wow!" Nate said. "I wonder what he did."

You are something Mr. McNamara, that's for sure. But it was the man Andy had saved that was foremost in her mind. She remembered the day she'd met Garrett. It was during her sophomore year at OSU. March 3rd, 1978. The day he'd planted a seed that grew and got her thinking about the arts. It wasn't so much the science in his lecture, but instead, his anecdotal stories. The man noted the presence of sustainability in nature and saw its perfection within its chaos; its beauty within its simplicity. His lecture changed the direction of her life.

At last, she shook her head and muttered, "I hope you're all right, Garrett."

"You know this Garrett what's his name?"

"Umm…Yes, I do." She turned the radio down and saw him eyeing her with a raised brow. "He's a noted folklorist. Addressed my Environmental Engineering class in my sophomore year." She smiled: saw Garret's thin, clean-shaven face in her mind's eye. How was it she'd forgotten him all these years?

Nate shrugged. "Oh." He fell quiet, then eyed her sidelong. "Wait, you were studying Engineering? You never told me that."

She shrugged.

"So, what made you change your mind…and Environmental Engineering? Somehow, I can't see you as an engineer, Mom."

"To answer your first question: Garrett changed my mind. His view of nature got me to see life from a different perspective. Instead of trying to engineer *it* and make *it* better, that *it* was fine just the way *it* was. I found it was better to protect *it* by telling *its* story through the lens of my camera. As for how I started out in engineering...well your grandfather was a Mechanical Engineer and–"

"You followed along...I get it."

From the corner of her eye, she saw him studying her. That she hadn't told him much about her college years when he was growing up had never occurred to her. Then again, they'd been turbulent years when she was battling to come to terms with who she was along with her parent's divorce and a father who was always holding her at arm's length.

"For a long time, I wanted to be an Architect like Dad, but..."

"It's never too late to follow a dream, Nate," she said, shifting away from dark memories to something more upbeat. In a rush, she continued, "You're only limited by your imagination, you know that, right? You're still–" She stopped herself from saying, *young,* and went on, – still able to get into the spring semester at Chemeketa. From there you can matriculate to OSU."

He shook his head. Looked away. "That's not my dream anymore."

"Okay, then something else," she said, trying to ignore the disappointment her beloved Neil would've felt or was it sadness or both? She didn't know. "How about engineering...or maybe something with computers. Programming or web design? You're good with that stuff and they have classes for that as well."

"Actually, I don't know." He abruptly shifted in his seat. "I just know what I don't want."

"Okay," she said, not wanting to pressure him any further. "We can talk about it later."

Janet pulled the car into the long, serpentine drive leading up through the tall grasses. At the end of the drive was the family cottage that had been passed down from Aunt June years ago. Now it was Trevor and Nadia's home. She parked in the turn-around off to the side of the modest A-Frame. A commanding view of the Pacific greeted her. She collected her purse and got out. Trevor came out from behind the cottage.

"How was the drive?"

"It was fine. Are we too early?"

"Not at all," Trevor said as he put his arm around Nate. "You hungry, big guy?"

Nate opened the back door and let Cleo out. "I could eat."

"Great, let's get inside," Trevor said.

He led them around the side of the cottage. When he opened the door, the tangy scent of vinegar brine leapt out. Janet's mouth watered as she stepped inside. She hung her coat on a gnarled, wooden coat tree and saw a rusted metal case the size of a banker's box on the Living Room floor.

That must be what I'm here for. She strode into the kitchen and found Nadia putting the final touches on dinner. Her daughter-in-law looked up as she covered the large roasting pan.

"Janet, how nice it is to see you," Nadia said in her exacting German accent. She removed her crisp white apron and tossing it on the counter, drew her into a firm hug. "You brought your appetite, right?"

"What about me?" Nate said as he entered the 'L' shaped kitchen.

Nadia let go of Janet and waved her hand in dismissal toward Nate. "You...I don't worry about. You are always hungry." She pointed the refrigerator out to him. "There's a bottle of wine in there. Pull it out and uncork it for us while Janet and I relax in the other room." She led Janet back into the expansive living area and motioned to the arrayed fixed windows overlooking the Pacific. "Trev's nervous about what is in that box over there. I told him, it is nothing to worry about. He does not listen to me though."

"Honey, I thought we agreed to deal with that after dinner," Trevor said, coming in. Nate straggled in behind him. They both carried a glass of wine. Trevor gave his to Janet and shot his wife a frown.

Nadia softened her brusque German accent. "What difference does it make Trev whether you show her now or later? Get it over with."

Nate looked on, puzzled.

Trevor eyed Janet anxiously. "I guess it doesn't matter," he said at last, going over to pick it up. "I don't know how long it's been buried.

Nadia found it under the flowerbed near the back deck. It's been there a while. Before you open it, I want you to know we had no idea what was in it until I opened it."

He set it on the dining room table behind them and stood back.

Janet turned to the box as everyone gathered beside her. She knew what was inside. Her hand went to the clasp on the lid and flipped it back hesitantly. Suddenly she was looking at a cardboard box. In large block letters, it was marked, "PERSONAL STUFF". She dropped her head and closed her eyes. "I wondered what he did with it."

"So you know about this?" Trevor said.

"I do," Janet said, looking back.

Frowning, Nate leaned his cane against the table and reached into the box. He took out a thin, brown book whose front cover was curled back around the edges and blew the dust off. "What are these?"

Janet put her arm around him. "They're your father's journals…memories of Trevor's mother. You remember me telling you about Sharon, right?"

Nate cracked the book, releasing the pungent odor of mildew. "Yeah, somewhat."

"Well, he wrote these before he met me, and they were very personal to him," Janet said. She gently pulled the book from his reluctant hands. *I'm sorry Nate, but this is a part of your father he buried for a reason.* "I think we should let these be and put them back where Nadia found them," she added, and set the book back into the box.

As the lid shut, Nate bunched his face up. "He's my father, too."

"I know," Janet said. "But he put them in there for a reason. Please honor it."

Trevor put his hand on Nate's shoulder. "She's right guy. Let it go."

"Easy for you to say," Nate said. "You probably read them."

"Only the first page," Trevor replied. "And it's our mother he's writing about, not yours. If I can let them be, so can you."

Nate grabbed his cane and held Janet with a withering stare. "Fine. Seems like I don't have a say. Just like Megan didn't when you sent Dad to the *Home!*"

The air went of the room. Janet gasped as the cry in her heart sucked her breath away. Trevor looked at his brother as if he didn't know him anymore.

Nadia spoke up. "Nate, that was mean."

But Nate kept his searing gaze on Janet.

Finally, Janet sighed. There was nothing more to say. Her son, whom she loved more than anything, had hurt her beyond imagination. Fighting to keep her tears in check, she walked out of the room.

The ride home from Trevor and Nadia's was long and quiet. Janet kept looking over at her son as she drove. Did he really mean to hurt her? Or had he just lashed out and didn't know how to retract the words.

The memory of the fight she'd had with Megan over committing Neil to Hazelnut came roaring back. Suddenly Megan's pleading voice was clanging in her ears. *'He's not gone, not all the way. You're abandoning him. He'd never do it to you, and you know it! Please, Janet, don't do this. Don't put him in one of those fucking places.'*

Janet closed her eyes; saw Megan in her mind's eye stalking back into the house. And she KNEW!

Megan had called Nate!

Had told him their mother's plan to place their father in a nursing home. Reminded him how their father feared ending up in one.

She pulled into their driveway, parked and sat with the car running, trying to find a way to bridge the gulf that had widened exponentially between them. That she'd been holding the floodgate of tears back wasn't helping.

"I'm sorry, Nate," she said at last, not knowing what more to say. The words came out just above a whisper, but they clanged in her ears.

He just stared ahead though with his jaw clenched tight. He glanced at her, and opened the door. Got out and marched awkwardly with his cane toward the house. She sat watching him as the added weight of his silence threatened to crush her. At last, she turned the car off, got out with Cleo bouncing along behind and followed Nate to the front porch where he stood like a wooden soldier.

Why are you doing this to me, Nate? I know you're angry. I know you're hurt about not being home when your father was near the end. And I know something bad happened over in Iraq. But why take it out on me? You know I had no choice with your father. You said so yourself when you came home. And now...this?

She opened the door and Nate slipped in ahead of her. Without looking back, he hobbled through the Great Room for the hall leading to his bedroom.

She felt her throat tighten. "Nate...I loved your father," she said with all the strength she could muster.

He stopped briefly with his back toward her. Stood in the hall as the monstrous silence ruled, then opened his door and went in. As the click of the latch echoed in the house, her tears crashed through.

Chapter 10

ANDY HEADED down the busy corridor of the cardiac wing of Salem's Hospital to visit Garrett. On the way, he'd picked up a basket of goodies for the man: paperback books and puzzles. When he came to Garrett's room and heard raised voices coming from inside, he hesitated, deciding whether to head for the waiting room for a few minutes to wait the argument out.

"Dad, you can't keep driving. You need to give your license up."

"Before what, Michael? I kill myself," the old man softly said. "I have one little incident and you'd think the whole world was falling apart. I'm fine–soon as I get out of here, that is."

"You're not fine! You just had a major heart attack and damned near killed two people in the process."

"I'm truly sorry about that, but how am I supposed to get around," the man muttered. "I have places to be. I can't live being locked up in a house, Michael."

"Where, Dad? Where do you have to go?" The son said raising his voice.

"The Alzheimer's Gala, for one. They've invited me to talk about your mother and hand out an award."

"That's not until January. As far as getting you there, I'll take you. And, for being locked up, there's alternatives and you know it as well as I do."

"Right! Assisted living or whatever they're calling it these days."

"I'm trying to help you."

"I'm not selling the house, and that's final."

Andy had heard arguments like these before. Tragedies did things like this to families, stressing frayed and anxious nerves. The man's son burst out of the room, his face red and skewed in bewilderment. He eyed Andy then turned back toward his father. "Well, you won't be driving anymore."

There was no reply. Just empty silence. As if being silent would make it all go away.

The son shook his head and rolled his eyes at Andy as he walked out of the room. "Looks like you have company."

He pressed his lips together and went in. Garrett's gaze was turned toward the window. He set the basket he'd bought for the man on the small chest of drawers. "Hi, Garrett."

The man turned his head toward him. "And who might you be?"

"Name's Andy. I was there the other morning, and I … well, I wanted to come up. See how you were doing."

The man flashed a smile. "Oh, why thank you, I appreciate it. I'm Garrett. Pleased to meet you."

"How you feeling?"

Garrett tried to pull himself up in bed so he was sitting upright, but was having a hard time. Andy reached over and helped him up. As he did so, Garrett winced. "Ahhh … My ribs, they feel like they've been kicked by a mule."

"I bet. Can I get you anything?"

"What I'd like, they don't have up here," Garrett said. He rubbed his chest, took a deep breath then sank into the pillows and shut his eyes. "So you were there, then? Word has it someone pulled me outta my car and saved my life."

"That's what they say." He pulled the blanket up around the Garrett's shoulders.

Garrett opened his eyes and considered Andy for some time. At last he said, "You're him, aren't you?"

He smiled. "Just happened to be at the right place at the right time."

"Lucky for me," Garrett answered looking off toward the door. "My Michael, he wants me to go in one of them homes across town. He says I'm too old to be driving. That I need help. Maybe he's right, but I'm not ready for a rocking chair … at least not yet."

Andy nodded.

"I know, he means well. But I could never leave my home." Garrett reached over and took a cup of water from the rolling tray table beside him. After a long, shaky sip, he continued. "I built it myself for my Annabelle, God rest her soul. Every beam and stud in that house has a part of me in it and every flower a part of her. He doesn't seem to understand that. I guess it's all this modern thinking: out with the old and in with the new. It seems no one appreciates the value in old-fashioned things anymore. They just toss out whatever doesn't work for them." He was quiet a moment. "You have children?"

He shook his head.

"A wife?"

"Nope."

Garrett studied him. "So sad. If you did, you'd know what I'm talking about."

He reached over and put his hand on Garrett's shoulder. "I don't think he's trying to toss you away, Garrett. He just wants you to be safe."

"So he doesn't have to worry, don't you mean?" Garrett paused then sighed. "Forgive an old man, that probably wasn't fair…but it's how I feel," he said raising his voice an octave. "I need to be free to go about doing the things I love. I can't do that when people are hovering over me like the proverbial hawk watching the mouse," he continued, emphasizing the last word. He glanced toward the door where a nurse was standing. "Speak of the devil, here comes one now."

"Now, now, Mr. Anderson, we aren't all that bad," the slender red-head said sweeping up next to him.

That was his cue. It was time to say good-bye, so he patted Garrett's shoulder and let himself out.

After Andy got back to the store, he retired to his office to return phone calls and go over emails. The last two days had been a hell of a ride. The accident and its subsequent aftermath had derailed his plans to catch up on all the little things crying for his attention. On top of all that, he was dealing with the barrage of reporters wanting interviews. How odd, he thought, that when he was saving lives on the force he was never pursued for interviews. It appeared one had to be a regular Joe in order to be noticed when it came to doing the right thing. He sucked down a gulp of coffee and picked up the latest trade magazine from Penguin Publishing as the background headache buzzed in his head. As he scanned the upcoming January releases, looking for a fresh title, the phone rang. *Christ, another reporter.* He had a mind to let it go to voice mail, then thought better of it and picked up.

"McNamara's."

"Is this Andy McNamara," said a female voice.

Wait for it. Andy mused, picturing a young journalist. He flipped the magazine page. "It is. Can I help you?"

"I hope so. I'm Janet Porter."

He sat forward and dropped the trade journal onto his desk. "Janet!" He cleared his throat. "What can I do for you?"

She was quiet a moment and he wondered if she was still on the line. Finally, she said, "Is there a chance we could meet for coffee?"

"Umm...yes," Andy said, delighted and a lot curious. "What's up?"

"It's my son Nate. I...I know you've been talking with him... and well, I just need to talk to someone."

He leaned back in his chair. "Sure. I have tomorrow afternoon free. Say around one?"

"That would be great. I could come to you."

He chuckled. "Looking for that free scone, I see."

She was quiet on the other end, then said, "Oh, that. No. I just thought it might be easier for you." She paused. When she spoke again, her serious tone brightened. "Besides, it would give me a chance to check out your store."

"It's not much, but it's growing." He made a mental note to have her books placed front and center in the display window.

"I'm sure it's wonderful," she said. "By the way, I heard what happened the other day at Riverfront City Park. Is the old man you rescued okay? Did he make it?"

"He did, thanks to God and a few good folks."

He heard an audible sigh. Finally, she said, "Oh good. He's such an amazing man. Such an influence on so many people."

"Sounds like you know him."

"Garrett Andersen? Yes...well, sort of. He was a guest speaker at my college when I was a sophomore. Anyway, you are a man of many hats."

He was intrigued. "How do you mean?"

"Well, a volunteer at the VA, a book store owner and a paramedic," she said. "What else do you do in your spare time?"

"Oh, that," he said. Obviously, she'd heard about his being a paramedic from Nate. He cleared his throat. "That's a part of my life that's over with now. Retired, and no other trade secrets, scouts honor."

She laughed. "You sure about that? I heard you've got connections with the Trailblazers."

"Yeah, the assistant coach and I go back some. He throws me a few tickets here and there."

"So I understand," she said. "My son tells me you've invited him to a game. On the 23rd...is it?"

"Yes. He mentioned he's a fan, so I thought it'd be a good diversion for him. We're going up with a couple friends of mine. I could see about grabbing another ticket if you're interested in tagging along."

"No, that's all right, but thanks. I have family coming in for Christmas and there's a crap-load of things I need to do," she said with a sudden shift of tone. Almost sad, Andy thought. "Well, I'll let you get back to work. You take care. Bye now."

The connection went dead but his heart was soaring.

Janet showed up promptly at 1:00. Andy led her to an out-of-the-way table in his café and took her jacket. As he did so, the scent of vanilla wafted out at him. He inhaled it, basking in the scent and sat casually taking in her soft cashmere cream-colored sweater accentuating her graceful figure. What he noticed more though was the necklace she wore. It was an antique piece of silver with a heart-shaped topaz stone in the center. She fingered it as she crossed her legs and offered him an unassuming smile.

She cast her glance around the room. "Thanks for taking the time to talk. I really appreciate it."

He sensed her anxiety. "Let me get you a cup of coffee and that scone."

"Not to be a pain, but do you have tea?"

"We do, but nothing fancy," he replied, getting up.

"That's okay. Whatever you have will be fine."

He left her sitting there and went over behind the checkout counter. His sister Amanda was changing the filter in one of their coffee makers. As he grabbed a pair of tongs and placed a scone on a plate, Amanda flipped the top lid back down and started wiping the counter. Without looking up, she said, "You sure you know what you're doing?"

He glanced back at Janet, who was perusing a book. "What do you mean?"

Amanda turned toward him and gave him one of her classic Doubting-Thomas gazes. Although he loved his sister, she had a tendency to be guarded of people. Not that he could blame her. Their whole lives, when they were growing up in foster care, had been one of survival. Trust came hard when all you knew was fighting for your place in a family where the other kids come first. Finally, she said, "Well, you always told me it's never a good idea to get involved with patients and their families."

"Yeah, I know," he said. He wasn't overly fond of the reminder. He snatched a couple napkins and a fork. "But sometimes you make exceptions. Would you mind grabbing me a cup of tea and a coffee?"

"Right," she said, drawing the word out while pulling out a couple of mugs and setting them on the counter. As she poured his coffee, she added, "I suppose it has nothing to do with the fact she's drop dead gorgeous."

When Jonah looked up with a knowing grin, Andy frowned. She was half right and he couldn't deny it. "No, it has nothing to do with it."

She gave him a crooked smile the way she always did when she knew he was bullshitting her and threw a tea bag into the mug. "She take cream and honey?" When he hesitated, she rolled her eyes. "Never mind, I'll bring it over."

He snitched another scone for himself, eyed her sidelong and shuffled back over to Janet. Pushing the plate with the scone toward her, he said, "So, what're ya looking at?"

She set the book down and turned it around so the cover was right side up for him.

"Snow Falling on Cedars. Heard it was a good read," he said picking it up. He turned it over and glanced at the back cover as Amanda came to their table.

"Hi there," Amanda said, setting Janet's tea in front of her along with a creamer and a jar of honey. As she did so, he saw her furtively giving Janet the once over. "I like your necklace. Where did you get it?"

"Thank you. It was a gift from my late husband," Janet said, looking up. She tossed Amanda a smile and drew her shoulders inward around the silver braided strand as she poured cream into her tea.

He put the book down and sipped his coffee as the women exchanged small talk about the upcoming holidays. As he looked on, Janet casually sat back, nibbling on her scone while Amanda prattled on about never having enough time to get things done. Finally, he eyed his sister and said to Janet, "So how's Nate?"

Taking his cue, Amanda thanked Janet for her compliment on the pastry and left. As she walked away, Janet pushed her plate aside and toyed with the simple yellow band on her ring finger, turning it around and around. She took a sip of her tea. "He's angry."

He tilted his head and nodded but kept his mouth shut and waited for her to continue.

"He's...well..." She paused, pressed her lips together. As her gaze drifted toward the window, her tone took on a reflective quality. "Nate's father was much older than I was when I met him and he had grown children. One of them was my best friend before I met him. Anyway, it started as sort of a business relationship. He was a tenant of mine.

"At the time, I wasn't looking for anyone. I was happy being on my own." She turned back to him and smiled. "But things happened and well...we fell in love and Nate was born shortly after we were married. My pregnancy was a surprise for both of us, but Neil was delighted. I remember him telling anyone who would listen he was gonna be a father again. He was a good father; bathed and fed Nate, read him stories, helped him with his homework, but...he just...well, he just didn't know how to get down on the ground with Nate when Nate was little. Play with him at his level, you know."

She narrowed a sobering gaze on him, cleared her throat and went on. "And then he developed Parkinson's." Again she paused, and as she did so, her shoulders sagged. She took a deep breath. "As it progressed, it interfered with his work. As an architect, my husband's life revolved around being creative. When he couldn't draw anymore, it crushed him. His life, and how he defined it, was taken from him, so he turned in on himself. Became frightened. Consumed with his failing body. The toll it took on our family was huge, affecting Nate most of all. He didn't understand what was happening to his father."

Now things are making sense, he thought. He looked down, pitying this proud woman whose story was firing bullets at him.

"But it was 9/11 that really hit him and Nate the hardest," she went on. "It devastated my husband and enraged my son. He was supposed to go to OSU that year, but changed his mind and enlisted. Shortly after Nate was deployed, my husband's memory began to fade. At first we wrote it off as him getting older, but as time went on, it became apparent it was more than that. His mother had died not knowing her own children, and the fear of it happening to him was terrifying. He wouldn't go to the doctor."

There was a long silence and he wondered if she was finished. At last, she swallowed. "I realized I...I was losing him when he started getting lost during walks around the neighborhood. I had to watch him like a hawk because he was leaving the stove on and walking away. Eventually, I had to take the car keys away. That was the worst. He...he just gave up after that."

He waited for her to collect herself then leaned forward. Gently, he said, "And Nate was away when all this was happening?"

"Yes. I didn't tell him what was going on with his father. He had enough to contend with. When he came home on his first leave and saw his father's condition, he closed himself off from everybody. I tried to tell him there was no way he could know what was going to happen, but he wouldn't listen, at least that's what it felt like. He went back to Iraq moody and quiet. I should've prepared him before he came home. It's my fault. I was scared."

She looked at him with desperation in her eyes. As a tear rolled down her face, her voice cracked. "He likes you. He'll talk to you. Please help him."

Chapter 11

J ANET TOOK the extended napkin from Andy and wiped her eyes. She hadn't intended to give Andy the nickel tour of the last twenty years of her life, and she certainly hadn't intended to beg him for his help with Nate. Now that she had, she felt a strange sense of release mixed with a discomfort of being exposed to a man she barely knew. She wondered what was he thinking as he sat across from her, leaning back in his chair with legs out stretched and crossed in front of him.

At last, he said, "He doesn't tell me as much as you think, but sure, I'll do what I can. For what it's worth, I don't think his anger has anything to do with you not preparing him about his father." He paused then said, "You mentioned earlier he's getting an apartment. Is he working?"

"No, not yet." she said, balling the napkin up in her hand. She saw him cock his head thoughtfully and wondered what he was thinking.

Finally, he leaned forward, set his coffee down and splayed his arms out on the tabletop. "Then, I assume you're footing the bill?"

"Well…yes. Why?"

"I have an idea. I need to fill a position here at the store and…" He hesitated then as if he was uncertain of what he was about to say, went on, "…and though I'm not sure how long it would last, how 'bout

I offer it to him? It's part time, mind you, but it'd give him something to do. Take his mind off things a bit."

She felt a weight lift from her shoulders. "You would do that?"

"Sure," he said, kicking back. He looked at his watch and rolled his tongue around the inside of his cheek. "I have to get back at it right now, but would you be opposed to grabbing a bite later on? Talk a little more about this?"

Her stomach fluttered. Finally, an ally! She drained her tea. "No, not at all. I have a project I have to get to tonight, but I have tomorrow free."

"Tomorrow it is then, say for breakfast?"

"Okay. Where?"

"You pick," he said, getting up.

Feeling hopeful about Andy, Janet left to meet him the next morning. A job wasn't exactly what she had in mind for Nate, but anything to take his mind off whatever was chewing him up inside was better than nothing. She pulled out of her driveway praying Nate would take Andy's offer when it came. But it was the unloading of her personal life to Andy that was foremost on her mind all last night. What had possessed her to open up like that to him? Had she said too much? She felt her gut tighten. Saying what she had said left her vulnerable to being pitied, and pity was the last thing she wanted or needed. As she turned onto Old Cypress Road, she wondered how he'd so easily disarmed her and then what he'd thought of her. Did it matter?

The thought that had hit her sideways last night was still there. Was there more than just her concern for her son roiling inside her? Sure, Andy was handsome, but was it more than that? He had a way of looking at her that left her feeling like she was listened to. Her husband had had the same manner, and that mattered!

She pulled into the lot of *The Pompeii Café* and parked. It was 8:45 AM and hopefully she wasn't too late. She'd told him 8:30, but a detour on the main road waylaid her coming in. Stepping out of her car into the cold December drizzle, she hoofed it to the warmth of the art deco coffee shop. Once inside, she searched the lavender painted dining room with its black and white checkerboard tile floors. Saw him sitting at a table opposite the old-fashioned soda-fountain bar.

The morning crowd huddling around their coffees and Danishes were regulars. A few of them she knew, like Ed and Harriet who lived down the road from her. A few of them looked up and smiled when they saw her. Most hid behind their morning papers ignoring her as she wove her way around them to Andy.

"Hi there," he said, looking up through a pair of large aviator sunglasses. He shut the day planner he was writing in. "Have a seat. You hungry? I'm buying."

"Tea would be great for right now," she said, removing her jacket and laying it over the back of a nearby chair. She sat wondering if he was trying to make a statement with the shades. But from what she'd gleaned of him so far, he wasn't that kind of man. Obviously, he'd forgotten he still had them on.

He pulled a menu in front of him. "So, what do you recommend?"

She smiled. "Well, you could remove your sunglasses."

"Oh, yeah. Joe cool, I guess I'm not." He took his glasses off, shoved them in his shirt pocket and picked up the menu. As he read down it, his brow wrinkled.

"The *Cubist* is good," she ventured watching tiny expressions of bewilderment wash over his ruddy face.

He pursed his lips and set the menu aside. "I don't suppose they have anything like an omelet?"

"I'm afraid not," she said.

He took another look at his menu. "Okay, guess I'll take your suggestion and go with the rice and meat filled pastry thing." He set his menu down, dug in his pocket and pulled out a small glass vial. He popped a couple caplets from it into his hand, looked up and said, "For my damned headaches...So, I've been thinking about Nate after we talked last night. Does he know you've talked to me?"

"No," she said, "Why?"

"Good. The last thing you'll want is for him to think this is a set up. If he catches wind of it, he'll walk away." He washed the pills down with a gulp of water. "Now, I could have him work the front counter, but what I really could use help with, is the computer."

Her heart lit up. "That's perfect. He practically lived on that thing before he went in the Army."

"Fantastic!" He smiled. As he did so, his deep blue eyes sparkled. "I'll give it a week or so and ask him."

The waitress came over and they ordered. After the woman left, she reached over and laid her hand over his. "Thank you."

He nodded, was quiet a moment then softly said, "It's the least I can do for another soldier. Our boys all need a leg up coming home. Too many of us end up falling through the cracks."

Janet felt the conviction in his voice and realized that until now, she'd never considered the homecoming plight of men and women who'd put their lives on the line for their country. She eyed the man sitting across from her and saw his rigid jaw, the far away gaze coming back. He was a man of steeped depth and the urge to go hide from him coursed through her, but her legs wouldn't move. And even if they could, she'd remain. Finally, she said, "When you came back from Nam, what was it like?"

He shot her a sobering glance. "I pretty much kept my mouth shut about it when I came home and tried to blend back in."

She sensed she was brushing up against a touchy subject. "So, you never talked to your parents about it?"

He looked off over the crowded room. "No, I didn't. There was nothing to say, really. I just got on with life."

"Becoming a paramedic?"

"Yeah, something like that," he replied, as the waitress brought their orders to the table. After she left them alone, he grabbed his fork and poked at his breakfast. He reached for the salt and pepper. "Actually, I started off as a fireman."

She unwrapped the napkin around her silverware, intrigued. "If you don't mind, my asking, what got you interested in that?"

He chuckled. "You won't believe this, but ole dumb-dumb here got stuck in a tree when I was a kid. "

"Oh, my God," she said, bursting out in laughter. She envisioned this six-foot-plus man in front of her stuck in a tree. It was a good thing she didn't have anything in her mouth otherwise it would've been all over the table. "Stuck in a tree?"

"Yeah, I was a regular Tarzan," he said, grinning. "The higher the tree, the better. Then one day I turned my ankle fifty feet up a gnarled oak and couldn't get down." He took a bite of his breakfast, wiped his mouth and shook his head. "So there I was out in the woods behind our house, screwed cause I couldn't put my weight on my foot. Fortunately, I was with my buds and they went running for help.

"Twenty minutes later, firemen show up, and before I know it I'm being rigged into a harness. As they lowered me down, I thought 'this is something I want to be'. After that, it was a done deal." He paused. "And you? What interested you in photography?"

She cocked her head. "I think it was in my blood the minute I was born. Just didn't know it until one day a man came and lectured at my university."

"An epiphany of sorts, huh? So what were you studying at the time?"

She sipped her tea. "Environmental Engineering, if you can believe it."

"Really? Somehow, I can't see you doing that. What started you off down that road?"

"My father, I guess. He was a Mechanical Engineer, so it sort of rubbed off on me growing up."

"I can understand that," he said. "So what did this guy who came to your college say to change your mind?"

"He talked about sustainability, but in a different way. Said the best way to sustain things was to observe how nature sustains itself, and for that, all you needed to do was look and see. So I started taking my camera out into the field afterward, and the more I did, the more I realized what my real calling was. Taking pictures of nature doing its thing spoke to me in ways nothing ever did. By the way, the man you saved, Garrett Andersen: that was him."

"Really?" He cocked his eye. "Small world isn't it? You never know how your paths are gonna cross. So, you shoot all digital or are you the last of the die-hards that sticks with film?"

She shook her head. *You're right Andy, you never know what the universe has in store.* "I'm pretty much digital now, but I have to confess, I prefer film. There's just something about getting in the dark room and doing your own developing. Makes you feel more in touch with the photo. My husband used to say the same thing about drawings. He hated the computer programs. 'Give me a sheet of paper and pencil!' He'd say all the time." She paused and cleared her throat. "So, I'm curious, what got you out of the fire department and into the book selling business?"

He flinched at the unexpected question. "An accident. I'm disabled. I have a TBI. Ummm … traumatic brain–"

"Injury. Yes, I know what it is," she said and instantly regretted the tone of it. "Sorry, I didn't mean that to come out like it did."

"Like what?"

"Smart-ass, I guess you would say."

"Didn't sound 'smart-ass' to me." He finished the last of his breakfast, pushed his plate away and sat back.

An elderly man a few tables away stumbled and fell. As his cane clattered to the floor, the crack of a coffee cup reverberated around the room. Everyone looked up, but Andy sprang from his chair and bolted over to him.

She tossed her napkin on the table, shoved her chair back and followed along with a couple nearby waitresses. As they knelt down beside Andy, she heard Andy asking the man if anything hurt while looking him over from head to foot. The EMT in him was kicking in. *You might be retired, but a paramedic you'll always be,* she thought as he guided the man to his feet and over to a chair. Once he was satisfied the man was okay, he turned to the waitress. "Get him whatever he wants. His tab's on me."

She smiled as she snatched a paper towel from one of the waitresses and dipped it in a water glass. *What a sweet gesture. Who are you?* She thought as she blotted the coffee stains on the old man's white shirt.

"I hope he'll be okay," she said when they finally returned to their table.

He glanced in the direction of the old man who was looking back at them with an appreciative smile. "I think he'll be just fine," he said, waving back at the man.

She leaned forward, "By the way, that was real nice; what you did back there."

"It's what I do," he said in a matter-of-fact tone. He looked off over the crowded dining room and was quiet for a moment. Turning back to her, he said, "So, what we were talking about?"

"Which was? I don't remember."

He frowned. "Damn, I hate it when I forget things I just talked about...Oh, hold on. I got it, your photography. Did you start out freelancing?"

She picked her mug up, tapped her nails against its ceramic side. "Sort of. I worked for a couple of small presses for a while. Meat and potato shoots mostly. I hated them–not the companies–the shoots. I wanted to be outside capturing mountains and rivers, not fundraisers and parades."

"Have to start somewhere." He took a gulp of coffee.

"I guess."

They fell into an awkward silence for a moment. She didn't know what more to say and he appeared tongue tied as well. She glanced over at the elderly man they'd helped. "Well, I've errands to run."

"Me, too," he added. He tossed his napkin on his plate and walked her to the parking lot where they stood under a slate sky. There, in the cacophony of traffic motoring along the byway, they watched a flock of starlings settle into the barren trees across the lot.

Finally, she said, "Well thank-you again for all you're doing for Nate."

"You're welcome."

She smiled and put her hand out to him. "Drive safe."

"I will."

She felt his hand slip away and watched him turn toward his car. Suddenly, he turned around. "Hey, would you mind having dinner with me sometime?"

She cocked her head in surprise. "Umm ... I–"

"I'm sorry, I shouldn't have."

"No, it's all right," she said, and her thoughts went immediately to Nate. *Will he resent me if I go, feel like he's a means to an end? I don't think so, but who knows. But it's just dinner. It's not like we'd be going out dancing and tearing up the night.* She looked down. He wasn't wearing a ring, at least not that she could tell. *And, I do like him. Oh, what the hell, what can it hurt?* "Well, with the holidays coming up, a gala I'm working on and all, I'm gonna be real busy... but maybe after the first of the year?"

Chapter 12

ANDY SHOOK his head as he pulled out of *The Pompeii Café's* lot into traffic. He'd never intended to ask her out. Now that he had, he didn't know what to do about it. *You're just a volunteer down there, but your priority is still to Nate. He doesn't need you sniffing around his mother. He needs a friend like you had when you came back from Nam. Someone to listen. I should probably call her and back out. But that would be awkward. Damn, you really screwed the pooch on this one, Bud.* He turned the radio on and listened to the morning show babble as he merged onto the main arterial running through town. Fifteen minutes later, he was walking through the front door to McNamara's.

Shedding his jacket, he tossed it behind the front counter. Jonah came out from the stockroom carrying a box of new paperbacks.

"Morning," Jonah said with a toothy smile. He set the box on the counter.

Andy shifted gears, pushed his dilemma with Janet to the back of his mind and nodded. "Morning. How'd your appointment go at the VA yesterday?"

Jonah shot him one of his trademark 'don't-get-me-started' looks and poured himself some coffee. "You want a cup?"

"No, thank-you. I'm coffee'd out."

"Okay," Jonah stirred a heaping spoonful of sugar into his cup, slurped a sip and smacked his lips. "Well, I'm off to work." He picked up the box of paperbacks, tucked it under his arm and took a couple steps. "Oh, I almost forgot." He turned around. "Some guy named Jack called. Said he can't make the game. I asked him for his number, but he said you already have it."

Damn! "Okay Jonah, thanks," Andy said. Suddenly he wondered what to do about the extra TrailBlazer ticket in his desk. He looked up and saw Jonah shuffling toward the book stacks. *Idiot!* "Hey, Jonah? You wanna go?"

"Go to what?"

"The game," Andy called back. "TrailBlazers are hosting the Celtics, night after tomorrow. I have a free ticket."

Jonah opened his mouth, paused and said, "Really?"

Andy nodded. "Would I BS you?"

Jonah's dark eyes narrowed then lit up a pocked face that had seen too much of what life could throw at someone. "I don't know what to say."

"Umm...'Yes', works."

Jonah ran his hand over his head and down the back of his neck. "Yes, it does...okay sign me up!" He took a deep breath and blew it out. "I've never been to a game." He grabbed his coffee and the box back up. Taking a few steps toward the book stacks, he stopped and turned around.

Andy saw the look of 'thank-you' on the man's face. *You're welcome brother.* As Jonah turned away toward the stacks, Nate came to mind. Though the kid came from an affluent family, he was no different from Jonah or from himself for that matter. They all shared one thing in common: dark secrets.

Finally, he turned and went into his office. In twenty minutes, it would be time to open up for the day. Being a Sunday, Amanda was in church and wouldn't be in until after 1:00 PM. That was all right. He needed time to think about how he was going to manage the eighteen-bazillion things on his plate. Chief among them was his pre-trial conference with the lawyers and the Stewart family on the 29th. Hopefully, the department and the family could come to terms and leave him out of it. If not, then everyone would be headed for a trial and an uncertain future. His gut churned at the thought of it.

While it was true the store wasn't tied to the accident, it was an asset and he'd be forced to liquidate to comply with a court order. Why hadn't he incorporated? A personal bankruptcy he could deal with. But as it was, being a sole proprietor left his store wide open to being swept out from under him, and those who depended on him. He eyed the pre-trial conference date on the calendar, circling it over and over with his pencil and sat back. Maybe he was worrying for nothing. His lawyer was confident he'd escape being tied to the settlement if the department and the Stewarts reached an agreement. He looked up and closed his eyes. *All my life, I've tried to do the right things. Tried to be a good soldier, tried to be the best husband I could, tried to help people. Yet everything I've done has turned to shit. What am I doing wrong?*

The phone rang, jolting him out of his musing. He picked it up. "McNamara's."

"Hi, Andy. How ya been?"

"Hey Matt," Andy said, bracing for another of Matt's well-aimed conversations regarding the accident. He knew it wasn't intentional. Matt was just doing his due diligence, but he wished Matt would talk about other things besides the God damned lawsuit. "I'm doing. What's up?"

"Same ole, same ole. What about you? Been thinking of you big guy."

"Just trying to keep my head above water."

"How's biz at the store? You making it?"

"Yeah, we're doing all right. Food's what's bringing 'em in right now, but book sales are picking up. I think by the end of the year, we'll be making a profit. How's things at the station?"

"Not bad. Couple fires in town, nothing major. Oh, and Toady finally got his EMT cert."

Andy smiled. Dan Revit, affectionately known as Toady, had been trying for the certification for the last five years. It wasn't that he didn't know his stuff; he just froze up when it came to test taking.

"Wow, he finally did it," Andy said, "Give him a pat on the back for me. Who you partnering him with?"

"Gonna put him with Bob. They're tight these days, so might as well." He paused. "So...umm, you ready for the 29th?"

There it was: the lawsuit...again. He drew breath. "I guess. You gonna be there?"

"Plan on it. Maybe we can grab a drink after. What d'ya think?"

"Sure. So you're thinking we're going to be celebrating afterwards?"

"Hope so. Don't need this going to trial," Matt said with a warning in his tone.

Andy saw red flags waving. "Something you're not telling me."

Matt cleared his voice. "The lawyer for the Stewarts, Mr. Reed, has requested the duty logs for that day."

"And..."

"Andy, you and Bob just came off a sixteen hour shift fighting a blaze down at the Johnson farm. You know the rules about required breaks."

"There was no one else available. What were we supposed to do, let the guy die?" Andy said, raising his voice.

"I know, I know...but the law's the law," Matt said and the friendly tone went out of his voice. "Get this thing settled!"

Andy sighed. "I'll do my best."

"I know you will." Matt warmed back up. "Don't worry Mac. Things'll turn out okay. Keep your chin up."

"Right," Andy said, daring to believe him.

Andy tried to ignore the upcoming pre-trial conference and concentrate on work for the next two days. But as hard as he tried, the ominous meeting with the Stewarts dogged him. *Maybe tonight's game would will take my mind off it*, he thought as he picked up his nephew, Tim, and headed to Salem to get Jonah. He pulled his Suburban in front of the St. Francis Shelter.

"Looks like we're gonna be fighting the snow awhile," Andy said to Tim as they waited for Jonah to come out. He watched the mix of sleet and snow spatter against his windshield. He felt a chill run down his chest. "You warm enough?"

"Getting t-t-there. You want me t-t-to sit in back?" Tim said as his body swayed side to side.

"Only if you want to," Andy said.

Tim cupped his hands over his mouth and blew into them. "Maybe I'll st-stay up here until we pick up...umm...what's his name again?"

"Nate," Andy said, as the front door to the shelter opened. Jonah popped out into the wintery downfall with a cigarette dangling from his mouth and wearing his tattered green army jacket. As the man heel-toed it toward them with his hands in his pockets, Andy pulled an envelope down from the visor. Nudging Tim with his elbow, he said, "I gave you your ticket, right?"

"Yup, right here." Tim tapped his jacket breast pocket with a shuddery motion as the back door opened and Jonah got in.

"Hey, Jonah," Andy said.

"It's cold out there," Jonah replied, tossing the butt into the wind and shutting the door.

"It's wintertime," Andy said. He handed Jonah his ticket from over his shoulder, put the car in gear and pulled back into traffic. "You remember my nephew, Tim, right?"

"I sure do," Jonah said. He extended his hand over the front seat for a handshake. "How you doing?"

"I'm d-d-doing good," Tim said, gripping Jonah's hand. "And you?"

"Couldn't be better," Jonah said, sitting back. "Well, maybe a little better. Could be a tad warmer out there."

"I hear that," Andy said, pulling back onto the arterial. He snatched up the paper with Nate's address and directions and glanced at it. As they motored along under the falling snow out of town into the countryside, the conversation bounced from the game to the upcoming inauguration of President-elect Obama until they all fell silent.

At length, Andy turned off the main route onto Old Cypress Road. As he drove down the tree-lined lane, he glanced at Jonah through the rear-view mirror and saw him looking out through the passenger side window.

"Damn…there's some boo-coo bucks out here," Jonah said.

Darn right, Andy thought, following the gentle bend in the road that ran through the wooded land of cypress, oak and pine. Now and then, through the snow-laden trees he caught glimpses of sprawling cedar wood contemporaries, craftsman lodges and log cabin chalets. As he passed them, he started paying attention to the numbers posted on the roadside mailboxes. When he came up to Janet's address, he slowed down.

"5787," he muttered. "Next driveway's it." He sped up and turned down a long serpentine drive through the wooded lot.

"Look, over th-th-there. Dah-dah-deer," Tim said, pointing to a couple of does and a yearling nibbling away on a rangy bush.

Andy eased his Suburban around the loop toward the front porch of the modest lodge-style home tucked away in the woods. As he came to a stop behind Janet's Highlander, Nate hobbled out the front door. Janet followed close behind with arms crossed over her sweater.

Andy rolled the window down, letting in the resinous scent of pine as Nate opened the back door. "Who ordered this crap?" Andy said to Janet.

"I don't know," she replied, rubbing her arms fiercely. "But be careful driving. I heard there's a chance Portland may get socked."

"Will do," Andy said as Nate pulled the door shut behind him. He waved back to her, rolled his window up and started back down the drive. As he pulled back onto the road, introductions were made. For the next hour the conversation centered on the game.

Jonah turned to Nate. "I saw on TV, you're up for a Cross."

Nate shrugged and let out a sigh. "I guess."

"You don't sound happy about it," Jonah said. "Then again, I was never excited about mine either. Just did what needed doing."

"What's a Cross?" Tim said.

"A Distinguished Service Cross, Tim, is for showing up under heated combat at risk to life," Andy said. He turned to Jonah. "You never told me you medalled, you old dog."

"You never asked," Jonah said. He turned to Nate. "So I hear they held a parade for you. It's nice to be recognized…isn't it, Andy?"

Andy knew exactly where Jonah's anger was coming from. Coming back from 'Nam a hero was nothing to be bragged about in the days when soldiers were, at best, dimly viewed by the public. He viewed the man in his rear-view mirror. Saw piercing dark eyes staring straight ahead.

Nate huffed. "Right."

Silence stalked the inside of the car until Jonah coughed and said, "It sure is snowing out there."

"Don't worry, Jonah. This old beast has gotten me through a lot worse than this," Andy said, glad Jonah had changed the subject.

But Nate said, "So, what is it? Your medal?"

Again silence filled the car. Finally, Jonah said, "A Bronze Star."

Tim turned around and looked over his seat at Jonah. "What's t-t-that medal given for?"

"Heroism in combat," Jonah replied, his tone flat and direct.

Tim said, "What dih-dih-did you do-do-do?" Andy turned to Tim. Nudged his arm and shook his head. Tim's face tightened. "I'm sorry. I dih-dih-didn't mean to be nosy."

"It's all right, son," Jonah said.

From his rear view mirror, Andy eyed Nate looking out his window. "There's things we just don't talk about, Tim." *Isn't that right, Nate?*

Nate spoke up, "Yeah…like the injured private taken prisoner at the beginning of the war. It was blown out of proportion. All the hype was political bullshit. Not saying she didn't deserve a medal…but really?"

"Maybe it was because she was a woman," Tim said.

"Probably," Nate replied. "I don't have anything against women. It was just overdone."

Andy tapped his fingers on the steering wheel as he listened to what Nate said. The kid was angry, but there was something else in his tone he couldn't quite place; something disturbing. He thought of Jonah then and the job offer he was going to make to Nate. He hadn't considered the benefits or the consequences of bringing the kid and the old black veteran together. Was it wise? He didn't know, but he'd promised Janet. The rest was out of his hands.

An hour before tip-off, Andy exited the I-5 interstate and followed the signs to the Moda Center. The parking lot around the twenty thousand seat arena the TrailBlazers called home was filling up quickly. He parked the car and they all got out into the falling snow. As they trudged to the main gate, Andy dropped back with Nate.

"You've never been to a game until you sit right behind the bench," he said as he tried to figure out how to bring up the subject of Nate coming to work for him. If he was too obvious, Nate would shut him down.

Nate nodded. "Looking forward to it."

"You're in for a treat," Andy said, trying to keep the conversation going while gauging Nate's mood. After the discussion in the car about medals, Nate had grown distant. "Anyway, there's a lot that goes on most people never see when they huddle around strategizing."

"I bet," Nate said, his misty breath rising into the darkening sky. He stopped and pulled his gloves out of his jacket. "Damn, it's cold. Hard getting used to winter again."

"I imagine." They started walking again. "I remember when I was in 'Nam. The humidity and heat were brutal some days, say nothing of the nights. You couldn't get comfortable no matter what you did because everything was always damp and smelled like week old diapers."

Nate smiled. "Iraq was a frying pan. You stayed in the shade as much as possible unless you wanted to be a crispy-critter."

"There's a term I haven't heard in a while," Andy said. "Had a different meaning in 'Nam."

"What's that?" Nate said.

"In 'Nam, a crispy-critter was someone who got torched, usually by *nape*. Not pretty."

"Nape?"

"Napalm. They used it in warfare against Charlie. Not nice stuff." Andy paused, not pleased with himself for bringing the subject up. "Say...umm...you know anything about computers and the internet?"

"Some. Why?"

"Well, I'm having a hell of a time getting my website up for the store."

"Who you using as a host?" Nate said.

"Moma-Web."

"Shit, you don't want them. They're a pain-in-the-ass," Nate said. "You need to hook up with WebBase-1."

Andy cupped his hands to his face to ward off the chill wind. "Never heard of them."

"Google them. They're the best."

"I'll do that." Andy coughed and rubbed his hands together as they walked. "Say, umm...would you be interested in helping me out?"

"In what way?" Nate said with a hedge in his tone as he trudged along beside Andy with his cane.

Andy slipped between two parked cars with Nate trailing behind. Over his shoulder, he called back, "I was thinking: being my *webmaster*? I'm an idiot when it comes to writing html. I'd make it worth your while."

Nate was quiet a moment and Andy worried if he'd rushed things. He stepped out between the cars. When Nate joined him, he turned around. As he was about to say, 'or not', Nate spoke up.

"Sure, what the hell? Got nothing better to do. How much you paying?"

"How much you want?" Andy said as they joined Tim and Jonah, who were standing in a short line waiting to get through the front doors to the arena.

Nate shrugged. Shot him a crooked smile. "Nothing too far out of my pay grade. Twenty, an hour?"

Andy pulled his ticket out. "How about fifteen."

"I guess," Nate replied.

Tim turned around in front of them. "You going t-t-to work for my uncle Andy?"

Nate pulled his gloves off. Shoving them in his pocket, he reached inside his jacket and pulled his ticket out. "Thinking on it."

"Cool," Tim said. "He's pretty easy. What are you going to–"

"Hey guys, got to move along," Andy said, cutting in. He was guessing what his nephew was going to say. *No, Tim, I don't want Nate finding out you're a computer wizard; at least not until Nate's been with me awhile.*

They passed through the turnstiles into the congested lobby and wove their way through the masses into the outer hall rimming the arena. As they walked against the flow of humanity toward the stairway leading to the courtside seating section, a group of teen boys ran past them. One of them bumped into Nate, nearly knocking him off his feet. Andy grabbed Nate's arm and steadied him as the boy melted into the crowd ahead.

"You all right?" Tim said to Nate.

Nate winced. "I'm fine."

"Damned kids," Jonah muttered, shaking his head.

Andy let go of Nate's arm and kept an eye on him as they started ahead again. The last thing he wanted was Nate limping back home to his mother. After his first few gimpy steps, Nate was walking right again and Andy's concern fell away. Up ahead, a vendor was selling programs. Andy dug into his wallet. As he was about to pull out a twenty, a loud cry echoed down the hall. He looked up and saw a crowd gathering near the stairway. He turned to Jonah. "I'm gonna check things out up ahead. Can you–"

"Don't worry. I got this," Jonah replied with a knowing look.

Andy ran up and cut through the onlookers. A boy, maybe ten or twelve years old, lay on the floor with his ankle turned back underneath him. He knelt beside the nasal wailing child. "I'm a retired EMT," he said to the distraught, brown haired woman across from him. She looked up from running trembling fingers through the boy's dark, curly hair, not seeming to comprehend him. Assuming she was the mother, he nodded toward the boy's leg. "May I?"

The distraught woman ran the heel of her palm over her tear stained cheek. "Thank you, some kid ran into my son and knocked him down." She glanced toward the boy's foot. "Do you think it's broken?"

Andy reached under the boy's leg and gently palpated the ankle. As he did so, a security man brought a litter over and set it by Andy's side. Andy turned to the uniformed man. "It feels like a bad sprain," he said as he immobilized the joint with a steady hand. "It needs to be x-rayed though."

As other staff members and medical personnel showed up, Andy backed away and prodded the mother to move aside so her son could be administered to. She looked up at him with glassy brown eyes then back at the boy. It was as if she was in a world of her own, orbiting her son. "He'll be fine," Andy said to her.

She didn't answer though. Instead, a large, bald headed man in an old faded TrailBlazers jersey broke through the crowd. In his vice-like grip, he held one of the racing teens by the arm. He handed the sullen-looking boy off to one of the guards. "This is the punk that ran into my son and knocked him down." He sneered and stuck a large, fat finger in the kid's face. "You're lucky I'm not your father. I'd kick your ass all the way home."

The man turned and walked over to the mother who was standing next to Andy. Sweat was beading on his furrowed brow. He drew her into his arms. "You all right baby?"

As she melted into him, she nodded.

The man shot Andy a passing glance then escorted her over to her son, who was strapped to the litter. As they stood by their whimpering child, Andy saw the boy sign something back to his father. Suddenly, the fated accident with the Stewart boy flashed before him. He sighed as Nate, Jonah and Tim walked up and joined him.

Well, so much for this game distracting me from court tomorrow.

Andy turned off the coastal highway into the crowded parking lot that fronted the county courthouse. With every mile that had passed on his way in from Salem, it became harder and harder to breathe. He just wanted this over with. He looked for his lawyer, Ed Reynolds', silver Lexus and found it beside a barren basswood tree near the front entry. As he headed his way, the burly, bald-headed counselor got out of his car.

"So anything more from the Stewarts' lawyer?" Andy said, when they were headed to the front doors.

Ed shrugged. "Nope. Like I said, I don't think they have much of a case. You did everything you could to avoid that child. It's plain and simple, and backed up by an unbiased investigation. They're fishing and the judge is hoping not to waste people's time adjudicating a case that's dead on...I mean a foregone conclusion."

"So, he'll push them to reconsider their suit?"

"He'll try and impress that upon them, yes."

"What if they don't come down?"

"We say nothing," Ed said, "and wait to see what happens. I had a chat with the department's counsel, Mr. Stanton, and the counsel for the insurance company. They're anxious to get this behind them, too, but they said anything more than two hundred K and we're going to trial. But one thing at a time," he cautioned as they headed to the elevators.

Andy's heart drummed as they entered the large conference room. He eyed the Stewarts, who looked up in unison as he entered. They were a blue-collar couple. Stout and just shy of six feet, Mr. Stewart had a bulldog face with ice-blue eyes and dark heavy brows. A wide nose tilted slightly to one side: maybe one too many fights? Seeing how he worked at the cannery in town and had thick calloused hands to prove it, Andy didn't doubt he'd gotten into a brawl or two over the years.

As for Mrs. Stewart, she was a wiry woman; maybe an inch or two shy of her husband's height and she wore her fading brown hair up on top of her long, thin face. A faint hint of rouge brushed her cheeks and no eye shadow accented her muted hazel eyes.

Mr. Stewart frowned. Held him in a suffocating gaze. Mrs. Stewart just stared blankly at him, ripping his guts out. Ed and the department's counsel took their seats across a long mahogany table from the Stewart's lawyer. As he sat, Andy sucked a deep breath and swallowed the burning lump in his throat.

After introductions were made and business cards were exchanged, the Honorable Steven Connors cleared his throat and expressed his opinion on the merits of the case to the Stewarts. Afterward, the judge leaned forward in his leather-upholstered chair, took off his wire-framed glasses and set them in front of him.

"Make an offer Mr. Reed," Connors said to the Stewarts' lawyer then followed it up with a firm exhortation with a hint of a warning in it. "A reasonable offer."

Mr. Reed turned to the Stewarts and whispered something into the ear of the father. After the father whispered back, Reed, said, "With all due respect, your Honor, we don't feel what we're asking for is out of line. A child died because of the negligent acts of Mr. McNamara."

The memory of the boy lying motionless on the pavement flashed before Andy as Reed's words stalked the room.

As Ed opened his mouth, Judge Connors waved him off. "Whether or not negligence is involved Counselor, is a matter to be determined." He turned his attention to the parents. "I'm very sorry for your loss, and I don't mean to minimize your grief, but I urge you to make an offer they can respond to."

The mother and father looked at each other and broke into whispering between them. Finally the father leaned over to Mr. Reed. After a brief conversation, Reed said, "In the interests of showing good faith, we'll accept seven-hundred-fifty thousand."

Stanton leaned back in his chair with a hawkish expression and darted glances with the insurance lawyer. A short private conversation ensued. At last he said, "Our offer is a hundred thousand, which we think is very generous considering the evidence."

Mr. Stewart bolted forward in his chair. "Generous! Are you serious?"

Andy tightened his grip on the armrests of his chair. Reed held his hand up and urged his client to sit back. "Counselor, a child's life was lost here. Surely, you can do better than that?"

Stanton sat forward and eyeballed the attorney across the table. "And we sympathize. But the evidence speaks for itself. My client and Mr. McNamara took every precaution as required in the performance of their duties, which has been borne out by an exhaustive police investigation. But in the interest of moving this thing along we'll go to one-fifty."

Mr. Reed rolled his eyes, hardened his expression. Eyeing the Stewarts, he said, " A million-five."

Stanton rolled his eyes and shook his head. "Final offer, two hundred and it's a gift I might add.

Reed turned to the Stewarts. The bitter expressions on their faces told Andy this was going nowhere. The judge sighed as Reed glared at Stanton. "In that case, we'll be seeing you in court."

As Reed collected his files and shoved them in his brief case, Judge Connors pulled out his court calendar. "Very well gentlemen. Right now, we have a busy docket so I won't be able to get you scheduled until sometime in May. I'll have the clerk firm up a date with you in the next week or so."

Judge Connors got up and headed for the door with the department's counsel following behind. After they left, Reed cleared his throat and said to Ed, "It's unfortunate the department isn't willing to come to terms. We were prepared to possibly drop the suit against Mr. McNamara, but now we're left with little choice unless he wants to settle up. You have an offer?"

Ed leaned toward Andy. "Sure you don't want to go with a two-hundred-seventy-five?"

"I can't afford that," Andy whispered back, feeling like a shit.

"Okay one-fifty, it is then, but I don't think it'll go anywhere," Ed replied. He turned to Reed. "We're prepared to offer fifty."

"I guess not. Gentlemen, have a good day," Reed said. As he went for the door, the Stewarts followed, holding Andy in condemning stares.

Chapter 13

J ANET ROLLED over and eyed the alarm clock next to her bed. 8:22 AM. *Holy crap!* She threw a robe on, let Cleo out of his kennel and flew down the hall. Of all days to oversleep, Christmas morning was not the one of them. Not when a twenty-one pound turkey had to be done before people arrived. Then again, she'd been up past twelve the night before cleaning and gift-wrapping. She rounded the corner to the kitchen and ran into Nate, who was sitting at the breakfast bar. He was in a pair of jeans and a sweatshirt. In front of him was a gift he'd just finished wrapping. He topped it with a bow, reached down into the bag beside him and drew out a box of fragrant soaps, lotions and bubble-bath beads. Obviously, they weren't for her. Probably for Megan. As he set them in front of him, he glanced up at her.

"Morning," he said.

"Merry Christmas," she said and giving him a peck on the cheek, she went over and flipped the door open to the fridge. "Can you take Cleo out for his walk?" When he didn't answer, she turned around. "Nate?"

He set the tape dispenser down and took a sip from the mug beside him. "Yeah, sure. What's the rush?"

She took a deep breath and swallowed the sudden urge to yank him off his stool. But it wasn't the right time to have it out with him about attitude. Yes, he was mad about her refusal to let him read the letters his father had buried behind the cottage, but he was acting like a jerk. She wrestled the turkey out and set it in the sink. "I overslept, that's what's the rush. And I have a ton of food to prepare."

He turned his eyes upward and shook his head. "Mom, it's no big deal. No one's gonna be running the glove on you."

She whirled around, knowing what he meant, but not appreciating his making light of the impending disaster in front of her. "What?"

"The glove...inspection!"

"Just do it, please," she said.

"Yeah, whatever." He got up. Shuffled over to the patio door, shoved his feet in his slippers and snapped his fingers at the dog. "Come on, boy. Let's get out of here before she blows."

"Get a jacket on, it's cold out there," she said to the door shutting behind him with a click. *Damn him!* She closed her eyes, pinned her hands on the lip of the counter and leaned forward, clenching her teeth. This was the last thing she needed on Christmas morning. Even though the last week hadn't been easy between them, she'd hoped he'd be pleasant today of all days. But it wasn't shaping up that way. *I don't owe him an apology for respecting his father's wishes. Neil buried that box for a reason and I'm not going to feel guilty about it.*

Except she did, and there was more to it than that. She was angry and scared. Angry that Nate wasn't talking to her about what happened in Iraq. Scared she was being locked out of his life. Though she had Megan and Trevor and the house as reminders of Neil, Nate was hers and Neil's alone and losing him frightened her more than anything in the world.

At length, she pressed her lips together and frowned as she watched her son walk with Cleo in the back yard. The two of them zig-zagged along, Cleo leading the way with his nose down low while dragging his long ears over the snow cover. Suddenly, a long forgotten memory of Nate surfaced. He was a little boy, and in her mind's eye she saw him walking Barney in the lot behind the cottage in Lincoln City. Where had time gone? Her throat tightened, but she forced the tears away and went back to the turkey.

As she crammed the last of the stuffing into the bird, Nate pulled back the patio door and came in with Cleo. From the corner of her eye, she watched him kick his snow-crusted slippers off and go back to wrapping gifts. For the next fifteen minutes the only sound in the room was Cleo munching his morning kibble, her chopping onions and potatoes and Nate cutting gift paper and wrapping it around boxes. Finally, she set her knife down, wiped her hands on a towel and turned to him. "I'm sorry."

He stuck a tag on top of the gift he was wrapping, set it aside and looked up. "For what?"

"For being short with you. I just want everything to be ready when people arrive."

"Everything'll be good. It always is," he said in an off-hand tone. He put his wrapped gifts in the bag beside him and got up. "I'm going to put these under the tree and grab my shower. You need anything else before I go?"

Yes, I need my son back. "No, go get your shower."

He nodded, took a couple steps then turned. "Oh... by the way, I got a job... well, sort of."

"Really?"

"Yes, with Andy. Guess he needs a hand with his web site." He shrugged. "Doesn't pay much, but it's something to do, I suppose."

Thank you, Andy. She took a step toward Nate. When he stiffened, she stopped. "That's wonderful. When do you start?"

"Next week, after I get moved into my apartment. Umm... we have any boxes around?"

"I think so, in the garage. Why?"

"Thought I might start packing a few things for the move. Anyway, gonna get wet," he said, turning away from her.

Really, Nate? It's Christmas! Are you that much in a hurry to get out of here? She watched his back retreat from her and felt stripped to the bone as the space widened between them. She clenched her jaw. *He hates me,* she thought as she threw herself back into preparing the turkey for the oven. But she couldn't fight the tears collecting in her eyes. She wiped them away with the back of her hand. *Merry fucking Christmas, Janet.*

As the morning wore on, she battled to remain in control of the emotional roller coaster she was riding. But the more she tried to ignore Nate's going about the house, asking whether he could borrow this or that for his apartment, the more the dagger of his leaving twisted inside her. She basted the turkey for the third time, poured herself a mug of tea and stepped into the Great Room wondering how she was going to make it through the day.

In the far corner by the hearth stood a twelve-foot Austrian Pine, wrapped in silver garland. It had taken some time finding one this year, but there were still a few farms up north that grew them. On it, a cascade of twinkling white lights meandered around silver and golden ornaments. Crowning it was an angel dressed in white taffeta. An antique Hummel manger huddled beside festively wrapped gifts. Red and white stockings hung from the mantel. Jingle Bell Rock rang from the CD player. A fire crackled in the hearth. But her gaze was pinned on the picture above the mantel. It was a picture of Neil and her that was taken shortly after they moved in. She gazed longingly at it, studied his robust nose, his full lips, his laughing blue eyes and fiery red hair. Felt herself transported back in time.

It was the Christmas of '96. She was a nervous wreck, worrying if her surprise for Neil was going to backfire. He hadn't seen his son, Trevor, in over twenty years. A lot of dark water had flowed between them during that time. The doorbell rang. She led Neil to the foyer, waited breathlessly in the eternity that passed between them. She would never forget the embrace that finally came. Father and son reunited. Outside of Nate's birth, it was the finest moment of her life.

"Mom, I think your friends from San Fran are here," Nate said from the end of the hallway.

She started then turned and saw Nate standing with a box tucked under his arm. He pointed at the front window as the grandfather clock in the foyer chimed the noon hour. Stepping to the front door, she saw Mick and Sandra getting out of their car.

Christ, they're early!

She ran to the mirror over the pedestal table in the foyer and combed her hair back with her fingers. Not her best face forward, but they were here. She stripped the stained white apron off and tossed it to Nate. "Can you throw this on the washer for me honey?"

He stuffed the wadded apron under the box he was carrying and left as the doorbell rang. Glancing at the mirror one last time, she stepped to the door and opened it. "Come in," she said with as much excitement as she could muster.

"Hi!" Sandra cried as she stomped her feet, knocking the snow off her boots. She shed her coat as Mick followed her inside. "Merry Christmas," she said wrapping her arms around Janet.

She lingered in the woman's embrace. "It's so good to see you. How was the flight?"

Mick kicked his boots off. "It was good. I was able to get us on an earlier flight so voila, here we are!" He panned the room. "Is Megan here yet? I haven't seen her in like…forever."

"She'll be here soon," Janet said.

Sandra walked into the room and ogled the tree. "Is that a Scotch Pine?"

"No, it's an Austrian," Janet answered, joining her. She stood beside Sandra as the memory of her first Christmas with Neil flashed before her–remembered him dragging in a massive ornamental evergreen that took over the entire living room. Said it needed no decoration. Only his family heirloom angel on top. She smiled. "It was Neil's favorite, so it became sort of a tradition."

Mick handed her a gift bag with a large red bow. "A little something for under the tree."

She came to herself. "Oh, thanks. Can I get you guys something to drink? I have wine, coffee, soda, tea or beer."

"I'll take a glass of wine," Sandra said.

"Beer works for me," Mick said.

Sandra said, "Where's Nate?"

Janet glanced toward the kitchen, remembering him with the box containing some of his belongings: belongings that were going to his new apartment...away from her. She shrugged. "Oh, he's around here somewhere." She set the gift under the tree. *Come on Janet; get it together.* "Hey, why don't we head to the kitchen? I picked up some jumbo shrimp we can nibble on while we talk."

"Mmmm...lead on," Sandra said. As she walked beside Janet, she dropped her voice. "How is he?"

Janet shook her head. "Later."

Sandra nodded as Nate rounded the corner with Cleo padding beside him. The two of them came to an abrupt halt. Nate said, "Oh, hi."

"Hi, Nate," Sandra said.

"Honey, you remember Mick and Sandra, right?" Janet added.

"Sure." He turned to Janet. "Any idea where my baseball card collection is?"

Really Nate? Can't this packing wait? "Should be down in the basement," Janet said, feeling her stomach knot and wanting to throttle him.

Mick slid up beside them and extended his hand. As Nate shook it, Mick said, "Looks like the leg's coming along good."

"Working on it," Nate said.

Suddenly, the front door opened. Janet turned around and saw Megan coming in with Ben. When Megan looked their way, her face lit up. "Mick!" She cried, rushing in, coat and boots still on. She threw her arms around him. "How the hell you been?"

Mick smiled. "Getting old. He glanced at Ben, who was removing his coat and tilted his head toward the man. "Not bad."

As the reunion took place, Janet saw Nate's jaw tighten, giving the impression he wanted to be somewhere else. She tapped his arm. "Mind helping me open a couple bottles of Pinot?"

Nate started, wrinkled his brow. "Yeah, sure."

She followed him in and when they were out of earshot of everyone, said, "Can we please be done with your packing for the day?"

He took down a couple of bottles from the wine rack. Set them on the counter. Leaning forward, he stared ahead. "Don't worry, Mom, I'm not going to ruin Christmas."

"Never said you would," she answered quietly. She opened the cabinet drawer and took out a corkscrew. Stepping beside him, she set the opener down. "I'm trying really hard here, Nate."

He pressed his lips together. "Shall I open both of these or just one at a time?"

She peered haltingly at the ceiling as the memory of his condemning her at Trevor's house roared in her head. That he'd accused her of being cold and callous had crushed her. She loved his father more than anything and putting him in Hazelnut Manor had been the hardest thing she'd ever done. At last she said, "I'm not going to apologize to you or anyone else for honoring your father's wishes. You hear me?" She grabbed his arm. "Your father buried that box for a reason so get over yourself and stop acting like a child."

"Acting like a child?" He gritted his teeth. "Really?"

He ripped his arm out of her grasp, tore the seal off one of the bottles and jammed the corkscrew in it. But behind his sullen glare there was something more. She studied him as he held her in a withering gaze. As she did so, she realized there was more to his anger than what had happened between them at Trevor's.

Her heart faltered. "Nate, there's more to this than that box, isn't there?"

He broke away and shook his head. "Doesn't matter, I'll be out of here in a few days."

Trevor and Nadia were the last to arrive. Janet braced herself for the inevitable coming together of Megan and her brother. But by the time everyone had finished dinner, what had always been the most stressful part of the holidays–Megan's animosity toward her brother–had failed to materialize. Instead, it was she and Nate who had the problem. She eyed her son from across the room as people were opening their gifts. He was sitting quietly beside Mick near the tree, nursing a beer while watching the commotion going on around him. A stack of gifts next to him were untouched. She spotted her present resting at the bottom of his pile and wondered if had ended up there by accident or by intention.

At length, she glanced down at her stack of wrapped boxes and gift bags that were strewn about her feet. She sighed. Unwrapping gifts was the last thing she wanted to do right now. Her stomach churned, threatening to erupt at any minute. At last, she bent over and lifted a thin, hefty package onto her lap. After reading the attached card from Mick and Sandra, she peeled the wrapping away and gazed down at a Swarovski crystal frame. Her brow went up. *Holy crap!*

For some time, she stared at the gift dumbfounded, then called across the room to Mick. Holding the frame up, she said, "Thanks. It's beautiful."

"You're welcome," he answered as he opened a gift of his own.

"Hey, Nate, thanks," Megan blurted out, holding up a cellophane wrapped collection of toiletries.

Nate raised his beer in salute and stretched his braced leg out in front of him.

"Hey, guy, you gonna open a gift?" Trevor said to Nate. "You've been sitting there for the last twenty minutes with nothing to show for it."

"I guess." Nate picked up a gift bag, reached inside and pulled out a bundle of army green dishtowels.

Megan leaned toward Nate. "I figured you could use a few house warming gifts for your new apartment."

Nate set them aside. "I like your choice of color."

"There's another bag there that goes along with them," Megan added.

Janet watched her son peer over the side of his chair and pick it up. Fifteen minutes later, he had a pile of towels, potholders, tablecloths, bedding and blankets by his side. Up until now, his leaving had been a distant thing, something airy, but watching him gather item after item had suddenly given substance to it and it hammered home in her heart. It was just too soon, but more than that, she couldn't bear the thought of ill feelings harbored between them. Somehow, someway, she had to reach him, but she didn't know how.

She eyed the final unopened gift at his feet. Her gift. She'd spent a lot of time on it last year, making it special, meaningful, something to transcend the chasm between them since the war. Originally, it had been intended as a homecoming gift after his first tour, but he'd re-enlisted. Now it sat there waiting to be opened and she had all she could do to breathe.

Nate set the last gift he'd opened–a set of silverware–with the others, and turned her way. For a second, she thought she heard an anxious tone in his voice. "You're behind," he said nodding toward the three unopened gifts in her pile.

"You want me to open yours now," she said as Sandra suddenly cried out. The woman was waving a travel brochure for Tahiti over her head, then turned and threw her arms around her husband. Shouts erupted all around about how jealous they were of her gift.

But Janet was watching Nate as he casually observed the mounting excitement. It seemed as if he was in his own world, watching things from afar. As if he'd been evicted from his own life. Every bone in her body ached for him and she desperately wanted to reach out, to fix him, to make him whole and happy again. At last, he turned to her. As everyone prattled and ooh'd and ahh'd around them playing show and tell, their gazes connected. She mouthed the words, 'I love you.'

When he shrugged, she bent over and found a tall, thin box wrapped in silver paper. On top was a royal blue bow. A card was attached. She picked it off, opened it and read the short verse that said:

Christmas comes but once a year, but your gifts are forever
And while the distance between us oft times may be far,
We're always together,
For now, tomorrow…forever -

It was signed: Merry Christmas, Nate.

She set the card down wanting to believe the words. With renewed hope, she tore away the wrapping from the white glossy box inside. Running her nail under the flap, she opened the box and took out a slender glass bottle with a spritzing dispenser. A caramel colored liquid glistened inside.

Nate said, "It's pure nard. It's very strong, so be careful how much you use."

She gave the balloon ball on the dispenser tube a squeeze and inhaled the earthy fragrance with a woodsy hint. *Wow, I guess so,* she thought as the powerful perfume threatened to overwhelm her.

"Pure nard. Isn't that what Mary poured on Jesus' feet?" Megan said, as Janet passed the bottle to her.

"Yes, it is," Trevor replied. "Back then, it was rare and expensive."

Janet shuddered. "Oh my God, Nate."

"You like it?"

"I love it," She got up. Went over and hugged him. But the embrace she thought she was going to get never came. She pulled back slowly, trying to conceal her disappointment and motioned to her gift for him. "Open it."

He picked up the package wrapped in gold, slipped the card out that was tucked under the red ribbon out as she looked on. After he read it, he turned his lips up slightly and put it back in the envelope.

"I mean every word," she said.

But he only nodded as he set the card aside. A minute later he was looking down on a dark blue album with a silver filigree leaf and tendril design around the edges. In the center of the album were the embossed words: *Your Family Roots.*

He picked it up, pulled back the cover as everyone gabbed about their holiday treasures. On the first page, she'd fixed the handwritten letter Neil had sent her when she was pregnant. It expressed how happy she'd made him. On the next page, she'd drawn Nate's paternal family tree, listing his father's parents, grandparents, great grandparents, aunts, uncles, and cousins.

As she watched her son leaf through the pages, studying the faces of his ancestors, the works of his father and those of his grandfather, the holiday music and ongoing conversations faded to nothing. Suddenly, it was just her and Nate as he perused post cards from England, Holland and Scotland signed by people he didn't know. But what caught his eye the most were the letters his father penned to her.

Last of all was the photo Neil had torn from a family album and clutched savagely to his breast just before the monster stole the last of his memory. Beside it, was the letter she'd written to him from her hotel room in San Francisco after she'd accepted her Ansel Adams Award. She didn't need to see what was written. She knew it by heart and she mouthed the words to herself as Nate read it.

You sleep five hundred miles away, yet I can almost feel you here beside me. I wonder if you know I'm gone or if you miss me? Sometimes I think you're evaporating right in front of my eyes.

I remember the night we met. You came along in that big old truck of yours and pulled me out of the snow bank. Who would've thought we'd ever meet again, let alone get married? We put up with a lot from each other, didn't we, husband?

Do you know I can still see you wading into the surf the day I first took you to my beach? It's like yesterday—you rolling up your pant legs and splashing in the water.

I'll always love you, and I'll keep telling you that so you won't forget. I'll tell you about our wedding on the beach and how you kissed me when you found out I was pregnant. You'll know how you looked at Nate when you held him right after he was born.

And I will tell you about the house you built for me, the excitement in your eyes as you planned every detail, right down to finding a place for Barney to rest.

These are the things I'll tell you every day so you won't forget. Ever!

At length he closed the book and looked up. He didn't need to say anything. His moist eyes and trembling lips told all.

Chapter 14

NDY PUSHED the elevator button for the second floor of the VA clinic and took a sip of coffee from his travel mug. It was barely warm, but he didn't care. Coffee was coffee, hot or cold and he had an appointment to get to. He looked at his watch. It was 9:15AM. He was late and he wondered if he'd have to reschedule with the neurologist. It had taken him a month to get this appointment. Then again, if he hadn't kept putting it off to begin with, he could have gotten in weeks ago. If his appointment were canceled, would he feel better? He wasn't sure, only that he was afraid of what he might learn. Brain injuries were tricky at best. Avoiding treatment was foolish and damned right dangerous. But that sage advice had always applied to others – not *him*!

The bell dinged and the elevator door slid back. He stepped out and followed a short brightly lit corridor to Dr. Lattener's office suite. Pushing back a tall solid glass door, he went in and checked with the receptionist. A few minutes later, he was shown to a tiny exam room where he waited until the doctor showed up.

Dr. Lattener was a small, sharp-featured man with a receding hairline. A pair of dark-rimmed glasses was pushed up on top of his head. He greeted Andy with a cursory 'hello'. Taking a seat on the stool across from him, he pulled his glasses down on his nose and took up Andy's chart. "So, tell me about your headaches."

As the doctor scanned the notes in the folder, Andy thought about how to begin. "They started about a month after the accident. They weren't bad in the beginning. Just

an annoyance. We figured it had something to do with my vision, which was affected by my concussion. Eventually we thought they'd go away."

The doctor looked up. "We, being you and Dr. Steffens?"

"Yeah. Anyway, she put me on Imitrex. For a while it seemed to be working and the headaches happened less and less."

Dr. Lattener sat back and crossed his legs. "But they came back?" He eyed Andy with a steady gaze.

"Yes, sometimes so bad I can't think straight."

Dr. Lattener pulled a pen from his pocket and scribbled something in the chart. "You were probably getting rebound headaches.

Andy sat back. "What are those?"

Dr. Lattener leaned forward. "They're headaches that may occur after long term use of certain medications specific to your condition. Tell you what, why don't we try alternating Relpax with Imitrex. These two medication used in conjunction with each other often solve the problem."

Andy smiled, liking that solution.

Dr. Lattener wasn't through yet. "Okay, a couple last questions. Tell me about the headaches. Are they worse in the morning or the afternoon?"

Andy blinked. He'd never thought about that before. He pinned his hands on the exam table he was sitting on and leaned forward. "Now that I think of it, usually, worse in the morning."

Dr. Lattener jotted down another note. "If you bend over too fast or strain when you go to the toilet, what happens?"

Andy chuckled, but it was no laughing matter. "My head explodes. Thought I was gonna pass out once. I figured it was high blood pressure. I've been teetering on the edge of it for a while now. My GP now has me on Lisinopril."

"And is that helping?"

"Well, I just started it."

Dr. Lattener nodded. "What's the dosage?"

"20 mg."

"Any nausea?"

"No."

The doctor nodded. "Who's your GP, Andy?"

"Dr. Palmer."

"Good man." Dr. Lattener set the chart on the exam room counter-top, rolled his stool forward and did a routine check of Andy's vitals followed by a good, long look into his eyes. When he finished, he said, "I assume, no seizures, loss of muscle control?"

"No, none that I can think of."

Dr. Lattener reached up and snapped his fingers near Andy's ears. When Andy jerked back, he said, "Well, your hearing seems fine. Any ringing?"

Andy shook his head as the doctor backed away. The man pushed his glasses up onto his head. "I'm pretty sure we're dealing with re-bound headaches, but just to be sure, I'm going to schedule a brain scan for you just to rule out anything more serious." He handed Andy a referral to a local diagnostic clinic and closed the folder. "I'll see you next month, okay?"

Andy folded the referral, put in his shirt pocket and hopped off the table. As he shook the doctor's hand, he couldn't help feeling better about the whole situation.

After his appointment with Dr. Lattener, Andy headed to the VA. As he drove, he chastised himself for getting worked up about nothing. How many times in the past had he feared the worst only to discover he'd worried for nothing? He put the whole issue to rest as he pulled into the VA lot and parked. Getting out of his car, he saw Nate hobbling into the building. He looked around for Janet's Highlander and saw it pulling out into traffic.

Damn! I was hoping to run into her.

It was then he realized the lines had blurred between Janet and his responsibility to Nate. Yes, he'd met Janet prior to Nate showing up at the VA, but it was only in passing. And while the rules about fraternizing with patients didn't apply to volunteers, they still mattered all the same. That he was attracted to her shouldn't matter. Except, turning off feelings was easier said than done. The question then became, where did his motives lie? Was his attraction to Janet the reason he'd taken more interest in Nate over other patients? The answer to that question made him uncomfortable as he joined Nate in the elevator.

As they ascended to the second floor, Janet's face continued to flash before Andy while he chatted Nate up asking him how things were going with the new apartment. But Nate was quiet, supplying only the bare minimum replies. It was clear the kid didn't want to talk so Andy took the hint and squashed the impulse to press further.

When the elevator door opened, they headed to Physical Therapy. Nate's routine consisted of a brief consult with his physical therapist and the usual test for range of motion. Once that was done, it was onto the treadmill. He set Nate's speed for a practical two-mile per hour pace. Nate frowned. He'd been pushing to up the speed since before he left for Yosemite.

Andy had seen this kind of drive in other soldiers returning from war with injuries. What was confusing him was Nate's brooding behavior. Anger, he understood. It often drove men to exceed their limits. But depression usually elicited the barest effort, if any at all. It didn't make sense.

But he had other patients to look after. He left Nate alone and went over to 'Old Man Horace' (as he was affectionately known to all the staff). Horace was a double amputee who'd served in Korea. The sharp-eyed old black man from the south saw more than most with his sky-blue eyes. As Andy helped him into his wheelchair, Horace flattened his ever-present smile. "I see ya hovering over that young feller over there the last few weeks. You worried about him, aren't 'cha?" Horace said with a raspy drawl.

"Just looking out for him," Andy said, not wanting to get into a drawn out conversation.

Horace cocked a burnished brow. "Looks like more than that ta me."

Andy smiled. "That so?"

"Just saying." Horace buckled himself into the chair. Peered around Andy's shoulder. "Mark me, lot's going on in that boy's head an' none of it good."

Andy glanced over at Nate who'd jacked up the speed on the treadmill, defying the PT's orders. Seeing the kid's knotted brows and pressed lips, he knew Horace was right.

It didn't take a lot of arm-twisting to get Nate interested in having a beer after PT. Apparently, Nate and his mother had argued recently and Nate was in no hurry to get home. He pulled into the parking lot next to Trent's Bar and Grille and found a spot near the front entrance of the quaint, one story understated brick building catering to the local veteran community.

Shutting the car off, the two of them got out and went in. In one corner, a muted TV was turned to a local news channel. A couple of grizzled war dogs named Lenny and Dan were nursing beers as they watched a young blonde woman wave at a weather map. At the back of the room, Dexter and Drew were playing a game of pool on an old beaten coin-operated table. Somewhere, a juke-box was cranking out Johnny Cash's *Folsom Prison Blues*. The stink of spilt beer comingled with the lingering odor of burnt burgers and potatoes.

Andy watched Nate survey the room before taking a seat on one of the varnished wooden stools. The kid pulled a ten from his wallet and hung the crook of his cane over the lip of the bar.

"Put your money away," Andy said, taking a seat. He ordered a couple of beers. Turned to the young man. "You wanna grab a bite?"

"Think I'll pass." Nate panned the room again as if to assure himself he hadn't dropped into a Twilight Zone episode. "So, this where you hang out when you're not volunteering or running your book store."

Andy shrugged. "I come here from time to time. Food's not bad."

"Yeahhh," Nate said, drawing the word out. The bartender set their beers in front of them. Lifting his glass, Nate threw back a gulp and wiped his chin with the back of his hand. "Beer's good."

"That it is." Andy took a sip of his own. "They have a Super Bowl Board here if you want to get on it. Ten spot a square."

"What's the payout per quarter?"

"Two hundred a quarter, four hundred final score, I think."

"Sure, why not."

Andy called the bartender over and Nate picked a square. As the kid wrote his name on the board, Andy brought up the Seahawks and the NFL draft. He needed to buy time to get Nate comfortable and get him talking about what was going on in his head. At last, he said, "So, how was your Christmas, it went well?"

Nate glanced at him. "It went." He took a gulp of beer, looked down and was quiet a long time. "So, I was talking to Jonah. He told me he was in college working on his engineering degree when he was drafted. He looks a bit old for Nam."

Andy wondered what happened between Nate and his mother as he sucked his beer, but decided to stay on point. "Life's been rough on Jonah."

"I guess...Did you–"

"No, we didn't serve together. I met Jonah shortly after I landed in Salem. I was at a stop light, running a load of lumber and rock from Kilgore's back to my store, when he came to my car window and hit me up for a few bucks. I would've brushed him off, 'cept for the patch on his jacket. 1st Marine Division, 3rd Battalion. My division!" Andy said, thinking back to the long talks he'd had with Jonah on city park benches over the ensuing weeks. Mostly, they'd been about life after the sweltering jungles of Nam, but occasionally they'd veered into the dark days when living was determined by lucky chance, because no matter how careful you were, there was always a bullet out there with your name on it.

"So, he was a panhandler?" Nate said, breaking into Andy's muse.

He started and turned to Nate. The kid was staring at him with knitted brows. "Umm...yeah."

"Wow!" Nate shook his head. "What happened to him? I mean, he's not stupid–he was in college working on an engineering degree."

He took in Nate's $300 Trail Blazer jacket and $175 pair of Air Jordan's. "Jonah's one of the 'unlucky ones'. He did his tour but never got his footing back on life when he came home."

"No family?"

"Not that he speaks of and I don't ask."

Nate was quiet a moment. "Were you ever scared...when you were over there...in Nam?"

Andy stared ahead to the mirror behind the bar. *Well, that was out of the blue.* "Yeah. We all were."

Another a long silence passed. Andy grabbed a handful of nuts from the glass dish between them and popped them in his mouth.

Nate drained his beer and set it in front of him. "I never gave getting scared a second thought 'til we got ambushed. Bullets and shit flying all over. Not knowing which way to duck. But the silence afterward. That's the worst, isn't it?"

Andy closed his eyes and saw a kaleidoscope of dead Viet Cong soldiers slowly spinning before him. Some no older than fourteen. Boys he'd gunned down from afar on orders from above. The ringing sound of bullets leaving his rifle and the smell of cordite akin to freshly lit fuses came thundering down upon him. He looked over at Nate. For the young soldier beside him, the horror lived in the silence. For him, it had, and would always reside in the deafening bang of the rifle. And while the silence and the ringing of the rifle's discharge were at opposite ends of the spectrum, they resonated all the same.

Nate grabbed a handful of nuts and pushed his glass aside, seeming not to care he hadn't answered him. "I remember being in that Hummer...Parker, Kendall, Cunningham all gone or bleeding out around me, and all I could do was deal with what was coming next." His swept his shoulders back and shook his head. "And they want to give me a medal for that shit? I'm no hero."

Nate snatched his cane off the lip of the bar. Climbed down from his stool. "Gonna hit the head. Be right back."

As the kid shuffled toward the Men's Room, Andy watched him. During the war in 'Nam he'd seen the toll of battle in men's eyes after months of brutal firefights. For some, it had etched a vacant, dull gaze of a dead soul that looked out at the world. He'd seen it in his own mirror many times after he came back and knew what it meant. That look was rearing itself more and more on Nate's face lately and it concerned him.

Chapter 15

THE ANNUAL Alzheimer's Gala to raise money and for remembering those who'd passed on from the dreaded disease was one of Janet's most sacred events. She looked down at the long, white banner rolled out over her Great Room floor and nibbled her lip. She'd been working on it, off and on, over the last two weeks, placing pictures in a whimsical fashion of those who'd passed away. That Nate was helping her right now meant the world to her. She looked up and saw him eyeing her. A lopsided smile was on his face. That was his way. He apologized with actions. Suddenly, what he'd said at Trevor's didn't matter that much anymore.

She handed him a tag with a name written on it and pointed to a picture of a frail old woman. Megan came in from the dining room where she was stuffing place cards, glitter, ribbons, candles and single stem bud vases in boxes.

"Wow, that's nice," Megan said.

"You think so?" Janet replied looking up. She was unsure the banner was as good as it could be.

Megan cozied up beside her. "Yes, I do, and you need to stop being Ms. Perfect already. Come on you two, we have to be there in an hour. I'll help you roll it up."

Janet sighed as her eye drifted toward the picture of Neil in the upper left hand corner. Had she placed his picture too prominently?

She didn't want anyone to think she was being biased. "Okay. Guess I don't have much choice anyways."

"No, you don't," Nate said pasting the nametag under the picture.

Janet and Megan joined Nate and the three of them rolled up the fifteen-foot long banner and slid it into a long plastic tube.

Two hours later, they were with a dozen volunteers in the banquet room of the Marriot Hotel putting the final touches on the tables waiting for the invited guests. As a man warmed up on a piano, Janet placed name cards on dinner plates along with disposable cameras. Wine glasses glistened and silverware sparkled. All that was left, besides lighting the candles, was a quick confirmation that the overhead projector was working properly. Currently, that was in Trevor and Nate's gifted hands. She looked at her watch as slides of the Alzheimer's volunteer staff flashed on the screen. Things were coming down to the wire.

"Janet? What do you think," said Megan's fiancé, Ben, who was standing on a ladder in the front of the room.

She stepped back as Trevor retracted the screen and looked at the banner. "Can you move it down a bit? And the Alzheimer's banner, too?"

Ben nodded to the volunteer and they dropped them. She gave them the thumbs up and went back to placing name cards while Megan arranged bouquets of lilies around the podium. A sound guy from the hotel stood on the elevated platform thumping the microphone.

"Everything looks perfect," Nadia said, coming up beside her. She moved a spoon a micrometer to the right of one of the dishes and shot Janet a smile. "Has it been decided who is going to be awarded volunteer of the year yet?"

"No, it's done by secret ballot."

Nadia took up a napkin and refolded it. "Maybe you will be chosen, no?"

Janet shook her head. "I don't think so. By the way, thanks for helping out."

"No problem. Why don't you go to the ladies room and freshen up. I will take care of the rest, hmmm?"

Janet looked up and suddenly realized she'd been running a hundred miles an hour since she got there. *I must look like hell.* She handed Nadia the rest of her place cards. "You don't mind?"

"Not at all."

"You're a sweetie. Okay, these are numbered according to table. See the '10' on this top card here with the name, Anderson. That would go with table '10' over there, and so on and so on."

Nadia nodded. "Okay, go now. Not much time," she said and shooed her away.

When Janet returned from the Ladies Room, people were filing into the Hall and talking amongst themselves. A pianist played a George Winton melody in the background. Its tinkling notes floated over the gathered crowd adding to the growing cacophony. She looked over the decorated candle-lit tables wondering if there wasn't more she could've done. Megan and Nate stepped beside her.

Putting her hand out to her son, Janet drew him close. "Well, it is what it is."

"You did a good job, Mom," Nate said. "If dad were here, he'd be smiling right now."

She turned to Nate. For a split second, she saw Neil's soft probing gaze looking back through her son's eyes. She caught her breath. "Thanks. You don't know what that means to me, honey. I guess I'd better get up there and start mingling, huh?"

"'Fraid so," he said.

She filed around the tables, greeting the survivors who'd come to pay tribute not only to their loved ones but to those who'd freely given their time and energy to walk with them through their darkest valleys. Some of them she knew personally. She took many of them into her arms and held them, renewing the unbreakable bonds only those who'd gone through the journey could understand.

And then she saw him. He was standing near the doorway. Garrett Andersen! He was wearing a button down white shirt and red tie. She went to greet him. "Garrett, how nice to see you."

He turned away from the man he was talking to and studied her with dark gray eyes. "Do I know you?"

"No, but you changed my life once upon a time."

"Oh, my goodness!" He reached out and clasped her hand. "I hope it was in good way."

"Of course it was," she said, delighted beyond her wildest dreams. "I was this unhappy engineering student who didn't know what she wanted until you showed me the way."

"And what way was that, dear?"

"Photography. It changed my life."

"Well, I'm not much of a photographer, but okay." He looked at her hard then. "What's your name, dear?"

"Janet, Janet Porter."

His bushy gray brow cocked and his smile widened. "The Janet Porter?"

She felt sudden heat come to her cheeks and looked down. "Well, yes."

He turned to the man beside him. "This young lady here, I'll have you know, inspired my last collection of shorts."

She froze, dumbfounded as Garrett turned back to her. That he'd based some of his short stories on her photography left her feeling validated.

"So, who are you here for; your mother or father maybe?"

"Umm…actually, my dear husband. He passed away a couple years ago," she said, looking up.

"Oh, my heavens. He was too young to have suffered such an awful thing. My deepest sympathy to you." He shook his head. "Alzheimer's an awful thing. It steals your loved ones right out from underneath you and all you can do is stand by and watch. My dear departed Annabelle, gone from me twelve years now, God rest her soul, hardly knew me when she went to the man upstairs."

He let go of her hand. Turned to the man beside him. "This is my son, Michael." They exchanged greetings. Garrett said, "Someone's been busy in here. Place looks like a weddin' hall. You sure we're in the right room?" He winked and shot her a knowing smile.

"Oh, yes," she said, suddenly feeling at ease with him as he gazed out over the vast room of large round tables.

"So where'm I sitting in here tonight?"

She went over to the reception table and found the sheet of paper with the seat arrangements. When she saw Garrett's name at her table, her breath caught.

A loud, sharp, Pfff…pfff, rang out overhead. Everyone averted their gaze to the front of the room where a rail-thin, dark-haired woman stood on a raised platform. She looked out over the gathered guests and volunteers and smiled.

"Ladies and Gentlemen, thank you for coming out on this chilly January night. It's so good to see so many friendly faces. As you all know, this is our 21st anniversary gala. Twenty-one years, can you believe it?" She paused, encouraging a sudden burst of clapping. "This year has been a great year financially and I'm happy to announce we are more solid than ever because of the generous contributions of people like you, who know how important it is to help struggling families dealing with this insidious affliction.

"But we're not here to talk money and finances tonight. Instead, we're here to remember our loved ones and those who are still among us in heart and soul. It's because of them we're here, and I wish with all my heart for a day when we come here not to remember but instead to celebrate the defeat of Alzheimer's."

"Here, here!" Someone said in the back of the room.

A sudden burst of applause. When it died down, Olivia went on, "Here, here, indeed. That day will certainly come, but tonight we will remember…and…honor our selfless volunteers who tirelessly give of their services, professional or otherwise.

"To help me this year, I have a very special guest." She paused as if for dramatic effect. "A man who has been a fixture here in Salem and the Willamette Valley for over fifty years. A man who's written words have shone a light on the land and the people who live within it. A man we're lucky to have with us after a narrow escape from an accident three weeks ago.

"Thank God for the tireless Salem Fire Department and its staff of exceptional EMT's who happened to be around the corner when it happened, and thank God for the staff at Salem Memorial who tended him night and day afterward. They really are the best! But you already know that, so without further ado, please join me in asking Mr. Garrett Andersen to present the Volunteer of the Year Award."

As Garrett got to his feet, the room erupted in applause. Janet was dumbfounded. How was this arranged under her nose? She watched the old folklorist shuffle to the front of the room. Obviously, President Olivia decided to have a surprise this year. *But why keep it a secret from me*, she thought. She looked over at Megan who was clapping. Remembered seeing her and Olivia having a conversation off to the side earlier. Did Megan know about this ahead of time? When Megan glanced back with arched brows and stretched lips, Janet knew. The ovation dropped and the room went quiet as Olivia gave way to Garrett.

Stepping up to the microphone, he tapped it. "Thank you, Ms. Chamberlain for inviting me here tonight." He turned to look back at her. "Such kind words." Facing front, he went on, "What Ms. Chamberlain is alluding to is that I had a heart attack while driving. I don't want to make a big deal about it, but when I was lying in the hospital bed, I thought about how precious life is... and more importantly, how lucky I was there were regular people who risked their lives to pull me out of a burning car. People, like you and you." He pointed out to the gathered guests.

"It's very restorative to the soul to see what we are all capable of when another person is in grave danger. It's what makes us human. We take that for granted until one day it's stripped away from us or from someone we love. That's why I come here with a new sense of urgency.

"This monster, Alzheimer's, robs us of our humanity. It whittles our memories away, strips us of our dignity and tortures our loved ones who take care of us. I don't need to tell you what it's like watching it eat away at someone you love. You already know that. But I'd like to share a few things about my Annabelle.

"Before it descended on her, she was a vibrant beautiful woman. I can still see her sitting on our back porch painting flowers or tromping over to our big oak tree to add birdseed to the hanging feeder. And I have a secret for you, she wrote a bit of poetry – and she was better at it than I was, but she refused to let me show it off. I adored the little things she did around the house that made it a home. Things like keeping the flower vases filled with daisies and zinnias, decorating the house around the holidays and lighting a candle or two on the fireplace mantle.

"There were so many things I loved about her that were stolen from not only her, but from me! She just faded away until she wasn't my Annabelle anymore. I took care of her the best I could, but in the end, it wasn't enough. I often look back now and realize I didn't have to do it alone. But I was a stubborn old fool—and still am—so I missed out on getting the help I so desperately needed, but didn't know I did. This organization and the volunteers who give of their time helping people take on the burdens they are saddled with is a Godsend, and I'm so happy to be a part of it now."

He glanced back at Olivia. "And now, I guess I better get to it and announce this year's 'Volunteer of the Year' award."

Olivia stepped beside him. Handed him one of two envelopes in her hand. He tore back the flap and pulled out a folded sheet of paper. Holding it in front of him, he said, "This year's recipient has been with us for over fifteen years and has gone miles beyond any expectations of a volunteer, taking on a case load of four residents. She has organized outings and parties for the respective families and essentially become part of them, all while raising two sons and a husband." He smiled.

"Husband indeed! Anyway, would you all please give a warm welcome of applause to Ms. June Kellog; this year's 'Volunteer of the Year'?"

The large curvy woman rose from her chair with the grace of a ballerina and wove her way around the tables as everyone clapped. Janet knew June well. The woman could talk for hours on end and had spent many afternoons at Hazelnut chatting Neil up in the cafeteria during lunch. That it had always been a one-way conversation didn't matter. Janet knew her husband enjoyed it and that was all that counted. As June accepted the wood engraved plaque from Garrett commemorating her efforts, Janet sat back, crossed her legs and prepared for a lengthy thank-you speech. She wasn't disappointed.

Finally, Olivia gently wrestled the microphone from June and congratulated her one last time. As June swished and swayed her way back to her table with her plaque held tight to her ample body, Megan leaned toward Ben and whispered something. Whatever it was, it brought a smile to his face and a quick glance toward Janet. Suddenly, she felt like the brunt of a secret, but before she could decide how she felt about it, Olivia spoke up:

"Thank you June…Usually, we move into honoring our loved ones at this time, but this year, we have one more recognition to make. Two years ago, I ran into a very special woman at Hazelnut Manor. She was there for her husband, who was in the end stages of Alzheimer's. After a few short conversations with the staff, I found out she'd become an integral part of the residents' lives there, enriching their days with art and music. After a little more investigation, I knew she'd be an excellent addition to our association.

"So, like any good president, I badgered her until I wore her down." The room giggled. "Since coming on board, she's not only maintained her arts program at Hazelnut, she's also grown our fundraising two hundred percent by knocking on every door and leaving no stone unturned. Her love and dedication toward the families and those who are afflicted is unparalleled and so I'm proud and pleased to present this little memento of the association's gratitude for all she's done. Janet, would you please come up and accept this gift of our appreciation?

Janet froze and felt her heart thump as she tried to comprehend what Olivia had said. Everyone at the table turned and looked at her with broad smiles. Even Nate was grinning. Megan eyed her brother, jerked her elbow back and forth, motioning him to do what?

"Mom, get up!"

Janet shuddered, came to herself and stood. As she walked haltingly to the front of the room amid the rousing adulation she felt naked and humbled.

Olivia waved one of the association volunteers toward her. In the man's hand was a large red and white gift bag. Taking it from him, she joined Janet and gave her a warm affectionate hug. "Thank-you so much," she whispered into her ear. Letting go of her, Olivia took out a twelve-inch solid crystal star and handed it to her.

Janet glanced down at the award and wiped an unbidden tear away. "Thank you, I don't know what to say." She drew breath and gathered her wits. "This is a complete surprise, and I'll never trust you again, Olivia Chamberlain." A chorus of laughter burst out from the room. She turned back to the audience. "You know, this honor goes to more than just me. Numerous people have been involved in what we've accomplished. Chief among them, is my best friend, Megan Porter. I couldn't have done any of this without her help and support. She's been a constant source of strength for me over the last two years."

She paused. "And last of all, I'd like to introduce my son, Nate, who's home now from serving our country in Iraq. In doing so, he made an unwitting and painful sacrifice. You see; he missed the last years with his father, defending our right to be free. Honey, would you please stand up?"

Nate blushed. Rolling his eyes, he looked up at the ceiling, sighed then reluctantly stood. The room erupted with applause and everyone stood. A woman cried out, "We love you, Nate."

Olivia stepped beside Janet. Took the microphone. "In case some of you didn't know, Nate's up for a medal! How great is that?"

Janet saw Nate stiffen and his brow furrow at the mention of the medal. She shouldn't have brought up the war and his sacrifice. But it was too late. His thin forced smile made her heart sink. The only thing she'd wanted to do was shine a little light on him. Let him know how much she loved him. That he mattered. But her best intentions had turned against her and tarnished a beautiful night.

Chapter 16

ANDY DREW his jacket collar around his neck against the biting winter wind and strode across the VA parking lot to his car. Thank God he was done with that accursed MRI scan. Even now, twenty minutes later, he could feel the loud rat-a-tat-tat of the machine reverberating in his ears. The sound brought back unwanted memories of *Kate*. Along with them was the pungent odor of cordite rising from her long steel barrel. He fished his keys out of his pocket, unlocked the car door and got in. For a moment, he just sat there, closing his eyes in the chilled silence surrounding him until at last he started the car.

Merging into traffic, he turned onto 25th and followed the snow-plowed road north through town. What he needed right now was something to snuff out the mind-numbing headache raging between his ears. He pulled in front of McNamara's and saw Jonah come out the front door dragging a snow shovel behind him.

"Hey, Jonah," he said, getting out of the car.

Jonah pushed a pile of snow across the walk, turned and thumped the blade on the curb. "Morning. How'd it go?"

"Just wonderful," he replied as a gust of wind slammed his face. "Damn, it's cold out here."

"Tell me about it." Jonah reached into his jacket pocket, took out a cigarette and a lighter. After he lit up, he pushed another swathe of snow to the curb and shuffled back. "Supposed to drop to single digits by afternoon, too." He stabbed the shovel down and propped a hand on its handle. Dashing the ashes off the cigarette, he looked up at the falling snow and blinked. "Don't think there's gonna be a lot of business today, but never can tell, right?"

"Nope, never can," Andy said, noticing Jonah's bare hands. "Don't you have gloves?"

Jonah puffed away and licked his crooked, cracked lips "Naw, I'm good. By the way, we're out of salt."

Andy yanked his gloves off and tapped Jonah's arm. "Here, put 'em on." When Jonah glanced at him sidelong, he added, "I insist."

Hesitantly, Jonah took them. As he put them on, Andy opened the front door. "Good man," Andy said. "Okay, I got to get inside. My head feels like a *Bouncing Betty* ready to explode, right now."

Andy hung his jacket on the coat tree and joined his sister at the front counter. She raised her brow as she boxed up last month's returns.

"What?"

"Nothing… So, how'd it go?"

He winced. "It went."

She taped the box shut she was working on and set it on the counter beside her. Fixing her flashing blue eyes on him, she tilted her head. "Headache?"

He grabbed a soda from the refreshment case. "Oh, yeah!" Without looking back, he went in his office and rifled through his desk drawer for the bottle of Relpax. Shutting the door, he flicked the light off, went to his chair and closed his eyes, waiting for the medication to do its voodoo. The next thing he knew, a hand was on his shoulder.

"Andy, Andy?"

He blinked. Looking up into the shadowy darkness, he saw his sister's silhouette blocking the light spraying in through the crack of the door.

"Why don't you go home?"

He licked his lips, slowly took account of his body and oriented himself back to the present. To his relief, the banging in his head was gone. Taking his time, he sat up and patted her hand. "No, I'm fine. How long?"

"It's past three."

"Shit, I've wasted half the day." He rubbed his neck. Reached to turn his desktop computer on then thought better of it. "Any mail?"

"Some," she said, her tone provocative. He saw her shadow pass in front of him and heard her take a seat on the other side of his desk.

"Some? What's that supposed to mean?"

In the filtered light, he saw her lean forward. "I've been keeping a secret," she said, her voice laced with excitement. "Remember the article in the paper about the city initiative promoting business startups and expansions?"

He shrugged. "Yeah, but as I remember we didn't qualify because we weren't in the selected business corridor."

"Well, I looked into it further and I found a sister grant for businesses within the Arts district. Long story short, I petitioned for a grant and guess what?"

He leaned forward. "We got one?"

"Yep. The notification came in the mail today. There's still some paperwork to do, but we're in."

"How much," he said, daring to believe it. Dollar amounts flashed in his head.

"Don't know right now, but it's in the five figure range," she said. "Think of what this means. We can do some of the things we talked about, like hire another employee. Or we can renovate or buy fixtures and equipment."

Suddenly he remembered Nate. He'd forgotten to tell her he'd hired him. Well, no harm, no foul. They had the grant. How could she get mad? "Umm...well, I sort of already hired someone."

She sat back in her chair and he felt her condemning gaze drilling into him. "Who?"

"Janet's son, Nate."

She cleared her throat. "And you were going to pay him, how?"

He hesitated, knowing there was no good answer. "Out of my own take-home."

"Which is barely meeting your expenses. Christ, Andy, you can't keep hiring people without discussing it with me."

"If you're referring to Jonah, I seem to remember you being pretty damned happy about that," he said, sitting forward again. "And, how do you know I'm barely making it or not?"

"I'm your accountant, remember?"

"Oh…yeah, there is that. Still, it's my store."

"Yes it is, but it's my job to make sure it remains that way." She paused. "As far as Jonah, you, my dear brother, have a selective memory. I was more than unhappy! I was petrified your customer base was going to vanish. The man was living on the streets. Not exactly, how should we say, employee material. But, I'll admit, he fooled me. He's smart and he's cleaned up fine."

"And you like his company, admit it," he said, sharper than he intended.

He saw her fidget. "Well, of course I do," she answered, her tone bordering on the defensive.

He knew his sister pretty well and was damn sure she wasn't judging Jonah on his looks. It didn't hurt to hammer home the point though. "There you have it then. And as far as Nate goes, it's just part time."

"Doing what?"

"He's gonna get our website ship-shape and operational."

She was quiet a moment. "What about my Timmy? He could help you."

He anticipated her suggestion. "I know he could, but he's got a lot going on in his life right now. And besides, Nate could use the distraction. He's gone through a lot and well, I'm worried about him."

"I don't get it. What's so special about Nate? You've worked with lots of people over the years who've gone through things. I've never seen you get involved like this," she said. "You sure it has nothing to do with his mother?"

He frowned. Again, his sister had hit near the mark. Was he that damned transparent? He sighed. "No, she has nothing to do with it. Nate had a bad time of it over in Iraq. I have a feeling he went through something horrific. Let's just say, I can sympathize."

He heard her sigh. Finally, she said, "Okay," but her tone wasn't convincing.

"By the way, please don't mention Timmy's computer skills to Nate when he comes in tomorrow."

"Don't worry. I'm not unsympathetic." He could sense her rolling her eyes at him. "You like taking on the hard cases, don't you," she said. "Don't answer that. And no more going behind your accountant's back. Understand, mister?"

"I promise. And Panda."

"Yeah?"

"You're aces."

"Thanks, but you've already buttered me up enough, don't you think?"

He laughed as she let herself out the door.

The following morning, Andy pulled in front of McNamara's with Jack riding shotgun. Jonah was outside by the door smoking a cigarette, waiting for him to open up. When the old veteran saw him, he stubbed his butt and pocketed it.

"Gonna be a cold one today. But at least the snow's let up," Jonah said as Andy unlocked the door.

Once inside, Andy turned the lights on and adjusted the thermostat. Jonah bee-lined it for the coffee maker to start the morning Joe. As the coffee brewed, Andy went about his morning business of cashing in the morning drawer and restocking the beverage cooler. Jack did his paw-patrol around the book stacks. Breaking down an empty box, Andy called over to Jonah. "Hey, when you're done straightening up over there, mind looking in on the Johns? I never got to 'em last night."

Jonah looked up and whistled for Jack. When the dog came running up, he said, "Come on boy, let's go sniff a toilet."

Andy smiled as he watched his dog and the old veteran toddle on back. *You certainly have a way with words my friend.* When they were out of site, he went back to filling the cooler. Orange-cranberry juice and chocolate yogurt flips were hot items and he was having a hard time keeping up with demand. He emptied his last box just as the front door opened. Turning around, he was surprised to see Tyler, his ex-semi-regular part-time help. The freckle-faced, lanky young man fidgeted as he stood in his tattered parka.

"No school this morning?" Andy said, eyeing the teen. He wondered why the boy was bleary-eyed like a lost runaway. He hadn't seen Tyler in a while, not since he'd had to let him go. Ditching work without calling in the morning of Garrett's accident had been the last straw. He'd felt bad about it, because he liked the kid, but he needed dependable help. Tyler was neither dependable nor especially helpful. Fact was, he'd heard Tyler was running with a loose crowd, smoking dope and dropping pills. Whether it was true or not, he didn't know, but he wanted to give the kid the benefit of the doubt.

Tyler shook his head and looked down. The kid was working up the nerve to say something. Andy refrained from pressing him further and waited. Finally, Tyler said, "My mom kicked me out."

Andy drew breath. "What happened this time?"

Tyler's glance darted around as he shrugged.

Andy crossed his arms. "What do you want, son?"

"I need a job," Tyler said, averting his gaze as Jonah came walking back with Jack. He glanced down at Jack who was sniffing his shoes.

Andy shared a knowing glance with Jonah. "I'm sure you do."

"I'll do better this time, you'll see," Tyler said.

"Look, I don't know what to say Ty. I gave you several chances and you tossed 'em back in my face. You need to get your life in order son," Andy said. "Where you staying?"

Tyler scuffed his feet. "Friends."

"Right," Andy said. He had a good idea that his so-called friends were no friends at all. He felt himself starting to acquiesce. *Panda's gonna kill me.* He shared another knowing glance with Jonah. "Okay, if we try this one last time, there's going to be some conditions attached."

Tyler looked up. "Like what?"

Jonah cocked his brow. Pursed his lips.

Yeah, I know Jonah. She's gonna kill me, Andy thought. To Tyler, he said, "You will show up on time and you will pay attention to the tasks I assign you."

"No problem, I promise," Tyler said.

"Don't promise me, just straighten yourself out," Andy said. He nodded toward the shovel next to the door. "Okay, you can start by clearing off the sidewalk."

After Tyler went outside to shovel, Andy strode into his office. Jonah followed him and leaned against the doorway with arms folded across his chest. A wry grin was on his withered face. "You really like pissing off your sister, don't you?"

Andy booted his computer up. "I just know what it feels like to be in Ty's shoes."

"Yeah, but being an orphan wasn't your choice," Jonah said, pointedly. "That boy made his own decisions. Not that I'm one to talk."

"Not arguing with you there, believe me," Andy said. He opened his email provider page, signed in and read down the laundry list of spam mail. There, he saw a note with Janet's name attached.

Andy,
We still on for tomorrow night?
Janet

His heart leapt. Suddenly he envisioned her sitting across from him at a candle-lit table. The thought of her looking back at him with her smoky brown eyes while they swapped details of their lives almost made him forget the conflicted feelings he was having about her. For the hundredth time he debated whether he should go through with the date. His fingers hovered above the 'N' on the keyboard. *Fuck it. I deserve it!* He typed back his reply. Hit the send button just as Amanda announced herself at the door. She squeezed past Jonah and pulled a chair in front of the desk.

Andy saw a frown looking back and braced himself for the oncoming offensive. "Hey Panda."

She crossed her arms. "What's Tyler doing outside?"

"Umm... shoveling," Andy minimized the application window as she drilled into him with a piercing gaze.

Jonah said, "Getting a bit hot in here. Think I'll go reshelf a few books."

She ignored Jonah's remark. "I can see that. Interesting thing is, Ty tells me, he's working for us again." She paused. Tapped her nails on the armrest. "So..." She cleared her throat. "I have a question."

"What's that?"

"Did you not hear one word I said last night?"

"It's just a trial period to see if it works out. You said we have a grant coming and well, the kid's in a bind."

She rolled her eyes. "Everyone's always in a bind with you, Andy. You can't keep spending money like a drunken sailor." She leaned forward and appeared ready to say more when a knock came to the open door.

"Hi," Nate said, standing just outside looking in. "I'm sorry. The kid outside told me to just come in."

"It's all right, we're finished here," Andy said, and instantly regretted it when he saw his sister's face darken. *Oh, shit. I've screwed the pooch again,* he thought watching her get up. He didn't need to hear the words: 'Really-did-you-just-say-that?' riding on the tip of her tongue. He knew he'd get an earful when they were alone. But that was later. Right now, he was upbeat. They were getting a grant and he had a date with Janet. He grinned. To her retreating back, he added, "I suppose the new oak shelving I saw in Falcon's catalog is out of the question."

There was no reply and he didn't expect one. He motioned Nate to come in and take a seat and reached into his desk drawer for an application. Pushing it across his desk, he had him fill it out. When Nate finished, he said, "Come, sit next to me."

He moved his chair aside and positioned the computer screen so they both had a good view of it. When he brought the Internet connection back up from the application dock, he froze. To his horror, Janet's note was staring them both in the face. He switched away from the window. Scrolled to his web page link. Prayed Nate either hadn't read the words or hadn't made the connection it was his mother.

For a moment Andy held his breath until Nate asked him to go into his website preferences. Clicking on the radio button, Andy blew a silent sigh out. *Holy crap Old Man, that was close.*

Chapter 17

J ANET SAT in her car in the parking lot of Sal's Bistro looking out at the failing blue sky. Tonight was dinner with Andy. She'd dressed conservatively. A gray cashmere pullover and black slacks. A topaz necklace dangled from her neck and a pair of studded silver earrings dotted her ears. She took a deep breath, got out of her car and headed for the front door of the mission style restaurant. As she walked under the soft yellow incandescent glow of the overhead lantern lights, she fixed her gaze straight ahead. The bistro was busy tonight. Through its divided, paned windows she saw people gabbing around candle lit tables.

It'd been a while since she'd been here, reserving visits for family birthdays and anniversaries. Why she'd suggested Andy meet her here for dinner when he'd called was beyond her. She pulled back the wood planked door and stepped into the warmth of the cozy, cream-colored stucco lobby. There, she found Andy sitting on a cushioned window seat. He got up and met her by the coatroom.

"Here, let me help you with that," he said, stepping around behind her. He slipped her jacket off her shoulders and darted into the Coat Room beside them.

She wrapped her arms around herself and rubbing her elbows, fidgeted as she waited for him to return. "Been waiting long?" She called back to him.

"Just a few minutes," he said. He came out and stood in front of her. "You look lovely tonight."

She twitched, fighting the urge to look away as he drank her in with an adoring gaze. "Thank you."

"You're welcome." He escorted her to the receptionist. There they checked in and were led to their table. He glanced at the window beside them. It overlooked the pond on the treed lot. "This is nice."

"It's one of my favorite restaurants," she said as she watched his gaze sweep the room, taking in the ambiance of candlelight, European table settings and the blazing fire in the hearth.

At last, he said, "How was your holiday?"

"It started out not so good, but ended up wonderful," she replied, remembering the look on Nate's face when he finished looking through the book she'd made for him. Even now, three weeks later, the memory tightened her throat and made her heart swell. She smiled, knowing Andy would understand how she felt. "I made a connection with Nate."

He smiled. "How so?"

She took a sip of water. "A year before he re-enlisted, I'd started a genealogy search on his father. It was supposed to be a gift for him when he came home. But of course he never came home so I kept working on it. And…well…with everything going on between us, it just made sense to give it as a Christmas present. It worked!"

"That's fantastic. And what a great idea," he said. He drank a sip of water, set his glass down and sat back in his chair. "I know how worried you were about him."

"I still am, but he's less distant now." She unfolded her napkin. "So, Nate told me he has a new job."

"Yeah. He's my new webmaster; started this morning. It's really something watching him buzz around my site, pointing out things I could do using this other provider he's going to get me on. I don't understand all the html stuff, but I get the gist of it. You have a very bright son."

She beamed as Andy pulled a pair of wire-rimmed glasses from his pocket and took up the wine menu. As she watched him peruse it, the last of her jitters subsided. Furtively, she studied the solidly built man with a square jaw and full lips. Tiny creases formed in the corners of his eyes when he smiled. Dimples dotted his ruddy, windburnt face. When was the last time she looked at a man like this? She couldn't remember. At last she said, "Thank you for that."

The waiter approached their table. "Good evening, I'm Sean, and I'll be serving you tonight. Would you care for anything from the bar, perhaps a glass of wine?"

Andy looked up. "Could we have a minute?" When the waiter left them, he lowered his wine menu. "Would you be interested in a bottle?"

"Sure, what did you have in mind?"

"I was thinking a Cab might be nice. They have a Montelena Cabernet here."

She blinked. *That's a pricey bottle.* "Yes, that'd be fine."

He gave her a friendly wink, set the menu on the table and pushed it aside. She could tell he was nervous. Fact was, she was, too. She reminded herself it wasn't a date. Just two people having dinner. Nothing more, nothing less. But still...

"So, anything else going on in your life?"

"Well, I organized an award ceremony here in town," she said.

"Oh, really? For what?"

"The Alzheimer's Association. I got shanghaied into volunteering a couple years ago."

He chuckled. "I know what that's like."

"The VA," she said, as the waiter arrived with their bottle. The man uncorked it and poured a splash in Andy's glass. After Andy accepted it, the waiter gave them the rundown on the specials, then retreated.

"The salmon looks good," Andy said. "And, yes, the VA, although it didn't take a lot of arm twisting on their part."

"It didn't take much for me either." She scanned down her entrée selections. "I can't decide if I want the Lobster Thermidor or the filet, although the Veal Piccata looks good."

He grinned. "Maybe we should just order page one of the menu."

She giggled. "So, I'm a piggy?"

"Not at all," he said. "Gonna have to watch myself with you aren't I?"

She smiled as she enjoyed watching him scramble for a comeback. At last she said, "That would a good idea. Anyway, I'm going with the lobster."

By the time the band started in the next room, Andy had her laughing so hard she could hardly contain herself. It was good to laugh. She couldn't remember the last time she'd felt this way. They talked on and off, sharing pieces of their lives as they listened to music by Billy Joel, Kenny Rogers, Air Supply, and Hall & Oats. By the time the second set started, it was like they were old friends.

He polished off the bottle of Cab and leaned forward. "Can I interest you in a dance?"

The question caught her off guard. "I don't know...I–"

But he got up and came around the table. He extended his hand. "Promise I won't step on your toes."

She looked up and saw his beguiling smile and didn't have the heart to say no. She took his hand and they strode to the other room. As they hit the dance floor, the band launched into Billy Joel's *Piano Man*. He drew her to him and before she knew it, she was totally lost in the moment. She pulled her head back, looking at the man who continued to surprise her, felt the warmth of his body pressed against her. Suddenly she wondered if she could get used to it.

He winked and twirled her around. "See, I told you, you had nothing to worry about."

"Worry about what?" She was confused.

"Me stepping on your toes," he answered, and swung her around again.

"Oh, that. Never doubted it." She moved her hand down his shoulder onto his back, felt the dampness of his sweater and his taut muscles beneath. "You've done this before, anything else I should know?"

He shrugged. "If I tell you everything now, how will I get you out again?"

"Oh, so your plan is to lure me along, huh?"

He tilted his head. Grinned and spun her around. "Is that a problem?"

"Might be," she said as he pulled her back into his arms. "Depends."

"On what," he said as the song came to an end.

She let go of him and patted his shoulder. "I need to make a visit to the ladies room." She left him scratching his head and drifted through the crowd to the far side of the restaurant. Things were moving just a little too quick, but it wasn't Andy who was responsible– not entirely anyway. It wasn't his fault her body was tugging at her for more. She needed space to collect her thoughts as she entered the powder room.

The wine was definitely a factor, but she couldn't deny the feelings that were running rampant through her body. She took a deep breath and stared into the long mirror across the vanity, glad they'd driven separately. The evening was supposed to be just dinner, but now everything was turned upside down. She thought about the impending 'goodnight parting' at her car door. Would he lean in for a kiss, and if he did, could she stop herself from wanting another? How in the world was she going to make a graceful exit? The idea this night could turn out the way it did baffled her. Yet here she was, contemplating what it would be like to see him again–and again.

She took a deep breath, gathered her wits and told herself to snap out of it. But the minute she left the room to head back to their table, her heart revved back up. When he saw her, he stood and waited for her to take her seat. "I was about to send the troops in after you."

She slipped into her chair. "Afraid I got lost?"

"Something like that." He paused and the smile left his face. "I can't tell you what a good time I've had tonight. I'd like to do this again, if you're interested."

There it was! A second date, which would lead to a third and a fourth, until what? Yet, how could she say, no? He'd been a perfect gentleman. "I had a wonderful time, too. Can I think about it and give you an answer later?"

He nodded. "Sure, I'm in no hurry."

"Okay then." She glanced outside at the full moon. "It's getting late."

"Tab's taken care of." He got up and they wove their way around the empty tables to the coatroom. After helping her on with her jacket, he guided her out into the cold, crisp air. "Where you parked?"

"Over there." She pointed to a parking lot lantern raining light on her car. When he put his elbow out for her take hold of, her breath grew short. *Well, here goes.* Her mouth went dry as he escorted her under the blackened sky. When they got to her car, he turned toward her and for a moment she couldn't breathe.

"Well, I guess this is good night."

She smiled. "Drive safe."

"I will." He nodded, and with a slow, easy movement, leaned in and kissed her gently on the cheek.

A rush of air gushed out of her as he pulled back. Not what she had expected, but then, nothing about him was ordinary. She pulled her keys from her purse and opened the door. After she was in and safe, he turned and headed into the night.

Janet thought of Andy all the way home. It was supposed to have been a simple dinner. She shook her head as she turned onto Old Cypress Road. *He's nice, okay better than nice, but this was a mistake. It can't happen again.* Except, she couldn't get him out of her head. She sighed as she saw his smiling face in her mind's eye. It had felt good being in his arms. *But where can it go, and how would it look to Nate?* She turned into her driveway and followed the snow-covered pavement through the wooded lot to her home. Inside, she saw lights on in the Great Room. Megan's car was parked in the turn around. *Why is she home?*

She got out of her car and pulled her coat snug around her neck as she shuffled through the freshly fallen snow to her front door. When she opened it, Megan was waiting on the other side.

"Well, look what the dog dragged in and the cat turned down," Megan said with a lilt in her voice. She glanced at her watch then looked back up at Janet with an impish grin.

Janet ignored her and tossed her purse on the pedestal table. She hung up her coat. "Thought you were spending the weekend with Ben."

"Yeah, that was the plan," Megan said, shutting the door behind them. "But his daughter Angela popped into town out of the blue. Seeing how she's never met me, we thought it'd be a good idea to keep things on the Q-T. So…how was the date?"

"It was dinner and it was good," Janet said. She glanced at the TV as she headed to the kitchen. It was, at present, airing a car commercial. "So, anything interesting on?" she called back over her shoulder.

"Umm…Saturday Night Live."

Janet opened the cupboard door. Took a mug down. "Oh, that's right."

"Where'd he take you?"

"Sal's." She put a kettle of water on to boil, opened a canister and tossed a bag of chamomile in the mug.

Megan pulled a stool out from under the island countertop and sat. "Sal's? He really pulled out all the stops."

"I was the one who suggested it."

Megan blinked. "Really?"

"Well, he asked me where I wanted to go and I sort of blurted it out."

"Right," Megan said, drawing the word out.

"What's that supposed to mean?"

"Nothing. It's just that Sal's is a couples place on Friday nights."

Janet rolled her eyes, but knew Megan had nailed her. "It was just dinner."

"Uh-huh. How was the band?"

"They were fine," Janet answered, wanting to get out of this conversation. The teakettle whistled. *Saved by the bell!*

But Megan tilted her head and gave her the look she'd seen so many times before: the one that said, 'Go on, I'm waiting'.

Janet poured her tea and stirred in a dollop of honey. "Ok...we danced to a couple of songs."

Megan cocked a brow.

"That's all!"

"You don't have to apologize to me, Jan. Dad's been gone two years now. But, Nate: he's a different story."

Janet sighed. "Yes he is, which is exactly why nothing is going any further with Andy."

"You keep telling yourself that," Megan said. She grinned as she tapped her nails on the countertop.

"Will you stop? Look, even if it all worked out, how does it end? I mean, at some point he'd want to..."

"Screw your brains out?" Megan said, and snickered.

"That's not what I meant, and you know it," Janet said. "You know, you're getting slutty in your old age."

"And I think my dad has rubbed off on you a little too much. You overthink things."

Janet frowned. "Really? Look, if I were to go out with him again, I'd be sending a message I don't want to send. Say nothing of what Nate might think."

"True statement," Megan said, getting up. "Personally, I think it's no one's business what you do or don't." When Janet opened her mouth, Megan cut her short. "I'm not done yet." She reached out and squeezed Janet's hand. "I saw how you loved dad. That's forever, but it doesn't mean you can't love someone new. You know you wouldn't be replacing him, just creating a little more space for someone else."

Janet blinked. Those had been Neil's exact words to her years ago, regarding his deceased wife, Sharon. Suddenly, the memory of him saying them to her came roaring back. Could she do what her husband had done: find a place for him to live inside her while making room for another?

Chapter 18

NDY STEPPED up to the doorway of his office and looked in on Nate. The kid had holed himself up behind the computer for the last three hours. Hadn't said a word to anyone. Crossing his arms, he watched Nate's fingers fly over the keyboard. As he did so, he thought of Janet. In his mind's eye, he saw her looking up at him as they danced the other night. He could almost feel the warmth of her body against him and the softness of her delicate hand on his shoulder. She had unwittingly hooked him and there was nothing he could do about it. He hadn't thought of anything else but her for the last two days. At length, he went over and viewed Nate's progress on the home page of his web site. A picture of the storefront with the name McNAMARA'S was pasted across the top in big block letters.

He walked in and leaned over Nate's shoulder for a closer look. "Look's great. Can you liven up the text a bit on the name?"

Nate sipped his coffee. "It's a rough draft right now, but yeah, sure." He switched to another screen and scrolled down. "You know, your system's ready to get waxed here, right? You should raise a firewall before you get a case of the crabs."

Andy sat beside him. "That bad, huh?"

Nate tilted his head and raised a brow. "Wide open."

Wonderful, one more thing for Panda to nail me on. His sister's unhappy face flashed before him. He sighed. "Okay, do it. You need my card again?"

"Nah, that's all right. I have all I need to clean you out," Nate said with a knowing glint in his eye.

Andy laughed. "I'm sure you do. Just remember, I know where you live." He paused. Felt his stomach rumble. Looked at his watch. "Say, it's getting around lunch. You hungry? I can throw something together or I could order out."

Nate shrugged. "Whatever." He closed out of the 'preference window' and hopped on the web. Pages flashed across the screen. Andy got up and started for the door. Nate called after him. "Pizza wouldn't be bad."

"Pepperoni?"

"That works," Nate said, looking up over the computer screen. "Extra cheese, thin crust, if you don't mind."

Andy smiled. *Of course you do...* "And to drink?"

"I suppose a beer would be out of the question."

Right, how'd I know that was coming next? "Yes, it would. We have soda, juice, ice tea or water."

Nate ducked back behind the screen. "Root beer works."

Andy turned and joined Amanda and Jonah. They were working the café counter. Presently, Jonah was waiting on a young woman and her small boy. Amanda was tending the cash register. Tyler was bussing tables. Jonah set a mug of hot chocolate in front of the boy and winked companionably. The dark haired, freckle-faced child ogled the steaming mug. Glanced up with a shy smile.

"Looks yummy, doesn't it?" Amanda said to the boy as she handed the woman her change. The boy pressed his lips together. Dimples punctuated his round, cherubic face. Amanda laughed. "You want whipped cream on that?"

When he nodded, Amanda added a dollop of frothy, white topping on top. A smidgeon of chocolate sprinkles was added for good measure.

"Say, thank you, Mathew," the woman said as she grabbed a napkin from the dispenser. She picked their mugs up and stood back to watch her son.

Mathew's gaze on Amanda darted back to Jonah. At last, he said, "Thank you."

"You're welcome," Amanda replied.

Andy watched mother and child find a seat in the café then turned to Amanda who was wiping the counter down. She threw the rag in the service sink below the counter and slipped past him without a passing glance.

She removed the filter basket from the coffee machine. "So, how's he working out?"

"Great," Andy said, trying to gauge his sister's mood. She hadn't said but a dozen words to him since he summarily dismissed her yesterday. Maybe he deserved the silence, but still. 'Having it out' about Tyler in front of Nate yesterday wasn't appropriate. She needed to get over it. He cleared his throat. "Say, I'm gonna order a pie. Pepperoni with extra cheese. You want in?"

She dumped the coffee grounds in the trash and set a new filter in the machine. Refilling the water reservoir, she flipped the switch and started the coffee maker to brewing. "No, thanks." Her tone was flat and abrupt.

Okay. But it wasn't okay. She might be his sister and his accountant, but it was his store and he didn't like the feeling of walking on eggshells. He called over to Jonah, who was busy restocking a napkin holder. "Hey, what about you. You interested?"

Jonah looked up. "Yeah... sure, why not?"

Andy dragged his cell phone out, dialed 'Pizza-Man' and ordered. Ending the call, he slid over next to Jonah and dropped his voice. "She say anything to you?"

"About what?"

"About me."

Jonah snapped the napkin holder shut. "Nope. What'd you say to her, anyway?"

Andy glanced over at his sister. She was loading mugs in the dishwasher. "Nothing."

"Must'a been something. She's pretty pissed," Jonah said, keeping his voice low. He shot Andy a lop-sided grin. Clicked his tongue and slapped him on the arm. "Gonna empty trash now. Give a shout out when chow arrives."

Andy watched Jonah walk away then turned to see Amanda cleaning up. He nibbled his lip. *The pizza won't be here for another twenty minutes. We're alone, well sort of, there's a few customers milling around.* He eyed Tyler, who was straightening chairs. *Can I iron this out before lunch arrives? It's worth a shot.* "Hey Ty, take care of things up here for a minute." He turned to Amanda. "Got a minute?"

She stopped what she was doing and crossed her arms. "Yeah, sure."

He led her to a secluded corner and looked into her expectant blue eyes. "I'm sorry I cut you off yesterday. I just didn't want to hash things out in front of Nate."

"You don't get it, Bruddy!" She bowed her head then looked up. "That's not it. I keep telling you we have to be careful with money, but you don't listen."

"You said we have a grant, so what's the problem?"

She waved her hands in front of her. "I don't know how much or when." She grabbed his wrist and eyed him sternly. "I'm doing everything I can to keep us from sinking and you're hiring people, left and right, behind my back. You can't keep doing that!"

"Yeah, but–"

"But, nothing! You need to stop this or you won't be in business long. As it is, we're in for a hell of a ride for the rest of this year."

"You mean, the trial?"

"I didn't say that. But yes, it might come into play. Look, I'm sure it'll turn out all right. You didn't do anything wrong. But as far as the store's concerned, you've got to start acting like a businessman or you're going to end up broke. You've poured your life savings into this store. Don't lose it on foolish whims."

Her words slammed into him. It was more than just acting like a businessman though. He suddenly realized he'd gone soft over the last couple of years and lost control, floundering in the 'should haves' and 'could haves' of his past. Where had his confidence and determination gone? Maybe the accident had something to do with it or maybe it was losing Brenda or maybe it was both. He didn't know, but his sense of direction, his self-assuredness had abandoned him. He had to get it back, had to start fighting again, man up and take control of his life if he was ever going to be happy because that was the bottom line.

"You're right, Panda," he said at last. "I've been wallowing in self-pity, minding everyone else's business but my own."

"You've been through a lot. You're still going through some tough stuff. But you're not alone... Don't give me that disparaging look. Mc-Namaras stick together!" She paused. "Look, I'm not saying you have to be cruel and uncaring, but you have to look after this store. That means making hard decisions. Think of it this way: Jonah, Tyler and now Nate, they're your troops. If you're going to take care of them, you need to take care of this store, otherwise you'll lose it and they'll be out on the streets. I know you don't want that. I don't want that.

"Tell you the truth; despite my reluctance in throwing in with you on this little adventure, I like working here now. And it wouldn't hurt to pull a small paycheck now and then." There was a hint of a smile on her face. She reached out. Took his hand. "Things are going to work out. The trial will be what it will be and we'll go from there. The good Lord looks out for people who do good things. Remember that. We're McNamaras, Bruddy, and we love fiercely. We just have to balance our feelings with reality sometimes."

Andy nodded. "McNamaras to the end!"

"Exactly!"

After the pizza arrived, Andy dug out plates and silverware and threw slices of pizza on the plates. Licking a bead of sauce off his thumb, he poured himself a glass of soda as Amanda shut the storage room door. She trudged over to him and opened the cabinet carrying an armful of paper cups and plastic ware. He glanced over at Tyler, who was parking the media cart in front of the book stack and tapped Amanda on the shoulder. "You sure you don't want a slice? There's plenty here."

She looked up. "Well, maybe just one."

"That's my Panda." He scooped up a plate and handed it to her. "You want a soda?" To Tyler, he said, "What about you?"

The kid nodded.

Amanda stood and snatched a knife and fork from the counter. "Yeah, a diet cola would be nice." She leaned in close to him. "So, umm…you never said how your dinner with Nate's mother went."

The comment caught him off guard. He waited while Tyler grabbed his plate. When the kid took it to a table, he said, "It went good. She's great company."

"So, where'd you go?"

"This place called Sal's Bistro." Andy popped the lid off his soda. He took a swig and cranked his head toward the back of the store. "Hey, Nate, Jonah…chow's here!"

"Sal's?" Amanda cocked a brow. "You really went all out."

"Actually, she picked," he said as Jonah and Nate shuffled up to the counter. He motioned to the plates with the slices piled on them. "Hurry up and get it while it's still hot."

Jonah grabbed a plate. "We're getting low on toilet paper. Better order some."

"Ouch," Nate said sliding another piece of pizza on his plate. He grabbed a soda and said to Andy, "When we're done here, come on back and I'll show you what I've done."

"You want to take a peek?" Andy said to Amanda as Tyler came shuffling back.

"Maybe later," she said. "I have to drop by home and switch cars with Tom. He's taking it into the shop for its 30,000 mile checkup," A customer came to the cash register counter with a couple of books. She set her plate down and went to take care of him.

After she left, the guys fell into an easy conversation about the up-coming NCAA basketball tournament. "UCLA looks like a tough out this year," Tyler said.

"Yeah, but look out for Butler," Jonah said.

Andy wasn't much of a basketball fan, but he enjoyed listening to the lively back and forth between Nate, Tyler and Jonah. Finally, he said, "Okay guys, back to work."

Nate grabbed another slice and took it into Andy's office. Andy followed and pulled a chair up next to him at the desk. Nate opened McNamara's web page. "I've changed the title text and added several links to your new social media accounts."

"New accounts?"

"Yeah, like Goodreads and MySpace," Nate said. "Right now, you have zero presence out there. Can't sell stuff if no one knows you're there."

"So...these are free accounts," Andy said hesitantly. In his mind's eye, he saw lightning bolts racing at him from Amanda's skull.

Nate nodded as he flipped through the website pages, showing Andy options he could add to enhance a shoppers experience. When he was done, he sat back, looked away and was quiet. At last, he said, "You ever do something you weren't proud of?"

Andy nodded, took a sip of soda. "A time or two. Why?"

"Just wondered." Nate bit into his slice of pizza, chewed and studied Andy intently. Finally, he said, "My mom and I got into it before Christmas and I...well, I said some things; things I knew would hurt her."

"Okay," Andy said. He crossed his legs and waited to see if Nate would say more.

Nate took another bite of pizza and darted his glance around the room. "It was about my Dad. He had this fear of ending up in a home. Something about grandma being in one, I guess. Anyway, near the end, he got dementia and it got too hard for mom to handle, so she ended up putting him in one. I knew it killed her to do it. She tried real hard to take care of him for as long as she could."

"I'm sure she did."

"Anyway, my step brother, Trevor, he found this box of letters and stuff my Dad buried in their back yard. They were written before I was born. I wanted to look through 'em, you know, see what my dad wrote. But she wouldn't let me. Said it was private! Anyway, I got pissed. I said she didn't care about anyone but herself."

Andy crossed his arms. "Which is untrue."

"Yeah, but I still don't see why I can't see 'em. I mean he's my father."

"I'm sure she has her reasons, Nate."

"Maybe." Nate knotted his brow, picked a piece of pepperoni off his pizza and popped it in his mouth. "Doesn't matter, it's her call. She's gonna do what she's gonna do, and I'm gonna do what I'm gonna do."

"And that is?" Andy said, wondering what Nate meant.

Nate blinked, obviously not expecting the question. Andy saw him scrambling for a passing answer that would hide the truth buried behind the brooding expression. "I was just saying, was all." He paused. Took another bite of pizza.

"So, you're still mad at her?"

Nate narrowed his gaze. "Some, yeah." The flash of irritation in his eyes melted into a shrug. "She gave me this book. It's a family tree thing with pictures and letters and stuff she'd been working on, like forever. Hard to stay pissed at that."

"Yeah, mothers are like that...doing the unexpected," Andy said, looking off. He thought of his foster mother, Mrs. Adams. She'd always been kind to him. But there had never been the love he craved. She reserved that for her children. Growing up in the Adams' household meant receding into the background when the family opened birthday or Christmas presents. Although there were gifts for Amanda and him, it was the smile on his foster mother's face as she watched her boys rip through the wrapping paper that he wanted. How he yearned for just half of that smile to be shined upon him.

At least that's what he thought until five years ago before she passed on. He gazed off into the memory of her giving him a box of photos. They were of him and his sister along with cards he'd hand made for her. She'd kept everything he ever gave her, even dried leaves and dandelions preserved in wax paper.

The phone rang outside the office, stirring him from his musing. He collected his thoughts and remembered Nate's last words. "So, did you apologize?"

"Not yet. It's not like I don't want to," Nate said. "But she's always in my face begging me to talk to her about what's wrong. I don't want to talk about it. It's all over and done. There's nothing to say. But she just can't stop. Maybe you could talk to her. You know, clue her in about the situation."

Andy eyed him. That Janet had begged him to talk to Nate, only to have Nate turn the tables was almost laughable. He suppressed a smile. "I can try. But you need to give her a break. She's worried."

"I know, but she doesn't need to be. I'll be fine if people leave me alone."

"People?"

"Yeah, the AEA is hounding the shit out of me."

"Ah, the Army Engineers Association. I've heard about them. Bugging you about your medal?"

"They're calling every day. I guess I have to go in for some kind of interview or something."

"They're just dotting their 'I's and crossing their 'T's," Andy said. He sat back in his chair and drank in Nate's plaintive expression. Finally, he said, "As far as your mom's concerned, don't ever wish for her to leave you alone. There will come a time when she'll be gone and you'll be wanting to talk to her."

"Yeah, I guess." Nate paused. "I take it your mother's gone?"

"Yeah."

Nate polished off the last of his pizza. "What was she like?"

Andy looked off, wondering if he should go there. Then again, maybe the kid needed to hear it and get some perspective. "I never knew her. She died when I was a baby."

Chapter 19

J ANET AND Nate arrived at the Ahwahnee Lodge five days ago for her photo shoot. The cabin they'd rented was neat and clean. Draperies, towels and quilts of Aztec design scattered themselves on rustic wood furniture reminiscent of the pioneering days. All of this was part of the charm of the legendary national treasure.

But getting her son to join her had been a herculean task. Okay, she'd played the guilt card on him. So be it! She was scared for him. Especially after she'd dropped by his apartment and found him sitting on the roof parapet three stories up.

Apparently getting him a job at Andy's store hasn't helped.

She tied her hair into a ponytail as she heard the shower turn off in the bathroom. The door opened and he hobbled out bare to his waist, his dog tags hanging around his neck. He dug a T-shirt out of the dresser drawer and pulling it over his head, stepped to the window and parted the curtains. A warm buttery light of the porch lantern trickled into the room.

"Looks like we got some more white stuff out there."

"Yes, a couple inches," she said, eyeing the alarm clock on the bedside table. It was 4:03 AM. "Should make for some nice shots today. You hungry?"

He shrugged. "I could eat."

His faraway look wasn't lost on her nor was his tossing and turning during the night. She refrained from asking him if he was okay. He would only nod anyway. How was she going to reach him if he wouldn't talk? It was like he'd locked himself away and hid the key. She threw a couple of lenses along with the filters into her daypack and zipped the camera case back up. Planting a kiss on his cheek, she got up. "We'll grab a to-go breakfast taco on the way to Glacier Point. Okay, hurry up dressing. I don't want to lose the morning light."

The snow danced in the chill drafts strafing Glacier Point. Janet parked and she and Nate got out under an oatmeal sky. They pulled the sable collars of their parkas snug around their necks and stood behind a broad stone rampart wall looking north toward Half Dome. On the other side was a thirty-two hundred foot drop to an undulating evergreen forest. Currently, it was swathed with a thin, white, lacey veil. Nestled within it stood the Ahwahnee Lodge. She leaned over the broad stone terrace wall and looked down. From where she stood, the great American lodge was no larger than a postage stamp.

To her right, Half Dome's massive upthrust of granite loomed over the valley floor like a God. She inhaled the resinous scent of the towering evergreen spires around her and brought her camera up to her critical eye. Although these were cliché touristy shots, she couldn't help herself. The view of Half Dome was so damned pretty. She aimed her camera lens west, framed a shot of North Dome and snapped a few more. Maybe she'd get something decent to add to her great room walls at home. Next she turned the camera southward for a shot of El-Capitan.

Her heart came to an abrupt halt.

Frozen, she stood terrified as Nate sat on the rampart wall kicking his braced leg back and forth against the sheer granite face on the other side. He turned and looked at her, holding her in a suffocating gaze. For a moment, the world stopped revolving. Finally, he smiled, turned and gazed across the chasm. "Hell of a view, isn't it?"

She swallowed the breath she'd been holding and struggled to master herself. "Yes, it is," she said as her heart pounded. "And would you do your mother a small favor?"

"What's that?"

"Could you please come down from there," she said as calmly as she could. "You're scaring me."

He turned back to her. When she saw his naked pain bleeding out from his beautiful brown eyes, she knew what he was thinking. *Oh, my God...No Nate, don't...don't do it...please!*

He studied her, penetrating her with a haunting look of a beaten child. She'd seen that look before: saw it in the mirror when she was thirteen after her uncle had raped her. There was no pain worse than the one that cut at your very soul, leaving it to bleed out into the dark abyss of a hopeless future. She stared back at him, holding him there by sheer will until at last, he swung his legs around and hopped down to the terrace floor.

From the time they left Yosemite until their final approach at Salem's Airport, Nate said little if anything. What bothered Janet most though were his actions at Glacier Point. They terrified her. Obviously she needed to talk to someone about them. But who? If Nate found out, he'd shut her down. She gazed out the window at the approaching runway, and thought of what to do.

The plane landed and they picked up their baggage. After throwing it in the back of the car, they drove to his apartment in silence. She dropped him off and headed for home. First thing she did when she arrived was go to her room. There she stripped out of her clothes and put on a soft pair of pajamas.

She wanted to lie down and take a nap, but she knew Megan would never stand for it. How much should she tell her? She didn't know. Maybe she should talk to Andy. Since that night at Sal's, they'd been swapping emails about Nate...and to be truthful, sharing things about each other's lives. Maybe that was a bad idea, but she couldn't help it. Andy was so easy to talk to.

As she padded into the Great Room, the memory of Glacier Point replayed itself in her mind's eye. It had been trapped in her head: a horrifying vision of Nate sitting on the rampart wall, his feet dangling 3,200 feet above the valley floor. His wretched gaze looking back was burnished into memory. She knew deep down, had she not been there, he would've slipped away. The unthinkable was devouring her from the inside out. Somehow, she had to reconnect with him.

She sighed and went to the kitchen and found Megan talking on the phone.

"Yeah, she's home," Megan said, looking out the patio door. "Haven't had the chance to talk with her yet…I hope so, too. She's really worried about Nate, and so am I…Yeah, I hear ya. I don't know if she'd be interested. I could ask."

"Ask me what," Janet said.

Megan turned around and slid the phone away from her ear. "Oh, I didn't hear you. Jean and Bob invited us over for dinner tomorrow night. You interested?"

A dinner party was the last thing Janet was interested in. She shrugged. "Sure, why not?"

"Great," Megan said. "Yeah Jean, we're in. What time?" She paused. "Six?" She eyed Janet with a look of, 'Is that all right?' When Janet nodded, she confirmed and hung up. "So, how'd it go?"

Janet knew she was asking about Nate. "It went well. I think Mick'll love the shots."

Megan put her hands on her hips. "I meant with Nate. Did he open up to you?"

Janet went over and pulled a bottle of wine out of the fridge. "No, and I really don't want to talk about it. I'm exhausted."

Janet pulled into Bob and Jean's driveway and parked next to their white Escalade. Ben's olive green Jeep was in the turnaround. As she got out of her car, the front door of the large contemporary home opened and a Great Dane came loping up to her. Janet patted the massive dog that was busy sniffing her pant leg.

"Brandy! Behave yourself," Jean said, wrapping a thick cardigan sweater around herself as she walked up to Janet.

"It's all right, Jean." Janet reached back into her car and brought out a magnum of Merlot. She handed it to Jean. "Something to get the party started."

Jean held it up. "Anam Cara Vineyards, Bob's favorite. He'll like this." She nodded toward the front door. "Let's get inside."

Janet shut her car door and followed Jean and Brandy along the snow dusted walkway. When they went inside, Jean took her jacket and closed the door, shutting out the cold. "Something smells good," Janet said as Jean led her through the airy lobby. They walked down the hall lined with photos of family and friends. When they came around the corner, Bob looked up from setting dishes out on a long granite topped island.

"Janet!"

"Hey Bob," Janet said, falling into a warm enveloping embrace. She pulled back and looked at the rugged, muscular man. He was in his trademark dark green khaki shirt and his sleeves were rolled up to his elbows. He was Tom Selleck and Russell Crowe rolled into one.

Tending a broad stainless steel stove was Ben. Athletically lean with sandy brown hair and green eyes, he projected a Johnny Depp appearance. A black apron covered a white button down shirt. Megan was setting out crackers and cheese on a plate.

Jean held up the magnum of wine. "Look what Janet brought."

Bob's eyes lit. "I think I love you, Janet!" He took the bottle, reached into his shirt pocket and pulled out a pair of wire-rimmed glasses. Holding it up to the ceiling pendant light, he perused the label. He turned to Ben. "My favorite. Wait until you have a taste of this nectar.

You'll never think of Merlot the same." He grabbed a corkscrew from the kitchen drawer.

Jean slid over to the liquor cabinet by the sliding patio doors and brought out four wine glasses as Bob popped the cork off the bottle. "So, tell us how your shoot went. Inquiring minds want to know."

Janet fixed a gaze on Megan, letting her know the topic of Nate was off limits. Shrugging, she said, "It went all right."

"It must have been beautiful up there," Bob said, pouring the wine. "I've seen pics of the valley in winter. They always blow me away." He turned to Jean. "We really need to get there next year and do some hiking. Maybe you guys could join us. It'd be a blast."

"I'll stick with hiking the malls," Megan said.

"So what are we having for dinner, exactly?" Janet said.

"Skillet spaghetti with a twist," Ben said. "Jean, hand me the oregano would ya?" He stirred a handful of pasta into the basin of boiling water and another dose of olive oil went into a large searing pan.

But Janet barely heard the answer because of what she suddenly noticed glinting back at her on Megan's hand. She stared at the bright silver ring on a finger where none had been for quite some time. "Megan?"

"Yeah."

"What's that on your finger?"

Megan flashed a coy smile and bit her lip. "An engagement ring."

Janet got up and went to her. "Oh my God! How wonderful for you. Have you set a date yet?"

"Not yet," Megan said. "Probably next fall. We don't want to steal the kid's thunder."

Ben said, "So, Janet... I hear you have a new man in your life."

Janet coughed. *Megan, you are so dead!* "Don't know where you're getting your news from Ben, but I'd check your source." She stared back at Megan who was averting her gaze to the ceiling.

"Uh oh, I stepped in doo-doo, didn't I?" Ben said.

"It's all right," Janet said. "Someone just got a little too enthusiastic about a dinner out."

"Getting home past midnight is more than just dinner out," Megan said, giving Jean an insider look. She tossed an evil grin at Janet. "He took her to Sal's. On a Friday night, no less."

"Will you stop?!" Janet cried.

"What's his name? Jean said.

Megan grinned. "Andy McNamara."

Janet sighed. "Okay, okay. I had dinner with him, that's all."

"He volunteers down at the VA," Megan put in, "works with the physical therapist helping Nate."

"I heard he saved a man's life a little while ago," Ben said. "Apparently, he's getting a Good Samaritan Award from the mayor."

"The guy deserves it, too. He's been through a lot," Bob put in.

"Oh?"

"Yeah, he was involved in an accident in Lincoln City a while back," Bob added. He earned a frown from his wife. "Something about a child dying. Very tragic. Apparently he was at the wheel when it happened."

Janet widened her eyes.

"I think we should change the subject," Jean said. "It's really not our business to talk about stuff we know nothing about."

Agreed, Janet mused. *Oh my God, Andy, I'm so sorry.*

Chapter 20

NDY KICKED his shoes off and plopped on his couch. It had been a long day down at the store and his head was banging. He knocked down a gulp of beer and bit into a burger as Jack sat at his feet hoping for a handout. On the coffee table in front of him was today's paper. He picked it up, stared at the headlines and set it back down.

He took another bite of his burger when his cell phone rang. He picked it up and looked at the screen. *Janet!* "Hey there, this is a surprise."

There was a pause on the other end. Finally, she said, "Hi, I hope this isn't a bad time."

He set his burger down and leaned back. "No, not at all. What's up?"

"I was wondering if you had some time over the weekend. I'd like to get together for a chat."

"Umm...I'm working Saturday. Sunday, maybe?"

"Yeah, sure."

He splayed his arm over the back of the couch, sensing her wanting to get together was more than just a friendly chat. "Anything the matter?"

She paused. "Umm...I'd rather wait if that's okay."

He wondered what it could be, but didn't want to press her. "Sure. Where would you like to meet?"

"I was thinking the Pompeii?"

Not his favorite place, but she'd be there and that was all that mattered. "Yeah, that works. What time?"

"How about around ten? The crowd thins out around then so we'd have some privacy."

"Ten's fine," Andy said. "So, how are things? Staying busy?"

"Oh, yes. I have a boatload of photos I have to plough through. You?"

"Trying to keep my head above water." He thought of their date and remembered how good she felt in his arms, then reminded himself how impossible it'd be for anything more to come of it. She probably knew it too, because when they'd talked about having dinner again, she'd put him off.

Suddenly, he didn't know what more to say. Awkward silence followed until she spoke up. "I hear we know someone in common...Jean Steffens?"

Andy was surprised. "Yeah, she's my eye doctor," he said, wondering if the good doctor had mentioned him to her.

"For your concussion, I assume?"

"Yeah, she keeps me pointed in the right direction. By the way, I saw one of your photos on her wall. Very nice!"

"Oh, thank you. Her husband does my yard work," she said. "She and I go back some. Hey, how's your vision coming along? Any better?"

He shrugged. "A little. My doc put me on some medication that's supposed to help."

"Can't be much fun dealing with that. Have they figured out what's wrong?"

"He thinks it's a thing called rebound headaches. I guess they happen when you take one kind of med too long. So we're switching back and forth to see if that works."

"Well, hopefully that'll work," she said. "Hey, look, I should let you go. I'm sure you have things to do. See you Sunday, then?"

"I'll be there." He bid her good-bye, flipped his cell phone shut and picked up the last half of his burger. He looked at it, felt his gut grumble, and fed it to the dog.

Andy turned into Pompeii's lot, parked and flung the car door open. He was late. As he marched toward the entrance of the café, a cool morning air buffeted his face wafting the citrusy scent of his aftershave cologne about him. He wrinkled his nose as he put his sunglasses on. Had he slapped on too much? Scanning the lot, he looked for Janet's Highlander. Hopefully, she hadn't left. He'd sent her a text message but hadn't heard anything back. He looked at his watch, and felt his body tighten when he opened the door and walked in. How was it she could make him feel like a teenager?

Unzipping his jacket, he panned the dining room. The place was dead. Bus boys were clearing tables as waitresses gabbed amongst themselves behind the front counter. Paul Anka crooned from overhead speakers. Janet was in a back booth. When she looked up, she raised her hand. He took a deep breath. "Relax, old man," he muttered as he strode toward her.

"Sorry, I'm late. There was an accident on the arterial coming out of town."

"Nothing bad, I hope."

"No, just a fender-bender." He removed his jacket and glasses. *Damn woman. What you do to me.* "I sent you a text."

She offered him a diffident smile and pushed an empty mug toward him. "Yes, I saw it."

"That for me?"

"Yep. Coffee's over there on the back wall."

He shuffled over, drew himself a mug of decaf and returned. "So, what's going on?"

She eyed him hesitantly then averted her gaze toward the window beside them. As she stared at the cloud studded morning sky, he sat back and saw the lines around her mouth deepen. Finally, she said, "Nate scared the hell out of me."

"What'd'ya mean? What'd he do?" Andy said leaning forward.

"There's a stone wall around the cliff at Glacier Point in Yosemite," Janet said.

"Yes, I know of it. What of it?"

She turned back to him. "He swung his legs over it and sat."

"Jesus," he muttered. He wondered where this was going and what she expected of him.

"The way he looked at me, I thought... I thought he was going to..."

He reached out and grasped her hand. "Don't go there."

"How can I not go there, Andy? If you'd seen his face, you'd understand. And that's not all. He's been doing lots of risky things lately."

"Such as?"

"Well, last week his landlord caught him sitting on the patio railing. He lives on the third floor! And then there's the speeding ticket he got. He was doing 112 on the 5. The only reason he still has his license is 'cause the cop recognized him from the press story when he got home... Oh, and yesterday... his sister, Megan, drops by to say 'Hi' and catches him shaving with his scout knife. You know how sharp those things are. Who does that?"

He sucked his lip unsure how to answer. He wanted to tell her it was just Nate being young and feeling invincible, but that wasn't the truth and Janet would have none of it. Still, how could he worry her any more than she already was? He let go of her hand and sat back. "I know you're worried, but don't make too much of his shaving with his blade. When I was in 'Nam, I used my blade a time or two in a pinch."

She stiffened and needled him with a steely gaze. "He's not in 'Nam, Andy!"

He knew whatever he said had to be served with a dose of caution. "I know that, and I'm not trying make less of this than it is, believe me. I'm just saying if he got used to using it over there, he might prefer it to his razor. It can happen."

She eyed him skeptically and her shoulders dipped a tad. "Okay, I'll give you that... maybe."

He felt a little wiggle room opening up and went on, "As far as the railing's concerned...yeah it's not healthy, but there's a million stupid things young guys do."

"Like driving 112 and sitting on rampart walls," Janet retaliated, lurching forward. "I don't think so."

He put his hands up. "I agree, they're something to be concerned about," he confessed, "but...okay, can I ask you...what exactly you want from me?"

"I don't know," she said, feeling defeated and sitting back. She wrung her hands and shook her head. "I'm sorry. I didn't mean to do that. It's just that I'm scared and I'm at my wits end. I shouldn't have bothered you."

"You don't have to be sorry. I'm no therapist, but if I can help, I will. Somehow, we'll figure this out," he said, having no idea of where to begin. But there was no way he was going to let her feel abandoned. He leaned forward, placed his hand over hers, wanting to wave a magic wand and make everything go away. Glancing out the window, he felt cramped in this unbearable conversation. There was nothing either of them could do about Nate right now, but he could distract her: make her feel better, maybe even laugh. "Hey, you up for a walk?"

She cocked her brow. "A walk? It's a bit wet out there, don't you think?"

"Just puddles, and the sky's clearing."

She hesitated. "I don't know."

He felt her hand slip away and he scrambled for something more to say. In a rush, he grasped at the first thing that came to his mind. "There's ice cream involved." *Did I really just say that?*

"Oh, really?" She eyed him sidelong. "It's still morning."

He peeked at his watch. "Yeah, but by the time we get there it'll be afternoon." When she hesitated, he added, "I'm buying."

"You don't give up do you?"

He grinned. "I'm a Marine."

"Right." She crossed her arms. A tiny lopsided grin creased her face. "Okay Marine, you win, let's go."

He winked, got up and threw a ten spot on the table. As he helped her with her coat, he got a whiff of a sweet, earthy fragrance. "What's that perfume you're wearing?"

She looked back over her shoulder. "It's nard. My son gave it to me for Christmas."

"Nard? Really?"

"Yeah, he brought it back from Iraq. I guess it was used in biblical times."

"It was," Andy said, dumbfounded as he escorted her toward the front door. As he walked beside her, he wondered if she knew it was also used in anointing the dead. Probably better not mention that. "So, I'm guessing you're a chocolate kind of girl."

"You're close, but you're missing something," she said reaching for the door.

He slipped around in front of her, pushed it open and they stepped into the cool, crisp air. "Umm...peanut butter?"

"There you go. And you?" Janet said as they strode toward the road.

Andy took to the outside shoulder and hemmed her away from traffic. "I'm a bit of a strawberry fan myself, but chocolate works fine, too." He buried his hands in his jacket pockets. "So, what do you like to do when you're not photographing the world or volunteering, at the Alzheimer's Association...is it?"

"Yes, the Alzheimer's Association." Janet stepped around a puddle, looked up and tilted her head. "I like to cook, try new things." She laughed. "Which is ironic considering I never cared much for it 'til Neil came along. He was a 'foodie' before anyone knew the word...always in the kitchen cooking up something."

"I bet you have quite the house, him being an architect and all," Andy said, happy to keep Nate out of the conversation until he had something substantial to add. That, and he wanted to know more about her because despite everything going on in his life, say nothing of the conflict of interest staring him in the face, he couldn't help wanting to be near her.

Again Janet laughed. "Oh, you don't know the half of it. You could start a restaurant out of it. Sometime, maybe I'll show you."

Sometime! "I'd love to see it. So what's your specialty?"

"I don't know if I have a specialty. I am partial to scallops."

"Ah, one of my favorites. All my meals lately are pizza or burgers. At least I don't have leftovers."

"Oh?"

"Jack takes care of those for me."

"He's a little darling," she said, striding along beside him. "Speaking of him, you bring him to work with you every day?"

"Pretty much." The sound of a car coming up behind them grew louder as they trudged along. He motioned her over toward the grass. "I hear you have a dog. A Bassett, right?"

The car passed them and its tailwind sprayed Janet's hair over her face. She pulled it away. "Yep. Name's Cleo."

"How old is she?"

"Cleo's a 'he' and he's thirteen this year. And yes, I know, Cleo's a girl's name, but Nate wanted to call him that when we got him. I have no idea why." She was quiet a moment. "Long story, short, we got him after my Barney passed away. Barney was my dog when I met Neil." She chuckled, but it had a wistful quality to it.

He eyed her furtively, wondering if he should say more when she spoke up. "What about you? How long have you had Jack?"

"A year and change. Closer to two, probably. I got him after I separated from my wife. The house seemed empty with just me bumping around inside."

"I know the feeling," Janet said. They walked for a minute in silence, each in their own thoughts until she added, "So, you never had children?"

"No. Brenda was too busy with her career and with me always being on call, it never seemed like the right time."

"There never is the right time," Janet said. "How long were you married?"

168

"Seven years, give or take. I thought we were good, but one day she up and says good-bye." He shrugged. "Guess she got tired of my rat race."

"Is that why you retired from being a paramedic?"

His gut knotted. "Some of it." He was glad she wasn't looking at him. *Should I tell her? She's been sort of open with me.* He hesitated then said, "I was involved in an accident with a fatality."

She spun around and took a step toward him. "Oh, Andy, I'm sorry. I can't imagine what that must've been like."

He dipped his head. Scuffed the ground. "He was just a kid running for a ball. I should've seen him...I came around the wide sweep in the road right after the performing arts theatre, you know the one near the bluff, and there he was. I swerved...flipped the truck, but it was too late...too little...sometimes I wonder why..." he said, and felt her hand wrap around his arm.

Looking up, he saw her staring back. Suddenly, he felt connected to her, and with it came the feeling of losing control if he took yet another step saying what he was really feeling. Yet, looking at her staring back with such tenderness and compassion, how could he back away, even though he firmly believed they could never be anything more than friends?

At last he said, "Let's get that cone."

Chapter 21

J ANET BAGGED a roast beef sandwich and put it in her daypack. A couple of hard-boiled eggs, a bag of trail mix and her camera went in along with it. As she zipped up the pack, she ruminated on her mounting feelings for Andy. Until three weeks ago, she hadn't thought beyond the dinner they'd had in January. There'd been no point in it. But ever since he'd opened up to her, she hadn't been able to get him out of her mind. She wondered how anything more could come of their friendship. Nate was her priority. He trusted Andy. She had to be careful, especially now when Nate was so unpredictable.

She went to the sink, drew water and filled her camelback. The grandfather clock in the Great Room chimed. Eleven o'clock. Andy would be over with Jack shortly. Could he reach Nate? He was a veteran, gone through a war, seen more than most.

She fitted the water-filled container in the pocket of her daypack, and set the canvas carrier by the front door. Glanced out the window. As she watched the spindled pines sway against the slate sky, she sighed. *Am I asking too much?* She wondered, not for the first time. Andy had gone above and beyond to help Nate, more than she had a right to ask considering all she knew. *He's going through so much of his own stuff: the lawsuit, the concussion, the accident… My God! And in spite of it, he makes time for Nate! Gives him a job, takes him out to dinners, games, the movies. I should back off, find someone else, but who?*

"You ready for a hike, Cleo," she said to the dog at her feet. She grabbed his harness off the hook. As he sat wagging his tail, she heard a car pull into the turnaround outside. Cleo jumped to his feet, and let out a booming bark. Janet glanced out the side lite and saw Andy getting out of his car. "Shh…it's just Andy and Jack. Now, you be a good boy. Jack's just a puppy, so we need to be tolerant, okay?"

A low, guttural complaint rumbled from the dog as she attached his harness and leashed him. It was the first time the two dogs had met, and she wasn't sure what to expect. In his old age, Cleo could be temperamental. She choked up on his leash. When the doorbell rang, the dog bellowed. Holding him close, she opened the door and held her breath until Cleo gave Jack a friendly sniff.

Andy grinned. "It appears we have approval."

"It does," she said, spying the darkening horizon. …*Better throw a couple ponchos in the bag just in case.* "Come on in. I'm just about ready."

He stepped inside and she watched him take a long, sweeping look around the vaulted great room. At last, he whistled. "You could get lost in here."

"I don't know about that, but I'll admit it takes some getting used to."

He strode over to the broad, slate fireplace and gazed up at a large, gold framed portrait of Neil, Nate and she. "That your husband?"

She stepped beside him. "Yep."

"Nice looking family."

She stared up at the picture, remembering the day her old friend and mentor, Mick, had taken it. It'd been a difficult morning for her husband. His Parkinson's had been raging and his hands wouldn't do what he'd wanted them to. Having thrown the razor across the bathroom, he'd sat on the toilet seat with his head bowed and hands trembling. When she'd come into the room, he'd looked up at her with a defeated frown. The expression on his thinning face had threatened to crush the both of them. "I can't shave," he'd said. "What's next? Wiping my ass?"

She'd held him, loving him with all her might. Picked up the razor and performed the simple act he'd done all his life. It'd been the beginning of the end, but she'd refused to acknowledge it then, denied the inevitable.

At last she forced a smile and let the memory fade. "Thanks. Come, I'll give you the nickel tour."

"Mind if I let Jack off his line?"

"Not at all," she said and let Cleo off his leash. As the dogs continued getting to know each other, she led Andy through the house, pointing out the cedar-framed pergola off the master bedroom that led to an enclosed gazebo out back. "My husband loved a 'rustic feel' and adored wide open spaces."

"I can see that." He ran his hand over a polished timber column and followed her into the kitchen. "You were right. You could run a restaurant out of here. I like the skylight above the island with the ferns hanging over the ledge. Nice touch. Your husband certainly had an eye for detail."

"Oh, you don't know the half of it. He drove the contractor nuts. But in the end, it turned out just the way he wanted it." She collected her house keys from a dish on the counter and turned the small TV off next to her. As she attached Cleo's leash, she added, "I'd show you the studio, but it's a holy mess and we really should get out there before we lose half our daylight."

They collected their gear and locked up. "The trail runs behind the property line," she said over her shoulder as they walked past the flowerbeds just coming to life in the back yard. "It hooks up with the Baskett Trail out back."

"Pretty yard," he said, behind her. "Did your husband design the landscaping?"

"Most of it, but I've added a few touches of my own."

"My goodness, you have a creek back here!"

She stepped onto a wooden bridge leaping over the waterway. "Yep, flows into Morgan Lake, north of here. We'll be following it for the next thirty minutes 'til we get to the loop. You'll like the lake, I think."

"What's that over there?"

She looked the direction he was pointing and smiled. Daffodils and hyacinths were in bloom around the waist high granite marker, their yellow and lavender faces swaying in the breeze sweeping over the yard. "That's where my beloved Barney is buried."

He ambled up beside her on the bridge. "He was the dog you told me about before, right?"

She nodded.

"Well, he was certainly loved."

"Oh, yeah," she said, drawing the word out. She continued on a thin, winding footpath with Cleo leading the way. As she walked, she breathed in the cool, resinous air and panned the understory of the awakening woods. Bunchberry, forest clover and brambles were putting out the first shoots of spring. Wild viburnum and flowering quince decorated the path with delicate red and white flowers. Their honeyed perfume floated about her.

Coming to the main trail, she veered left and before long came to a wide-open meadow. As she took a drink from her camelback, he joined her and they looked out over the golden fields that shivered under a scudding gray sky. Cleo and Jack nosed around in the tall grasses beside them. She pointed to the green hills beyond the field. "The lake's a forty-five minute hike from here."

He nodded. "Can I ask you a question?"

"Sure." She turned and saw him studying her.

"You've been widowed now for how long?"

She wondered what he was leading up to. "About two years."

He took a pull from his water bottle and capped it. "That's a big house to bang around in all alone. You ever think of downsizing?"

"If you mean, sell it," she said, "Never, but I don't exactly live all alone. Megan's been with me for over a year."

"She's your step daughter, right?"

"Technically, yes, but we don't think of each other that way. We were friends long before I met her father."

"Oh!" He was quiet a moment. "She's about your age, isn't she?"

"Two years younger."

Jack ran ahead, crossing himself up with Cleo's leash. "Jack, what are ya doing buddy?" Andy said untangling the two dogs.

She laughed. "Marrying her father wasn't exactly what either of us had in mind, but it was what it was."

"True love," he said as they started back off.

The way he said it, as if he didn't believe in such things, niggled her. "Yes, true love! It does happen, you know."

He drew breath and his shoulders dipped. "I don't doubt you at all. I'm sure it happens. I just haven't found it or it hasn't found me. I thought I had it with my ex, but I guess I was fooling myself. And now…in my old age, it's probably not in the cards."

She rolled her eyes. "Oh, please! Come on, you're not that old." It occurred to her then that he'd never told her how old he was. In fact, there were a lot of things she didn't know about him. His birthday for one, where he grew up and the music he liked for another.

"Old enough," he said, shuffling along behind her. He cleared his throat. "Ask you another question: you think you'll ever marry again?"

It was a question she hadn't given a lot of thought to over the last couple of years and it startled her. A month ago, the answer would've been an emphatic 'no'. Neil had taken part of her with him when he died. But now, she wasn't so sure. She shrugged. "Who knows? I never planned on falling in love with my husband, but it happened."

"How much older was he?"

"Twenty-one years." They walked a while, each in their own thoughts as a dark blue lake began to make an appearance beyond the rolling fields. Finally, she said, "So, where'd you grow up? Out here?"

"Yeah, Lincoln City. You?"

She took another drink from her camelback. "When I was young we lived in a little village in New York called Liverpool. Then, when my parents divorced, my mom brought me out here."

"Long way from home," he said. "You have family out here?"

"Yeah, my Aunt June had a bungalow outside of Dallas. She's passed now. What about you? You have other family out here besides your sister?" she said as Cleo ran ahead, stretching his retractable lead line.

"No, she's it."

"So, mom and dad have passed on?"

He was quiet a minute. "They died when I was a baby. My sister and I were raised by foster families."

She stopped and looked at him, her eyes wide and jaw slackened. The dogs shook themselves and looked up expectantly, as if to say, 'what's going on...why are we stopping?' She ignored them and said, "You're an orphan?"

He shrugged and looked off, watching a flock of blackbirds spiral in a wide looping arc then head north. "Yeah," he said, fading the word out. "I don't like to think of it very much. My sister, she was my mom in a lot of ways. She kept us together. Not that our foster parents were bad. They just had their own priorities to look after."

"Their children?"

"Yeah, something like that. But hey, we had a roof over our heads, clothes on our backs and three squares a day. Could've been a lot worse."

All at once, her thoughts went to her father as she tugged on Cleo's lead line, drawing him back to her. "Most people take their connections to their parents for granted. They believe their mother is their mother and their father, their father. They can't begin to imagine what it's like to feel disconnected, living with a parent who isn't your real mother or father." She paused. "They say it takes more than blood to be a parent, and maybe that's true, but knowing you're not blood, not physically part of them...it keeps you wondering who you really are, if that makes any sense."

"It does," he said and held her with a penetrating gaze. "You seem to have first-hand knowledge of this."

Now it was her turn to look away. "I do. I never knew my real father," she said, her voice just above a whisper.

"Did he pass away?"

She turned back to him. "No. My mother had an affair I never knew about. It was the family secret until one day, I found out. Long story short, it shook me to my core. I felt like my whole life was a lie. But in the end, the man I thought was my father growing up became the father I wanted." She felt her throat tighten and swallowed, forcing away the urge to break down and cry. Taking a deep breath, she stiffened her jaw and said, "Despite knowing everything, he loved me as his own!"

Andy remained quiet, as the dogs stirred below them. Maybe it was the way he listened to her, never interrupting or trying to fit her into some box that put her at ease. At last, she reached out, took his hand and stepped onto the trail. As they meandered along the footpath, she said, "He gave me away when I got married and then in the end, helped me take care of my husband. What kind of man does those things?"

"A real man," Andy said, squeezing her hand.

"You should've seen the two of them together," Janet said. "Getting into all kinds of trouble."

Andy grinned and nodded toward the approaching lake. Overlooking it was a tiny bluff with an old wooden picnic table. "Looks like we've arrived. Wanna grab a bite up there?"

"Why not?" She followed him up a narrow footpath. Once they reached the top, he dropped his pack and took Jack and Cleo for a sniff around the pampas grass bordering the tiny clearing. As he did so, she unpacked their lunch and set it out. "You want a turkey or roast beef sandwich? I brought both."

He reined in the dogs and hitched their leashes to the table. "Roast beef works," he said, digging into his pack.

"And for a salad; mac or potato?" She removed lids from containers. She stabbed a spoon in each and looked up just in time to see him set a bottle of wine on the table. "Oh, my goodness."

"Mac works fine. White or red?"

"I think white," she replied. "I assume you brought something to put that in or are we drinking straight from the bottle?"

He reached back into his pack and set a pair of mugs on the table. "Will these do?" He pulled a corkscrew from his back pocket.

Janet took a seat and smiled. "They'll do just fine. Anything else in that bag of tricks you brought?"

Popping the cork, he looked up and waved a finger at her. As he poured their wine, he said, "You'll see soon enough." He handed her a mug and sat down beside her. For the next twenty minutes, they looked off over the ruffled lake while they ate.

"Oh...oh, I felt a rain drop," he said.

She blinked. "Crap! The ponchos, I forgot to pack them." She looked up at the brooding cloud cover. Saw darkness closing in over the way they'd come. *I guess we're going to get wet. Oh, well.*

Janet ran through the driving rain across her back yard with Cleo, Andy and Jack in close pursuit. When she came to the garage side door, she threw it open and they ran inside. Sopping wet with his hair matted to his face, Andy dumped his backpack on the garage floor and unlaced his shoes. She raced for the laundry room.

When she came back, he was bare to the waist. A small silver scar tattooed his abdomen. She pretended not to notice it, tossed him a robe and motioned him to follow her. "There's a bathroom on your left at the bottom of the stairs," she said, handing him a basket. "Towels and washcloths are in the linen closet to the right as you enter. Just leave your wet clothes outside the door and I'll get them in the dryer after I shower."

He threw his shirt in the basket and shot Jack a pointed gaze. "You behave yourself up here 'til I get back." He turned back to her with a lopsided smile. "I suppose you don't have a pair of men's shorts hanging around?"

She grinned. "Sorry...just ladies. You're more than welcome to borrow a pair of mine. I don't think you could get into them. Be fun watching you try, though."

"I think not. Besides, I don't trust your camera."

"Oh, really," she said with mock indignity. "I'll have you know, I don't take pictures of just any old willy-nilly thing."

He stared at her wide-eyed and she felt sudden warmth flood her face. "You're dripping," she said then quickly excused herself.

"Come, Cleo," she said, padding down the hall. Once she was behind closed doors, she stripped out of her wet clothes and threw them over a laundry rack to dry. As she did, Cleo stared up at her. "Did you see the look he gave me?" she said to the dog. "You and I both know I wasn't referring to you know what!" The dog yawned and licked his chops. "Okay, maybe the thought crossed my mind, but really..."

Suddenly her body stirred, and not for the first time. The memory of when they'd met for dinner back in January flashed before her. She didn't know what to do about it then nor did she now. She stepped into the bathroom, turned the shower on, and tried to vanquish the racy images rampaging through her mind. But no matter how she tried, his wet, naked, broad shoulders remained. A shiver ran through her as she stared into the mirror and saw her flushed complexion.

Thank goodness he's not here right now.

She wrestled to get control of herself and stepped into the warm spray of the shower. As she washed her hair, she thought about what he'd told her on the trail and what she'd revealed to him of her own life. Andy had grown up fighting to claim a place in an indifferent world, while she was a reminder of a betrayal. Had she said too much? She didn't think so. She turned the water off, stepped out onto the tiled floor and wrapped her hair in a towel.

Throwing on a pair of cotton sleep shorts and a tee shirt, she went to see how he was making out. To her surprise, he was already in the kitchen wearing a robe and fiddling with the coffee maker. "I found the filters, but I can't seem to find the coffee," he said, turning toward her as she stepped into the room.

"In the fridge," she said. "It keeps better there."

He wrinkled his laugh lines and opened the refrigerator. As he bent forward and pawed around inside looking for the coffee, his robe parted giving her an eye full. She caught her breath and looked away, quite sure if he turned around, she would've turned five shades of red. "How was your shower?"

"It was great." He poked through the leftovers on the bottom shelf. "How do ya find anything in here?"

"It's in the back. To your right."

He held a bag of Hawaiian dark roast over his head. "Ah...this all you got?"

"Afraid so. Why?"

"I'm not used to the fancy stuff." He stood and opened the bag, peering down into it. "Guess I have to grind it, too. Where would I find one of those?"

"Cabinet on your left, bottom shelf. Measuring cups are in the drawer to your right," she said, amused. "Okay, I'm going to go put your clothes in the dryer. Be right back. Don't go anywhere."

He tilted his head and pursed his lips as if to state the obvious as she turned to leave. As she strode down the stairs, she grinned. It had been a long time since she'd had a man bustling around in the kitchen. She thought about that as she loaded Andy's clothes in the dryer. After turning it on, she skipped up the stairs and when she reached the top, heard voices. Pricking her ears, she froze. *Oh, my God. What are you doing home, Megan?* She looked up, wondering how she was going to explain Andy in her kitchen making coffee wearing nothing but a robe.

Chapter 22

A NDY KNEW a shit-eating grin when he saw it, and right now, Megan was wearing one on her heart shaped face. He sat at the kitchen island wearing just a robe, feeling more than a little awkward. Not a great first impression to be sure. Megan didn't seem to care. In fact, she seemed to be reveling in Janet's predicament. Over the last two weeks, Janet had warned him about Megan. Her stepdaughter was out there, spoke her mind and at the moment madly in love, which meant Janet needed to have someone, too. 'Don't pay her any mind,' Janet had told him. Apparently, she was right. The woman was obviously having fun watching her stepmother act like a cat in a litter box trying to explain why he was in a bathrobe with nothing on underneath.

Megan said, "Whatever you say, Jan. Really, I believe you." But her arched brows and lopsided grin said quite the opposite. She squatted down and gave Jack an itch behind the ears. "You're a cutie, but I think you already know that, don't you boy?" Jack put his paws on her knees and stretched his head up to give her a lick on the chin. "How old is he?"

"Going on two," Andy said, getting the distinct feeling he was going to be under an intense inquisition very soon.

Megan petted Jack and stood. "You're right Jan, he does remind me of Barney." She went over to the fridge and took out a bottle of wine. "Anyway, will Andy be staying for dinner with us?"

"We haven't really talked about that." He shot Janet a fleeting glance as she got a dish down for Jack. Clearly, she was trying to ignore Megan's leering gaze.

Megan popped the cork on the bottle, poured herself a glass and turned around. Leaning back against the counter, she crossed her legs and sipped her wine. "Well, we have plenty here to share, and Jan's a hell of a cook. What do you think, Jan?"

Janet looked up from pouring kibble into Cleo and Jack's bowls. "Yeah, sure. But it's up to Andy. He might have some place to be."

Which means what? He thought. *Does she want me to leave or is she just being polite?* He hesitated, sipped his coffee. "I wouldn't want to impose."

"Nonsense, we insist," Megan said, fixing her flashing green eyes on him. As he sat there feeling like a link of salami at a delicatessen, she added, "I bet you're a steak and potatoes guy. We have some strips in the freezer don't we, Jan?"

"Don't go to any trouble on my account," he said, snugging the robe a little tighter around him. *On second thought, maybe I should get out of here.*

"Not sure, take a look. If not, I'll can hop down to Clark's and pick some up," Janet said with a diffident smile. But her tightened jaw and creased brow were anything but casual. "So, something come up with Ben? I thought you were there for the weekend?"

Megan tore her gaze away from Andy and opened the freezer. As she pawed around inside, she said, "His sister's husband's tractor or something broke down and he needed Ben's help getting it back to the barn. Since it's an hour to Lebanon plus however long to get whatever it was back to the barn, it didn't make sense for me to hang around. Besides, I needed to get back anyways…ah, there they are!"

"There, what are?"

"The steaks," Megan said, taking them out. She set them on the counter. "So, Andy, Janet tells me you're separated."

Janet coughed as if food had gone down the wrong way. "Megan!"

"It's okay, Janet," He drained the rest of his coffee. "Yes, I am."

"How long?"

Janet rolled her eyes, mouthed the words, 'I'm sorry' to him. But he didn't mind. In fact he liked Megan's direct approach. "About a year and a half." He paused. "I hear you're engaged. Congratulations. When's the big day?"

Megan blinked, obviously surprised. "August 29th, and thank you. Gonna be a busy summer."

"Oh, how so?" he said, happy to keep the conversation on her and off of him.

"My son's getting married in July," Megan said. "One wedding is enough to plan for, but two! Already, I'm meeting myself coming in and out the door."

"Should combine them," he said. "Save yourself a lot of headaches."

Megan looked at him as if he was insane and chuckled. "Right, and lose the rest of my mind. I don't think so."

"I'm going down to check laundry," Janet said. On her way past him, she leaned in close and whispered, "Be careful what you say to her. She'll use it against you."

He laughed. "I'm sure we'll be just fine," he said, observing Megan watch Janet walk out with Cleo trotting close behind.

When they were alone, Megan walked over and sat across from him. Glancing at the empty doorway, she said, "So, tell me, what's going on between you and Jan?"

You do get right to the point, don't you? "Just friends."

She narrowed her eyes and he could see her turning his answer over in her head. Finally, she said, "For being friends, you see each other a lot. Not that it's any of my business, except that she's been my best friend since forever. The two of us have been through a lot of shit. I love her like a sister. Anyone who screws with her, screws with me."

"Point taken."

"Good. Now that we understand each other, I won't have to worry about her, will I?"

Janet's right, Megan's a handful. "Not to worry."

He saw her assessing his response. At length, she sat back. "Jan's a wonderful woman, a fabulous mother, but she spends too much time on everyone else and not enough on herself. And now with Nate home and injured like he is, well…it's taking a toll on her." She leaned forward. "She told you about my father, right?"

"Some."

She drained her wine and lowered her voice. "He had Alzheimer's. It was hard on all of us, Jan most of all. She did the best she knew how. Did she tell you, she had to put my dad in a nursing home?"

"She mentioned it."

"My father hated them. Said people were treated like crap there. Anyway, Jan and I got into a huge fight when she placed him."

"It must've been hard for the two of you."

"It was. I didn't see how bad it was for her. I was too focused on my father's fears. It wasn't until later I understood how difficult it'd been for her. She loved my dad and it crushed her to place him. Needless to say, I felt like a shit.

"Anyway she's been through a lot, Andy, and now with Nate home and injured and everything, she needs someone to lean on besides dopey old me," she said. She leaned forward. "If you're just friends, make sure you don't send the wrong message, if you understand me."

The remark landed at ground zero and it gave him pause to think about the path he and Janet were on. Megan hadn't said anything he hadn't already considered, but hearing it aloud and coming from Janet's best friend carried a lot more weight, especially now with his trial looming next week. Was it wrong to foster a relationship that could go nowhere, hurting a woman who'd gone through so much?

April 30th raced toward Andy like a fire truck on a 911 mission. He rolled out of bed, rubbed his eyes and blotted out the bright sunshine streaming through the window. Today would begin the opening arguments of the trial. He hauled himself out of bed into the shower.

As he washed up, his stomach knotted. For the last week, he'd tried to ignore the angst building up inside him, but it wouldn't go away. It was like a brush fire, gathering strength and spreading with each day that passed.

He turned the water off and leaned back against the wet tile wall. His future life was at the whim of a dozen people he didn't know. If he lost, everything would go away. What that would look like, he didn't know, and he didn't want to. He drew breath and gritted his teeth. As he did so, Amanda's words echoed in his head. 'Man up Marine, we got a fight ahead and I need you to be on your 'A' game.'

He toweled himself off, shaved and got dressed. A plain blue suit with a white shirt and a dark blue tie would have to do. It was the only suit he had and he hadn't worn it since the funeral for the Stewart boy. He thought about that as he combed his hair and checked himself in the mirror. Was it a harbinger of things to come? How things had changed. Back then at the gravesite there'd been no accusations. Only grief and trying to grapple with the tragedy that had changed so many lives that day.

Andy grabbed his keys and headed out the door with Jack bouncing ahead. After dropping off the dog with Tom, he and Amanda would make the ninety-minute drive to Lincoln City. He'd have her drive so he could close his eyes and avoid the glaring sunlight. The last thing he needed was a migraine. As it was, he'd hardly slept last night thinking about today. He popped a couple of Imitrex as a precaution, threw the car in reverse and backed out of his driveway.

Andy sat looking out the passenger side window as Amanda turned into the courthouse parking lot. Outside of a few encouragements from her, the ride had been a quiet one. Then again, she knew him well. When things demanded his attention, he went inward. He opened the door and got out. As he marched toward the front entrance, he panned the lot and looked for his lawyer's silver Lexus. What caught his attention instead was a maroon Highlander. Blinking, he checked the license plate and shook his head. Despite his urging her to stay home, she'd come. He couldn't say he was disappointed she'd ignored him.

Amanda said, "Something wrong?"

He nodded toward the Highlander. "Janet's here."

"I know," she said, smiling.

He stopped and feigned annoyance. "You knew she was coming then?"

"I did, and stop pretending you're upset. You know as well as I do, you wanted her here," she said without breaking stride.

It was a true statement, but he wasn't going to admit it to her. "She doesn't need my drama in her life right now, Panda," he replied, catching her up. "She's got enough of her own."

She didn't answer him or wouldn't as she stepped to the front door, turned and straightened his collar. Patting him on the shoulder, she looked up at him, her sky blue eyes in seeming amusement, then smiled and went in ahead of him.

The courtroom was bathed in morning sunshine that rained through the windows. Murmured voices of officers and guests floated about. Andy panned the whitewashed room with drawn back red drapes and spied Janet sitting near the back. She waved to him as Amanda took a seat next to her. Nodding back, he made his way to the long defendant's table. As he did so, he felt the condemning stares of the Stewarts who'd parked themselves next to Mr. Reed, Esq. The pencil-thin lawyer glanced over at him, his tacit expression and sharp red tie sending a clear message of power and indifference. The man turned back to the Stewarts and muttered something before going back to reviewing paperwork in front of him.

Andy felt his chest tighten as he found his seat next to his lawyer, Ed Reynolds. The large burly man looked up, greeted him with a friendly smile and a handshake then went back to studying a document. Beside Ed sat the department's council Stanton and beside him, the lawyer for the insurance company. The two suited men sporting black ties were quietly conferring with each other as they dug files out of their penda flex folders.

But it was the twelve individual padded chairs in the jury box that got Andy's attention at the moment. At present, they were empty, along with the judge's high-backed leather chair behind the bench. Andy took a deep breath and tried to calm his nerves. How odd, he thought, that a room full of suited men and women could exhort the same feelings as a sortie of armed Viet Cong.

At length, the door beside the jury box opened. Seven men and five women came filing out. He watched them take their seats. Their faces were looking straight ahead, their expressions, grave and unreadable. A minute later, the door behind the judge's bench opened and Judge Connors stepped out of his chambers in his judge's robe.

"All stand," cried the bailiff. "The Honorable Judge John T. Connors presiding."

The gallery and the court officers got to their feet as Connors stepped to the bench and took his seat. As the bailiff released the audience to their chairs, Andy made brief eye contact with the man before the gavel was swung and the proceeding got officially underway. After the jury was sworn in, Mr. Reed gathered his notes, stood and facing the jury, said:

"Ladies and gentlemen of the jury, we're here today not to right a wrong, because ultimately there are no winners here, but instead to hold our public agencies which act in our behalf responsible for providing the services they do in a manner consistent with their standard of care. The tragic events that led to the death of young David Stewart could have and should have been prevented had the department followed the standard of care they are duty bound to hold. They didn't though, and because of it a young innocent child lost his life," Reed said. He glimpsed down at his notes and as he did so, Andy glanced back at Janet and Amanda. They were eyeing him sympathetically.

Reed looked up and continued, "In the upcoming testimony and evidence you'll hear and see how protocols were ignored and chances needlessly taken by well-meaning individuals. The department and Mr. McNamara's council will argue that time was of the essence, but we say rushing out without taking the time to follow the proper standard of care is negligent. And it was this negligence that resulted in a cost too great to bear."

Reed went on for the next five minutes. When he finally ended his opening argument, Andy felt like he'd been dragged through a napalm doused rice paddy.

By the time Judge Connors swung the gavel down ending the first day, Andy had a roaring headache. To say that Reed had made a convincing case for the Stewarts so far was an understatement. He got up, and received some encouraging words from his lawyer that things were only half done. They'd have their say in a short time. But it didn't help. After he shook hands with Ed, he shuffled to the back of the gallery and joined Amanda and Janet. There, his sister gave him a friendly bump on the shoulder and offered him a reassuring smile with a thumbs up. Janet put her arm around his waist and gave him a squeeze.

"Let's get out of here and get something to eat," Amanda said. "I'm starved."

He wasn't hungry though. All the fight in him had been whittled away to a nub. He reached into his shirt pocket and dug his sunglasses out. "Sure, why not?"

"You okay?" Janet said to him as Amanda led the way out into the late afternoon sunlight raining down on the coastal city.

He looked down at Janet's watchful eyes as they walked to their cars. "Yeah, I'm fine. Thanks for coming."

She took his hand. "No need to thank me. You've been there for me and Nate. It's the least I can do."

Suddenly, he wanted to roll up in her arms and never let go. "Well, it means a lot to me," he said as they came to her car.

Janet called to Amanda, "Want to ride together? We can take mine."

Amanda shrugged and they got in Janet's Highlander and drove along the winding coastal highway past shops and eateries until they came to the Cove of the Coast Restaurant. Janet parked and they all got out and strolled into the comely clapboard and brick building with a sweeping gabled roof. Perched on the bluff overlooking the ocean, its quaint family style dining room offered spectacular views of the coastline.

He followed his sister and Janet to a table beside the band of windows at the back of the room. He'd eaten here more times than he could count over the years and knew the menu by heart. As he sat, it occurred to him maybe Janet had crossed his path here a time or two. Perhaps they'd even sat at opposing tables. He leaned toward her as she took the seat beside him.

"I take it you've been here before," he said.

"Oh, just a few times," she answered as she looked at the menu.

Amanda said, "What's good here?"

"More like, what isn't," Janet said.

The waitress came and they ordered. While they waited for their entrees, they avoided talking about the trial, and focused on the upcoming Salem Art Fair and Festival. Amanda suggested McNamara's should have a tent there. He knew she was trying to downplay the trial. That it was only a formality to get over and past. He couldn't blame her. He'd been telling himself the same thing over the last few weeks.

At length, Amanda sipped her water and sat back with a discerning expression. As she looked at them, he got a feeling he knew what was coming. His sister wasn't one to mince words. Seeing how he and Janet were pretty close lately, he braced himself and waited. Finally, Amanda said, "I have to tell you Janet, you two look great together. I'm so happy for you both. My brother deserves someone who's supportive and willing to go the distance."

Bingo! He thought and glanced at Janet. If the assumption his sister had made bothered her, she wasn't letting on.

At last Janet said, "Andy's a sweetheart. What's not to like?"

"Oh...we've got a lot to discuss there," Amanda said, eyeing him sidelong. He was then treated to watching the women carry on a conversation about him for the next ten minutes. By the time their food arrived, they'd somehow, someway, managed to paint a silver lining on one of the worst days of his life.

Mr. Reed rested for the plaintive the next day just before noon. It was then left to the defendants to present their case. An accident engineer was called to the stand first who detailed the events for the next hour. The man's professional opinion was Andy had done all he could to avoid the child based on the speed he was going, which was within the accepted range of an emergency vehicle on route to a critical situation. That he'd missed the deaf child sign was of little consequence considering all the factors. Following the engineer was Bob Lightfoot's testimony, which backed up Andy's deposition.

Andy sat beside his lawyer, heart pumping as his stomach churned, watching the proceeding. While he'd testified before in cases, and knew the feeling of anxiousness that proceeded taking the stand, this was different. This was about him. He eyed the clock on the wall. 2:24 PM. He was next. Court ended at 4:30 PM. That left two hours of grilling if Reed ended his cross-examination of Bob right now. He looked on as the lawyer questioned his partner and waited for him to bring up the issue of the time logs. But the cagy lawyer never brought it up. In fact, to this point Reed had said nothing about it. Andy knew Reed was waiting for him.

Well, he'd done the only thing he could in an impossible situation. A man's life was at stake: time log be damned. He leaned over and whispered to his lawyer, Ed, "He's waiting for me to make his point."

Ed nodded. "You'll be okay. Just be honest, be yourself."

He shrugged, sat back and glanced at Janet and Amanda sitting behind him as Bob left the stand. As his partner strode up the aisle, he shot him a thin smile. He nodded back. Took a deep breath.

"The defense calls Mr. Andrew McNamara to the stand," said Mr. Stanton.

He got up, tugged on the bottom hem of his suit jacket and strode to the witness stand. After he was sworn in, Mr. Stanton led him through the painful events of that day two years ago. As he repeated his version to the jury of what had happened, he felt the angry, dark eyes of the Stewarts burrowing into him. Thankfully, 4:30PM drew near and Judge Connors adjourned for the day.

The following morning, Andy had Amanda ride in with Janet while he rode in with his lawyer. On the way, they discussed how Andy should handle Reed's cross-exam. "Don't let him rattle you. Stick to the facts as you know them," Ed had said as they pulled into the courthouse lot. Andy nodded and got out of the car.

They walked into the courthouse as Janet and Amanda pulled into the lot behind them. "Stay focused Andy," Ed said leading him to the defendant's table. Stanton was already there with the insurance lawyer. The jury box was empty and so was Connors' chair.

Stanton reached over and shook Andy's hand. "How you doing?"

"I'm good," Andy lied. He looked across the aisle and saw Reed going through his papers, sharpening his teeth for his turn with him.

The jury door opened and the men and women filed in and took their seats. Right after them, Judge Connors came out of his door. He took his seat, brought the court to order and had Andy take the stand.

"I remind you, Mr. McNamara you're still under oath," Connors said, and turned to Reed. "Councilor, your witness."

Reed stood and pressed his lips together. "Morning, Mr. McNamara. I'm not going to ask you to repeat what you went through yesterday again. That had to be difficult."

"Thank you," Andy said, bracing himself for the storm that was about to come.

"I do have a few questions that maybe you can help me with, but first," Reed said, pulling a document out of a file folder. "Your honor, I'd like to enter this 'time log' into the record as exhibit '8'." He handed it to the bailiff who in turn gave it to Connors.

Connors read it, and said, "So, entered," and handed it back to the bailiff.

Once Reed had it back in hand he explained the rules and regulations on permissible shift lengths to the jury then stepped forward. "On the morning of April 25th, 2007, where were you?"

"I was at a three alarm structure fire on 3rd street," Andy said.

Reed nodded. "Was the whole department there?"

"Most of us, yes," Andy said. "We left a skeleton crew at the station."

"I see," Reed said. "And you came back to the station when?"

"Around noon."

"You came back alone?" Reed said.

"No, Bob Lightfoot came with me."

"And the rest of the crew?"

Andy took a drink of water from the glass on the witness stand rail, set the glass down and said, "They stayed behind cleaning up."

"Why didn't you stay?" Reed said.

"I'd been there all night, and Captain sent me back."

"Because you were exhausted?" Reed said, pointedly.

Andy knew where this was going and there was no way out of it. He shot a glance at Ed and the department's council at the defendant's table and saw them draw a collective breath. "I don't recall."

"Right," Reed said. He stepped up to Andy and handed him exhibit 8. "Do you recognize this, Mr. McNamara?"

Andy looked at it; saw his name typed on the top and the times in and out of service. "I do."

"And what is it?"

"It's a time log."

"Can you please tell the court what your in-and-out times were for the 25th of April 2007?"

Andy didn't need to look at the log to know the times. "I logged in at 8PM on the 24th. I never logged out because I was in the hospital on the 25th due to the accident."

"That's right, you were injured. I'm sorry about that," Reed said. "Now the call for the cardiac arrest came at what time?"

Andy took another sip of water. "2:25PM."

"On the 25th?"

"That's right."

"Hmm…that's an eighteen hour shift so far and you're going out on a call," Reed said. "Besides being outside the rules and regs, I have to believe you were just a little bit tired…hmm?"

"I was perfectly alert and aware," Andy said as firmly as he could eyeing the men and women of the jury.

Reed tilted his head and tapped his fingers on the railing in front of Andy. "Ask you another question, Mr. McNamara. What time did you get up the morning of the 24th?"

Andy saw Stanton, the lawyer for the insurance company and his lawyer, Ed lean forward. Biting his lip, he bowed his head then looking up, sighed and said, "I believe somewhere around 7:30 AM."

"7:30!" Reed said, rolling his eyes. "That's what…umm…thirty-one hours? And you insist you were alert and aware? You know what I think. I think you were sleep impaired Mr. McNamara. I think you had no business climbing behind the wheel of a car let alone operating a large rescue vehicle. Let me ask you another question Mr. McNamara. How come you didn't have Mr. Lightfoot drive? Was he over the service log time limit?"

"No idea!" Andy said, balling his fists in his lap as the muscles in his shoulder knotted. "And I wasn't interested in asking. We had a code 99, er…a cardiac call to attend to. Every second mattered."

"I'm sure it did," Reed fired back, "except all that hurrying ended up in what, never making it to the cardiac call and ended up with a dead child."

"Objection," Stanton said.

Reed smiled. "Withdrawn."

Connors said, "Strike the comment from the record. The jury will disregard."

Reed turned away from Andy, paused then turned back. "As I studied the logs, I saw Mr. Fuller was at the station that day and there was another man named Mr. Dan Revit. Care to comment why you didn't seek them out. Certainly you knew they were there?"

Andy felt his gut tighten. "Yes, I knew they were there, but I was already at the truck and so was Bob. It didn't make sense calling them down when we were already geared up and ready to go so I made a decision."

"Well, we all see how that decision played out, don't we?" Reed said. He panned the jury for added effect then said, "No more questions."

Chapter 23

J ANET TURNED into her driveway and parked in the turnaround. Andy was looking out the window from his passenger seat. For a moment, he didn't move, just stared at the budding hawthorn. Finally, he turned and smiled, but it wasn't a sincere smile. She reached over and gripped his hand. "It'll be all right."

He shrugged. Opened the door. "You sure about me staying the night? I don't want to put you out."

"Of course." She led him up the stone path to the porch and let him inside. "Why don't you wash up? You remember where the guest room is?"

"I think so," he said, loosening his tie.

"And get out of that suit."

He eyed her sidelong. "Where's Megan?"

Janet chuckled. "Up north."

Andy slipped his suit jacket off and flipped it over his shoulder. As he shuffled down the hall, she watched him. *Amanda's right, he's a good man,* she thought as he slipped out of view. She put in a CD of her favorites and went to the kitchen to peruse the scattered collection of take-out left overs in the refrigerator. Eggplant parm, Moo goo gai pan, Chicken quesadilla–no, no, and no! "The man deserves something better," she muttered, popping the freezer door open.

A couple of Delmonico steaks stared her in the eye and she dragged them out. Twenty minutes later they were sizzling on her *Jenn-Air* grille. She took a sip of wine and turned them over as he walked in. "Feel better?"

"Much, thank you. That smells heavenly," he said sliding up next to her.

She felt her breath catch as his arm brushed her back. "You take your steak medium or well done?"

"A little in-between. What's that herb I detect?"

"Rosemary. Get you a glass of wine?"

"Sure, but I can help myself," he said, ducking away. She heard him uncorking the bottle and poking around behind her. "Wow, you're going all out. Asparagus, salad, taters!"

She smiled, enjoying the playful intimacy flooding the space between them. "I'm glad you're hungry."

"I am. I like your choice of music."

"Yeah, James Taylor's a favorite of mine," she said, plucking the steaks off the grille. She set them on a platter, took them to the table and lit a taper she'd placed in the center. Backing away, she considered the pair of opposing square, ceramic plates, mandarin-green linen napkins and bone-handled silverware. Had she overdone things? The candle gave it style, but also gave it a romantic tone. Was that what she wanted and would he sense it? Well, it was too late now and to be truthful, she didn't care. She tipped her wine glass back and drained the last sip.

"Why don't you bring yourself over here and sit." She removed her apron and tossed it on the kitchen island. From the corner of her eye, she caught his glance racing over her pastel blue blouse and black slacks. It had been awhile since a man had given her the 'up and down' or rather since she'd noticed it. She discovered she missed the feeling of being appreciated.

Apparently he realized he'd been caught looking her over because he turned to the bottle of wine, picked it up and joined her by the table. "Get you a refill?" Again, her body prickled as he stood inches away.

She tried to ignore the flood of warmth running rampant through her. The hint of citrus soap lingering in the space between them was quite distracting. *Steady, girl,* she thought, as he poured more wine into her glass.

She avoided his impossible blue eyes, knowing if she looked into them, she'd be gone. "Sit while I bring over the rest of our dinner."

With the bowls in front of them, he dug in, piling a generous helping of potatoes onto his plate. "I have croutons for your salad if you want," she said as he plowed into his dinner.

"No, I'm good," he said.

She looked on wondering where things might go later on. He looked up, caught her watching him, set his knife and fork down and sat back. For a minute their gazes locked as James Taylor's 'Carolina on my Mind' trickled in from the other room. Finally, he picked up his glass and took a drink.

"This is good wine," he said, breaking the spell between them.

"It comes from Anam Cara Vineyards," she said, struggling to catch her breath. "How's your steak?"

"It's great." She smiled, took a bite and realized she was in trouble as he leaned forward and laid his hand over hers. "Thanks. I needed this."

"You're welcome," she said, fighting to keep control of herself. The warmth of his hand and his heartfelt sentiment had her heart racing. "You had a long day."

"Yes, I did," he said, turning the stem of his wine glass around and around. "Can I ask you something?"

She sensed a bombshell coming her way and her heart thumped. "Sure."

"I don't know how to ask this other than to come right out and say it." He cleared his throat. "Since I've been alone, I've been bumping around; keeping to myself. Nightlife has been a date with a TV and a pillow." He drained his wine. "So, my question is: what about you? You been getting out there in the dating rat-race since your husband passed?"

Checking to see if the coast is clear, huh? "Haven't really thought about it. Guess I've been too busy taking care of business."

"I hear ya," he said in a casual tone and took up his knife and fork again. "Tell you the truth, the idea of getting out there and starting over is exhausting."

"I know," she said as he went back to eating his meal. She stabbed a tomato off her salad and waited to see what else he might say. But he changed the subject to the trial. As he analyzed his testimony and the jury's take-away, she felt the tension between them die away.

Andy finished his steak and worked on his potatoes, picking at his salad in-between bites. "So, what do you usually do at night?"

"Depends. If I'm on contract, I'm working. But if I've got nothing going on, I read, bake, try new recipes or putter around. Sometimes, I write. I do like Saturday Night Live, so I catch that whenever I can."

"Maybe we can check out a movie or something later on…if you're interested."

"Yeah, I'd like that. Megan has a ton of DVD's. I'm sure we can find something."

After they finished dinner, Janet dragged out Megan's movie collection and they pawed through it, settling on National Treasure. As the movie started, she curled up on the couch and watched him take the recliner next to her. She found herself disappointed he wasn't joining her, but kept her mouth shut. But then that was his way, not presuming anything. She adored that aspect of him, but right now, what she really wanted was to feel him sitting next to her.

"How's things with Nate?"

"Okay, I guess. We haven't seen each other much the last couple of weeks. I've called him a couple times." She shook her head. "Short conversations."

"Yeah, he's like that. He'll come around."

"I hope so. We talked about taking a day together and driving down the coast sometime. Not sure when."

"Did you?" He stirred in his seat. He glanced at the movie, which was more a distraction than entertainment and was quiet a minute. Finally, he said, "Nate's doing a great job down at the store. Hopefully, I'll still have it after next week."

She rolled her eyes and her body tightened. "Don't go there, Andy. Everything will work out." *Enough. Get over here!* "You know, I don't bite."

He eyed her and she saw a tiny smile creep over his face. "I take up a lot of space."

"It's a big couch," she said, staying put. She didn't want him finding refuge at one end with her at the other.

The snick of a door shutting stirred Janet from a dreamless sleep. She arched her back. Stretched her legs. Felt an arm wrapped around her. Her hand went to her waist. Andy! They'd dozed off on the couch watching the movie. The sound of footsteps nearby opened her eyes and she saw Nate standing by the TV. He didn't look happy.

She jostled Andy and sat up. "Nate, what are you doing here?" She blinked and looked to the grandfather clock. Saw it was after ten. "It's...late."

"I might ask you the same thing, Mom."

She didn't like his tone. "We were watching a movie and fell asleep."

"Apparently," he said, glaring back.

Andy righted himself and sat up awkwardly beside her. She didn't need to see his face to know he was surprised. Nor did she need to ask Nate what he was thinking. It was fairly obvious. But she'd done nothing wrong. And she reminded herself she was his mother. Did she owe her son an explanation? Not really, except he was under the impression Andy had befriended him for friendship's sake. She eyed her son as she thought about how to handle the situation. "Why are you here? Is there something wrong?"

Nate looked off. "Never mind. I wouldn't want to interrupt your date."

Janet bristled. "It's not a date! He had a long day in court, so I invited him back for dinner."

Andy leaned toward her. "I should go. I'll call a cab."

She turned to him. "You'll do no such thing." Turning back to Nate, she said, "Why am I explaining myself to you?"

"I don't know Mom. Why are you?" He eyed Andy despairingly. "I thought you were my friend, but I see it was all about getting in her pants. But hey, it's all good."

Janet reared up. "Nate–"

"Don't! Just don't, okay?" Nate said. He pulled his shoulders back. Stared at the both of them. Nodded disdainfully. "I hope things work out for you. I really do. Just don't coming around blowing smoke up my ass anymore, Andy, okay? I'll see myself out."

As he tromped to the front door, Janet got up. "Nate!" But the only answer she got was the sound of the door slamming behind him.

She collapsed on the couch. Put her head between her hands.

Andy sat beside her. "I'm sorry. I should've had you take me home instead of coming back here."

"It's not your fault," she said, sitting back deflated and trying to think of what to do. Her first thought was to call Nate, but she knew he wouldn't answer. Chasing after him was ridiculous. She needed to talk to him, but waiting until morning felt like an eternity. She turned to Andy and saw the far away look in his eyes. Knew he was feeling like a shit and felt the space between them widen. Her heart sank. They'd had such a nice evening together. Instead, it had ended in a crushing silence with her fighting to breathe.

At last, Andy got up. "You should get some sleep."

She shrugged and dragged herself from the couch. "I'll see you in the morning." She watched him retreat down the hall. As he went into his room, she wrapped her arms around her waist. It was going to be a long night and she was fairly sure she wouldn't be sleeping through much of it.

It thundered and rained during the night, and by the time morning peeked through Janet's bedroom window, she felt like she'd been dragged through a knothole. She got up and scampered to the thermostat. It had gotten unseasonably cold overnight and with the heat turned back it was a chilly fifty-three degrees in the room. She jacked it up to seventy-two and ducked into the bathroom. After she checked her cell phone for email and messages, she turned the shower on and stepped under the warm spray. What she wanted to do, was linger in the comforting steam rising around her, but now was not the time. She had to find Nate and set things right.

Forty minutes, later, she was sliding into the driver's seat and starting the car. As she cranked up the heat, Andy got in and said, "He'll come around."

"I hope so. He's not answering his phone," she said, putting the car into gear.

"I think he's more upset at me than you," he said as they pulled out onto Old Cypress Road.

"What I don't understand is why he stopped out so late," she said. "That's not like him at all. Something must've happened."

She glanced at Andy and saw him looking back. There wasn't much he could say and she knew it. "So, warm enough?"

"Getting there." He yawned. "Looks like we're gonna have a soaker today."

"Yeah, and a cold one." She turned the radio on low and they were quiet for a minute. As a rule, she didn't mind just being with someone and not saying a word. But the space between them was a minefield of unsaid fears. The longer it lasted, the more the silence gave substance to them. Finally, she said, "I always find it hard to sleep on a bed I'm not used to."

"For me, it's the pillows. Give me an old beaten down one I can bury my head into." He looked off over the passing landscape of flowering meadows and ragged evergreens. "Beautiful country out here."

She turned onto Farmstead Road. Headed south toward Route 22. "Yeah, I like the woods," she said as they drove along the rolling straightaway littered here and there with clumps of soil from farm tractors. She turned onto the arterial and headed east toward Salem, keenly aware his hand rested on the console between them.

Her hand drifted toward him, but she quickly drew it back. "You want me to drop you off at home or the store?"

"Home will be fine. Make a right after you cross the river," he said.

She followed his directions from there and said little more until they reached his driveway. As she pulled in and parked, he turned to her. "It'll be all right. God never gives us things we can't handle," he said, reaching over and taking her hand. "If you need me, call," he said and letting go of her hand, he opened the door and got out "Drive safe and let me know how things turn out, okay?"

She nodded. "Bye, Andy."

After dropping Andy off, Janet headed for McNamara's to see if Nate had gone into work. But he wasn't there, and nobody had heard from him. She got back in her car and rang his cell phone. Got his voice mail. She'd already left two voice messages so she hung up and swung into traffic. His apartment building was ten minutes away. When she turned into the lot, the rain was coming down in sheets. She reached over the back of her seat and grabbed her umbrella then ran to the front entry of the building and flung the door open. She thought of how to open a conversation with Nate as she took the elevator up to the third floor.

Nate's apartment was at the far end of the transecting hallway, near the exit stair. Striding toward it, she felt her body tense up. By the time she was standing in front of his door, she found it hard to breathe. She raised her hand to knock, hesitated, then rapped softly and listened for stirring inside. When there was no answer, she knocked again, harder.

"Nate! It's me," she said.

She waited a moment as her heart thumped. Still, there was no answer. Glancing down the hall, she suddenly felt naked. But the longer she stood there waiting, the more her nerves frayed. *Why isn't he answering? Okay, you were mad last night, Nate. I understand that...but really? Stop acting like a child and answer the door!*

Suddenly, Megan's story of him sitting on the balcony railing gripped her. *No, he wouldn't do that. He's just hurting and trying to punish me.* But the tale grew louder and before she knew it, the memory of him sitting on the rampart wall kicked in. She knocked one more time and clenched her keychain as visions of him lying dead on the floor terrified her. She had a key to the apartment. *Come on, Nate, open the door! Screw it!*

The key slid into the lock and a moment later she was inside the tiny apartment. Panning the tidy kitchen and living room, she turned and went to the bedroom. Pushing the door open, she saw the made bed and exhaled. *I can't believe I just overreacted like that.*

The question then became, where was he if not there? She didn't know if he had new friends or haunts. Then again, she hadn't asked, and even if she had, she was fairly sure she wouldn't have gotten an answer. She pulled her cell phone out and dialed Andy. He had no idea either, but he tried to reassure her, Nate would be okay. Well, she knew he was trying to help, but this was her son. She hung up and called Megan but held off on hammering her over what she'd said to Nate. When Megan didn't know anything either, she hung up and felt her fears jackknife back on her.

She turned, pulled the door closed behind her and nibbled her lip. As she tried to plot her next move, she saw an envelope on the kitchen counter with an open letter beneath it. From where she stood, she could just make out a blue rimmed seal on the cream color stationary. Walking over, she picked it up. *What's this?*

Dear Nate Porter

I'm writing to let you know how proud of you we all are here in the great state of Oregon and that I'm personally going to walk your medal process all the way up to the top chain of command. If there's anything at all I can do for you, please don't hesitate to contact me.

Sincerely

Jeff Merkley

United States Senator

Janet set the letter down, having a good idea of what Nate's reaction to it must have been. He wasn't keen on getting a medal and it wasn't because he didn't like being in the spotlight. It was because of something that happened over *THERE*. She locked up and left. Wherever Nate had gone, it was to be alone.

She drove through the rain heading toward home racking her brain. Had he taken to a trail somewhere? It was raining, but that had never stopped him in the past. Before he enlisted, he'd spent hours out on them, traipsing around the countryside near their home. A chime went off in the car. She was low on fuel. Before she went much further she needed to gas up. She pulled into Cain's and ran into her next-door neighbor Ed, who was sitting in a booth near the front door reading the Salem Gazette. When he saw her, he waved.

"Hey there, Janet," he said, setting his paper down.

She forced a smile. The last thing she wanted right now was to get entangled in a conversation with the old man. "Hi Ed, how are ya?"

He studied her with discerning gray eyes. "Well enough. You don't look too happy though. Everything okay?"

She put her hand to the door to go out. "Oh, just one of those days, you know."

He nodded. "Seems that's going around. I saw your boy in here a little while ago. He said pretty much the same thing."

"When? How long ago?" she said freezing mid-stride.

"Maybe thirty minutes."

He came back to talk! "Thanks, Ed," she said and ran out. But when she got home, Nate's Camry wasn't in the driveway. Bewildered, she sat in her car. Dialed his cell. When there was no answer, she tried the store again. He still hadn't shown up for work. Maybe call Andy? No, Andy would be the last person Nate would want to talk to. *Should I head back into town, try his apartment again? Maybe Ed saw which way he went. Shit, why didn't I ask him? Damn it, Nate, where are you?* She scolded herself as she jammed the stick into drive and shot out of her driveway.

The trip back to Cain's took forever. At least that's the way it seemed to her. She flew into the lot praying Ed was still there. She hit the brakes, parked and ran for the front door. The man, who was sucking down a gulp of his coffee, looked up in surprise as she entered.

"Forget something?" he said.

"No...umm...by chance, you didn't see which way Nate went after he left here, did you?"

He shrugged. "No, I didn't. Why?"

"I did, Ms. Porter," said the cashier, who was bussing a table nearby. "He went west on 22 toward Dallas."

Fogarty! Of course! Idiot! "Thanks, Jimmy."

As she drove west, Janet imagined a variety of scenarios on how things would play out. The ones where Nate stalked off, accusing her of betraying him, she tried to ignore. Unfortunately, those were the ones that nagged her the most. But they were the least of her worries. What was really at stake was her son's life. Being young and reckless was one thing, looking for ways to up the ante was another thing altogether.

She turned into Fogarty State Park and felt her chest tighten as she parked. The rain had given up twenty minutes ago and had left a world veiled in mist. Getting out, she marched under the swaying oak and cottonwood canopy to the underpass leading to the beach.

There, she stepped onto a broad mat of sand stretching out to a surging gray ocean. She looked south first; pretty sure he hadn't gone that way. North was where all of their history lay on this beach. At length, she turned and panned the sweeping coastline to a jagged arm of boulders jutting out into the roiling water. The tide was coming in as birds circled overhead, their wings outstretched in the swirling wind. She pulled a lock of hair from her face and started walking. Her altar rock was well down the beach. A brisk fifteen to twenty minute walk on a good day. Today it would be at least that and more.

Striking for it, she passed the soughing grasses nesting in the rolling dunes. But her gaze went mostly out to sea. She told herself she was overreacting; that *he* would never go there, but she couldn't tear her eyes off the dark gray ocean. Then she saw it: a duffle bag. It was maybe forty yards upwind lying on the beach and beside it was his leg brace. She stopped, narrowed her eyes on the up-thrust rock breaking the surf beyond the bag and froze. Walking astride it, knee deep in the surf, was Nate and he was heading away from shore...away from... *her*. For a minute, the world shrank and her heart raced. She knew the wild thoughts rampaging in her mind were just that: wild. Nate would never....not when he had his whole life ahead of him. Would he?

Suddenly, she burst into a dead run across the sand. "Nate...Nate...stop!" she cried, hitting the rolling white caps pounding the beach. As she sprinted into deeper water, she felt the grit shift beneath her feet and the powerful draw of the receding ocean.

A large wave that was rolling in slapped her and swept her feet away. All at once, she was upside down. Tasted salt as another wave crashed in and sucked her breath away. As she struggled to get to her knees a hand grabbed her arm. When she looked up, her son was staring back in bewilderment.

"What are you doing?" he cried, helping her to her feet.

She caught her breath as they walked back to dry land. "I saw you heading out to deep water and I thought..."

"Jesus...you thought I...really?" He rolled his eyes. Pointed to a ledge on the rocks. "I was going out there to sit. I come here to think!"

Suddenly she felt embarrassed. "I didn't know," she said.

"Well, now you do. What are you doing here, anyway?" he snapped.

"I want to talk to you about last night," she said.

"Right," he snapped. "Hey look, I don't care…whatever. If you want bang him, go ahead."

She stared at him, stunned, not believing her ears then slapped him across the face, startling him. In all his life she had never struck him and it surprised her, but she wasn't going to apologize. "You will not talk to me like that, do you hear me? He's my friend, that's all and he's gone out on a limb for you," she shot back then turned and headed off down the beach with her hands balled.

"Mom, Mom," he said, calling after her. He caught her up and grabbed her arm. "I'm sorry. I…it just came out."

She spun around and looked at him. Saw the bare contrition on his contorted face, and said, "You need to think about things before you shoot your mouth off. And you know what: what I do and don't do in my personal life is my business and I won't have you or anyone else judging me. Like I said, Andy's my friend and he's been there for me when I needed him." She paused. "Like it or not, I'm your mother, and I worry about you. It's my job. It comes with the territory, and it doesn't end just because you're a grown man."

"I know, I know," he said, looking down and scuffing his feet on the sand.

"Then what? Talk to me. What's going on? You don't have to hide what happened from me. I'm here, and I love you." When silence followed, she reached over, grasped for his hand. "The longer you keep whatever's bottled up inside the more it'll eat at you."

"I really don't want to talk about it." He gazed off into the distance then turned back with a far away look. "What do you want from me?"

She studied the taciturn expression he'd inherited from his father. "What I want, I can never have again, but I'd settle for your trust."

He glanced at the ocean as the wind tossed her hair around her face. "I do trust you. I just don't know how to talk about it, okay?"

"You start with one word at a time, Nate." She looked upward. That she was even contemplating what she was about to say dumbfounded her, but if she wanted him to talk she had to raise the ante and that meant baring her soul. She looked at him hard. "What I'm going to tell you, only two people in the world know. One of them was your father and the other your sister." She took a deep breath, let it out and said, "Nate, when I was twelve, I was raped." She paused and watched her son's face darken as he drank in the bitter words. When she felt her confession had hit home, she went on, "I kept it a secret for over twenty years and it almost cost me the greatest love I ever knew."

"Why are you telling me this?"

"Because, you need to know you're not alone." She reached up and cupped his cheek with her hand. As she studied his searching expression, she said, "I read something in a book once. It was in one of your father's devotionals, I think. It said people are like pebbles on a beach. Life comes in, bathes and scours them, shapes and refines them leaving beautiful, shining stones in its wake."

"There's no beautiful, shining stone here, trust me," he muttered and started walking again.

"Oh, I don't know about that," she said. "I've seen more than you know behind that armor you wear."

He scowled. "Not this. You don't want to know this."

"Don't pretend to know what I can handle and what I can't!" she cried, seizing his arm. "I don't need your protection. I need my son back!" She stared at him, holding him stock-still by the sheer force of her gaze until at last he said, "Okay, you win."

She'd heard that phrase before and not by him. Megan had screamed it at her three years ago after she'd pulled rank by placing Neil in Hazelnut. Now, as then, her answer was the same. "There are no winners, Nate. Love doesn't keep score."

He chewed his lip, seeming to mull over what she said and started walking again. "I suppose you're right." He paused, looked off again as if he couldn't bear to see her face. She watched him draw breath as he tightened his jaw. At last he said, "You sure you want to hear this?"

"I want to hear whatever you tell me."

"Okay. But first you should get out of those wet clothes before you freeze to death." He marched back and grabbed his duffle bag. As he did so she noticed he wasn't favoring his leg. She scratched her head. *Wow, he's come a long way. When did I miss that?*

When he returned, carrying his bag, towel and brace, she said, "You're walking really good."

"Yeah, rehab's done the trick." He paused and took his sweatshirt off. Handing it to her along with the towel, he looked up and down the empty beach. "Here, get out of your wet top, dry yourself off and put this on."

"Nate!"

He looked upward. "Oh, come on. Really, Mom?"

"I suppose." She turned, surveyed the beach for herself and stripped out of her soaking blouse. Toweling herself off, she put his fleece on, and said, "Aren't you going to be cold?"

He strapped on his brace and picked up his duffle bag. "You kidding? After three years over there, this is paradise."

They started off down the beach and as they walked along the water's edge, she reached out and took his hand. "You know I love you more than anything, Nate. You're my world. If anything were to ever happen to you, I would..."

"I know, I know."

"Now, out with it."

He shimmied his duffle bag higher on his shoulder and glanced at her from the corner of his eye as they walked. "We were on our way back from rounds in Falluja. Cunningham was riding in back with me. Kendall was shotgun and Parker was driving. Things were quiet in Al Nasr...a town on the way back to Bagdad. Anyway, people were out, going about their business. Nothing out of the ordinary. One of them was Hadid. Big round guy. He ran a little Ali-kabob in town. Always had a smile on his face when we stopped for grub. Real nice man."

"It happened so fast. Bullets flying," he said looking out over the water with a thousand mile stare. "Poor Hadid, he never had a chance.

Parker hit the gas and we hunkered down in the 'V' trying to get under cover. Freaking IED, blew our front end off and threw Parker out in pieces."

He came to a stop, paused and was quiet a moment before going on. "I was pinned down in back. Cunningham was slumped over my lap bleeding out. There was nothing left of his face. Kendall though, he grabs my *Kate* and starts firing away. Takes down maybe ten of the *Mooj's* before he gets hit. And me...I do absolutely nothing"

He shot her a haunting look. "Kendall was down, and I hid under Cunningham wondering if I'm next... Long story short, I passed out and by the time I came to, the story in the field hospital was that I'd taken on the *Mooj's* all by myself. And the tale grew taller down the line. I'm a hero! Yeahhh," he said drawing the word out. "You see my problem now, Mom?"

She eyed her son as her heart broke. Understood the position he'd been put in, that there was no easy out. She reached up and wrapped her arms around him, holding him fiercely. When she drew back, she saw the man he'd become melt into the boy he'd left behind, and loved him more than she thought possible.

Chapter 24

ANDY CLOSED his front door, shutting out the driving rain and tossed his umbrella on the floor. *I should've never gotten on the couch with her. In fact, I shouldn't have allowed her to talk me into coming home with her. What was I thinking?* He thought as he drifted to the window and watched Janet drive away.

He'd come close to telling her how he felt last night but couldn't find the words. Or was it he didn't have the courage? Anyway, it didn't matter now. He'd screwed the pooch big time. Whatever they had was slipping away before it had even begun. Maybe he was overreacting, but there was so much against him he couldn't see clearly. All he knew was he'd put her at odds with Nate, and that bothered him more than anything. He knew better. As far as he and her son were concerned, well...

Anyway, there wasn't a damned thing in the world he could do about it. His life was spinning out of control, but he refused to buckle under to his fears. The last thing he needed was to sit around the house holing up and licking his wounds. Besides, it was time he got to the store. He went to his room, changed out of his rain-spattered suit and grabbed his keys.

McNamara's was humming with the morning crowd; many were regulars he was getting to know by name. But he wasn't in a chatty mood so he made a beeline for his office. As he walked around the occupied tables, folks shouted out hellos and how-ya-doings to him, oblivious to his drama unfolding around them. He waved back, rounded the front counter and hung up his jacket.

Amanda cashed out a customer and looked up as he passed by. "How's things?"

"They've been better," he said as Jack came running up. He glanced down at the dog that was on his hind legs pawing him. "Down boy...so, anything I need to know?"

"Not especially. Oh, Janet stopped by looking for Nate. She looked flustered. Was he supposed to be here today?"

"Don't believe so," he said as his gut tightened. "That fresh coffee?"

"Umm...yeah," she said and eyed him sidelong. "You sure you're okay?"

"Yeah, why?" he said, grabbing a mug and a Danish.

"Well, you don't look it. Don't worry, things'll be okay, you'll see."

He appreciated her sentiment, but she didn't know what had gone down the night before and he wasn't about to tell her. He forced his foul mood into a dark corner and poured a cup of decaf. "I'm sure you're right. By the way, do me a favor?"

"What's that?"

"Figure out how big a hit we can take if I sell my house...just in case."

She turned and looked at him as if he'd lost his mind. "Where would you live?"

"Not important, just do it okay?" he snapped and stalked into his office. As the door slammed behind him, he balled his fist. It wasn't Amanda's fault his world was crashing around him, but he didn't have the strength or the will power to apologize.

Andy unlocked the front door to McNamara's just after dawn Monday morning. As he lingered inside with Jack beside him, he panned the darkened store, drinking in the shadowed shelves, the tables stacked with books, and the empty chairs sitting around the cafe. This is what he'd wagered his future on, and as he stood there, it all felt surreal that he could lose it with one single word... guilty. Two months ago, the word would've clanged in his head, but now it took a back seat to Janet.

For the hundredth time, he thought back to Nate walking in on them. If only "this-or-that" had happened ran through his mind all weekend. He had fallen prey to the proverbial insanity of ruminating over it again and again, and it hadn't helped she didn't call like she'd promised. He just wanted to know she was okay. Except, to be honest, it was more than that. She had touched a place deep inside him, a place no one had ever reached. When they were together, he felt whole and understood. The thought of anything happening to her frightened him.

At length, he unzipped his jacket and poked his way through the maze of empty tables. When he first opened the store, he loved this time in the morning when he could listen to the little creaks and clacks weeping in through the still silence. It was a time ripe with promise and possibilities. Now, it felt like a funeral hall draped in sullen gloom. He looked down at Jack who was padding along beside him with his nose to the floor. Somehow Andy felt himself smiling. Then again, Jack always seemed to raise a sliver of hope things would get better even on the worst days of his life.

"You're a good dog, you know that Buddy?"

Jack looked up, licked his chops and wagged his tail, as if to say, 'What can I do? Name it!'

"I'm afraid nothing right now," he said to the dog as he stepped behind the front counter. For a minute, he thought of turning the lights on then decided against it. Instead, he started the coffee machine and helped himself to a blueberry muffin as Jack lingered nearby. A loud yawn followed, then a 'rat-a-tat' of nails tapping the tile floor as the coffee machine came to life. "Don't give me that look. You had breakfast before we left home." Not that it meant anything. Jack was always in town for whatever was on a plate.

He bit into his muffin and pulled a copy of yesterday's paper on the counter in front of him. The death of a thief from a deputy's Taser commanded the front headline. He scanned down the story and leafed through the Opinion and Sports sections as the clock overhead ticked and the coffee maker gurgled. By the time he looked up from reading, the sun was spraying warm buttery rays through the front window across the floor. He glanced at his watch. It was a few minutes before 6:00 AM. Amanda and Jonah would be showing up in another thirty minutes. His lawyer, Ed, had said he didn't need to be in court for the verdict. Up to now, he thought maybe he should stay away, but as he stood there looking out over the tables and book stacks he realized he couldn't wait for the phone call that would decide his future.

"Come on Jack, we're gonna take a ride."

The ninety-minute drive on the highway to Lincoln city slid by as he ruminated on the past. His tour in Nam, his life growing up in Lincoln City, the accident, they all came roaring back. At length, he came to a light on the awakening street cutting through town and he petted the dog sitting beside him. "Got another bad feeling, Bud," he said, watching the people going in and out of Stella's diner. He'd drop Jack off with her later when it was time to find out where his life was heading. The light turned and he drove down the main drag until he came to a public lot. Pulling in, he found a place to park and sat mindlessly looking out at the muted green and gray coastline. Its draw on his troubled mind was stronger than ever.

"Come, boy," he said, opening his door. As he stepped out, his cell phone vibrated in his pocket. He pulled it out and eyed Amanda's number flashing on the screen. He was hoping it would've been Janet calling.

Sighing, he flipped it open. "Yeah."

"Where are you?"

He locked the car door and strode across the lot to the stairs leading down to the beach. "Lincoln City. I decided I had to be here."

"I know." She paused. "It'll be all right, Bruddy, you'll see."

He sensed worry in her consoling tone. "Right. Hey look, I'm going to take a walk."

"Okay. Keep me posted? Please?"

"Yeah." He ended the call and descended the stairs with Jack leading the way. As he started off down the beach, he tried to believe maybe this time God would finally give him a break. But the reality was he'd probably get shit on again, because up until now, the Man upstairs had taken a dump on every good thing he tried to do. Why was it God had chosen him to be His proverbial Job? All he'd ever wanted was to live a quiet contented life surrounded by family doing the things he loved. Was that too much to ask? Why was he always the one on the outside looking in? He felt his chest tighten as he balled his fist.

"I've always done the best I could! What do you want from me?" he cried into the wind.

There was no reply and he didn't expect one. He looked down at Jack who was staring up at him. "Yeah, I know. He's answering: I'm just not listening good enough." He laughed sardonically, bent down, grabbed a stick and throwing it ahead with all his might, sent the dog racing after it. As he watched the dog run, he clenched his jaw. "Either make Your point or leave me the fuck alone."

The courtroom was subdued as Andy sat next to the department's counsel waiting for the jury to make their entrance. Stanton had told him when he called that the short deliberation meant good things. Though he was encouraged, he was nowhere near as confident as the department's lawyer was. The jury door opened and the jurists filed in. Andy studied their faces looking for some kind of clue of what was to come. The tall dark haired man leading them in was looking straight ahead, his long face serious and unreadable; the expression on the blond woman behind him, hard and smug, the portly red head in the back row, looking sympathetic or was it apathetic? Did it even matter? The seven men and five women sat as the Judge's door opened.

"All rise," cried the bailiff as Judge Connors entered the room.

Connors took his seat and brought the court to order. "Ladies and gentlemen of the Jury, have you reached a verdict?"

"We have, your Honor," said the tall dark haired man rising to his feet. The bailiff walked over, took the envelope from the Jury foreman and delivered it to Connors. After he opened it and looked it over, he handed it back to the bailiff, who delivered it back to the foreman. Connors said, "How does the jury find?"

The foreman stood and pulled the slip of paper from the envelope. "On the charge of wrongful death, we find the Lincoln City Fire Department and the codefendant guilty."

The courtroom suddenly shrunk, squeezing the air out of Andy. He blinked, trying to wrap his head around what he just heard. He thought he'd prepared himself for it but as he stood there amidst the murmurs and whisperings of those around him he discovered he'd seriously misjudged his reactions. He tried to draw breath, but found he couldn't.

Again Connors spoke up. "Has the Jury determined the compensation to the plaintiffs?"

"We have your Honor."

"How do you find?"

"We find that the Lincoln City Fire Department shall compensate the Plaintiff in the amount of $1,500,000 dollars and the codefendant, Mr. McNamara, shall compensate in the amount of $250,000."

Andy sat in his car staring straight ahead. He didn't remember picking up Jack and driving home or anything else for that matter. All he kept hearing over and over in his mind was, "Mr. McNamara, shall compensate in the amount of $250,000." At last, he turned the car off, trying to wrap his mind around what the future was going to look like. *I better secure that gutter before it tears away from the house. Trim needs a coat of paint, too. Did I pay Salem Electric?* Jack stirred beside him as his cell phone vibrated in his pocket. Digging it out, he saw Amanda's name blinking back and let it go to voice mail. He turned the phone off, tossed it to the back seat and threw the car into reverse.

An hour later, he was in the thick of the Cascade Range, driving directionless through the quaint homely town of Idanha. Along its dated main street corridor were buildings rooted in the '50's and '60's: two and three story masonry and stone structures with decorative cornices and whimsical stone-carved pendants above darkened windows. As he passed the general store and the hotel beside it, he suddenly felt the weight of the verdict come down full force on him. He hit the brakes, came to a stop on the empty road and sat there gripping the wheel with white knuckles.

"You fucked me again!" he muttered, gritting his teeth. He pounded the steering wheel as he saw his future sliding through his fingers. "God damn You! Yeah, I'm talking to You!"

Jack jumped back and barked as he hit the gas, spun the car around and sped out of town back to Salem. As he drove, his anger spiraled and by the time he got home he was livid. He tromped into his tiny living room, tossed his jacket over the sofa and marched out to the tidy little kitchen. Throwing the cupboard door open, he yanked down the half empty bottle of Johnny Walker. Slugging back a gulp, he grabbed the bottle and hurled it across the room. When it hit the wall, Jack went into a fit of barking. But he didn't care. Suddenly, he was throwing plates and glasses from the dish drainer in every direction. A wild sweep of his arm sent canisters of sugar and flour exploding on the floor. A toaster went hurling against the microwave as Jack cowered in the corner.

When at last his rage was spent, he bent over with hands on knees trying to catch his breath. He looked at the broken glass, dishware and spattered food on the floor as his body shook. Sinking to the cold tile floor, he closed his eyes and felt Jack sidle up beside him. How long he sat there taking refuge in the love of the little dog, he didn't know. The only thing he knew was Jack was the only thing right now standing between him and the dark emptiness inside.

At last he got up, dragged himself through the wreckage into the living room and plopped on the couch with a thunk. Jack jumped up and sat in his lap as he snatched the clicker on the end table and turned the TV on. He scrolled through the channels, settled on 'Law and Order' and sat back mindlessly watching the district attorney grilling a person on the witness stand.

Suddenly Jack stirred in his lap, and Andy looked up to see Amanda pushing through the front door and sweeping into the room. "Well?!"

He looked up at her and tried to answer, but couldn't find the words. It didn't matter though, his expression obviously told her all she needed to know."

"Oh, God. How bad?" she said taking her coat off and sitting beside him.

Again, all he was left with was a shrug.

Her face darkened. "This is crazy. You didn't do anything wrong!"

"Doesn't matter," he muttered. He felt a long rant coming on from her. "I'm tired and I don't want to talk about it, okay?"

She frowned. "Yes, it does matter. Now, certainly the department will appeal, and so will we." He looked away bristling and took a deep breath, not wanting to get into a fight. But she tugged at his arm. "Don't you dare give up on me, you hear me?" she said.

He turned back to her. Held her with a defiant gaze. "What am I supposed to pay Ed with, huh?" he said, daring her to strike back. When she didn't answer, he said. "What I thought. Now please drop it!"

She was quiet for a minute then finally said, "You're angry. We'll come at this later in the week after you've got your head on straight. Have you eaten? And by the way, how come you didn't answer my calls? I was worried."

He patted his pants pocket as his annoyance with her subsided. Couldn't remember where his phone was for a moment then said, "Oh, I think I left it in the car." He got to his feet and ducked outside. When he came back in, Amanda was standing in the archway leading to the kitchen. He traded glances with her in the awkward silence that followed. Finally, he said, "I was a little upset."

She nodded, surveyed the remnants of his rampage and said, "Understatement of the year."

When she started for the closet, he said, "Leave it. It's my mess. I'll deal with it later."

If she had a notion to protest, she kept it to herself and stepped away from the disaster. One thing both of them knew growing up was to step back and give space when the other was in a mood. She walked over and stood toe to toe with him. "Are you going to be okay?"

He looked away. "I'm going to have to be."

"I hope so. We'll get through this, you'll see," she said putting her arms around him. She held him for some time as the TV babbled in the background then drew back. "Law and Order? Really?"

He smiled despite his mood. "Yeah, I know." He led her to the door and walked her out to her car. "Drive safe, okay?"

Reaching up, she patted his face. "Get a good night's sleep and behave yourself. Oh, and give Janet a call. She's been trying to get a hold of you."

Chapter 25

J ANET LAY in bed thinking about Nate, imagining for the hundredth time what he must have gone through in Iraq. She couldn't say she was disappointed he'd hid under his fallen friends, but she knew it had come at a terrible price. She wanted to pay that debt for him, take it all away, but she couldn't and she knew it. All she could do was love him, be patient (not one of her stronger suits) and support him in his long arduous road back to the young man he'd left behind six years ago. At least the first hurdle had been cleared; he told her what had happened. Now it was a matter of keeping him talking so the healing process could continue. She stared at the ceiling. If only there was a way of retracting the tale of heroism by those who had found him. But in truth, she knew that even if she could wave a magic wand and make it all go away, it wouldn't erase the guilt and shame her son was dealing with.

She sighed. *How does one deal with the instinct to stay alive while friends are fighting for their lives? Why is it that some could suspend fear and turn it into blind rage? Some call it courage, but I'm not so sure.* To her way of thinking, it boiled down to fight or flight mentality. No one could know how they'd react until the moment was at hand. *Nate isn't a coward. He just reacted and fell into the instinct for survival.* But what she thought didn't matter. The only thing that mattered was what Nate believed and there was no changing it as far as she could see. What she hoped for was for Nate to start forgiving himself and find his way back, at least partially, to who he was before he left her and Neil six years ago. For now though, she'd take whatever he was offering, which was more than she'd gotten over the weekend from Andy.

She rolled out of bed, wondering why she hadn't heard from him. Was he mad she'd forgotten to let him know she was all right? She'd left two voice messages yesterday without a peep back. She slipped into her robe and let Cleo out of his crate. The dog yawned and stretched as she drew back the curtains, letting in the morning sunshine. To her stilted amusement, a squirrel was busy trying to figure out how to rob the birdfeeder hanging off a large shepherd's hook attached to the pergola. She watched the creature for a moment bobbing here and there then headed for the kitchen, debating whether she should call Andy one more time. She was getting the feeling things didn't go well in Lincoln City.

As the coffee pot gurgled, she put Cleo on his lead line and let him out for his morning walk. It was cool outside and the morning dew was glistening on the grass. In the trees out back came the shrill of cardinals as they bounced from branch to branch. The grandfather clock in the great room chimed. She glanced at the digital numbers on the stove that said 6:30 AM. Shutting the sliding glass door, she went and filled Cleo's bowl then booted up her laptop and poured a cup of coffee. Scrolling down her email, she saw a message from Mick.

She opened it and read he was finally retiring and was she sure she didn't want the post of Editor-in-Chief for the Sierra. She shook her head as her fingers flew over the keyboard. Five minutes later a reply was on its way back. She let Cleo back in and for the rest of the morning she worked on the Siletz River shoot. Currently she had a photo of the river on her desktop. As she started tweaking the light saturation, her cell phone went off. *Well, finally!*

"Hi there."

"Sorry I didn't get back to you. Had sort of a bad day yesterday," Andy said.

She pushed back from her desk. "I take it the verdict came in?"

There was a long pause. "It did."

"How ya doing?" Janet said, avoiding the word she was sure neither of them wanted to say.

"I've been better." He cleared his throat. "How'd you make out with Nate? Did you get ahold of him?"

If he didn't want to talk about the trial, she wasn't going to press him. "After a bit of a hunt, yes," she said. "He opened up to me about Iraq and we're working things out."

"Good, glad to hear it."

She stared out the window, wondering what to say next. What she really wanted, was to see him. "Hey, interested in doing lunch? I can come into town," she said.

"Sure, when?"

She nibbled a fingernail. "Say around two at that little Italian place you like down the street? I'm buying."

"You mean Dominic's? Yeah, sure, that works."

She fidgeted in her chair, wanting to find words that would make him feel better. "Hey Andy, everything's gonna be all right, you'll see."

"Yeah. Okay, got to get back at it here. Bye now."

Shit!

Janet entered Dominic's shortly before two and sat in a booth toward the back of the long, narrow restaurant. While she waited under the light of a hanging swag lamp, she glanced at the paper menu offering Italian fare. Not that she was going to order. With her concern for Andy growing by the minute since his call, she couldn't eat even if she wanted to. She sipped her water, took a deep breath and tried to think how she could possibly help him.

She peered over the opposing seat back, down the shadowy, narrow dining room toward the front door and saw staff setting tables and waiting on guests. *Where are you?* Glancing at her watch, she saw it was quarter after two and wondered if she should call him. But as she went to dig her phone out, it buzzed in her purse. She pulled it out and read the text message telling her he was running a few minutes late.

She texted him back and took another sip of water as the waiter showed up. Maybe a glass of wine would take the edge off. She looked up at the smiling blond waitress and ordered a scotch, neat. While she waited for it, Andy came in and when she saw him, she got up and gave him a hug, which wasn't returned anywhere near what she'd wished for.

Pulling away, he offered her a tight smile. "Sorry, I'm late."

She watched him slide into the booth and glance down at the menu. His shoulders were pressed back tight against the seat and the paper rattled in his hands. Finally, he looked up, shifted abruptly and set the menu down. Pushing it aside, he said, "You been here long?"

"Only a few minutes," she lied. She swallowed, refusing to feed into his guarded attitude and smiled. "You've had a busy morning."

He set his hands on the table and laced his fingers together. "Not really. Did you order?"

"Just a drink," she said, and as if on cue, the waitress showed up and set her scotch in front of her.

He darted his eyes at it and looked up at the girl. "I'll take a beer. Whatever's on tap'll be fine." After she left them, he turned back to Janet. "So you and Nate are good now?"

"Yes."

"Good, I'm glad. I know how worried you've been about him."

She took a sip of her scotch. "More than you know."

Andy paused. "He called in. I take it he spent the weekend with you?"

"He did. Went home last night. He's gonna be okay." She looked at him trying to discern his stoic expression, "What about you, though? Are you all right?"

He looked off then turned back to her. "Not so much."

"You want to talk about it?"

"Not really," he said as the waitress came around.

Janet stirred the ice in her drink, not sure how to respond as he pulled his menu back up and glanced at it again. "You want anything?"

"No, I'm good."

"I guess I'm good, too," he said and sent the girl away. He was quiet a minute and she could see him working up to something. Finally, he drew breath. "Over the weekend, I've had a lot to think about and the truth is, I've been going along with my head in the clouds." He took a pull from his bottle and stared at her long and hard.

"What do you mean, head in the clouds?" Janet said, although she had a good idea he was talking about them.

He glanced away and turned back to her. "I'm not going to lie to you. I like you...a lot. Way more than I should," he said.

"And what's wrong with that?" Janet said and frowned.

He gritted his teeth. "Your son. I'm not supposed to get involved with patient's families."

"Oh, please, Andy. If you have something to say, say it," Janet said, setting her glass down and bracing herself.

He looked off again and she saw him take another deep breath. "I've been battling with this since I met you. I kept telling myself, how does this all work? Where I would ever fit in? You come from a different world than I do."

"Meaning?"

"Well, look where you live. You're a famous photographer, have all the comforts of life and have nothing to want for..."

"Don't fool yourself, Andy," Janet snapped. "I have plenty I want for."

"I know—you worry about Nate," he said conceding the point. "But..."

She leaned over the table and grasped his hand. "Look at me. If you're worried about the money or your lack thereof, think again. I don't care about money. I care about you!"

"I see," he said, pulling his hand away. "Okay, for the sake of argument, tell me this," he said as his knuckles whitened from his grip on the beer bottle. "What happens if we become more than just friends, hmm...what then? I have nothing to offer. What am I supposed to do? Just move in and live in a house your husband built? Pretend it doesn't bother me?"

She blinked. Up until now she hadn't thought that far ahead. Suddenly, she found herself grasping for an answer. "Why do we have to solve that right now?"

He knitted his brow. "Because, damn it, I'm in love with you!"

The words clanged in her ears and she opened her mouth dumbfounded. *How did I miss all the signs?*

He lowered his voice. "Janet, I can't deal with you deciding at some point I'm not worth it and still be able to deal with the mess my life is in!" He gulped his beer down, peeled a ten from his wallet and throwing it on the table, got up. For a moment, he gazed at her with longing in his eyes, as if wishing things could be different. At last, he said, "I'm sorry, I can't do this right now," then marched out.

Holy crap, he's in love with me. Janet shook her head as she pulled into her driveway. Suddenly everything had forever changed between them. She sat in her car, remembering him saying the fated words then throwing the twenty dollar bill on the table and stalking out. Yet, as quickly as things had changed, she wondered if they were over before they even had a chance to begin. *But he loves me…really?* She couldn't get over it and bit her lip as her heart thrummed. It wasn't something she was prepared for and it was forcing her to rethink her own feelings.

Well, how do I feel about him? I like him…okay, a lot. But do I love him?

She sighed and turning the car off, got out. Seeing Megan's car parked in the turnaround, her walls shot up. The last thing she wanted was to be interrogated on why she was home so soon.

Megan sauntered out from the kitchen with a dishtowel in hand as Janet shut the front door behind her. "You're home!" she said. "I thought you were having lunch."

"No, just a drink. He's got a lot going on right now," Janet said, hoping her tone wasn't betraying her.

"Oh…So, I take it things went okay with the trial," Megan said wiping her hands.

Janet hesitated. "Not really."

"He lost!" Megan's eyes widened and her mouth fell open.

"Yeah."

"He's gonna appeal, right?" Megan said as if it was a foregone conclusion.

Janet slipped past her on her way to the kitchen. "Don't know."

"What do you mean, you don't know?" Megan said, following her.

"Just what I said. He didn't say and I didn't ask," Janet snipped. Suddenly, she needed space and air so she pulled the sliding glass door back and went out onto the deck.

Again, Megan followed and behind her, came Cleo. The dog lumbered over and stood between them at the railing. Megan said, "Are you okay? Talk to me."

From the corner of her eye, Janet saw Megan watching her. "Not now, Meg, okay?"

"Yeah, sure," Megan said. She pinned her hands on the railing and for several minutes they stood in awkward silence looking out at the backyard. Finally, Megan said, "Trevor called while you were out this afternoon, asking if you were around. Seems we're invited to a surprise birthday party for Nadia on Friday."

"That's nice," Janet said, glad for the change of subject. "Should be fun."

Megan shrugged. "Maybe."

Janet turned to her, suddenly confused. She'd been under the impression Megan had been getting along with her brother. "Maybe what?"

Megan said, "I'm trying, but it isn't easy. You don't simply forget some things."

Cleo stirred beside them. As the sound of his tags jingled below, Janet searched Megan's faraway gaze and tried to find the right words. "No one's asking you to forget, Meg. But people say and do things when they're in bad places they regret later on. Don't let what happened so long ago keep you apart."

Megan turned to her. "Are you talking about your father now?"

"Actually, my mom, but it bled onto my father," Janet said.

"Your mom? What happened?"

Janet blinked. *Didn't I ever tell her?* She dug back into her memory and to her surprise, realized she hadn't. "My mom had an affair when she was married to my father. And I was...well, the product of it."

Megan stared back, seeming unable to wrap her head around what Janet said. "Oh my God...Wait, you told me your mom and dad didn't divorce 'til you were thirteen. So, are you saying he thought you were his daughter all the time?"

"No, he knew from day one."

"Holy shit," Megan said and let out a big sigh.

"Anyway, it became the big family secret, kept hush, hush from me."

"When did you find out?" Megan said shaking her head.

Cleo stirred again, leaning heavily against Janet's leg. She nudged the dog to the side and motioned for him to sit. "A year after I met your father."

Megan blinked again and for the first time Janet could remember, the woman was speechless. Any other time, she would've laughed, but not now. She stared out over the yard, watching the birds visit the feeder and said, "All my life, I wondered why he held me at arm's length, making me feel like I wasn't good enough, no matter what I did. All I knew was the dance of anger we were in, constantly hurting each other until it was almost too late. I hate to think what I would've missed if I hadn't let go of how I felt."

She felt Megan's hand cover her fingers as she gripped the rail. "I'm so sorry you went through all that," Megan said.

"Don't be," Janet said, turning her head and eyeing her best friend. "For better or worse, it taught me to look deeper into the wounds and start the real healing. You have a chance with your brother...right now. Talk to him, listen to each other."

Megan nodded and looked off over the yard. At last, she said, "I loved my brother, Janet. I looked up to him. Hell, I idolized him. I just felt so betrayed. I mean, how could he walk away from Dad and me like that?'

"I don't know. It hurts when people you love walk out on you," she said and waited to see what Megan would say back.

"My father loved him more than anything."

There it was at long last: the truth! Janet put her arm around her stepdaughter and best friend. "Your father loved you very much. You were never second best to anyone in his heart: believe that!"

"How'd you know I felt that way?" Megan said barely above a whisper.

Janet shrugged. "A guess,"

Megan looked up and studied her a long time. "You really do get me, you know that?"

"Some of you, not all," Janet said, and grinned.

"I love you," Megan said, leaning in closer. "You know, I haven't asked you if you'd be my Maid of Honor. Would you?"

Janet tightened her arms around her. "Why, of course."

"Good, because there's no one else in the world I want beside me." She smiled and looked upward. "I think I just felt a raindrop. We better get in."

"Yes, let's. Cleo, come boy."

The dog scrambled to his feet and yawned. As they all walked inside, Megan said, "How about we have a girl's night in, throw a sappy movie on, get drunk and order a pizza?"

"What a great idea," she said. "And maybe chocolate ice cream and cake for dessert?"

"Yikes. You wicked thing! I have a wedding dress to get into, girl-friend," Megan said, cuffing her on the arm.

Janet snickered as she dug in the cabinet drawer for Jumpin' Johnny's takeout menu. "It's three months away, Meg, and I'm sure you can get Ben to work an extra pound or two off you." She hesitated then with a smirk, added, "Just don't whittle him down to nothing. As it is, you're running the poor boy ragged. You really should consider getting yourself one of those rabbit things."

Megan's jaw dropped and her eyes almost popped out of her head. She broke out in raucous laughter, then said, "Oh, my God. Did you just say that?"

Janet tossed her a saucy grin. "I think I just did."

Chapter 26

ANDY BLEW out a breath, shoved his hands in his pockets and felt his shoulders sag as he turned and headed back to the store. He said the words: actually he blurted them out. Why? Did he really mean them? He thought about that as he went and as he did so, the memory of the hike to Morgan Lake with Janet flashed before him, giving him a glimpse of how things could be if only... what? *Get over it*, he reprimanded himself as he walked with his head down, ignoring the sounds of the busy city street.

At length, he came to McNamara's. Stopping, he peered up at the canopy with his name scrolled across it in big block letters, wistful of the plans and dreams he'd made. They were being washed away now in the foaming tide of an impermanent life and taken back out to sea. He glanced at the front door then went in. Amanda looked up from bussing a table as the door shut behind him. Mercifully, she hadn't badgered him about trying to appeal the verdict.

"That was a quick lunch," she said passing by him with a stack of dishes.

"Wasn't very hungry. Mail here yet?"

She nodded at the front counter. "Over by the register."

He strode over and picked it up. Going through it, he said, "You cancel the Harper Collins order yet?"

"This morning, yes."

"Good. When Tyler comes in at four, I'll get him started helping Jonah with repacks."

She put her hands on hips and frowned. "I think you're overreacting Bruddy. You don't know how things are going to pan out until we talk to Ed, who by the way, called while you were out."

"What about?" Andy said, looking up from separating junk mail and setting it aside.

"I imagine our next steps," she said, and turned away to start loading the dishwasher.

"Next steps indeed," he muttered and went to his office. After he booted up his desktop, he sat staring off at the picture of Toad, Matt, Bob and him down at the station. It was taken five years ago after they were all awarded a medal for valor for going above and beyond in risking their lives to save a family in an apartment fire. It seemed an age ago when life was good. He heard a knock on the door and looked over to find Jonah filling the doorway. The man's arms were crossed over his chest and his intense blue eyes were drilling into him.

"Mind if I come in?"

He motioned Jonah forward as he opened his email account. "What's up?"

"I heard about the verdict. You okay?"

"No, not really, but I guess that's the way it goes. Sometimes, you win and sometimes you lose," Andy said, scrolling down and deleting junk mail.

Jonah was quiet a moment then said, "What're you going to do?"

Andy looked up, wondering what part of the verdict Jonah didn't understand. "Well, I thought I might have a going out of business sale."

"So you're giving up just like that?"

"Umm... well, unless money starts falling out of the sky like manna from heaven, I don't see as I have much choice."

"I don't think your sister shares that sentiment."

"Yeah," Andy said, drawing out the word. "Well, she's more optimistic than I am at the moment." Jonah leaned back and there was judgment in his gaze. Andy bristled. "What?"

"Nothing. I'm just wondering where the man I thought I knew suddenly went. The Andy who badgered me into coming here to work for him would be fighting tooth and nail right now."

Andy leaned forward. "It's out of my hands, Jonah!" he said louder than he intended. "I'm wiped out. Broke. Finished!"

Jonah was quiet a moment and Andy could sense he was in for a carpet-bombing. Finally, he said, "I'm sorry, but you don't know what finished feels like, or maybe you do and you've just forgotten." He uncrossed his arms, got up and pinned the palms of his hands on Andy's desk. Leaning forward, the old veteran hardened his withered face. "Let me give you a newsflash. Having things out of your hands is coming back from defending your country and not being able to find a job because you're a baby killer or a murderer. Things are out of your hands when you don't have anybody you can stay with when you lose your home, so you end up sleeping on the streets.

"You ever wake up soaked to the bone, freezing your ass off in an alley? You ever wonder where you're going to get your next meal; whether you're going to be rolled in the night or where you're going to go to the toilet day in and day out? You ever feel repulsed by your own reflection and stink? You ever been walked over, walked on, walked away from and shit on by people who'd just as soon you go someplace else and die?"

Andy shrugged. There was nothing to say.

Jonah straightened up and nodded. "Yeah...I thought so." He softened his voice, eyed Andy companionably. "People think I gave up. I never gave up. I just worked on surviving. We're Marines and Marines never give up, so man up!" he said, with all the force of a seasoned drill Sergeant. "You have a family, and friends, remember that! That's more than I ever had when I came back. You remember 'Nam, right?"

Andy nodded. "Yeah, I do."

"Good. Then you remember when you didn't know from one day to the next whether you're going to be going home in a body bag. What kept you going then? Ask yourself that. If you can answer it, then you know what to do.

"You got people here who want to help and you're just shoving them away! You cannot win this war by yourself," Jonah said, stressing the words. "Let people step up, do what they can." He drew back and regarded him a moment with a wait-and-see-expression. When Andy nodded, Jonah softened the harsh lines in his face. "No shame in taking a hand up, Marine," he said and walked out.

After the man left, Andy sighed. It had been years since anyone had dressed him down like that and while the man had shown him no disrespect, Andy had felt small under Jonah's watchful eyes. He looked off, considering all the man had said. Jonah was right: it was time to fight.

He got up and closed the door, turning Jonah's words over in his head. What would the Andy of the 'Nam years do right now? He couldn't change the verdict, but he could throw up a Hail Mary and see what happens. He gritted his teeth and picked up the phone. As it rang on the other end, he brought up his bank's website.

"Reynolds and Rossi, may I help you?"

"Hi Nancy, Andy here returning Ed's call," he said, bringing up McNamara's bank balance. At the moment, it sat at just over $64,000.

"Hold on, let me find him," she said and put him on hold. A minute later, Ed picked up. "Hey Andy, how you doing?"

"Okay, considering."

Ed was quiet on the other line for a minute.

Andy went on, "You called. I assume you're trying to schedule a meeting to decide our next steps."

"As a matter of fact I was," Ed said.

"Good, the sooner the better. Whatever I can do to keep my store, I'll do it."

Ed cleared his throat on the other end. "Well, I'm already ahead of you there. There's a petition I'm working on to ask the court to structure the award so it doesn't bankrupt you if all else fails."

Andy sat forward. "You can do that?"

"Yeah, sure, providing there's compelling reasons and you can show need."

"Why didn't I know this before?" Andy said.

There was a long pause. "I thought I mentioned it."

"I don't think so," Andy said, trying hard to keep his hopes in check. "No matter, when can we meet?"

"How 'bout tomorrow morning at my office, say around ten?"

"That works," Andy said. "See you then."

Andy spent the rest of the afternoon doing inventory and tallying up values for fixtures and equipment just in case Ed was wrong and the judge refused to restructure the award. As for the appeal, where would he get the money for that? While he had known Ed since high school and had attended his kid's birthday and graduation parties, he didn't work for free, and Andy wasn't about to start asking him to.

Tyler poked his head around one of the book stacks. "I'm out, Mr. McNamara, unless there's something else you need me to do."

Andy glanced at his watch. It was near nine o'clock. He rubbed the back of his neck and set his clipboard down on the shelf beside him. "No, you go on home, Ty. I'll need you here right after school tomorrow though."

"Okay, see you then," Tyler said, and shuffled off to the front door.

Andy watched him go then collected his clipboard and headed to his office. As he walked out between the stacks, he saw Jonah tying a bag of trash by the front counter. "Front end's put to bed," the man said, looking up. "You about finished tallying? I'm hungry."

"Yeah, I'm wrapped. Let's get out of here," Andy said. He went in his office, shut his computer down and tossed his clipboard on the file cabinet. As he followed Jonah out the front door, he paused and panned the darkened store, drank in the shadowed shelves, the tables stacked with books, the empty chairs sitting around the fireplace.

"You're bouncing around a little bit better," Jonah said.

Andy glanced at him. "Yeah...I am," he said following the man out into the cool evening air. As he locked up, he felt Jonah's gaze on him. He turned and saw him lighting up a smoke. "Thanks for kicking my ass today."

The man shrugged. "Don't mention it. Just don't give up."

"Not planning on it. Okay, let's get some chow and I'll take you home."

They stopped at Trent's and went in for a burger and a beer. Being a Monday night, the bar was quiet. Andy panned the darkened room. The usual crowd: Roy, Don-Don, Whiggins, Johnson, Sanders, Beckett were all there, lined up down the bar like so many sparrows on a wire, all in their faded denims and embroidered baseball hats. They all looked up when Andy and Jonah pulled out stools then went back to their beers.

Andy crossed his arms on the bar, leaned forward and signaled Trent. The owner was a big man, built like a spark plug. A thick gray beard and mustache wrapped around a large round face. Friendly green eyes peered out from under bushy gray brows. A balding head glistened under the overhead lights.

"Hey Mac, Jonah," the man said, lumbering over. "What'll it be?"

"A couple burgers and Molson's to go with 'em," Andy said, slapping a twenty on the bar.

Trent looked at his watch and pressed his lips together. "It's 9:30 Mac. Help's gone home. I can order in a pizza if ya want."

Andy turned to Jonah. "What do ya think?"

Jonah shrugged. "Pizza's fine."

"Pizza it is then," Andy said and ordered them a medium pie with the works, less the fish. After Trent called it in, the man set them up with a couple tall beers and chatted them up about the local politics and what they had going on in their lives, which Andy kept a tight lid on.

When Trent left them alone, Jonah said, "So, what's the deal with the store?"

Andy sat back. "Well, I called my lawyer and apparently, if the appeal dies, the award to the Stewarts can be structured.

"What's that mean?"

"It means I can keep the store, and my house, providing I show need. Still have to get the blessings of the judge though."

"And what's your gut tell you about that?" Jonah said, and took a sip of his beer.

Andy shrugged. "I'm cautious, but hopeful."

"So you're still gonna go for the appeal?"

"I guess," Andy said. "Just don't know where I'm gonna get the money for it."

Jonah was quiet and Andy could sense him tossing something over in his mind. Finally, Jonah turned to him, and his penetrating gaze put him on edge. At last, he said, "Hey, I know things are tight, so I've been thinking…maybe it's best I step aside, you know. Besides, I've never been one to put down roots for long and to tell you the truth, I've been feeling a little cramped lately."

Andy drew breath. "Thanks for that, buddy, but I'm not accepting your offer and if you up and leave I will hunt you down. Understand?"

"Huh…what makes you think it's an offer? You work me like a dog and this five days a week shit schedule is affecting my social life."

Andy saw the man fighting to keep a straight face and elbowed him. "Look, if you really need to leave, I won't stop you, but you'll be missed and not just by me. You're like family, and you know I don't say that lightly. But it's up to you." He turned and called down to Trent. "Hit us again!"

Jonah licked his lips and averted his gaze toward the mirror behind the bar as Trent set their beers in front of them. After they were alone again, Jonah said, "Been a long time since I felt a part of anything. Got no family to speak of, no home to go back to. All my old friends have taken to the wind. Wouldn't know where to find 'em if I were to look." He turned back to Andy, searching him with piercing blue eyes that had seen too much. "I don't mind saying I'm grateful, cause I am, but you need to understand, everything I've ever had or wanted has been taken away from me in one fashion or another, so you'll have to excuse me if I'm a bit leery."

Andy nodded. "I know."

Jonah tossed him a lazy smile. "I think you do Mac. Now where the hell is that pie? I'm hungry!"

The meeting with Ed left Andy daring to believe he could weather the financial storm heading his way. He walked into McNamara's feeling cautious but hopeful and headed for his office to pull things together regarding the petition. As he began filling out forms Ed had given him, Matt called him and reminded him of Bob's anniversary. As he wrote down the date and the details, his door creaked back. He held his finger up to his sister and motioned her in.

"So, it's later in the week," Amanda said after he hung up. "Have you made any decisions yet?"

He set his pen down and looked up into her searching blue eyes knowing she was anxious about the future and he couldn't blame her. Having poured in a tidy sum of sweat equity over the last year, she had a stake in the outcome, too. At last, he said, "Matter of fact, I have."

When he didn't elaborate right away, she added, "And?"

"We're going to appeal, and if that doesn't work, Ed says we can petition the court to restructure the award so we can keep the store."

"We can do that?" she said, coming in and sitting down.

"As long as we can prove financial hardship, apparently so."

"Well, I guess that makes sense. I mean, if you lose the store, how can you ever pay the award? Can the Stewart's lawyer reject it? I mean, couldn't they still make you sell the store and your house, and then make payments?"

Andy shook his head. "Ed says it's up to the judge. There'd be restrictions of course."

"Such as?"

"Well, my salary and that of my employees would be capped to cost of living indices. All future profits would have to be disclosed and docked per a percentage to be determined. Also, any loans we take out would need to be approved. That kind of stuff."

"Well, that's something at least. Let's hope the appeal makes it all unnecessary. I'll tell you one thing, once this is all over and done with, you need to have Ed reorganize us and get insurance," she said.

"Us?"

"Yes, us," she said. "I talked with Tuck and we're gonna throw in with you as partners."

The pronouncement dumbfounded him, and he tried to decide how he felt about it. On the one hand, it took away the stress and pressure of trying to make things work all by himself; yet on the other, it felt like he was being rescued. At last he sat back and looked at her hard. "Sounds like I don't have a choice," he said, and his tone sounded edgy even to his own ears.

Her shoulders drew back as if he'd pinned them against her chair. "Of course you have a choice! It's just an offer, Bruddy, and one meant from the heart. Sounds to me like you don't trust me," she fired back.

Now it was his turn to backpedal. He looked away. "Sorry, I was just surprised. And you know I trust you. Has nothing to do with that," he said turning back.

"Hmm...okay," she said, eyeing him thoughtfully. She was quiet a moment then added, "Think about it, then?"

"Of course." But he already knew his answer to it or at least he thought he did.

She nodded and folded her hands together in her lap. "Good. Now, what about the grant? Did you tell Ed about it?"

"Umm...I forgot. I better let him know and see what he says."

"Yeah," she said, widening her eyes. "Cause the check came in. I put it in the safe while you were waiting to see what would happen. I'll keep it there as long as I can. But sooner or later, the corporation counsel will come asking why we haven't cashed it."

"Damn. Let's hope we don't have to give it up. That would hurt," he said

Chapter 27

J ANET SAT at Neil's pilgrim desk, writing checks and paying bills when her cell phone buzzed. She picked it up and when she saw Andy's name flashing on the screen, her heart jumped. *Finally!* It had been a week without a peep from him and despite wanting to answer right away, she let it go to voice mail. Maybe that was childish, but she wasn't going to give him the idea she was waiting by the phone for him. Then again, she felt justified. If he really loved her, he was going to have to prove it. Telling someone you were in love with them was serious business and he hadn't gotten off to a good start in waiting a week before ringing her up.

When the phone buzzed again, letting her know she had a message, she picked it up and listened to Andy's voice asking her if she'd like to go to dinner to 'discuss things' and to call him back when she had a chance. She smiled and decided to give it a couple hours before answering then went back to paying bills. As she wrote a check for her quarterly taxes, she heard a car coming up the driveway. She looked through the office window and saw Megan. She was coming back for another load of boxes full of personal effects and clothes. Megan's move to Ben's was almost done, leaving Janet and Cleo alone, in this giant 3,200 square foot house. Well, she'd done it before and she could do it again.

"I'm back!" Megan cried out from the front foyer.

Janet got up and went out to see if there was anything she could do to help. There wasn't much left: four boxes, a suitcase and a laundry basket full of shoes. Megan grabbed the suitcase and tossed a couple boxes on top as Janet picked up the basket and carried it out. As Janet shut the trunk, Megan went back in and grabbed the remaining boxes. When Megan returned and set them in the car, Janet said, "So, I guess this is it?"

When there was no answer, she turned to see Megan looking upward toward the overcast sky. Her jaw was trembling and her eyes were misty. Finally, Megan seemed to collect herself and taking a deep breath, eyed her and said, "As I was driving back from Ben's, I was thinking about us and all we've been through. Thirty-plus years–think of it, thirty years. That's a long freaking time and you know what: I wouldn't trade one second of it for anyone else but you."

Janet's heart swelled. "You've been my best friend, Meg. More than a best friend."

"I don't know about that," Megan said throwing her arms around Janet. "All I know is that even when I was angry at you, you still loved me." She drew back and wiped her eyes. "Now, you gotta promise me something."

"What's that?"

"That you won't let that sexy Marine get away."

Janet laughed. "I'm working on it."

"Good. Okay, don't forget we have Debbie's shower coming up. Let's go shopping for it."

"Sounds like a plan," Janet said as Megan got in her car. "Okay, you better get going so Ben doesn't worry. And if I find anything you leave behind, I'll box it up and get it to you."

It was late afternoon when Janet shut down the computer and turned the light off in the office. Rousing Cleo, she followed him out to the kitchen and started dinner. As she went about throwing a salad together for herself, her cell buzzed. She picked it up. It was Andy. She smiled. "Hi," she said, straining to keep her tone even and casual.

"Hey, I left a message earlier. Didn't know if you got it."

"Umm...sorry I meant to call you back but Megan was here and I was helping her load her car. She's moving in with her fiancé," she said, rather proud of her quick response.

"No worries. Anyway, I'm sorry I haven't been in touch, but I needed some time to get my head on straight."

"And have you?"

"That's what I'd like to talk about. I was thinking dinner, maybe?"

She sprinkled pine nuts over her salad and set the bowl on the island. "Okay. When?"

"Sometime this weekend?"

She thought about it and while she had the weekend open, she wasn't going jump at his beckon call. "This weekend's not good," she said and was about to make up an excuse before she stopped herself.

He paused, and in the silence she felt him waiting for an explanation, which wasn't going to come. Finally, he said, "Okay, what about sometime next week?"

She sat back and considered. *He waited a week to call me after dropping that bomb on me. He can wait a little while.* "I'm on contract, so I'm going to be busy," she said, which wasn't a lie. She'd landed a new client, Great Adventures, and had a shoot at Jackson Hole planned next week. And the weekend after was Megan's daughter-in-law's wedding shower. "What about sometime the week after next, maybe a Thursday or Friday that week?"

"Oh, okay," he said, and she felt the disappointment in his tone. "I guess Thursday would work. Umm...I had a chat with your son."

"Did you?" she said.

"He's not happy with me."

"We talked about what happened. He feels betrayed and used," Janet said. *I don't believe you'd do that, at least I hope not. That's not the man*

I was falling in love with. "It's gonna take a while for him to warm back up to you."

"I know. I never planned on any of this."

"Well, life's what happens when you're making other plans," she said and stabbed a piece of lettuce. "So, how are things with the store? Nate tells me there's some new plan in how to keep it."

"Yes, if the appeal falls through, I guess I can petition the court to restructure the award in a way I can pay it and still keep the store."

"That's great."

"You're mad at me, aren't you?"

Janet set her fork down. "I'm a bit hurt, Andy, but I'll get over it."

"Because I didn't call."

"Yes. Look, let's not get into this over the phone. It's been a long week and now I have some things to think about."

"You mean about us?"

She crossed her arms. "That's part of it."

There was a pause. At last he said, "You don't mind if I call you, do you?"

Men! Really! "Of course I don't," she said shaking her head. She picked her fork up again. "Hey, I just put dinner on the table. Talk later?"

"Yeah, sure," he said. "I've missed you."

Well you have a funny way of showing it. "Well, thanks. You have a good night." She ended the call and felt a smile come to her face. Yes, she was being prickly, but he deserved to be reminded there was more than just his feelings at stake. If he was going to win her back, he was going to have to earn it.

Janet hauled her camera bag into the kitchen, set it on the table and did a cursory inventory of her equipment while she waited for Nate to show up. He was taking her to the airport to catch her ten o'clock flight to Jackson Hole. As she went through her lenses and filters, Cleo stirred at her feet. He knew she was getting ready to go somewhere. She glanced down at him and saw his sad brown eyes looking up. She wagged a finger at him.

"Mommy's only going to be gone a few days and Nate and Megan will be here to look after you so don't give me that sad face, little man."

The dog swayed his robust body back and forth as his nails clicked and clacked on the tile floor. But when the sound of the front door opening came trickling in from the other room, he burst into a booming bark.

"I'm here, Mom," Nate called.

"Out in the kitchen, honey," she hollered back, checking the battery power on her camera. It was down to seventy-two percent. She looked up, puzzled then remembered she'd used it on her hiking trip with Andy to Morgan Lake. She opened the photo log on the camera and scrolled through the photos as Nate came into the passageway. On the tiny screen were photos of Andy. The one looking back at her right now was of him popping a cork on a bottle of wine with a devilish smile on his face. She smiled as the tender memory scratched her heart then turned the camera off.

"You about ready?" Nate said, as she stuffed the camera in the bag and zipped it shut.

"Just about." She threw the bag's strap over her shoulder, drank in the smile on his fresh washed face and saw the start of a beard on his chin. "You and your razor parting friends?" she said grabbing a granola bar from the counter.

"For a while." He nodded toward her bag. "Want me to get that for you?"

"No, I'm fine. But you can get Cleo in his crate for me."

She watched the two of them amble down the hall then grabbed her carry on and marched out the front door to Nate's car. Throwing her bags in the back seat, her thoughts went to that special day with Andy. A day akin to one so many years ago on a beach she loved. There, on her altar rock that overlooked the mighty gray waters, she'd fallen in love with a man twenty-one years her senior. Though she'd questioned her feelings on that day, and now also for Andy, she knew deep down fate had once again intervened. To what end she didn't know. She couldn't see that far. But she knew in her heart the chapter on Andy was far from over.

"Everything all right?" Nate said, suddenly beside her.

She started and looked up. "Oh, yes. I was just going over my mental list. Making sure I have everything."

He threw her overnight case in the trunk and slammed it shut. "You got your boarding pass?"

"Right here," she said, patting her purse as she slipped into the front seat. As he started off down the driveway, she noticed a bag from Kent's Pharmacy on the console between them.

"I guess Ben's out of town so Meg and I are hanging out tonight. Got anything decent in the fridge or are we ordering out?"

"Just leftover quesadillas and part of a quiche." She eyed the pharmacy bag again. "New medication?"

Nate yawned, grabbed the bag and tossed it in the back seat. "No, same ole, same ole."

She frowned. Having gone through her own bit of hell years ago, she knew the addictive power of Vicodin. "Your leg bothering you again?"

"Not really. But every now and then, it complains. I'm good. Don't worry."

Right. "I'm not. Just be careful with 'em. They're addicting. Last thing you need is to get hooked," she said studying him as he drove. To no surprise, his expression remained as usual: impassive. Whether he was telling the truth or not, she didn't know. But having made a breakthrough with him, she didn't want to press him any further. *A little bit at a time.* "By the way, Cleo has a touch of arthritis so he's getting a couple aspirin in his kibble these days."

He darted a glance at her. "He's getting up there... You going to get another dog after he... you know?"

"I haven't thought about it, really. Probably not... I don't know," she said. Truth be told, she'd been trying to ignore the telltale harbingers of Cleo's twelve years; the white hair spreading up his muzzle, his loss of step and the fact he'd been sleeping a lot more over the last year. But now that Nate had put words and substance to the warning in her heart, the idea of not having Cleo underfoot came hammering home.

"So, I assume you heard they're planning a big to-do about me in town next month. A parade, fireworks, chicken barbeque; the whole nine yards. Even Senator Merkley's coming to town."

"Yeah, I heard. Are you okay?"

"Gonna have to be, I guess. Don't have much choice," he muttered. "I just wish this would all go away."

"I know. Is there anything I can do for you?"

"Don't think so, but thanks."

Silence filled the space around them making it difficult to breathe. She'd been turning an idea over in her mind the last week. *Should I bring it up?* She thought about it a moment, then gathered her courage and said, "You know, I've been thinking about the medal."

"Have you?" he said, glancing back.

She appraised the lifted brow over his eyes. "You said Kendall was the guy who stood up fighting, right?"

"Yeah," he replied, and she felt the suspicion in his tone.

She took a deep breath. "What if you gave the medal to his parents? You know, privately, then tell them what he did," she said and waited to see his reaction.

He stared ahead for several minutes, his freckled face void of all expression as the rolling fields slipped past their windows. Finally, he nodded. "Maybe."

"No one would need to know," she added.

He turned the radio on to a local country music channel. "So, what do you think of Ben?"

Okay, I guess that ends that for the time being. But at least he didn't say no. "He's nice. I like him," she said. "You?"

"Nice to see Meg happy after her living in the dumper for so long. She deserves something good for once," he said as the road veered east. He flipped the sun visor down. "I have a question."

"What's that?"

244

He cleared his throat. "What's up with Trev and Meg?"

"What do you mean?"

"Well, it's pretty clear Meg's had a beef with Trev over the years. You know what that's all about?"

Dumbfounded, she looked at him. How could he not know? Certainly, Megan must've said something to him by now. Then again, he'd taken a liking to his half-brother after they met, so maybe not. And Trevor didn't dish on people, especially family. At last, she said, "You never asked her?"

He shook his head. "Figured it wasn't my business."

"Well, maybe. But I don't think she'd object to you asking her now," she said and wondered, what it was with her family and secrets?

Chapter 28

ANDY GRABBED his keys off the kitchen hook and opened the back door, letting Jack spring ahead of him. Today was Bob Lightfoot's twenty-fifth anniversary party and as his friend and partner for most of those years, he wanted to be there. Yet, part of him felt like a traitor and he was reluctant and nervous. Seeing the old gang again, brothers and sisters in arms he'd left for another life, left a sour taste in his gut. They'd all gone through so much together, knew things about each other no one else knew: private, personal things about marriages and children–things that required trust! And he'd let them down and what was worse had abandoned them. It had been over a year now since he'd walked into the station that had been his home away from home.

He steeled himself, started the car and pulled out of the driveway for the ninety-minute ride to the coast. Most of the drive would be in and out of the rain. Well, that was all right with him. His injured brain preferred dull gray clouds over blinding, blue skies.

He turned the radio on and an hour later, veered onto Rte. 101 toward Lincoln City. As he drove along the winding highway skirting the ocean, he saw whitecaps rolling in off the gray waters. Even though he'd been away from the coast for only a few months, it felt like a lifetime. There was so much that had shaped his life here; the local auditorium where he used to hang out as a kid listening to the local bands reeling off tunes by Bob Dylan, the Stones and the Beatles. And then there were late night beach parties around campfires, basketball at the high school gym and sandlot football in open fields.

Last of all were the people of Lincoln City, people he grew up with and knew most of his life. They were good folk, stout and sturdy, hard-working and always offering a hand to those they knew. It was a place where folks understood the need to pull together and help each other in hard times. It was home, and always would be despite his new life in Salem.

He pulled into the station lot and watched those who'd just arrived hustle from their cars to the front doors to get out of the rain. Engine number 1400 and Ladder 1402 were parked outside, along with Rescue Trucks 1404 and 1405. Notably absent was Truck 1406: his truck. He sucked his lip and sat in his Suburban, needing time to gather his courage to rejoin a family he was no longer part of. Finally, he pulled the keys from the ignition and got out with Jack trailing behind. The dog looked up at him, as if to say, 'I'm getting wet, let's go!'

A minute later, he stepped into the warmth and cacophony of the crowds milling around in the truckless garage bays. The large cavernous space had been set up with tables and an impromptu stage decorated with dark green ribbons. A life-size picture of Bob was tacked to the south wall and over it was a banner with the words, 'Twenty-Five Years of Service'. Twelve empty folding chairs were lined up below it on the stage.

Suddenly, a voice boomed out from the crowd calling his name. It was Dan Rebbet. The barrel-chested man with curly blond hair was built like a fireplug and had the appetite of an orca. He came marching toward him wearing a thick, red and black hunting shirt. "Hey Andy, how the hell are ya and where ya been?"

Andy shook Dan's thick, puffy hand. "Busier than a one-armed paper hanger," he said, giving the man a good look. "You've dropped some weight."

Dan shrugged. "The wife has me on some low carb shit."

Andy nodded toward the hot dog in Dan's other hand. It was loaded with the works. "I don't think that's on it." They both laughed. "Nice crowd. Where's the man of the hour?"

"Over there, talking with Matt and Cap. And who's this little guy here?" Dan said, looking down at the dog pawing Andy's leg.

"This here's Jack, my new partner."

Dan crouched down and ran a hand over Jack's back. "Cute little feller." He looked up at Andy and winked. "Better watch out, once Tammy sees him, she'll try and steal him away. Anyway, let's get you a beer." He stood and they drifted over to the beverage table where a couple of volunteers were pouring drafts from a keg. As Andy took a cup, Dan said, "I heard about the lawsuit. How ya doing?"

Andy shrugged. "Getting by. We're going to appeal."

"I heard. It'll be all right. You were doing your job; they'll see it eventually," Dan said, patting Andy's shoulder. The man grabbed a soda off the table as Andy's old firefighting partner, Eric, walked up wearing a standard issue flame retardant vest.

"Hey, Mac. Wondered if I'd see you."

"Couldn't keep me away," Andy said. "How's Martha and the kids?"

Eric grabbed a soda off the table and took a sip. "Doing fine."

Dan piped up, and jabbing Eric, said, "The old man here's gonna be a grandpa."

"You don't say," Andy said, surprised. "Congratulations. I assume it's Shelly, right?"

"Oh, God, yes," Eric said. "Don't even want to think about it being Mary. I'd slit my wrists." He chuckled as more of the crew came over and joined them. Among them was Tammy, a short redheaded, spunky EMT who ruled the roost: as she liked to call it. She dropped to a knee to pet Jack and was rewarded with a tongue washing to her neck and chin. Next to her was Marc. He'd joined the station a couple years ago and quickly endeared himself to all with his culinary skills.

On the other side of Tammy, stood Jean who was shooting dagger glances at Andy. There were those in the station who'd supported Andy after the accident, and then there was Jean. Then again, she was

Bob's wife and there'd been no secret she blamed her husband's injuries on Andy's carelessness. She pasted a smile on her large, round face as Bob showed up with the District Chief, Matt Fuller and Captain Alexander.

Bob wrapped his arm around Andy's shoulder and gave him a squeeze. Quiet, watchful and powerfully built, the son of a Nez Perse tribal elder exchanged a knowing glance with Andy and smiled. "Where's that attractive woman I saw you with at the courthouse? She someone new?"

"No, just a friend," Andy said, taken aback. He looked away wondering how Bob knew about her, then remembered she'd been there the day he'd testified. *He must have seen her sitting with Amanda and put two and two together.* Suddenly, Janet's face flashed before him, and it struck him hard in the gut. He forced a smile and turned back to his friends just as Bob's pager went off. Then so did Jason's, Dan's, Marc's and Jean's. They all looked at each other as the truck bay speakers brayed:

BEEP-BEEP-BEEP-BEEP
LINCOLN CITY FIRE, STATION 1400, STRUCTURE FIRE, BARN FIRE, 4208 ANDERSON CREEK ROAD, NEAR CROSS STREET OF SOUTH SCHOONER CREEK ROAD, TIME OUT, 14:48

Dan frowned. "Damn."

"Hey, isn't that Jonesy's Farm?" Andy said.

Matt nodded. "Sure is." He turned to Cap and kept his voice low. "That barn is full of hay if I remember right."

"And close to his propane tanks," Eric piped in. "If they go up…"

"Yeah," Cap said.

"Okay guys, grab your gear and let's saddle up," Matt said as the overhead doors rose. He drained his soda and crushed his paper cup. "Let's hope the rain gives a hand."

As the fire and rescue trucks pulled onto the highway with sirens blaring, Andy turned and melted into the crowd. Once again, the life of a fire and rescue responder intervened and while they'd all gotten used to it, there were certain times it was harder to take than others. He sighed, feeling bad for Bob, but in truth he felt disappointed. All his friends were gone; left him to be a stranger in a place he'd called home for years. He drifted in and out of conversations until at last he found himself by the front door watching a group of retired firefighters playing cards while listening to a two-way radio. Among them were Bags and Paddy, Woody and Trapper. As they slurped their coffees, they chattered about the local election for mayor.

"Hey Mac, you okay?"

He started and turned to find Tammy leaning against the wall beside him, staring back with arms crossed over her chest. "Yeah, I'm good," he lied.

"You sure? I heard about the trial. Sucks!" She shook her head and looked upward. "You know, there was a time when duty called and you just went because saving lives was what mattered. Now it's all about protocols and covering ass. Fatigue impaired, yeah, right. It's all bullshit. We could do sixteen hours standing on our heads."

While he appreciated her sentiment, he really didn't want to talk about the trial so he looked back off to the old men playing cards.

"Don't mind me and my big mouth," she said, laying her hand on his shoulder. She paused. "Why don't you join them?"

Why not? Got no place to be. He reached up, squeezed her hand and shuffled over to the table. "Hey, have room for another?"

The old men looked up. "Hey, Mac, sure have a seat," they said, making room for him.

Bags fanned his cards out in front of him and said, "I bid three."

"Pah!" Paddy growled and set his cards down. "Come on with ya then."

Bags threw out an ace of hearts, smiled and gave Andy a glimpse of his hand. A definite three bid.

Andy looked on as Bags swept the hand and tallied up the score. "Your deal Woody," he said then looked at Andy. "So, word has it you're working rescue operations up north."

How did he find out about me rescuing that old man? "Not much gets past you does it, Bags?" Andy said, suppressing a smile.

Paddy said. "What rescue operation?"

Bags cocked an eye. "Paddy, you really need to come out from that cave you live in." Then went on filling the men in on Andy's heroics up in Salem. As he came to the end, Tammy called everyone's attention to the small flat TV screen mounted to the wall at the back of the truck bays. A weather radar map of the state showed a sickle shaped green band with red blotches indicating severe thunderstorm activity approaching the coast. Scrolling across the bottom of the screen was a line of text within a thin yellow banner. As he moved closer to the screen, Tammy turned the volume up and a man's voice rang throughout the station:

"...*Yes, Tom, we're keeping a close watch on this band of thunderstorms that have been growing in intensity over the last four hours. If we can zoom in and look at the radar here, we see a powerful spiraling updraft at the leading edge. This is what's known as a mesocyclone. And here, at the rear of the storm, we have several small red ameba-like areas in the shape of a hook. This is all indicative of a super-cell thunderstorm, meaning high, gale force winds, hail and torrential rains. Right now, the leading band of this fast moving storm is about two hundred miles off shore and at its current speed and direction, we predict it will make landfall just south of Lincoln City around 8:45 tonight. Residents along the shore are advised to...*"

Andy glanced around at the knitted brows and slack-jaw expressions looking on. With the majority of the station out at Jonesy's Farm along with those from Station 1500, the remaining forces left to protect the city would be overrun if the storm slammed into them full force.

Tammy sidled up next to him and said, "Let's keep our fingers crossed things don't turn into a major C-F."

"Yeah, let's," he said, as his gut knotted. He pulled her aside and lowered his voice. "Can you set me up with a few odds and ends just in case?"

She pursed her lips and put her hands on her hips. "Like what?"

"Flares, rope, spinal board, trauma kit, you know...standard gear."

"Flares, harnesses and rope I can do, but the rest..." She shook her head. "No way, and you know better than to ask."

He bit his lip. "Okay, whatever you can give me then. First of all, we better get folks to safety. Get ahold of the Catholic Church down the road. They have a large basement that could be used as a shelter if need be. In the meantime, I'll get folks moving."

Once the crowd had been dispersed, Andy and the remaining crew settled in for the oncoming storm. There really wasn't much they could do other than wait it out and hope things didn't go all to hell, especially for those who were out at Jonesy's farm battling the fire. He looked on while Tammy checked in with Matt on her cell, giving him the latest weather updates. The supercell was ten miles off shore and picking up steam. By the time it made landfall, wind gusts could reach up to a hundred miles per hour. As of right now, they were in the middle of a torrential downpour.

He glanced up, listening to the rain and hail thundering down on the roof as the overhead lights flickered. A minute later, they went out and a loud bang-bang-bang pounded one of the overhead doors, prompting Jack into a fit of barking. Tammy called the dog and pulled him into her arms as the darkened world outside their garage door windows lit up bright as day. For what seemed like forever, the men and women of Station 1400 sat in darkness until the generator kicked on. But the returning light only seemed to piss the storm off, and it slammed the station with everything it had.

Ten minutes later, the bay doors were shuddering and flexing in their frames. Tammy shot Andy a knowing glance and called to him. "We need to get out of here. Any suggestions?"

Andy thought hard. "We could try the Supply Room," he yelled back as a loud pop-pop-pop strafed the air. The bottom three panels of the main overhead door blowing out into the inky darkness made their decision for them. As they ran to the back of the garage amid the hurling debris and trash flying around in all direction, Andy saw Paddy on his knees. "Paddy, Paddy, you all right?"

The man nodded and pointed toward the back of the room to where Woody was splayed on the concrete floor. One of the two rookie EMT's was hunkered over him as another deafening pop-pop-pop reverberated in the garage. Andy glanced back to see the remainder of the door rip away and disappear into the ravenous night. In its wake, a sheet of rain and hail rushed in, flogging everything in its path. He struggled to his feet and helped Paddy up, then staggered to the back of the garage as a bolt of lightning lit up the blackened night. A shower of sparks sprayed the concrete apron in front of the abandoned bay door opening. The generator sputtered and a moment later, everyone was in pitch darkness.

You've got to be kidding me! Andy thought as another bolt of lightning lit up the world. He handed Paddy off to Tammy who was waiting in the alcove next to the supply room and caught a whiff of burning oil. "Get him inside and dig out the flashlights."

"Stay here, I'll send Rick out to give you and Marty a hand," she yelled over the howling wind.

Suddenly the world outside lit up bright as day and for what felt like minutes to Andy, the dark of night was held back. Finally, the rookie came rushing out with his head bent down low and handed Andy a flashlight. As Andy took it, he suddenly remembered Jack. *Oh, my God, where is he?* He shot a panicked glance around the ongoing disaster surrounding them. The last time he'd seen him was when he was in Tammy's arms. But that was before everything went to hell. He grabbed the rookie's arm. "Where's my dog?"

The kid jerked his thumb back toward the supply room.

Andy's heart beat again and he let out a breath. "Thanks...Rick, right?"

The kid nodded.

"Okay, let's go get 'em," he shouted, turning back into the wind. But walking was near impossible against the powerful gusts sweeping into the garage. A folding chair sailed past his head and crashed against the wall, missing him by inches. He took the hint Mother Nature was sending him and dropped down into a crawl. When he came upon the other rookie, he said, "How bad?"

The kid looked up as another chair hurtled over their heads, missing them by inches. As it scraped across the concrete floor, he called back, "Concussion. He's out of it pretty good."

"We got to get him out of here," Andy shouted as Rick crawled up beside them. A loud screech pierced the air and when Andy looked up to see a thousand pound plus tool chest sliding across the garage bay floor, he knew it was time to get the hell out of there. "Here, take his arm, and I'll get the other. Rick you get his feet."

The kid hesitated. "Shouldn't we get a board?"

"Don't have time," Andy cried back as a sudden stream of rain poured down from above. He looked up and felt his heart stop again as he saw the metal roof deck getting peeled back from the joists. *Shit! No time to argue.* "Go, go, go!"

The men shoved their arms under the old man and dragged him out from under the failing roof as the large ventilation unit leaned into the opening and came crashing down. The rookies glanced back then looked at Andy with startled faces.

"That was fucking close. Holy shit!" Rick cried.

But Andy's attention was drawn to the natural gas line that was crimped and hanging down into the garage. If it was ruptured and lightning hit the station, it was going to get a lot worse. Was the supply room going to be a tomb? He didn't know, but it was better than where they were right now. He pointed back to the heavy metal door Tammy was standing next to with a flashlight in her hand. "Let's go!"

For the next thirty minutes, Andy and the men and women of Station 1400 huddled in the dark supply room hoping against hope it wasn't their time as the storm battered the station. Then, at last, they heard only the reverberating rat-a-tat-tat of rain pelting the roof. The raging wind and booming thunder had seemingly moved on, but in its wake it had rendered the station useless. Andy went to the door with Rick and

Marty, opened it and shined the light of his flashlight around. In the murky darkness, the garage bays took on the appearance of a sunken ship. Trash and debris, equipment and tools, and chunks of building were strewn about as if a bomb had gone off.

Andy sniffed the air and turned to Rick and Marty. "I'm not sure if that gas line is compromised, so whatever you do, keep your cell phones off until you're well away from the building."

Rick said, "We have a sniffer here."

Andy looked at him and then waved his hand toward the disaster outside the door. "Ummm...yeah. Where?" When Rick shrugged, Andy continued, "Right. Okay, I'm gonna go shut the gas off now, but in the meantime, I need you guys to get everyone out and I don't think I need to emphasize the words; be careful."

He went back to Tammy who was applying a dressing to Woody's head with assistance from Paddy, who was directing the beam of a flashlight on the affected area. The old man, who'd come to shortly after they got in the room, winced. Andy looked the old man in the eye and said to Tammy, "How's he doing? Can he walk?"

"He has a nasty gash on the back of his head. I've managed to stitch it up and get a dressing on it, but he needs to be seen by a doctor."

"Yeah. Hopefully we have hospital left."

"Hopefully, we have a vehicle to get him there," Tammy said. "I need to get a hold of someone."

"Not until you're well away from the building or you could get there before any of us," Andy said. "I'm going to go turn off the gas. I told Rick and Marty to help you guys get out of the building. I'll be out shortly, now go!"

The gas service was located in the Furnace Room. He panned the beam of his flashlight around the truck bay, drew a deep breath and caught a whiff of mercaptan. *Damn! This just keeps getting better.* He looked up. *Anything else You want to throw at me?* With the blown out openings letting in outside air, the gas concentrations were likely teetering toward instability. A downed electric conduit hung in front of the alcove leading to the service quarters. *Now would not be a good time for you to come alive,* he thought, skirting around the debris and scattered equipment.

When he reached the alcove, he turned and watched the silhouetted refugees make their way out of the building. When everyone was out, he put his hand on the knob and closed his eyes. "Okay, big Guy, I guess it's all up to you now," he muttered, and pulled the door open a crack. As he pushed it back, he held his breath, hoping the added fresh air wouldn't tip the balance and send him to St. Peter in a billion pieces.

But God shined on him, so with care he stepped in and pushed the door shut behind him. Barring any unforeseen catastrophe, from here on out it would be a matter of choking off the gas supply and leaving through the back service door. He picked his way through the dark, wet room, not counting on anything being that easy, and when he came to the gas shut off, he wasn't disappointed. For some unfathomable reason, the dedicated shut-off pipe wrench was missing. Playing his light over the room, he hunted for it and came up empty. Where was it?

Dumbfounded, he ran his hand through his hair. "Just great!" He contemplated going back out into the truck bays to look for it, but the one thing he didn't have right now was time. With the gas concentrations rising in the garage there was no telling when it could be set off, and as much as he hated the thought of the station going up in an explosion, it wasn't worth dying for. Sighing, he went for the rear exit door, but when he tried to open it, it wouldn't budge more than a couple inches despite his throwing his shoulder into it. He shined his light out the crack of the door and saw a waving jagged branch on the other side. The storm had dropped the large sugar maple behind the station against the back wall.

He pushed on the door again, but it wouldn't move. He looked up and shook his fist. "Will You give me a fucking break here, just once!" he growled. As if to stick His finger up at him, the scent of mercaptan wrinkled his nose. He was trapped with only one-way out: and that was through the midst of the living bomb. Reluctantly, he walked back to the interior door leading to the garage and as he put his hand on the knob, his heart pounded. But there was no second-guessing it. He could open it, and take his chances, or stay and die.

Turning his head away, he closed his eyes, turned the knob and pulled the door back. As he did so, the pungent sulfuric odor wafting in the room hit him square in the face. One wrong move creating a static condition or the tiniest of sparks would level the building and everything around it for a hundred feet in every direction. He swallowed and as he started picking his way past the wreckage and debris, he saw smoke then a burst of flames rise from the house across the street.

Suddenly, his brain screamed, *"Run"* and he bolted through the opening out into the night, and as he ran, felt the ground shake behind him before launching him into the air.

Chapter 29

J ANET PULLED up in front of Kyle's house in the south side of Portland and parked. It had been a long time since there was a wedding in the Porter clan, let alone two in the same year–a mere three months apart, no less. The next hundred plus days were going to be a blur helping Megan keep her head on straight with all the details surrounding not only her son's wedding but also her own. Today was Kyle and Debbie's wedding shower and as she and Megan rode up to Portland, she couldn't help but think of her late husband, Neil. He was such a family oriented man.

She got out of her car and collected her gifts from the trunk for the kids: a set of Egyptian cotton linens and a duvet along with a gift card for MacKenzie-Childs with a substantial credit balance. Megan grabbed her gift bag from the back seat and joined her. "Here, let me get that," she said.

Janet handed her the wrapped duvet. She'd struggled the last couple of weeks trying to figure out what to get her step-grandson and his fiancé. Nothing felt adequate or sincere enough. Finally, Megan convinced her one could never have enough bed linens. "I hope they like it."

"I am sure they will love it," Megan said. "Come on, let's get to the party."

She hoofed it up the driveway with her stepdaughter, past a line of cars to the porch just as Kyle opened the front door. As they walked, Janet gave the newly purchased red split-level ranch a cursory glance. The large picture window frame and trim work had recently received a fresh coat of white paint by the looks of it and the deck, a deep brown stain. A large flowering hawthorn was putting out white blossoms at the far corner of the house.

"Hi, Mom, Grandma," Kyle said, coming out. At six-three and a hefty two-fifty plus, he filled up a doorway. And as usual, he had his trademark Trailblazer jersey and jeans on. Reaching out, he took her package and let them slip past him.

Janet heard laughter downstairs. "You're the doorman, I take it," she said, as he set their gifts on the couch by the door.

"For the time being," he answered, giving his mom a hug. "As soon as my buds get here, we're gonna catch the game down at *The Home Plate.* Anyway, everybody's downstairs as you've probably heard."

"Sounds like the party started without us," Janet said, catching a whiff of tomato sauce. Again, there was more laughter downstairs and above it all was Debbie's high-pitched giggle. Apparently, they were chatting about some game they were going to play involving the honeymoon. She cleared her throat. "I hope you're not eavesdropping on what's going on downstairs."

Kyle shot her a lopsided grin and his face colored. "Wouldn't dream of it."

Janet smiled. *Right.*

"Come on, Jan, let's see what's going on down there," Megan said, grabbing her gift.

Oh boy, here we go," Janet thought. "Okay, Kyle, have fun," she said, taking up her gift, and followed Megan down the short flight of stairs to the family room. There she found eight of Debbie's closest friends along with a couple of Megan's friends of old sitting around gabbing amongst themselves. They all looked up when Janet and Megan came in.

"Hi, Mom," Debbie said, getting up and coming over. After placing their gifts on the table beside them, she hugged her mother-in-law to be. Afterward, she embraced Janet then made introductions to her friends before leading them to the long buffet table that had been set up at the end of the large decorated room.

Janet glanced around at the clusters of white and silver balloons and arrangements of pink and white hydrangeas set up on tables trimmed with streamers. She was never a fan of large parties, even at her own wedding so long ago. They overwhelmed her, pushing her back into the corners, making her feel awkward. But this was important to Megan. Her best friend's son was getting married. She drew breath determined to ignore the burn in her gut, and admired the prominent vase of pink and white roses sitting front and center among the bowls of salad and pans of Italian meatballs and pasta.

"There's a ton of food here, so help yourselves," Debbie said.

Janet grabbed a plate and helped herself as Megan drifted over to the dessert table. "Oh, my God," Megan said. "A chocolate lava cake! Really? Deb, you better be careful or you'll have to let your dress out come the big day."

"Don't worry, Mom. I've starved myself for the last three days so I can splurge," Debbie said. "Can I get you a drink? We have champagne punch unless you want something non-alcoholic."

Megan shot Debbie a crooked frown as if she thought the girl had lost her mind. "Umm…champagne, thank you very much."

"What about you, Ms. Porter?" Debbie said.

"Champagne works for the time being," Janet answered, and found her seat next to Michelle, Debbie's mother. The woman was a stunning brunette with large brown eyes and a killer figure. The two of them chatted while Janet ate her lunch and as they did so, she found out Michele was a teacher with more than a passing interest in photography.

The sound of silverware ringing against glass got their attention. Julie, who was Debbie's maid of honor, was standing with a large canvas bag in her hand. Poking out of the top of it were various items:

a beach towel, a parasol and a couple of things Janet couldn't quite make out.

"Hey everyone. It's time to let the games begin," she said. "This game is called 'What's in the Bag?' What I'm going to do is pull out each item and show them to you. Afterward, I will put them all back and you will write down everything you can remember on a slip of paper Amy is passing around. The one who remembers the most items wins a special gift over there on the gift table.

"Now the first item we have is..." She reached in the bag and snatched out a pair of red panties and showed them around, bringing about giggling and laughter.

Janet rolled her eyes. Not because she didn't expect something like this to rear its head during the party; it just showed up quicker than she anticipated. The next item was a box of chocolates and the next after that was a bottle of sun tan lotion. By the time the nineteenth item was pulled out of the bag, Janet was fairly sure she wouldn't be able to remember half of them.

"And now, for the final item in our honeymoon bag we have..." When Julie paused, rolling her tongue inside her mouth while bobbing her brows for dramatic effect, Janet braced herself. Finally, she popped her hand out holding a large tube, and cried out, "Ta-da...a bottle of Astroglide!"

The room erupted in laughter and Megan's eyes nearly burst from their sockets. Then the group seemed to remember the mothers of the bride and groom were in the room. They shut their mouths and turned to them. But when Megan burst out laughing and Michele grinned, laughter returned. "Oh, my God!" Megan squealed. "Julie, that is too damned funny."

Janet shook her head. It was definitely going to be an interesting party. She dug a pen out of her purse as Julie placed the items back in the bag. But as she went about listing the items she remembered on the slip of paper, a sobering thought of Nate's broken engagement to Tracy flashed before her. There was a time, not so long ago, when she'd anticipated attending a shower for her future daughter-in-law, and she'd looked forward to it. That bright expectation had been dashed away by the events in Iraq that changed her son's life.

She looked up, pretending to recall the items in the bag and studied the young women around the room. Tamara with her buttery coffee-colored skin and long, dark lashes, AnnMarie's long, thick, black hair, high cheekbones and subtle upturned eyes, and finally, Vanessa's polished ebony complexion, dark brown eyes and brilliant, white smile. They were a diverse group, coming from different walks of life, yet all interconnected by friendship, a belief in a bright future and a new-age ritual revolving around an age-old rite. A world apart from the war her son had lost so much in. A war she believed was predicated on intolerance and hate: the 'us-against-them' mentality and an unwillingness to listen.

Her phone rang in her purse, startling her out of her muse. She pulled it out, saw Nate's number blinking on the screen and got up. "Hi honey, what's up?"

"Have you heard about the storm coming off the coast?"

"Well, I heard we're supposed to get a good rain, why?" she said, drifting off into a corner.

"Umm…it's a lot more than that," he said. "Amanda closed the store and sent us home. You and Megan might want to get on the road before too long or stay up there tonight."

Janet frowned. Storms were a fact of life in the Pacific Northwest. Nothing she couldn't handle. "We'll be fine honey, but you're right, we should probably get on the road before too late. Umm…where's Andy?"

"Lincoln City. Guess there was some kind of celebration for one of his firefighting friends down there. They're supposed to get slammed from what I understand. Anyways, I wanted to make sure you knew about things. Be careful driving home okay, and give me a call when you get in."

"Will do, honey. Love you." She ended the call, and felt a twinge of concern for Andy. Inland storms were one thing, but when they hit landfall they could be destructive. She tried to put it out of her mind and rejoined the women who were comparing the lists to what was in the bag.

Megan looked over at her and dipped her brow. Mouthed the words: everything all right? Janet nodded as Julie called her name out. "Okay, Ms. Porter, your turn?"

Janet forced a half-hearted smile and read from her list as Julie kept tabs on her correct answers. When she finished tallying up the totals, Julie looked up bright-eyed and announced, "We have a winner, and it's Ms. Porter!" Getting up, Julie went to the gift table and brought back a slender, silver and blue box with a frilly blue bow and ribbon on top and gave it to Janet. Whatever was inside was feather-light.

When Janet went to set it aside, the women frowned. "Open it," they cried.

Janet rolled her eyes, uncomfortable with being the center of attention, and pulled the ribbon away. As she lifted the lid off the box, she got the distinct feeling it might be some kind of gag gift, but to her delight she found instead an elegant, silk rose. Surprised, she plucked it from the box and held the pink blossom up for everyone to see. "This is gorgeous," she said, and handed it off to Michele to pass around.

Julie said, "Megan picked it out."

As the rose made its way around the circle of woman, Janet's set the box down and as she did so, saw a small card peeking out of the tissue. She picked it up and read the note:

Thanks for always being there, carrying me when I thought I was alone.

Janet's throat tightened. The game was fixed. Why didn't that surprise her? She cast a furtive eye toward her best friend, who was chatting with Kyle's fiancé and wiped away the tear that trickled down her cheek. *And you've carried me as well. It's what best friends do, even when we're not liking each other very much, yet we deal with it and there's nothing in this world I wouldn't do for you, Meg, believe it. I love you.*

The rain pelted the Willamette valley in drenching sheets, reducing visibility on Rt. 22 to practically nothing. But then Janet was used to storms that could drop two inches of rain on a whim. It was the constant flashes of lightning that lit up the sky and the bursts of wind pushing her car around the road that bothered her. She turned up the radio and looked over at Cleo, who was riding shotgun. The dog was antsy in his seat, lurching at every booming crack of thunder. "We'll be home soon, boy," she said, more to convince herself than comfort the dog. As she turned onto Old Cypress Road, a loud buzzing interrupted the song on the radio.

ALERT...ALERT...ALERT. THE NATIONAL WEATHER SERVICE HAS ISSUED A STORM WARNING FOR LINCOLN, POLK, BENTON, MARION AND CLACKAMAS COUNTIES.

POSSIBLE STRAIGHTLINE WINDS IN EXCESS OF 90 MILES PER HOUR MAY OCCUR ALONG THE STORM'S PATH. HEAVY TORRENTIAL RAIN AND HAIL OF SIZABLE PROPORTIONS IS PREDICTED ALONG THE RAPIDLY MOVING STORM FRONT.

STORM SURGES MAY PRODUCE TSUNAMIS ALONG COASTAL AREAS AND FLASH FLOODING OF RIVERS....

Janet's hands gripped the wheel as the report rambled on. Her windshield wipers slashed back and forth in front of her in a futile attempt to dash the water off the glass. Now and then she felt the tires leave the road and heard the spray of water pound her wheel wells. All she wanted was to get home but the elements were working against her, slowing her down at every turn. Again another flash of lightning lit up the world and for a brief instant she saw the thrashing heads of cypress and pine whipping back and forth.

She cursed herself for not leaving Portland earlier, except it was Kyle's fiancé's wedding shower. The Porter clan was getting ready to grow again and as matriarch she wanted to be there for every minute of it. Who knew the storm would grow in such intensity so quickly. At last she saw her driveway and she let out a breath she'd been holding for the last half hour. She turned in, drove down the long serpentine drive and made a mad dash for the house with Cleo. Once inside, she put her back to the door and leaned onto it, collecting her nerve until at last, she turned the lights on and trotted to her bedroom. As she went, she peeled her sopping wet blouse off and hung it over a laundry rack.

After she changed and dried herself off, she wrapped her hair in a towel and retreated to the great room, where she turned the TV on to get the latest news on the storm. While she surfed the channels, Megan called.

"You get home okay?"

"Yeah, I'm fine," Janet lied, wondering why she never heard her phone go off. She pulled it away from her ear and sure enough there were three voice messages blinking on the screen.

"Good. I was getting worried. The news says the storm heading your way is growing by the minute."

"Yeah, I'm in the middle of it right now," Janet said, watching the weather reporter on TV waving over the radar map. "I guess we're supposed to get some serious wind." She waited for a reply, but all she got was silence. "Megan...Megan, you there? Damn. Dropped call." She called back, but all she got was Megan's voice mail. Sighing, she flipped her phone shut and went about toweling her hair dry. As she did so, the lights went out and she was thrown into darkness.

Wonderful! She threw the towel over her shoulder and groped her way to the kitchen with Cleo lingering underfoot. Pawing through the cabinet drawers she found a flashlight and tracked a path to the breaker box in the garage. But the power remained off after she reset the tripped breakers. "Okay, candles it is," she muttered with a huff, and headed back into the house. There, she rifled through the utility closet in the hallway, dug out a handful of tapers and set them out around the Great Room. With nothing else left to do, she hunkered down with a book and her flashlight in the candle lit room to weather the raging storm outside. But the comfort she sought from reading was ripped away by a loud crack. Suddenly the darkened world outside the cathedral windows was bright as day and Cleo jumped, letting out a sudden bark as the house trembled then shuddered. For a terrifying moment, she couldn't breathe as the outer walls flexed and relaxed from the surging wind. Then all went quiet and something deep inside her knew all hell was about to rise up.

"Come, Cleo," she said, getting up. She raced for the hall to get to the basement as a deafening howl rampaged over the house followed by a booming thud. Suddenly the cathedral windows in the Great Room burst from their frames showering glass throughout the room. As the raging wind flooded in, tossing furniture and debris about like confetti, she fought to keep her balance going down the hall. "Hurry, Cleo," she cried as they stumbled along the darkened corridor. But when she reached the basement door, the floor shook beneath her and she was thrown back. As she tumbled down, the roof opened above her and through it plowed a thick black shadow. It was just a tap, a nudge, a crack and then a sharp blinding shot that stole her breath. She lay there stunned as her body went numb. She watched the wind dismantle the house piece by piece then looked down and saw her body pinned by a massive limb. The world swirled around her as she lay exposed to the icy rain pouring down and as it pelted her, she began to understand she was in trouble.

Clenching her teeth, she reached down and pushed against the gritty bough, but her only reward was slicing pain that seared through her like a hot poker. Gasping, she fell back and staring up at the gaping black hole, heard the thunk, thunk, thunk of the wood deck being pried from the beams. Her home, the house Neil had built for her was being dismantled right in front of her and as she watched its destruction, a new terror swept over her. Smoke!

Suddenly her whole life came into clarity as Cleo nestled up close to her and nuzzled her face. All her memories started running past her in fast forward. So many things she'd forgotten were suddenly there as if they'd happened yesterday. Then she saw Neil's face and Nate's, and Megan's and her father's and all of those she'd loved and even those she'd only met for a brief moment; a kaleidoscope, a tapestry. Her whole life condensed into this one perfect moment. A photo of a lifetime, a masterpiece beyond the skill of any photographer was looking back at her. She coughed and felt the crushing pain in her chest begin to abate. Then an echo, or so it seemed, whispered in her ears.

"Mom…mom…where are you?"

"Nate," she muttered and closed her eyes as the rain drummed and pinged around her.

"Mom…mom. Answer me!" The voice cried, growing louder.

She blinked and licked her lips. *Nate. It's only right that you're the last thing I think of. I love you."*

"Oh, my God, Mom! I'm here," he said. She looked up into the bright beam of a flashlight then saw him. His face was beautiful in the white luminescent halo. Turning away, he yelled, "She's over here!"

She smiled as Cleo's warm tongue licked her face then gazed up at her son, grateful to have one last look at him.

"I have to get you out of here. Hold on, don't you dare go anywhere," he said. His face left her line of sight and as she lay there drifting into the darkness, she wondered if it had been a trick of the heart, wanting to believe she had seen her son one last time.

Chapter 30

NDY HIT the ground with a thud and rolled over on his back. For a moment, he didn't know where he was nor could he catch his breath, but then the air rushed back into his lungs like a raging fire. *The storm...gas leak...house fire...bright flash...explosion!* Coughing, he blinked and looked up at the blackened sky tinted in muted oranges and yellows, then felt a wave of heat wash over his face and hands as if the sun was beating down on him. At the same time, came the sensation of his head being underwater. He turned onto his side, winced then wiping his eyes, saw flames climbing high into the starless night.

Suddenly, a hand was on his shoulder. He looked back and saw Tammy leaning over him, her eyes wide in alarm. Her lips were moving, but he couldn't hear a word she was saying. For that matter, he couldn't hear the raging fire either. She patted him, urging him to lie back down but he waved her off and got to his feet. The breathtaking sharp jab in his side made him regret it. His eyes rolled up into his head as her hand gripped his arm. Glancing over at her, he saw her lips moving again, then felt another hand grip his other arm.

One excruciating step at a time, he walked with Tammy and Rick over to where the refugees were huddled under a portable LED light, well away from the fiery station. A large nylon canvas was staked down on the ground, its edges fluttering in the swirling whirlwind of heat from the billowing blaze. When at last he was lying down,

Tammy unbuttoned his shirt and palpated his ribs. As her probing fingers pressed down a wave of pain tore through him and he jerked back. But he paid dearly for the sudden movement and cried out, which made things even worse.

As tears leaked out from the corners of his eyes, he heard Jack's murmured bark and little by little the sounds of voices grew around him.

"I think he has a fractured rib," Tammy said. Her words were muffled as she reached into the large, canvas med bag at her side.

Andy watched her dig out a couple of instant gel packs, and after giving them a twist and a squeeze, she taped them to his injured ribs. As she did so, three trucks from Station 1400 came around the corner with sirens blaring with two patrol cars behind them. They came to an abrupt stop in front of the burning station and men poured out of their cabs racing toward the fire, running hoses out behind them. A moment later, Captain Matt Fuller came racing up in his car. He jumped out, barking orders then trotted over to Tammy.

"Everyone all right?"

"Mostly bumps and scrapes," Tammy said, getting to her feet. She swept a lock of hair off her forehead with the back of her hand. "Looks like Andy might have a broken rib and Paddy a concussion."

"You call PWA yet?"

"Yeah, but all their units are out" Tammy said.

"Damn," Matt said. He glanced around and chewed his lip as his radio chattered. "Okay, take my car and get 'em to Samaritan stat."

Andy peered out through the car window at the shadowy fingers of twisted branches, strewn chunks of roofing, trash, and fallen service lines as Tammy steered the captain's car around and past the wreckage. Occasionally, they passed people milling around with flashlights like characters out of one of those zombie movies that had become popular. Most of them were assessing the damage to their homes and property. In the inky darkness it was an eerie sight. As Tammy made a left, heading up NE 28th to the emergency room entrance lot, Andy worried about Jack even though he knew the guys at the station would look after his little buddy.

The car pulled up to the entry doors. Although the parking lot lights were dark, the hospital was lit up and bright inside. A couple of security guards came out to meet them. One helped Andy out of the car and into one of the awaiting wheelchairs, while the other grabbed a chair for Paddy. As Tammy pulled away from the entry, the men wheeled them inside the crowded Emergency Department and brought them to the triage nurse.

As the man looked Paddy over, Andy watched the doctors and nurses rushing about tending to the injured that were lined up against the hallway walls on gurneys. Yet despite all the commotion, he could only make out the conversations close by. The rest were muffled ramblings and noises. Right now, what he wanted was to breathe without being stabbed in the chest. He closed his eyes as a blanket was laid over him, trying to take small measured gasps as he waited his turn, but instead felt his chair moving. He looked up and saw he was being wheeled down the hall.

"Hey, Andy," said a woman's voice close to his ear. She parked him in an alcove, set the brakes on his chair, came around and kneeled in front of him. "I'm Dr. Sheldon. Can you tell me if you hurt anywhere else besides your ribs?"

He looked down at the green-garbed, blond haired doctor, licked his lips, and tried to respond, but he didn't have the strength so he winced and shook his head.

"That's okay," Dr. Sheldon said. She pulled his blanket aside and palpated his ribs, sending him on another adventure in pain. "I'm sorry, I know that wasn't a lot of fun."

You have no idea Andy thought, gritting his teeth.

She waited for him to collect himself then looked him over good. "Well, you're pretty banged up, but I don't see anything to worry about right now. Still, we'll get you x-rayed and try to make you a bit more comfortable." She patted his shoulder. "Okay, I'll check back on you later," she said, then turned and melted into the sea of chaos.

The next morning, Andy sat in his hospital room waiting for Matt to pick him up. He'd been released from care an hour ago. It had been a long night without a wink of sleep. He fidgeted in the wheelchair, trying to find a comfortable position. It was of no comfort that he would have to deal with being stabbed with every breath he took for the next six to eight weeks. He picked up the hand-held mirror on the tray and looked at the bright strawberry scrape on his cheek and the blackened eye under the bandage on his brow. *Well, none the worse for looks,* he thought.

He set the mirror down and rolled over to the window, looking out over Devil's Lake. The soaring blue sky betrayed the carnage sweeping the tiny coastal city he'd called home for years. For all practical purposes, the land below his window looked like a war zone. Trees were down everywhere and several wood framed buildings had been reduced to a pile of matchsticks.

He heard a knock on the door and turned around to see a nurse stepping in with a cell phone in her hand. "Hi," she said. "You have a call from your sister, Amanda?"

Oh, shit! "Thanks," he said taking the phone from her. He frowned when he saw the crack in the screen and put it to his ear. "Hey Panda."

"Are you okay?"

"Yeah, just a little banged up is all."

"Banged up?" She cried. Her tone was laced with incredulity. "I hardly think of a broken rib as being banged up! Why didn't you call me? You scared the bejesus out of me, Bruddy."

"Well, I was a little preoccupied at the time," he said. A sharp twinge took his breath away and he paused and waited for the pain to ease up. "Hey, it's a bit difficult talking right now. Can we do this later?"

She paused. "Of course, I'm sorry. It's just that you scared me."

"Scared me, too," he said. "Okay, I'll see you when I get back."

"Which is when?"

He shrugged. "Hell if I know. A few days, maybe. Depends on what the doc says. Don't you worry, I'll be just fine."

"You'd better be," she said. "Take care of yourself...Oh, and by the way, in case you're worried, the store made it through things just fine."

"Good. And what about you?"

"We lost a couple trees, a few shingles and some gutters. Tuck says it's nothing serious. But our friends in the valley got hit pretty hard and the Heights lost a lot of beautiful homes. Anyway, I'll let you rest for now. Love ya."

The line went silent, and as he pocketed his phone, his sister's news banged around in his head. He looked back toward the window. Janet lived in the Heights. What if she...? He'd call her as soon as he got situated, which was where? Maybe Bob could put him up until he was able to drive.

"Your taxi's here."

He turned back and saw Matt shuffling into his room wearing his beige turnout coveralls. He ran his thick fingers through his dirty blond hair. The man gave him the once over with one of his trademark sidelong gazes and shook his head. "You look like shit."

"So do you," Andy volleyed and bit back the sharp twinge.

Matt nodded. "Tammy told me what you did. There are better ways of getting out of that law suit than killing yourself off, you know."

"Yeah, don't I know it," Andy muttered.

Matt slapped him on the shoulder. "Thanks for giving it a shot. Don't worry; we'll get by. I don't think our insurance company is very happy though."

Andy winced. "Easy there," he rasped, trying to catch his breath.

"Oh, sorry, Mac."

Andy nodded and glanced around the room, wondering about the future. Every question he thought of brought about two more. *Holy crap!* "Where's Jack?"

"With me. The two of you will be bunking at my place 'til you're able to drive. Don't get too comfy there, either. I like my solitude."

Well, that takes care of one thing. "So, do I still have a car?" Andy said.

Matt nodded. "Yep, just a cracked windshield. We'll get 'er back to the house and I'll have the adjuster come out and add 'er to the bill."

Andy did the math. Between getting the car to Matt's, dealing with insurance and having the auto glass tech replace it, he could possibly end up being stuck at Matt's for a week. Then again, the doc would probably ground him at least that long. He frowned, "Okay, it is what it is. Let's get out of here."

Matt's house was located on a large parcel of wooded land off Drift Creek Road, south of the city. The two-story white colonial with black shutters stood back from the road behind a dense stand of rutted pine and cedar. Matt pulled up to the breezeway and put the car in park.

"You need a hand?" he said.

Andy pushed the passenger door open and swung his leg out. "No, I'll be fine."

"Okay, inside door's open. Make yourself at home. I'll be back around five, give or take," Matt said. He reached up to his visor and punched the button on his garage door opener. As Andy grabbed his goodie bag from the hospital and waited for Jack to scramble out, Matt's two-way radio came alive. He listened to the incoming call and radioed back he was on his way. To Andy, he said, "Accident in town. Okay, Bud, no rest for the weary. Stay out of trouble."

Andy watched Matt's car pull out into traffic, then turned into the garage with Jack trailing close behind. Until now, he hadn't realized what walking with a broken rib entailed, but his body was quick to let him know it didn't like it. Heel-toeing it down the cluttered hallway, he used his hands to steady himself. First order of business was taking care of a nagging bladder then hunting for some Tylenol, followed hopefully by a good long nap.

But lying down on Matt's much-used sofa was out of the question and the old leather recliner wasn't much better. Finally, he gave up, found the clicker among the magazines and junk mail on the faded, oak coffee table and turned the TV on. Thank God Matt had satellite. Otherwise, with the cable being out, he would've gone stir crazy. He surfed the channels and finally settled on NCIS. Although the show took liberties with how things really were in the service, Mark Harmon's character resonated with him. Quiet, stubborn, self-assured, and a man of integrity, Gibbs was a man of conscience. Yet, there was only so much NCIS he could watch, so he skipped around for a movie and decided on Independence Day. The next thing he knew he was being awakened by the sound of Matt's stirring in the kitchen.

"What time is it," he said, shuffling into the room.

Matt looked up from setting a plate of left over pizza on the floor for Jack. "A little after six. How ya feeling?"

"Like I got run over by a truck," Andy said, and frowned as Jack tore into the slices. "Pizza? Really, Matt?"

"He seems to like it," Matt said, watching Jack gobble it down.

"Well, you won't like what happens after it filters through him," Andy said. He reached into his pocket, felt a sharp stab to his ribs, and brought his wallet out. Digging a twenty from it, he gritted his teeth and placed the money on the table. "Would you mind picking up a bag of kibble. He's partial to beef and liver."

Matt shrugged and took the cash. "Sure. Probably should grab some groceries anyway unless you want to do take out."

"Take out works. And you're out of beer. Here!" Andy said, digging another twenty out. "My contribution."

"Thai or Italian?" Matt said, heading for the door.

"Thai works. Anything with beef or pork's fine," Andy said and winced. "By the way, you have any gel packs hanging around here?"

Matt pulled the door open. "In the linen closet. 'Kay, I'm off. Be back in a few."

Andy called Jack over to him and looked down into the dog's innocent, dark brown eyes. "You know, you're gonna pay for that meal, right?" Jack licked his chops and wagged his tail as if to say: 'that tasted good, but is that all there is?' Andy shook his head. "Right. Okay, let's see if I can find some relief."

Taking his time, he walked down the hall to the bathroom and went in. As he pawed around in the linen closet, his cell phone buzzed in his pocket. He looked at Bob Lightfoot's number flashing on the screen and realized he'd forgotten to call Janet.

"Hey, Bob," he said.

"How you feeling? I would've come up this morning, but we were mopping up down to the station."

"Don't worry about it, Bob," Andy said. "Total loss, is it?"

"Pretty much," Bob said. "I guess we're gonna work out of Station 1500 for the foreseeable future. They're really busy right now. That storm clobbered everyone pretty good, especially the valley. They lost a lot of nice homes up that way."

"Yeah, I heard," Andy said, his voice trailing off. He looked at his watch. It was going on six. Janet should be home by now if she ended up staying with her family up in Portland.

"Andy, you still there?" Bob said.

"Ahhh…yeah, yeah. Sorry, Bob. I was just thinking of something. "Hey, look, my ribs are killing me right now and it's hard to talk. Can I get back to ya?"

"Yeah, sure," Bob said. "You take care of yourself, and I'll see you as soon as things get cleaned up around here."

As soon as Andy ended the call, he navigated to Janet's number and hit send. But the phone just rang and rang until it finally went to voice mail. He chewed his lip, wondering if he should start calling around, but tempered his panic that she might just be on the phone or had it on charge. He'd try again in another half hour.

By the time the following morning came around, Andy was beside himself with worry about Janet. He'd tried her number every hour on the hour last night to no avail. Even Nate hadn't answered his phone. He shuffled over to the front window and pulled back the curtain. Tammy had just parked his car in the turn-around and was handing *his* keys to Matt. As the two of them chatted, Matt looked back toward the house.

"Oh, no you don't," he muttered. He rapped on the window pane and pointed to the car keys dangling in Matt's hand. The captain raised his arms in protest as if to say, 'What do you need 'em for? You're not going anywhere.' But Andy waved him toward the house nonetheless, and went to the door. As he opened it, Jack came running into the room from the kitchen. Andy pointed him back toward the hall and stepped out onto the porch as Matt came up the driveway with Tammy following.

"Don't even think of stranding me here," he said.

Matt shook his head. "Mac, it's probably just a downed cell tower. If she's anything like you told me, she's probably busy helping someone. Promise me you won't do anything stupid, okay?"

Andy snatched his keys and buried them in his pocket as Tammy asked him how he was feeling.

"I've been better, and thanks. You're a sport for bringing my wheels to me," he said glancing over at his car. A section of blistered paint was on the quarter panel. Turning back to Matt, he nodded toward the road. "Better get at it."

"Yup...and you better stay put! Hear?" Matt furrowed his brow, but Andy knew it was all for show. At last, the man turned to Tammy. "Okay, let's get at it. Got a long day ahead of us."

They scampered down the stairs and Andy watched them get in Matt's car and dash down the long driveway. When they were out of sight, he turned back and went inside and called again. Still no answer. He ran his hand through his hair. *Where are you? And why aren't you answering?* He turned on the portable TV in the kitchen and started picking up the empty take out containers on the kitchen counter and throwing them away...anything to keep busy. A minute later he was riveted with alarm as catastrophic shots of shattered homes in the Valley flashed on the screen.

Maybe Amanda knows something. He dialed the store and when Jonah picked, he said, "Hey, Amanda around?"

"Oh, hi there, Andy. I heard you're in the hospital. You okay?"

Andy clenched the pillow to his chest. "I'm over to a friends for a few days and I'm fine: just a few bumps and scratches is all. Where's Amanda?"

There was a pause. "Hold on, I'll get her for ya. Oh...I just got a call from Nate. Apparently his mother's place got hit by the storm and she's in a bad way up to the hospital."

As the words drilled into Andy, the world around him grew small. Stunned, he tried to make sense of what Jonah had said. He closed his eyes as his hands trembled. "I'll be right home," was all he could manage to say, and he flipped the lid on the cell phone shut, ending the call.

All the way back to Salem, Andy's thoughts revolved around Janet. He coughed as he stepped into the hospital lobby and was rewarded with a sharp jab to the ribs. Gritting his teeth, he waited for the pain to subside and marched over to the hospital receptionist, hoping against hope he wasn't too late. When the woman behind the desk said Janet had been moved to a private room, he looked up. *Well, for once, You listened!* He took the slip of paper with her room number on it and hurried to Janet's room.

Stepping inside, he saw her asleep in bed with her hair swept back over the pillow. A little white bandage was taped to her forehead and an IV drip was attached to her hand. He took care to be quiet as he looked down at her. She seemed so small and fragile. A section of blanket had pulled away from her leg. He reached down and drew it back over her.

She stirred, moaned, and opened her eyes. "Andy?" she said. Her voice was hoarse and barely above a whisper.

"I'm here," he said. "I didn't mean to wake you."

"It's okay." She wiped the sleep from her eyes. Can you raise me up a little?"

"Sure," he said. He hunted for the bed control and when he found it, raised the head of the mattress until she told him to stop about a quarter of the way up.

Licking her lips, she studied him. "How long you been here?"

"Not long. I came as soon as I found out." He studied her again: saw the pallor of her skin and the darkness around her eyes.

She reached up with her hand, pointing at his face. "You're hurt."

"Oh, just a few scrapes is all. But what about you?"

"I feel like I got run over by a semi." She twisted around, as if trying to get more comfortable, and winced. "I think I should've stayed in Portland."

Andy pulled up a chair. "I heard Nate brought you in."

"He did. He saved my life from what the doctor said."

"What happened?"

She turned her head toward the tray table. "Could you grab my water for me?"

As he held the cup for her to get a drink, Nate walked in. He nodded at him, said 'Hi' which wasn't returned, and looked back at Janet, feeling small and unwelcome in the judging gaze he knew was coming back. Then again, what did he expect of Nate? He'd betrayed the kid, led him to believe it was all about them being friends, not chasing after his mother. Well, maybe not chasing, but he certainly had made himself available and had encouraged things. For now, he'd have to live with the uneasy truce between them Janet had unwittingly engineered. Beyond that, there was nothing he could say or do that was going to change a thing. It was up to Nate and that was going to take time!

Janet spoke up. "There's my hero."

"Hi Mom," he said sidling up next to the bed. He put out his hand and swept away an errant lock of hair from her face. "I talked to the Red Cross. They're gonna board up the broken windows and tarp the roof until we can get someone out to the house to assess the damage."

Andy looked up. "How bad is it?"

Nate shot him a not-now look and said, "Like I said, they have to assess."

Janet said, "Is Cleo doing okay?"

"He's fine. Missing you though." He smiled at his mother and it was so tender, Andy had to look away. "So much for him being my dog."

It was time to leave. He got up and as he did so, his broken rib screamed at him, but he swallowed the searing pain and headed for the door. As he passed the foot of Janet's bed, he glanced at them and said, "Gonna head down to the cafeteria for some coffee."

Janet called out to him. "Why don't you go home? You look tired."

Andy gritted his teeth, fighting to keep his expression serene. "Don't you worry about me, I'm fine," he said.

Nate looked back at him and their gazes met. "What happened to you?"

"Took a tumble on the pavement," Andy said and walked out.

Chapter 31

FTER ANDY left to get coffee, Janet looked up at Nate. "He feels bad."

"Well, he should," Nate snapped. He softened his tone. "And why are you defending him?"

"What do you mean?"

"Well, Megan said he sort of blew you off."

Janet closed her eyes. *Megan, when are you going to learn to keep your mouth shut?* "He didn't blow me off. He had things to think over," she said, looking back up at her son's furrowed brow. But she couldn't deny she was leery and it prompted one of Neil's little sayings to come tumbling back. In her mind's eye, she could see him telling Nate that trust was a product of consistency multiplied over time. Well, Nate had learned that lesson well, and he held others to it with no apology forthcoming. As for herself, she had to admit she'd only known Andy less than a year.

She wriggled around, trying to get comfortable on the firm, unyielding hospital bed. What she wanted was to be home, cocooned in blankets. But that wasn't going to happen. The beautiful home Neil had designed and built for her was a wreck as far as she knew. She nibbled her lip as her thoughts spiraled into memories of Neil walking her around the house as it was being built, explaining how it went together along with the little details he was putting into it for her. It was as if the universe had stripped another layer of him away. Her throat tightened. It was one thing to move on, maybe even fall in love again: quite another to have the precious things that had been woven into the fabric of her life taken away.

There was a knock on the door. "Hello, how are you doing, Janet?" Nate looked up as the doctor swept in and walked to her bedside.

Janet eyed the coffee colored woman wearing teal green scrubs. Dr. Akua was her name, or something like that, she couldn't quite remember. "I'm okay, I guess...until I move the wrong way, that is."

The doctor smiled, drew the curtain around the bed and said, "Nate, would you mind stepping out for a minute?" Pulling the blanket back, she exposed Janet's blackened and bruised body along with the bandaged incision under her left breast. With an adept sure-handedness, she peeled the bandage back and after a good look, covered Janet back up again. "Your incision is healing nicely," she said. "Any light-headedness, blurred vision?"

Janet shook her head as the doctor checked the IV drip. "No, just a little nausea."

"A common side effect of the anesthesia," Dr. Akua said. "Have you been getting up and around?"

"A little," Janet replied then winced. "I feel like I've been stomped on."

"That's because you were. You're very lucky to only have a ruptured spleen," Dr. Akua said. "Had that limb come down on you a few inches to the right, it would've killed you. As it was, you were seriously injured. Thankfully, your son found you when he did, otherwise..."

"Yeah. I was supposed to call him when I got home," Janet answered as the memory of Nate's rain spattered face flashed before her. "I guess forgetting isn't such a bad thing sometimes."

"In this case, yes," the doctor said drawing the curtain open. "You can come back in, Nate."

"So, how long am I in for?" Janet said, figuring she'd be kept at least a week more. The problem was, she didn't have a home to go home to. Suddenly, a billion questions came rushing at her. Where would she stay: with Megan and Ben, Trevor and Nadia or would she live out of a suitcase in a hotel room or an apartment for an indefinite time? And then there was Cleo. Where would he go? Did she still have a car?

Dr. Akua broke into her panicked musing. "Let's see how the next few days go. By then we'll know when we can send you home."

Janet nodded, but her mind was going in circles thinking of all the priceless keepsakes: the picture of Neil and her over the fireplace, Neil's pilgrim desk, family photo albums and scrapbooks.

The doctor bid her good-bye and when she stepped out, Nate said, "Speaking of going home, you want me to chat with Megan? I'm sure she'd take you in."

"Oh, no. I don't want to burden her, especially with Kyle's wedding coming up," Janet said.

"Okay, what about Trevor then?" Nate said.

Janet shook her head as Andy came strolling back in. "Can we do this later?"

"Sure, Mom," he said as Andy pulled up a chair.

Janet eyed him sitting next to her. He was definitely uncomfortable. "Are you sure you're okay?" she said to him.

Andy nodded and smiled, but the easygoing expression on his face looked forced.

Nate turned the TV on and as they watched the news, a segment came on about the storm. A moment later she was looking at aerial footage that was panning the path of destruction the storm had left. She looked at Andy with widened eyes and as she did so, realized there was a lot he wasn't telling her.

But her pain meds were kicking in, and the next thing she knew, she was waking up to Nate's voice. "I need to get home, Mom."

She opened her eyes and saw him standing over her. "What time is it?"

"A little after six." He leaned in and gave her a peck on the cheek. "I'll see you tomorrow, but before I go, I need to know what to do with Cleo. My landlord says I need to find a place for him. He can't stay with me anymore. You want me to take him up to Megan's?"

Janet licked her dry, parched lips. "I really don't want him going up there. If he does, I'll be roped into going, too."

"So, a kennel?" Nate said and frowned.

"Oh, no, not a kennel. Let me think." She shimmied up in the bed. A sharp jab under her ribs reminded her not to do that again.

"I could take him in," Andy said, speaking up.

The suggestion caught her sideways and she eyed him. "Oh, I don't know, Andy."

"No, really," he said. "I have plenty of room and I'm sure Jack would love having a playmate in the house."

It was an intriguing idea, and the more she thought about it, the more it made sense, especially if she took a place in the city. Then again, she was pretty sure the offer wasn't made in a vacuum. She eyed Andy who was looking at her intently with a diffident smile that was confirming her suspicions. Then again, she couldn't say she minded seeing him on a regular basis, and it would go a long way in his proving whether he really loved her or not. Finally, she said, "If you're sure."

"I am," Andy said

She debated his offer one last time, except there really wasn't anything to debate. The question was: how would Nate react. Cleo had been his dog. Would it exacerbate the fragile truce between them? She hoped not. She glanced at Nate, trying to discern his mood, but couldn't read his inert expression. Finally, in a careful tone, she said, "Okay. That's really nice of you Andy. It certainly makes me feel a lot better knowing he has a playmate to pal around with."

Janet sat on her hospital bed waiting to be released. It had been a long seven days looking at the four walls. Sure, there had been TV when the kids or Andy wasn't there, but there was only so much of that she could endure. As she waited for Nate to pick her up, she called the Grand Hotel and made long-term reservations. The four star hotel on Liberty Street near River Front Park was near Nate and would be her home until she could find something more suitable. Ending the call, she looked out the window, antsy to get moving, except there wasn't much to look forward to. She picked up the mirror the nurse had left her and stared into tired eyes. Despite all the help coming her way from family and friends, she felt oddly alone and drifting into an unknown future.

Starting over: rebuilding her home, refurnishing it with all the little things that would make it a home again, to say nothing of possibly having to replace all her clothes, linens, camera equipment, TVs, stereo components and computers. It was overwhelming.

A knock on her open door drew her out of her musing. She looked over, and to her surprise, saw Andy standing with a nurse. "Hi, you ready to ditch this place?" he said.

She eyed the wheel chair being rolled in by the nurse. "I take it you shanghaied my son out of the job."

He pressed his lips together. "Something like that. I hope it's all right," he said as the nurse positioned the chair beside the bed.

Janet set the mirror down, grabbed her purse and eased into her ride. "I hope you know what you've just got yourself into."

"What do you mean?" he said.

"Oh, Nate didn't tell you? We're going shopping for a change of clothes. I can't keep wearing Meg's until they fall off," she said, waving her hands over her green loose-fitting blouse and dark slacks.

"Ah, that's why he finally gave in when I asked if he would mind," he said as the nurse wheeled her out of the room.

As they rolled down the busy hallway to the elevators, she heard Andy uttering short grunts beside her. She reached out and tapped his arm. "Care to share?"

"Share what?"

Janet rolled her eyes. *Men!* "You're in pain. What did you do to yourself, and don't lie to me."

He pursed his lips. "Can it wait till we get in the car?" he said.

"I guess," she said, glad he'd convinced Nate to let him come.

As Andy buckled her into her seat, she caught a whiff of citrusy cologne. It brought back memories of the night at Sal's. That night seemed like an age ago as she sat waiting for him to get in beside her. There was so much that had happened over the last nine months to bring her to this moment, she thought as Andy got in and pulled out into traffic. She put her sunglasses on and glancing over at him, noticed he had a pillow on his lap.

"That's interesting," she said nodding toward it.

"Yeah," he said with a sigh then glancing her way, paused and added, "It's to help cushion a cracked rib."

"Really…a broken rib," she said, shaking her head, "and you were going to tell me this when?"

He shrugged and bit down on his lip. "You were in the hospital and I didn't want to worry you."

He had a point, but still. She turned to him. "You shouldn't be driving."

"I'm fine. Just have to be slow and careful." He turned and headed down the arterial. "So, where we going?"

She sighed, reached over, and patted his hand. "Westgate. We're shopping, remember? So, how'd it happen? And are you okay, really?"

"I've been better," he said, "but I'll be okay, honest. How it happened, well, that's a long story. I'll tell you later."

After they picked up some essential items from Bennigans, they headed for the Heights. As Andy drove past waving fields of wild grasses comingled with flowering coneflowers, daisies, and roadside asters, and into the wooded land, she braced herself for what she imagined was going to be a complete disaster.

As he turned onto Old Cypress Road, he reached over to take her hand. "You okay?"

She swallowed. "I'll be all right."

They turned into the driveway, and as they rounded the stand of juniper and cedar sheltering the property, the house came into view. She squeezed Andy's hand as she took in the mayhem skirting the front porch. Her car was parked off to the side in the turn-around. It was plastered with leaves and fallen branches. The flowerbeds were mashed and outdoor tables and chairs were strewn about the yard. Jagged limbs, stripped of foliage, along with a smattering of roof shingles and window screens lay jumbled on the driveway. Sections of rain gutter, swinging listless in the breeze, hung down off the eaves. But what really hit her was the plywood across the top cathedral window in the expansive curtain wall. The stained glass pane depicting Frank Lloyd Wright's 'Tree of Life' was lying on the ground and other panes below it were boarded up. She put her hand to her mouth, stifling a gasp and tried to breathe.

Andy stopped the car and was quiet a long time until at last he said, "It'll be okay. The main thing is the structure looks intact. Neil was a smart man using post and beam construction."

Unable to drag her gaze from the catastrophe in front of her, she nodded. "I thought I could handle seeing this, but I guess I wasn't ready."

"You want to come back later?" he said. "You don't have to do this now."

"No, I think I do," she answered, and her voice sounded hollow to her ears as she opened her door and got out. Andy pulled the wheelchair out of the back of his suburban and brought it around. She sat in it and they walked around behind the house, eyeing the scattered debris and fallen limbs. Then she saw it. A shorn limb of the massive willow ramrodded through the kitchen roof with a flapping blue tarp tacked around it. Memories of Christmas and family gatherings rushed back. It was almost more than she could bear.

Andy stood beside her, his gaze caressing her, and he reached down and took her hand. "You can rebuild it, and I'd like to be a part of it, if you'd let me."

She looked up into the eyes of a man humbled by what life could throw at someone and finally felt her tears come. He understood what it was like to lose the things you loved, to grasp those you cared about a little too tight sometimes and what it was like to walk into an uncertain future...and that mattered!

Chapter 32

THAT NIGHT, long after Andy left, Janet stood by the window of her darkened hotel room with arms crossed, looking out over the sleeping city below. As she stared out at the starless night, she contemplated the enormous task of putting her house back together. Again the feeling of her life having been hijacked and her being hurled into a roiling ocean of uncertainty returned. She dipped her head, swallowed and felt her throat tighten as she covered her face with her hand. Stumbling back to her bed, she crumpled down onto it, and as she lay there in the dark of night, asking why, she felt a longing grow in her heart.

Suddenly, she NEEDED TO BE on her beach sitting on her rock! She looked up at the digital alarm on her bed stand as the powerful urge to go running out into the night surged through her. But a small voice in her head whispered, *It's ten o'clock! You just left the hospital. And... alone? Really?* She nibbled her lip as the urge warred with common sense. *I'll have Andy take me to get my car in the morning... no, better I get Nate. Andy would never let me behind the wheel.* She closed her eyes and wrestled with the pillow, trying to get comfortable until at last, her mind shut down and she fell into a dreamless sleep.

When she woke, the first light of day was filtering into the room. She eyed the slate gray overcast then glanced at the clock. 5:45 AM. Nate was an early riser, but it was too early to call him. In the meantime, she'd think of a way to convince him to let her drive. She got up, showered and shuffled down for her morning breakfast. The breakfast café in the hotel was on the first floor tucked away on the side of the spacious entry lobby. She walked across the marble tiled floor into the dated, yet inviting café and found a table near the windows. Outside of the staff working the buffet on the far wall and a few guests sitting at tables nursing cups of coffee along the windows, the only sound in the room was the soft piped in piano music.

Ninety minutes after she called Nate, he pulled up outside her hotel with Cleo in the back seat. He opened the door of his car and the dog popped out. Moving carefully, she squatted beside him and was greeted by a wet, slurping tongue. She hadn't seen him since the night from hell, so she gave him a thorough check up then ushered him back in the car. As she got in the car, she caught a whiff of seasoned French fries and a grilled cheeseburger. She glanced over her shoulder at the pile of crumpled Johnny Jack's Burger bags on the floor. When Nate got in beside her, coffee cup in hand, she pointed toward the mess in back with her thumb. "Please tell me, you're not feeding him that stuff."

Nate frowned. "No, that's for me," he said, pulling out into traffic. Grinning, he winked. "Breakfast of champions." He sipped his coffee and turned onto the arterial. "You sure you should be driving?"

"Don't start," she said. "I'm fine."

He eyed her with a raised brow. "Right. I'll follow you back to the hotel, just in case though."

The comment caught her by surprise. "Well, I was thinking about stopping by the mall to pick up a few more things," she said and waited to see how he'd react.

He sucked down a gulp of coffee. "Can't it wait 'til later?"

"No, it can't," she said, her tone firm and unyielding.

He frowned. "You know, sometimes you can be just like Dad."

"Runs in the family, I guess."

"Yeah, right." He went quiet for some time, and as he drove, the creases around his eyes deepened and his brow wrinkled. Finally, he said, "Can I tell you something without you going all nuts on me?"

She pasted on a smile despite the sudden warning in her heart. "You can tell me anything, you know that."

He turned and eyed her sidelong as they came to a red light. "I've been thinking about getting into firefighting and stuff like that," he said.

Where did that come from? She coughed. "Firefighting."

"Yeah. And I know what you're thinking: Andy has nothing to do with it, and don't you say anything to him about it either."

"Okay," she agreed as her mind did cartwheels. Every fiber in her body wanted to cry out and shake him to his senses, but the fear of him shutting down on her after they'd come so far seized her heart. "So...how'd you come up with that?"

"After I pulled you out of the house, I got this unbelievable rush as we were going to the hospital–I'd saved your life! Yeah, I know, you're my mother and all, but it's more than that."

I need to be happy for him, but... for the first time since he's been back, he's excited about something. He has a goal! But firefighting? She fought to maintain her composure. "Saving a life is a huge thing, honey. You should be proud of yourself. What about your leg though?"

"My PT, Barry, says if I keep going the way I am, I'll be a hundred percent in another four or five months."

"That's wonderful," she said, and reached over and grasped his hand. *One day at a time.* She repeated over and over in her head as he drove. *Don't rush him. Let him have his moment. He's had so few of them. In the meantime, maybe something else will come along. At any rate, he'd be home and not over there.*

He pulled his hand away as the light turned green, made a left onto the arterial and was quiet for some time. At last, he turned to her. "You like Andy a lot, don't you?"

"Yes, I do. But I'm not rushing things."

He nodded. "It's not that I dislike him..."

"I know," Janet said. "It's okay, I understand how it looked."

Again, he went quiet and his brows creased the way they always did when he was deep in thought. Finally, he said, "How would you feel if you were me?"

"Probably the same," she confessed and looked off at the fields passing them by. "All I can tell you is what I believe."

"And what's that?" Nate said.

She felt his gaze burn into her. "That for him, it was always about you." She paused; debating whether she should tell him she'd approached Andy first. Turning back, she said, "I'm probably to blame."

He shifted in his seat and glanced at her with a furrowed brow. "How so?"

"I sort of started things. When I was scared for you, I went to him," she said and braced herself. "I'm sorry, I didn't know what to do."

She watched him turn her confession over in his mind for some time. Finally, he said, "Well, I guess that explains things."

"Please don't be mad at me," she said, and reached for his hand.

He took it into his and smiled. "It's all right, Mom. I know you meant well." He paused. "Tell you something: I thought about quitting the store, but changed my mind."

"I'm glad you didn't quit," Janet said. "He needs you."

"Don't I know it," Nate said then chuckled. "The man's helpless around a computer. But that's not the reason I stayed." He drew breath and continued, "I stayed for me. I need to get my head straight. Start dealing with things. If nothing else, being in that ambulance as you were fighting for your life showed me that. You kept calling my name ...several times...and it made me think. I've been a dick to you and everyone. Time to man up and take responsibility for things."

"You mean the medal?" Janet said, as he turned onto Old Cypress Road.

"That's a big part of it, yes. But there's a lot more to it than that. You've always been there for me, even when I was an SOB. It's time for me to step up to the plate, take care of you for a change. So you tell me what you need done, and I'll do it."

She smiled as her sudden tears blurred his beautiful face. "You have no idea how much I love you."

"I'm sure I don't Mom," he said as they passed broken branches and ruined shrubbery stacked in piles along the shoulder of the road. A hundred feet shy of the driveway, he slowed down until they were moving at a crawl then brought the car to a stop and said, "Before we get to the house, I need to warn you, you're not gonna like what you see."

She patted his hand. "I've already seen it. Andy brought me here yesterday."

"Oh, okay!" He started ahead again, pulled through the treed opening and drove along the sweeping driveway. As the house came into view, he added, "The insurance adjuster and the structural engineer are supposed to come tomorrow."

"Have you been inside since…"

"No," he said. "The Fire Marshal doesn't want anyone inside 'til the engineer makes an evaluation that it's safe. After he gives the all clear, we can get in and start mopping up: probably next week sometime." He paused. "I called Trev and Meg and they said they'd come help, and so did Ben and Nadia, Jonah and Ty, but we probably ought to get a contractor involved. There's a lot to do, especially around the yard. That willow really made a mess of things."

Janet noted her son hadn't included Andy as he pulled around and parked. "I'll get Bob for the willow and the yard."

"Bob?"

"Yeah, he's my lawn guy," she said. "What about Andy?"

"He has a broken rib, Mom."

She reached over and patted his hand. "Honey, he'll want to be here, but if that's a problem…"

He shrugged. "No. I'll ask him when I drop Cleo off."

Good, it'll mean a lot coming from you. "I'll make some calls when I get back to my room," she said, digging into her pocket for her keys. Suddenly, she realized there were people that hadn't been told what happened to her and she made a mental note to call her brother Craig and also Mick and Sandra. She turned to Cleo. "You be a good boy for Andy, you hear?"

The dog licked her hand. Nate said, "Take it easy driving back and don't overdo it, okay?"

"I'll be fine," she said, getting out. "Love you. Okay, I'm off."

The drive to the coast was a long, achy affair, but the need for the connection with her sacred space overruled the complaints of her battered body. She turned onto the coastal highway running through Lincoln City, and passed tourists and town folk going about their treasure hunts and journeys. But it was the ocean to her right that pulled at her the most, and as she drove along side of it watching the white caps roll in, her scattered, anxious thoughts collected themselves and settled on all that had happened over the last nine months.

Foremost on her mind was her troubled son. He'd carry the tragic memory of that day in Iraq with him forever, but he'd turned a corner and finally let her in behind his armored walls. And then there was her treasured house, which had been built especially for her with love. It had been ravaged by the storm and could be rebuilt, but it would never be the same and perhaps that wasn't a bad thing. Like all things of impermanence, it would adapt the new while retaining the old: a marriage of memory and hope. And last of all, there was Andy. She hadn't ever planned on having another man in her life. Neil had been her all for so many years, but now she found her heart was stretching, making room for another.

She parked, watched a group of teens amble toward the passage burrowing under the highway then gathered her strength and stepped out under a soaring, blue sky. Home! She was home, where her heart of hearts dwelled. She walked across the lot to the footpath leading for the underpass and a far-reaching dun beach. As she poked along the winding footpath bordered with irises, asters and daisies, she breathed in the clean, resinous air and listened to the skittering and chattering of squirrels in the branches above. Looking up into the leafy canopy, she saw them bouncing around in a game of tag.

A moment later, the sonorous thrum of the ocean coursed through her body as she stepped out from the underpass into the bright sunshine. As the gentle breeze sweeping the grassy dunes tossed her hair about, she kicked off her sneakers and rolled up her pant legs. Barefoot with her sneakers in hand, she strode to the edge of the scouring surf and there sauntered along the matted sand. Here and there the ocean rushed up and washed her ankles before sliding back out. She looked over the restless waters, watching the birds skim the choppy surface. Suddenly it was just her, water, earth and sky and in that perfect moment, she felt whole again.

Looking toward her altar rock down the beach, she saw in her mind's eye her son, then her departed husband and her father. Along with them, were Andy, her friends and extended family and those who'd come and gone out of her life, and as their faces flashed before her, she began to understand the new direction the universe had plotted for her. The storm hadn't taken anything away, but instead was now giving her new insight. The things that really mattered were the people who had decorated her life and made her who she was. She would not forget that going forward.

Starting over wasn't the ending of one thing and the beginning of another. It was paying attention to what was important, and that was simply: BEING PRESENT!

Chapter 33

Ashville, North Carolina.
October, one year later...

J ANET GLANCED at Nate as he slowed their rental SUV down to a crawl on the curvy tree-lined, cobbled street. He was so handsome in his dress blues, but it was the medal in the purple case between them that held her attention. She eyed the case with the simple bronze cross with an eagle bearing its outstretched wings. He hadn't had it on since the President had clasped it around his neck. The memory of the ceremony was still fresh in her mind. He had stood tall and straight, but in her estimation, his shoulders sagged under the weight of the millstone lain around his neck. As soon as he could, he'd taken it off and put it in its case and it hadn't come out since. She was glad he'd soon be rid of it, but she worried about the errand they were on. Had she made a mistake in suggesting he give the medal to Kendall's parents? When the notion had hit upon her a year ago, she hadn't considered Nate needing to explain his reasons for passing the medal to Kendall's parents. Now his deep hidden wound, which had threatened to tear them apart, would be opened wide again. But he was determined to tell the truth and she couldn't argue; it was the right thing to do.

"I believe we're here," Nate said nodding toward the modest brick colonial set back from the road. A late model Ford pickup truck was parked in the driveway.

Janet eyed the manicured lawn; saw two large, fat pumpkins squatting in front of an assembly of dried cornstalks on the front stoop. While the festive, fall decoration was colorful and appealing, it felt rigid and artificial, as if it was there because it had to be, not because it wanted to be. She felt her gut tighten as he pulled up to the curb in front of the home and put the car in park. Turning the engine off, he sat back as if collecting his nerve and looked at her.

"Are you all right?" she said as she stared back, suddenly wanting to whisk him away.

He nodded. "Don't worry, Mom. I'm good." He flashed her an accommodating smile then turned and snatched his dress hat off the back seat. "You ready?" he said, grabbing the purple case and opening the car door.

She gathered her breath. "I'm proud of you," she said. "You're doing a great thing here."

"They deserve it," he said, and got out.

She opened her door and followed him up the slate stone path to the house, glad she'd decided to wear a sweater. Despite the clear blue skies and the bright sunshine raining down over the prosaic bedroom community it was quite cool. She joined Nate on the concrete stoop and looked at her watch. "We're a bit early."

Nate rang the doorbell and stepped back. "You worry too much."

As they waited for someone to answer the door, she saw his body stiffen and it took every ounce of strength not to reach over and grab his hand. Then finally, the sound of the latch turning stole the thought away. The door opened and a short, round woman with curly gray-brown hair and piercing blue eyes stepped into the opening. Behind her stood a tall, wiry man with thinning silver hair. For a moment no one said a thing as Nate and the woman stood locking eyes with each other with guarded expressions, as if the woman was searching for answers in Nate's gaze and he searching for words to tell. Finally, she smiled and stepped back.

"Come in, come in, won't you both," she said, her laid-back graceful voice beckoning them into the tiny foyer. As the man shut the door behind them, the woman led them into the living room. "Please make yourself comfortable."

Janet darted her glance around the muted beige walls, taking in the gallery of family pictures and framed official letters. Prominent among them was a large framed photo of a young man in his dress blues over the fireplace. A myriad of smaller framed photos were perched on a painted white mantel. A simple tan upholstered couch sat across from the large bow window looking out over the front yard. A glass top coffee table held a tray of cookies. Four porcelain coffee cups and a tall carafe sat on it.

"I made coffee...decaf...I wasn't sure. Or we have soda if you want or tea or juice," the woman said following them in.

The man joined them in the center of the room and rested his hand on the woman's shoulder. "Honey, it's okay." Shooting Janet and Nate a congenial smile, he said, "I'm Jimmy's dad, Roland and I guess you've already spoken to my wife, Elizabeth. Pleasure to meet you young man." He extended his hand to Nate.

"Call me Liz," the woman said.

Nate removed his dress hat and tucked it under his arm. Handing the purple case to Janet, he dipped his head to the woman and shook Roland's offered hand. "Call me Nate sir, and this is my mom," he said, nodding to Janet.

Janet put her hand out. "Nice to meet you. I'm Janet, and coffee's fine."

"Nothing for me, ma'am," Nate put in then glanced to the picture over the mantel.

Liz followed his gaze and they both stared at the picture of the young redhead with laughing blue eyes a moment until at last she said to Nate, "So... my Jimmy, he talked about you a lot."

"He was my bud," Nate said and pressed his lips together.

An awkward silence followed until Roland broke in. "Well, let's all have a seat, shall we?" The man sat in a wingback chair across from the couch and crossed his legs as Liz came forward and poured coffee. Janet found a seat on the couch, suddenly feeling like she didn't belong here, except she had to be; not because Nate needed her – he didn't – but because she couldn't abandon her son to face the evils of that day all over again alone. She folded her hands over her son's medal case, watching the mother. The woman's hands were trembling as she handed her husband his cup.

Roland said, "So, Liz told me when you called yesterday that you're from Oregon. That's pretty country out that way. Where 'bouts do you live?"

"Just outside of Salem," Nate said taking a seat next to Janet. "A place called the Heights in the valley."

"We have a friend in Portland we went to see a few years ago and he took us to the coast one day to see the Pacific Ocean. I'll never forget it; it was so beautiful. I can't imagine waking up to see that every day," Liz said and went on prattling, telling them all about their vacation for some time. As she spoke, Janet noticed the woman fidgeting in her chair, glancing now and then at the picture of her son over the mantle.

Finally, Roland broke back in. "So...you're a long way from home son," he said. "This a special trip or are you just passing through?"

Nate sat forward on the edge of the couch, his back rigid with his feet planted flat on the floor. "No sir. I came to see you...and you, ma'am," he said glancing at Liz as Janet looked on.

Roland sipped his coffee and Janet saw the man's eyes stray to the medal case on her lap. His gaze turned back to Nate. "Well...we're honored, but...uh...what brings you all this way?"

Janet saw Nate draw breath and felt the palpable tension radiating from him. "I'm here to right a wrong," Nate said.

Roland and Liz wrinkled their brow. Roland said, "Go on."

Nate cleared his throat, looked up at the picture of his fallen friend, then turned back to face the Kendalls. "I don't know how much you know about what happened to Jimmy, but I was there–"

"You were!" Liz burst out. Her eyes widened and she put her hand over her mouth then looked at her husband.

"Yes ma'am," Nate said.

"Oh, my God," Liz cried. "Did he, he…suff…"

"No ma'am," Nate said. He paused and Janet could see him collecting his nerve to go on. "He…umm…went…quickly." He took a deep breath. "But there are things that never came out that should've."

"Like what?" Roland said.

"It's a long story, and it's not an easy one to tell sir, so bear with me."

"All right, go on," Roland said.

Nate nodded, glanced back up at Jimmy's picture, and said, "We were on convoy and on our way back from Falluja that day. Jimmy was riding shotgun, Cunningham was in back with me and Parker was driving. Things were quiet when we got to a little town of Al Nasr on the way back to Bagdad. Jimmy was telling jokes, cracking us up."

Liz nodded. "That's my Jimmy."

Nate smiled but it went away as he resumed the telling. "We were always on our guard, but Al Nasr had never been a hot spot, so we weren't too concerned. Besides, most of the locals were merchants trying to eke out a living, and we were their biggest customers." He paused again, cleared his throat and went on. "When the shooting started Parker hit the gas and the next thing I knew, we were flying through the air. When we came down, the front end of our 'V' was blown off and Parker was gone."

An audible gasp from Liz filled the room.

"Anyway, I had Cunningham slumped over my lap and my leg was bleeding out from a hit so I couldn't do anything. Jimmy though, he grabs his *Kate*–rifle–but it jammed up. I tossed him mine, and said, 'keep your head down and don't do anything stupid' cause Jimmy, he liked hot-dogging it. He looked at me then, and I'll never forget it. It was like he was saying good-bye, then he stands up and starts firing away, taking down anything and everything he could. I was screaming at him. Get down, get down! He just kept firing away though until…"

Nate looked off as silence sucked the air out of the room.

Janet's throat tightened.

Nate swallowed. "And me…I took my rifle back from Jimmy and hid under Cunningham's body as the firefight went on. Then everything went quiet except the cries coming from the other trucks. For a long time I didn't know whether we'd run them off or not, but I knew the *Mooj's*. If they won out, they'd be coming around to plug the dead just to make sure."

As tears streamed down Liz's round face, Roland leaned forward. "But they didn't win."

"No sir, they didn't," Nate said. "Jimmy was a hero. He saved my life that day and others, too." He turned to Janet and took the medal case off her lap. "In here is a medal I received for heroism that day. I never wanted it nor do I deserve it. It belongs to Jimmy and I'm giving it to you."

"I don't understand," Liz said. "What medal?"

Nate's fingers trembled as he opened the case and took the bronze cross out. As Janet watched him, she could see he was having all he could do to keep from coming apart. He paused, stared at Jimmy's mother for a moment then said, "When the medics found me, I was unconscious and by the time I came to, the story was out that I'd taken on the enemy all by myself. Apparently some of the guys in the rear guard thought it was me firing, not Jimmy. Then when they discovered it was my rifle that had been used, it was a done deal. The C.O. pushed the paperwork up the chain and the wheels had been set in motion. No matter what I did or said, they didn't believe me. I was just being a good soldier acting like a hero. I'm here to make it right." He got up and walked over to Liz, handing her the medal."

Her hand shook as she took it from him. Reaching up she drew Nate into her arms and burst into tears. As they held each other, Roland's face crumbled. He came over and put his arms around the both of them. Watching them, Janet realized all Jimmy's parents had were a medal, memories and scraps of their son's life.

She'd been blessed.

She still had Nate!

Dear reader,

We hope you enjoyed reading *Starting Over*. Please take a moment to leave a review, even if it's a short one. Your opinion is important to us.

Discover more books by Ronald Bagliere at https://www.nextchapter.pub/authors/ronald-bagliere-author-new-york

Want to know when one of our books is free or discounted? Join the newsletter at http://eepurl.com/bqqB3H

Best regards,
Ronald Bagliere and the Next Chapter Team

About the Author

Ron is a practicing architect living in upstate New York. An avid hiker and photographer, he has traveled to Nepal, New Zealand and throughout the United States, Alaska and Hawaii collecting ideas for character driven stories of romance and adventure. Other novels by Ron are:

Loving Neil
The Lion of Khum Jung
Beyond the Veil

Connect with Ron via Facebook at R.J. Bagliere or on the World Wide Web at: www.rjbagliere.com

Starting Over
ISBN: 978-4-86751-552-5

Published by
Next Chapter
1-60-20 Minami-Otsuka
170-0005 Toshima-Ku, Tokyo
+818035793528
5th July 2021